**Sandro**

# CIAO, AMORE, CIAO

Based on a Heartbreaking True Story

Black Rose Writing | Texas

©2025 by Sandro Martini
All rights reserved. No part of this book may be reproduced, stored in a retrieval system or transmitted in any form or by any means without the prior written permission of the publishers, except by a reviewer who may quote brief passages in a review to be printed in a newspaper, magazine or journal.

The author grants the final approval for this literary material.

First printing

This is a work of fiction. Names, characters, businesses, places, events, and incidents are either the products of the author's imagination or used in a fictitious manner. Any resemblance to actual persons, living or dead, or actual events is purely coincidental.

ISBN: 978-1-68513-578-2
Library of Congress Control Number: 2025932186
PUBLISHED BY BLACK ROSE WRITING
www.blackrosewriting.com

Printed in the United States of America
Suggested Retail Price (SRP) $24.95

*CIAO, AMORE, CIAO* is printed in Garamond Premier Pro

\*As a planet-friendly publisher, Black Rose Writing does its best to eliminate unnecessary waste to reduce paper usage and energy costs, while never compromising the reading experience. As a result, the final word count vs. page count may not meet common expectations.

Praise for
*CIAO, AMORE, CIAO*

"A gripping saga that roots excruciating betrayals in a nation's tragic history."
*–KIRKUS REVIEWS*

"Vivid and chilling, this is a riveting tale of the horrors of war and a dangerous truth waiting to be unearthed."
*–SUBLIME BOOK REVIEW*

*For Alessandro Martini (1922-?), Natalie (always), my parents (Elisa and Giovanni), and Paola (who came when I was close to surrendering: forever thank you, you saved my life).*

# A Note

This is a story of a family of no ones.

The facts? They're mostly true. Except the ones that aren't. You can find out more about the story and the background at *ciaoamoreciao.net*.

Some names have been altered, some events invented, and some characters created. The only truth is that this is a work of fiction based around actual events.

For the war scenes, dozens of texts were consulted to recreate the retreat from the Eastern Front. Many of the scenes are taken directly from first-hand accounts, both published and privately held. Sources are available on the website.

Certain Italian words (and Venetian dialect) that don't lend themselves to translation have been retained: a glossary at the end explains their meaning.

The chapter titles are all songs "Made in Italy". You can listen to a playlist on Spotify: "Ciao Amore Ciao, by Alex Martini".

"You can lose your way groping among the shadows of the past."
– *Louis-Ferdinand Céline*

"We were the leopards, the lions; those who'll take our place will be little jackals, hyenas; and the whole lot of us, leopards, jackals, and sheep, we'll all go on thinking ourselves the salt of the earth."
–*Giuseppe Tomasi di Lampedusa*

"'The American army,' said the Prince of Candia, 'has the sweet, warm smell of a blonde woman'."
–*Curzio Malaparte*

"War is for men as maternity is for women."
–*Fascist Doctrine*

# CIAO, AMORE, CIAO

# ONE
# WE OWE GOD A DEATH

*There's nothing new except what's been forgotten.*
—Marie Antoinette's dressmaker

## "L'Appuntamento"—Ornella Vanoni

January

Just gone dawn and waiting on a moulded red plastic chair with raindrops like a rash on the skin of dawn-splattered windows behind me when WhatsApp pings on my phone. My wife's friend from New York thinks I should be over my mom's death by now. My wife agrees. *How long does this go on for? I've had enough of your sad pity box.* It's as I start to type a reply on what she can do with her network of shallow-water sharks in New York that a voice, firm but cool, injects its way into my being.

"Are you the accountant or the writer?" it asks.

I raise my head from the screen. There's a man standing over me with fuzzy silver hair and a mismatched trouser-and-sweater ensemble in earthen tones and gentle fabric that is all bafflingly soothing—a sedative in cotton with a vague, almost repentant smile creasing a tanned, inquisitive face.

"Dr Puccini?" I ask, shutting down the app like a guilty schoolkid.

He watches me stand and holds out a hand. "You must be the accountant," he says, "you seem so angry sitting here." He clasps my hand and I find I can't look away from eyes that are as soft as his flesh in my hand.

"It's not—it isn't anger," I assure him.

He takes a moment to gauge my face and then, seemingly content, lets my hand loose. "Come"—he places a limp, guiding palm on my shoulder—"let's get some coffee."

He leads me through a maze of white- and green-lined hallways on the noiseless oncology ward at the Alto-Vicentino Hospital, back toward the elevator-bank from which I'd been ejected twenty minutes earlier, weak-kneed and horrified. As we wait for the elevator, he takes a second look at me and suggests, "So you're the writer, then?"

"Word monkey would be more accurate."

He considers this and then says, "Your father spoke to me about you and your brother. The accountant, and the writer from Zürich."

I think, no. Neither is true. Neither a writer nor from anywhere at all.

"Your brother being the accountant from South Africa, yes?"

"Yes. He's the angry one," I add.

"He wasn't able to make it?"

"My brother? No. No, it's just—it's just me."

"And your mother," he says when the elevator doors split open like lips, "she passed a month ago?"

"Less," I reply, following him into the metal mouth. "December twentieth." I swallow the tremor in my voice and think I'm nowhere near the end of this sad pity box. He meets and traps my eyes with his—sensitive pillows for the lives that he, I imagine, slashes with cool reasonableness every day of his working life. A surgeon of the soul. He seems to want to linger in my gaze, as if deciding what tack he should take until I look away, down at his shoes. Sensible, brown suede ankle boots, worn and stained.

"What are you working on now?" he asks, pinching the lobby button.

I wave a hand as we rise from the basement. "A piece for a car magazine—in the States," I reply when the elevator doors divide, and I hurt after him through the white-tiled lobby now crowding with the sick and the damned in pools of new-day light that reeks of insulin. "A feature on Porsche. The generational thing, you know. On the Cayman and Boxster. The luxury of history," I finish, feeling a fool for mentioning a title I'd come up with three hours ago, at 3.30AM, while rolling down the long-pebbled drive lined by plane trees that leads to the old Palladio-style Villa Scacchi Hotel near Vicenza. I've been there every weekend since October, that villa rising from the flatness of the Veneto plain and out of the skin-like fog that seems always to hover ankle-high over the dark soil a base from where I come to supervise death.

We're in the café, a place in the scrubbed morning sun surrounded by windows and a glass ceiling that magnifies a pink-conch sky. The teen behind the counter seems to know the routine; she quickly assembles a jam brioche and a cappuccino on the counter for Puccini, and I ask for an espresso to his enquiring brow. He touches my arm lightly when I search for coins and pays for it all on a white card dangling from his belt.

"I have an old Porsche," he tells me when we head back for the elevators after a brief pit stop at the sugar counter. He watches me scoop a sachet of cane sugar into my espresso with an inscrutable gaze. "A 930 Turbo."

"Cool. The Widowmaker."

"I'm sorry?"

"That's what they called it in the States—the Widowmaker. Killed more yuppies than Black Monday."

"Is that right?" He nods wistfully as I follow in his footsteps. "My wife actually bought it for me," he says without a hint of a smile as he taps the elevator call button. "For our twentieth anniversary." We watch the blood-red digital numbers wink. "But I do love her—the car, I mean," he says, sipping at his cappuccino and watching me as if he's waiting for something.

"You need to be brave with it," I tell him.

"You really do," he agrees. "When she gets out of shape, the only way you're getting her back is to floor it. A car that teaches life lessons like that is more than just a machine, right? You must be brave, yes." He presses the Level -1 button and studies me with the brioche between his lips. He leads me back through the maze toward the oncology ward and the derelict red plastic chairs now devoid of even my life. "Your father told me you'd lived in New York—before Zürich, I mean. Is that right?"

"Twenty years."

"Why did you leave?"

"Fascism makes me nervous."

"And yet here you are, in Italy. Does that make you nervous?"

"Right now it does."

I'm not sure if he hears me. A nurse cuts us off the instant we step back into his ward, and I pause mid-stride as he nudges her away from me to have a whispered conversation over a clipboard. Then his head springs up and those tender eyes meet mine. There's something there that I can't read.

"Come," he says, "come," and leads me into an office across from the reception desk. It's a small, weirdly shaped room, narrow and stretched and claustrophobic, as if time is warped in here, coning away toward the sick light haemorrhaging beyond the window. The desk is entombed beneath dozens of files amassed about a central monitor. Two chairs wait before the desk, and a leather one sits behind it with some sort of back-support pillow.

"So hot in here," he says, shutting the door on us and striding to the window that he shoves open. He takes a plastic file and jams it between the window and the frame to keep it ajar, and the coldness seeps in with the mist. "Sit." He taps the back of a chair while rounding the desk. "Sit, sit." He shows me how on his chair and arranges the croissant and cappuccino like chess pieces between the files before clicking the monitor screen to life. "Tell me, has your father ever been around mines?"

I sit down, not knowing if I should lean forward or back. "I'm not...he was a, a mining engineer in Africa for thirty years, but ... he didn't work *in* the mines, no, not really. Why?"

"Asbestos." He opens a folder on-screen and clicks on a file. "This is his MRI," he explains, and by twisting the monitor's face further toward me, it affords me a reason to sit closer. "This," he points with a finger, "is his left lung." He dances the mouse icon on the screen. I don't have a clue what this is. And a realisation that Puccini knows more about engines and organs than I'll ever know about anything at all. "You see how misshapen it is? Here, compare it to the right lung." He clicks his mouse and gazes at me. "Do you see?"

I see the inside of my father's body. It reminds me of a Spanish omelette in monochrome. I swallow vomit that tastes of bitter espresso.

"Down here"—he shows me a slow-moving video of an alien landscape, and takes a bite of the croissant—"you see there, down in the sac, this is where the cancer is. We suspect mesothelioma."

Two words. I sit back and blink it away. The mist is orange-tinged out there in the cold, fingers rootling through the window. I can't even pronounce it. I can't even pronounce this.

"You'll recall that we removed a litre from his abdomen last week, yes?"

"Yes, a litre of fluid, he told me."

"That wasn't fluid." His eyes are dewy, puffy clouds on a summer's day. "That was blood."

I feel mine run up through to my brain and freeze right there.

"The cancer is aggressive. With mesothelioma, and a man of his advanced age, it's to be expected, of course. It's already spread to his bones, here," he clicks the mouse, "you can clearly see in this scan—like Swiss cheese in there, that's his femur, and here are his vertebrae, can you see? It explains the disintegration of his two lower vertebrae over the autumn. And the broken femur."

The broken femur. His fall. It all starts with the fall. The day they'd cremated my mom.

I'd gone down to the local *rosticceria* that evening and come back to the apartment with new roasted potatoes flaked in crisp fresh parsley, and two fillets of grilled orata. Funny how I recall that. We'd eaten in silence, my dad and I, in that apartment my parents had called home for a quarter century, haunted by my mom who'd been gone but six nights. Her chair at the dinner table was vacant; his chair, my dad's, sat hollowed out too. He'd chosen instead to sit where my daughter Natalie would always sit when we'd come visit, next to my mom back when ... back then, before she'd gotten sick, before ...

He sat across from me that night eating tiny morsels of cold fish and studied his fork as if he didn't understand anymore, as if everything had suddenly become a mystery to him. On his pinky finger, I noticed, he wore my mother's wedding ring, the wedding ring the undertakers had given him when she'd left the apartment that last time, carried away by strangers, still and dead. It made him seem like a pirate, this old man with his two gold rings, my father with whom I'd never bonded, having come onto the scene when he was just about forty and consumed by work and what I later came to imagine—for my own amity—as the regret of a life unfulfilled, a life scarred by a war that had meant nothing to me, a disfigured life that'd gradually metastasised into an indifference swayed by nothing, not even my mother's first signs of illness.

We spoke not a word. And really, what was there to say? Eventually, in that loud silence, I'd gazed not at him—not at the pain in his gaunt face—

but down at my cold white fleshy orata and said, "What you did—keeping her here…until—" he said not a word—"I never told you…you remember, back when you guys came to America, that last time…" That last time, when I'd picked them up at JFK and saw my mom walk out into the filth-haze of a summer's day with a strangely vacant smile, that was the start of the descent into the madness, and I told my father, the night of his fall, "She told me she wanted to be at home. She always wanted to be at home with you."

He said not a word. I'm not sure he ever really understood her illness—or perhaps he did and just couldn't accept because he just kept trying to rationalise with her even when she was dying right in front of him.

The night of the fall—before I'd left for my hotel to leave him alone on his couch with his ghosts and the red chair on which he'd found my mom dead less than a week earlier, the chair on which she'd lived out the last weeks of her life in diapers because she'd been unable even to stand anymore, the chair where he'd found her dead-still in the morning bright, the skin on her face sucked to her bones and he too afraid to touch her—that night I told him not to take the pills the doctor had prescribed to help him sleep.

"Don't take them," I told him, "don't take them until you get into bed."

"Okay, Sandro," he'd said, sitting on his couch, hunched forward with his palms on his forehead and his elbows on his knees. He was staring down at his slippers and rocking back and forth, back and forth in that gloom, broken only by a pool of yellow from the lampshade beside the couch, in pain from the crumbled vertebrae that'd barred him from leaving the apartment since back in the autumn when he'd shattered them trying to lift my mom, in that silence haunted by sixty years of marriage and memories I smiled and said, "Ciao, see you tomorrow," and left him alone.

Relieved, I was, to get out.

He'd taken the pills, of course, and then fell in the bathroom near midnight, snapping his femur. They'd taken X-rays at the ER before admitting him—there's no treatment for a broken femur aside from an operation (the things you learn)—and some wide-eyed specialist in orthopaedics had noticed a shadow in his lung. He had double pneumonia and, typical for the elderly, it had come without even a fever, and then they'd seen fluid in his abdomen which wasn't being dried by the battery of penicillin they shot into his arms via IV for a week prior to the surgery, fluid in the abdomen that they'd eventually sucked out, fluid that was blood dancing heavy with cancer. After that, they'd given him an epidural and set his leg, half-convinced he'd never make it through the procedure. They wheeled him back groggy to his room where I stood alone waiting for him in that ward that smelt of ripe shit and old piss and skin rot and flowers. Four days later, they'd taken an MRI. And a day later, Dr Puccini had sent an email asking me to call his office and set an appointment at my earliest convenience for me to now ask him, "What does this all mean?"

Puccini sits back in his chair as if this were a question he'd not anticipated and takes a moment to reflect. "Signor Lago, treatment options—scraping the lung or any other invasive procedure, even chemo—in every scenario, it would not only not extend his long-term prospects, but probably narrow them. There's nothing we can do to reverse this. I'm sorry. What we can do is make him comfortable."

"Comfortable."

"Palliative care. Medicine fails us all in the end," he says, and it sounds to me like genuine regret, "but we are competent at managing pain."

I glance up at Puccini through a film of tears. The office has the quality of the world on a misty morning in Northern Italy. Vague, tired. Ill-defined. "How much time?"

"We can't be sure. We can't even be sure it's mesothelioma unless we get inside and take a biopsy. Tumours, you see, they progress at different rates." His eyes are like rubber gloves when he gazes at my tears, and he doesn't look away and allows me the dignity of my pain.

"How long?"

"I don't believe he'll see Easter," he tells me, and watches me cry. "And if he saw the first day of summer, I would call it a miracle."

I feel my breath exhale. It comes out like a little moan. Like my soul is vomiting. "So—two, three months?"

"Optimistically."

My hand comes to my cheeks, and I squeeze hard so that my lips pucker and hurt but it doesn't stop the tears. "Does he know?"

"I spoke to him last night, briefly, when he asked about the results of the MRI. I told him, softly-softly," he says this in English, softly-softly, "that we'd found something. He seems a gentle man. He said to me, 'I can't accept'."

"He's dying."

"If he were a younger man, it would make sense, perhaps, to reveal the gravity of his prognosis. With your father—we must first get him set up at the rehab centre in Malo. Geriatrics will discuss this with you today, but you need"—he clips off the monitor and places a hand around the cappuccino cup—"you need to understand that, after an intervention and at his age, even with a typical patient, rehab will take one, probably two months, maybe more, and by then…do you follow?"

I follow him out. And thank him outside his office.

"I'm open to any communications," he tells me. "Anything at all."

"What do I tell him?" I ask.

Puccini holds my hand softly and the pillow-eyes absolve me. "There's no right or wrong here," he says, and he seems a giant to me then. "There's only what you can live with."

## "Ma Che Freddo Fa"—Nada

The black Porsche Cayman in the hospital lot burps out a haze of oil when I start her up and watch grey blue gun-smoke drift into the frying haze. I gun the throttle and clear out the oil that'd accumulated somewhere in the engine bay after my run up from Zürich though the night. There's a slight hesitation in the pickup of the flat-6 that I'd noticed in the soggy-lit Gotthard Tunnel, but she sounds keen enough when I bubble my way out of the lot through the prolonged shadows of the hospital. My phone lights up and the theme to *Magnum P.I.* comes on. I Bluetooth it to the cabin.

"Hey," says my brother's voice, calm and clear from sunny faraway Africa, "you spoke to the doctor?"

"Yes. I'm just leaving."

"I can hear," he says with something that sounds like reproach. And then silence for a while. "And?"

And. And he's dying. "It's…it's what we imagined."

"He's sure?"

"Who?"

"Who do you think?"

"…Yes. Yes, he's sure. He showed me…you know, the MRI, the—"

I make the turn around the traffic circle and take an arterial road west that runs through what had once been lush farmland. Strange thing about Italy—factories and farms and apartment buildings all built side-by-side, a communism of design and lechery on the frozen, flat, misty winter plains of the Veneto.

"How long?" he asks. I'm about to speak but my throat chokes up and I find a cigarette and light it up as I get to a set of traffic lights. "Hullo? You there?"

"Yeah. He said, two, I don't know, man...three months? Mesothemol—meso—"

"Mesothelioma," says my brother and then, "I don't understand—how?"

"Mines."

"He never worked in the mines."

I pull off from the traffic light and my voice has an hysterical edge to it when it says, "Does it matter?"

"Have you seen him?"

"Who?"

"Come on," he says, frustrated.

"No. Not yet."

"Where are you?"

"I'm headed for the apartment."

"Okay. And then—"

And then. "I'll go to the hospital. It's too early now—it's—he's probably still asleep."

"Okay."

"Okay."

I short-shift up and listen to the twangs and pops and grousing rasps from the engine just behind my head until he says, "There're some documents the lawyers want. They're at the apartment where Dad keeps his personal papers. Mom's testament. Can you WhatsApp them to me?"

"Sure."

"Sure. Okay. Well—"

"Okay," I tell him, and cut the call because he's clogging up and he's my big brother and I don't want to hear it. I slow for another set of traffic lights ahead, where two kids on bikes, attracted by the rhythm of the bubbling motor, turn to stare. One of them, big smile on his face, shouts, *"Bella macchina!"*

Intimidated by their youth, by the promise of all their tomorrows when all that remains to me is the misery which lies ahead on the other side of a winter's dawn dragged out there beyond my dirty windscreen, freedom withered to a stiff engine stretching time and memory like an elastic, I burrow further into my bucket seat and try to pretend they don't exist.

It's all gone, that's the thing—that mechanical freedom of childhood—it's all gone, and guys like me, who'd spent a lifetime driving and writing and dreaming, gone with it. Where once the number of pipes at the ass-end of a car was personal triumph, now their absence is the promise of dawn disinfected from the stain of our shameful history. White, male, straightish. And that's okay, that's how it works, this world, but it's all so far from the dirt and thunder of those worn-out, rusty grandstands at Kyalami racetrack in the '70s, pushed-up against my dad on summer days of *braaivleis*, sunny skies and Chevrolet where smitten boys came to worship at the altar of heroes on full-counterlock drifts through Crowthorne Bend with tight-packed Colombo V12s wailing mechanical bits that tore at your organs. So far from those hot metal bleachers in the Highveld heat, with me sitting close-up to my dad—my dad and his binoculars and his chronometer and his Marlboros and Mom's sandwiches in the blue cooler box lodged between his ankles.

My life, my career, my dad, all of it dying. Mourning my mom as my father dies, it's the price of life, I guess. I give the kids something to enjoy, popping the clutch when the light turns green, and pulling off in a dissonance of smoke and noise and rising revs, pushing first all the way up to 7,200 RPM and, too slow, I hit the limiter before thrashing it into second and that's when the torque, hollow and deep, gets the back-end seriously out of shape. But the adrenaline's kicked in good and proper now, and instead of slowing for the bend ahead, I just throw the Cayman in, trusting the front will bite and it does, rigid like a ratcatcher it bites. I come out the other side with the rear-end trying to get out front and the thin black wheel in my hand catching the slide, my heart in my mouth and my guts shouting more, more of *this* because like this I don't get to feel, don't get to remember. I hook it all up and then straitjacket myself on the seat belt as I boot the brake pedal to the floor and lock everything up to avoid rear-ending an SUV with Netherlands plates coasting down the road at some miserable speed.

I'm reminded of the ex-editor of *Cars Magazine*, a friend who'd signed off—before heading to Upstate NY three marriages and two bankruptcies down—with, *"The future is just shitty little cars for shitty little people."*

The Porsche crackles on an upshift and I'm into the gloomy winter landscape of the Veneto where concrete structures that'd once been factories vomiting the post-war Italian miracle—until the marrow had been sucked out by Brussels's eternal desire for German lebensraum east—rot in the mist aside cheap palazzi leisurely peeling and dying in place there amid the frigid fields of winter.

I take the right onto the road that joins Schio with Piovene—Piovene, where my parents had retired after almost four decades mislaid in Africa, Piovene that nestles forgotten where the motorway ends because it's where the Valdastico Autostrada stops, right here in this scrappy village of three-thousand souls. They'd had plans to extend the highway up into Trento and on to Austria, but that'd been scuppered by a coalition of environmentalists and right-wing separatists. And so it all stops here, in this derisory medieval village carved into a lush valley at the foot of the Dolomites, and sure to have disillusioned those foolish enough to have come to discover what waited at the end of the road.

My mother could've saved them the journey—she'd always said this was the antechamber to the grave.

End of the road that meanders past the old stone walls of the main cemetery in the shadow of Monte Summano where believers had been coming since the 15th Century on their pilgrimage to somewhere or something I no longer recall. There's a billboard stuck on the moss-topped stone wall that seals the dead in the cemetery, a woman smiling out at me. She's wearing a green T-shirt—a tight-fitting green T-shirt because Italy—her nipples nut-hard against the fabric, smiling out at me with so much promise. Her name, I read as I drive past, is Eva Fachin.

Vote Freedom. March 9. #ItaliaFirst.

They love their fascists here. But I'd vote for her now: I'd vote for the promise of that smile.

I take a left past the billboard and I'm in what my mom would joke as *il centro della cosmopolitana*, textile-baron Alessandro Rossi's planned worker village from back in the 1900s when the mills had employed almost fifty-thousand beings in the Lanerossi factory, then one of the world's largest textile mills and now just a hefty, shattered concrete-and-glass husk rotting high on a ravine above the Astico River.

The main road through the village is hushed, forsaken of life, flanked by a regiment of oak trees standing mute like surrendering troops with arms aloft to a milkshake sky, puzzling shadows collapsing against the deep-chilled stores that've been boarded up by rusted-metal shutters. Those shops had been put on the market when mom-and-pop had died by kids who'd long-since fled for Milan and Berlin and London and the new villa estates of better towns. The stores had been left breathless behind graffiti-slashed ramshackle shutters that shout of a world mislaid decades ago down here in the gloom of Monte Cengio. Monte Cengio, where once the Sardinian Grenadiers had fought their final epic battle and died for *patria* by grappling the invading Austrians and hurling themselves into a two-thousand-metre cavity of suicidal history.

The apartment is in a cycle of brutalist palazzi that'd been built in the '80s. Bauhaus meets cheap-ass. The original tenants are dying off now, and the cut-rate concrete buildings, in neat rows of tricoloured pastels wedged apart by pocket-sized gardens, are beginning to endure the same urban decay of the adjacent blocks that'd become home to refugees through the years—Sri Lankans first, and then West-Coast Africans who'd come when the tanneries were humming, and now swollen by refugees from America's failed wars in North Africa, all living out their tired lives behind scruffy-torn curtains and garbage-strewn verandas.

The Sri Lankans that'd managed to get a toehold back when times were good still meet up on Sundays to play cricket on a potholed football field down by the church dedicated to the Lady of Lourdes. My mother always said it reminded her of South Africa when she'd walk by and watch them play. My mother, from Foggia, from *il mezzogiorno*, watching cricket in Piovene, my mom who'd seen her first black man when the rapey Americans had come to town in '43 with their cigarettes and chewing gum and eternal optimism. But then she too had been an immigrant, starting that journey right after the war on the *Terroni* Trains to Torino that'd inspired her lifelong revulsion for the North. For this place. And these people. Because before Italy First, it was Padania First up here: it was the dream of secession, a place where Southerners like my mom—the first wave of immigrants that'd come to work the FIAT factories and the sweatshops of the Italian miracle bought by the Yankee dollar—would never be welcome. Trickle-down economics in the land of the mafia—only the Americans could ever have been that naïve.

Up here in the Nord-Est, here in the Veneto—the Tri-Veneto—they'd had a republic for a thousand years before Napoleon had forced them into unification with the rest of Italy, and their UNESCO-recognised language is still spoken in Istria where D'Annunzio had invented fascism, and Rio Grande do Sul and Santa Catarina in Brazil, and Chipilo in Mexico, and my mom had hated them as only a Southern Italian can ever hate, hate without parole, a life sentence of hate. The referendum of 1866 that'd forced them into the union was still seen as illegitimate up here where the neo-fascist Bossi and his spittle-lipped dream of Padania north of Florence had spluttered to the tune of *Dal Po in giù l'Italia non c'è più!*

The rest of Italy were just a bunch of Africans for these folks, Africans like my mom who'd gone to Africa for real one day in the spring of '61 to straighten bananas, or so her brother had suggested when he'd come up from Foggia to wish her well at the airport in Fiumicino where she'd boarded the Alitalia DC-5B, on her way to meet my father already in Johannesburg.

Athens, Khartoum, Nairobi, Salisbury, and finally Joburg, where she'd found a race even more terrorised and despised than she had been. Now they vote for the neo-fascists down South because they despise the immigrants from Africa as the Bossi-brigade had once despised them. Hate is a limitless commodity, and this place my mother had loathed. And it was here—in this valley surrounded by raw-knuckle mountains that rise through the Altopiano to Trento and on, up to the Dolomites and finally the Alps, on a fertile plain where the Astico River is a white gash of spiteful angry glacial water—here where she'd come to die.

She came because my father wanted to return to the land where he'd been raised in the disease and hunger of war, chasing—or perhaps, I think, being chased—by something he'd tried to outrun for a lifetime. In Switzerland and France and Brazil and Mozambique and the fucking Congo and finally South Africa, where my mom had built a life. Our life. A life abandoned when she'd followed my dad back here and where he'd paid by consuming himself at the altar of her madness. Amen, I think, slowly rolling the Porsche past the water-rotten concrete palazzi. A lifetime of being *auslanders*, and then they'd come here—they'd come back to where it'd all started—they'd come back home as immigrants to an Italy that had never existed beyond my dad's fantasies to die.

## "Il Sognatore"—Peppino Di Capri

I park down below the palazzi on a potholed access road and walk into a damp-stained concrete subway with garages on either side, and through a metal door that feeds into the apartment building. The stairs, beyond the door, are white marble. A decade ago, I'd told my dad to find somewhere with an elevator when my mom's knees had begun to play up, but he never did listen. "We'll see," he said, my dad's wrap-up to any argument for twenty-five years. *"Domani si vedrà."* But I've told myself already—there's going to be no resentment, no anger. Not now.

The second-floor landing is awash in light from a bulky glass-brick window over the stairwell. My mom's lemon tree has withered and died. I step by it toward the apartment door. There's no one in there now. I draw out keys, six of them, my mom's keys, and find one that fits the lock. How many times had she done this with my dad waiting inside?

I'd turned the gas off two weeks ago, and the freeze that rolls out with that familiar scent of home when I push the door open reminds me of the morgue. It reminds me of my mom, lying there in her coffin, the skin drawn tight over cheeks bruised purple, and mouth forever pursed in agony spent. I can't get that out of my mind. I can't get rid of her dead face, and the apartment gives me the chills, and it isn't the cold. The night when she'd died, I'd woken in the apartment in Zürich and seen a shadow, heavy with dance and malice, race across the wall like a spider. It'd terrified me and I'd known instantly: I'd gone upstairs and sat on the couch and waited. At seven—7.03AM—their doctor had called from this apartment, from that phone over there in the kitchen, next to my dad's contact-book that he's had for forty years. "Your father asked me to inform you…"

But I'd already known. There'd been so much malice, so much threat in that shadow.

I shiver when I walk into the apartment.

My mom had died over there. That red chair over there, there under the wall of windows in the lounge, there before the white lace curtains where the damp sunshine seeps in the plastic light of morning. She died on that chair—the red one over there. She went from Foggia, bombed during the war, to the hunger and cold of postwar Torino, to the big-sky promise of fading colonial Africa, to that red chair. That was her life.

It doesn't take long for an apartment to become a mausoleum, I think, walking to their bedroom. The wooden shutters are semi-closed and a thread of liquid sunshine cuts across the polished floor and over their made bed like an arrow. No one will ever sleep in that bed again. I steel myself and walk in.

On the wall above the bed hangs a crucifix. A relic of childhood. Mine. I was in a hospital, in my oxygen tent, and my mom had called for a priest. Who knows where she'd found him because she always hated priests, but he'd come and stood over my bed like a vulture and said his prayers and left the crucifix behind, a talisman, I suppose, and I guess it worked because I didn't die. But then these are my half-memories, and my mom, who would remember it all, is gone. And with her my childhood, my life before my own recollections, and maybe it's best that it's all gone, this yellow-tinged resin of memory of my mom taking me to a specialist and me asking to be carried in her arms, and I remember the world up there, safe in her arms, up there where the grown-ups spoke and rationalised, up there where the magic that kept me alive happened, the two vials she kept in the refrigerator now in her denim shoulder bag for the specialist to inject into my blood. Tetracycline. And then we'd get the bus back home, me lying with my head on her lap feeling the grumble of the bus beneath the hot, clinging plastic seat, and the abstracted stroke of her fingers through my hair as the purple jacaranda trees pulsed-on by. Shadow-and-light, shadow-and-light, down into Yeoville and the promise of another afternoon without the taste of honey-wet phlegm closing down my lungs, and a radio play on Springbok Radio floating in the light of my room with those voices from far-away lands as beautiful as the fancy of a sick boy in Africa who had nothing much left but his dreams. She died and took my history with her, my mom who'd come to Africa, pregnant with my brother on that flight from Rome, a twenty-two-hour ordeal down the spine of Africa where kids would come onto the plane at each stop baring exotic foods secreted in flies before finally meeting my dad in Joburg carrying, she once told me, seven red carnations, not a word of English between them, and somehow she'd given birth to a child three months later in a hospital where the only common word between her and the doctor and the nurse was spaghetti.

"I just looked at the doctor's face," my mom would say. "Words don't matter that much in the end."

My brother. Focus, I think, licking the tears on my lips, focus on the task.

I'd removed my mom's stuff after she died, stored them downstairs in suitcases in the garage while my dad sat on the couch in the lounge. A lifetime of work and sacrifice and all that remains now is my father's stuff. Not much of that, either. The old shed possessions like they do dreams.

I step to the drawer and find an old shoebox from a department store in Joburg that'd gone bust back in the late-'80s. Inside are all his personal papers. Well organised. There's a plastic pouch with all his work papers from Brazil in the '50s, Paris and Zürich and Torino, and his original papers from Mozambique, Zambia, Rhodesia, and South Africa, where he'd arrived in the winter of 1960. Another pouch contains the rest of his papers. Bank statements, all tidily marked, and the document my brother is asking for.

I slide it out of the pouch. *Last Will & Testament.*

Something slips out from the pouch and floats to the floor like tickertape. A photograph. I scoop it up. Monochrome. My father is of that generation who marked up photos on the back, but the handwriting here isn't his.

*July 1943. I leave this with you. You'll know what to do if the time comes. And what <u>not</u> to do. Yours in friendship—JC.*

I frown, turn the photo around and hold it up for a jet of light and dust to bring to life. Four men. Two are holding a third between them in the foreground while a fourth stands washed-out on the edge. Does he even belong to this scene? Behind them, murky with age, is a distant column of men marching off down a hill into a white-white world made of snow and ice, a zig-zag column of thousands of men like ants snaking off into a purity of glossed white. The four men wear blankets, and their feet are garbed by more blankets strung together by wire or rope. I glance closer. The man in the middle, the man being held up, looks a lot like my uncle. My uncle Alessandro, who'd vanished into that very hellscape in January of '43. He has a long icicle running down from his nostrils to his mouth like some sort of repulsive bone, and he stares out at me through the years with a longing that makes me focus-in on his eyes.

I spread the documents on the bed and use my phone to snap photos like a spy and send it all to my brother over WhatsApp. Strange that I've never seen this photo before. And who the hell was JC?

*Thanks. How you doing? I called dad-he didn't reply*, my brother pings back almost instantly. He's dying, I think, and don't bother replying. I snap an image of the photo and bundle everything up into the pouch and push it into the shoe box. The photo I take with me. In the lounge, on the armoire by the TV cabinet, is a red vase made of layers of ceramic tiles. My mom's ashes. They'd weighed more than I'd ever imagined when I carried them home in that vase. My father was already in the hospital when she'd come back from the crematorium: he's never seen the vase, never saw what became of my mom. His wife. Never felt the weight of her ashes.

Right then the TV comes blaring on and I suck up air, fright rushing like a needle through my veins. RAI Uno. Politics. "The neo-fascist right is the only response to the abandonment of the working—"

Jesus. The remote control is on the coffee table, and I grab for it quickly, shut the TV and head for the front door, feeling the sick come up. In my hand is the photograph.

I'd wanted to write this story once—even paid for an investigator in Russia who'd come up with nothing at all. My uncle Alessandro, swallowed by history in 1943. I'm a member of a few Facebook groups that post news items on dog tags and whatnot found in the killing fields of the Don River. I call up the image on my phone and share it to the ARMIR Group page—ARMIR was the name of the Italian Army sent to die alongside the Nazis outside Stalingrad.

*Anyone know who these men are and where this photo was taken?* I write and, sliding the photo into my coat pocket, walk out of the apartment just as the TV comes back on.

I shut the door fast and try to breathe.

"Bondì," says a voice.

I jump and feel a muscle twinge in my neck as I swivel round to see a woman standing in the shadows at the far end of the corridor.

We know each other by sight, but I can't remember ever swapping a word beyond hullo. She's always been here, though, the neighbour my mom always called "la matron". She's aged, silver-haired and hard-lined puffy face. "I just wanted to express my condolences." She takes a few uncertain steps toward me, slipping out of the shadows but leaving me a lot of space. "For your mother. *Mi dispiace.*"

"*Grazie.*"

"And your father?" she asks, silver-liquid eyes seeing a lot more than I care to reveal as she edges closer like a threat.

"He broke his leg."

"Yes, I know, how is he?" I try to find words, but she's old enough to understand and says, "Please let him know I send my best wishes."

"Of course."

My phone pings. I smile an apology and grab it. Messenger. Not a friend. Someone named Sofia. She seems pretty enough in her avatar. I accept the request and read the message.

*Please remove the image you just posted on the ARMIR page. There's copyright on that image. Take it down immediately. Thanks!*

I slide the phone into my pocket and look up. La matron's still there, lingering, about to walk away, unsure, searching for courage. I wish she'd just go, but she's found it now, and her words come to me soft and cool like the marble hallway. "You know, I saw your mom—it must have been September or early October—I remember because the weather was starting to turn, and she was wearing just a light coat. She was downstairs," she waves down the corridor, "she was downstairs, leaning against the door, where the postboxes are, you know, and I was coming back from the Co-op and I saw her, she looked so fatigued leaning there against the wall, and I asked her, I said, 'Lisa, are you okay?' and she said, 'Angela,' she said, 'Angela, I can't anymore, I'm so tired. I can't do it anymore. *Non ce la faccio più*'."

I swallow.

"That was the last time I ever saw her."

In October, my mom had stopped leaving the apartment, surrendering herself to that red chair where she'd sleep for most of the day and night, and who knows what sinister world she'd inhabited in those last weeks trapped by her secrets and ghosts—who knows what thoughts stuttered through her broken mind as she sat there on that chair and slowly died on me. But I'd been dead to her already, I guess. I'd died the day she'd forgotten who I was.

## "Ciao, Amore, Ciao"—Luigi Tenco

The Alto-Vicentino Hospital had risen from the mud of the Schio flatlands about a decade ago in a modernist totem of lime-green façades and aspiration with a massive rail of Brazilian hardwood arcing out of the mist like a mammoth tusk. The hospital had been built when the Veneto was still one of Europe's economic powerhouses, back before everyone found somewhere better to be, including the world-class doctors who were meant to have come along with the world-class hospital.

Schio was where my father had been born in the strange pause-years of Duce's Italy, a merchant town that hosts a Manchester-themed week once a year, the two linked by a shared history of mills, industrialisation, and organised labour, though I doubt anyone in Manchester has ever heard of it. Still, they'd exported their textiles and their Marxist revolutionaries around the world from this withered and once-wealthy provincial town nestled under the Dolomites, here where they'd built Italy's very first industrial-age factory.

I can see the roundabout down beyond the walls of tinted windows that accompany me through the sun-washed hallways toward the southern elevator bank. The second exit on the roundabout ends at the morgue, a bunker-like building whose roof is disguised by a shrivelled lawn, right behind the ER. It's where I saw my mom for the last time, lying there for six days before they'd taken her to Spinea, thirty minutes down the motorway, to one of only two ovens within a hundred-kilometre radius. Italians don't like to burn their dead. Or maybe it's just me. It'd been my father's decision to cremate her, but to me, it'd felt like a second death.

I recall the horror of that air-conditioned windowless white room and the gleaming polished-wood coffin with the glass-top like some sort of sterile greenhouse. Inside was my mom. In that electric-cold air tinged with the myriad aromas of flowers, I'd thought I'd gone into the wrong room, the tiny woman who lay in that coffin, that wax-like statue on its white satin bed, a stranger to me until I saw her crossed socked feet and her face and the flesh so tight. That deep purple bruise above the button of her lips that would darken through the days as she lay there waiting for the trip to Spinea, and abruptly I recognised her, my mother, and a sound came from me in that room scented by the sweet aroma of a bazaar, a sound came from me that I thought came from somewhere else, *someone* else, a strange dog-like sound, and I couldn't stop myself. I couldn't stop that sound for the longest time, that awful belch that came from me.

The geriatric ward spreads away like destiny down an airport-length corridor with rooms on either side beyond a busy-busy reception island. The smell here is of carbolic acid and iodoform and shit and piss. It's the scent of life broken down to its basics, and there's no more hiding here. No more pretence.

It's hard to imagine that these living corpses that I pass now in their murky rooms were ever infected by life. But there it is. Room after room of stinking flesh like dying fish and bulging eyeballs and shattered minds staring into an abyss that you can almost touch, and a man is shouting, *"Mama, mama!"*

I am suddenly reminded of being with my folks on chilly Friday nights, up late with hot cocoa and curled under coarse blankets watching American TV shows—*McCloud* and *Magnum P.I*—safe from the one thing she could never protect me from: her own transience.

My phone starts ringing. I grab it and check the screen. Italy number. "Hullo?"

"Is this Signor Lago?" asks a female voice in my ear.

"Yup. Who's this?"

"Hi, this is Sofia. I reached out to you on Facebook. This—"

"—isn't a good time."

"I understand, look, I need—"

"Sorry, how did you get this number?"

"That's not important. I really do need to ask you to take that image down, it's—"

"Not a good time," I repeat and hang up, thinking paradise is surely just an escape from this soulless mediocrity of the technological age.

There's a wilderness of hope on the ward, a madness that you can taste like bile, an afterlife of sorts tainted by the guilt of jonesing for the sweetness of the long walk out into the cold, leaving *this* behind, this stench, this putrid end, this suffering, leaving all of this behind. It's written on the faces of those who stand around gazing at the screens of their phones, waiting outside rooms for nurses to clean and doctors to assess, all of us trapped in a communism of despair. All we can do now is wait, knowing that soon it'll be our turn to watch those we love get rolled away on beds covered by drawn-up sheets as if the nurses were wheeling around the drinks trolley on an Atlantic flight, wheeled away through the doors behind the reception over there that lead down to the morgue.

My father is in the last room on the ward, the final room on the left. Beyond is a floor-to-ceiling window slapped by the smile of light that washes the scrubbed linoleum floor so brightly it hurts. My shoes have a rhythm on these floors, and I wonder if he can hear them as a condemned man hears the echo of his executioner.

My phone pings. I take it out. Messenger.

PLEASE *pull down the photo. I can explain everything but take it down* NOW.

At least she hasn't used a fucking emoji. I take a moment. And then type what I'd been wanting to type all day, and it feels good.

*Go fuck yourself.*

I slide my muted phone into my pocket and stall outside the room. Inside, the blinds are up, the daylight harsh and cold like a fever. It's a relief because I can hide behind my shades. My father lies on a single bed, on his back, under a shield of blankets. His eyes are shut, and I feel my heart stumble until I see his chest move. How had I missed how old he was? They have a delicate balance, that's what the doctor had told me when I'd brought my mom here, and once gone, the decline is always rapid. Better off dead, my wife said. My mom. My dad. And me, should I ever get ill. They're old, and they're better off dead. There's no room for emotions—they'll call it maudlin, and worse yet, sentimental, because life is only about the cold-blooded pursuit of simple happiness now, like lizards in the sun, licking up what it is to be human.

I stare at my father. He's changed in the two, three weeks that he's been here. His appetite has fled with his weight, and even the cakes and *macedonia* I bring from the hotel breakfast-bar go uneaten. My father. I recall him differently. I remember him back-when—in Africa—my age, and the thought scares me because he'd seemed so old to me then, and in these memories that haunt what I like to pretend is sleep in the spare bedroom in Zürich, I recall him as a man who'd come home with the night to sit there on his couch with a cigarette and a glass of Dimple whisky and *The Star* newspaper, waiting for the news on the Pioneer television set in its altar-like cabinet that would be unsealed in the evening to broadcast the filtered fascist news that he'd assess in a few chosen words as *"stronzate"*. This man lying in the bed here, under his blankets, is an imposter. He wears new pyjamas I'd bought for him from OVS, and his iPhone and spectacles and Bosch wristwatch lie on the airplane-style plastic swivel table clipped to his bed at chest-level.

His eyes blink open. It takes a moment before he recognises me and a tremble of a smile cuts across his lips. An unreadable smile tinged with so much sadness and regret that I have an overwhelming desire just to hold him. That anyone would smile when they saw me—that's the betrayal, that's what he'll take with him.

"Sandro," he says, "you here already?"

Usually visiting hours are later. But I suppose you get special times when you're the one chosen to condemn a man. We speak in English and Italian—it depends on the mood, on what we're trying to convey. If it's serious, I'll speak Italian, to ensure the information is not misunderstood. The language of immigrants, the borrowed and the stolen, alien words for foreign sentiments. Today will be one of those all-Italian days.

On the floor beside his bed is a plastic bag swollen heavy with his urine. At the bottom is blood. Crystals of blood float sluggishly in that soup, dancing and sinking.

I swallow down bile.

"What time is it?" he asks, his eyes shimmering.

"It's early." His hair is silver and wild and there's stubble on his pale-yellow face. "I came in late last night."

"Why you do that, Sandro?"

I step into the room and grab a plastic chair from near the door, drag it toward the bed. I've come to let you know you're dying, that's why.

"Help me up," he says.

The general rule, the orthopaedic surgeon had told me, is that anyone over eighty who breaks their femur will be dead in twelve months unless they're on their feet within the first three weeks. I step closer, smelling him, and wrap my arms around his body. I can feel his bones, sharp, and they make me want to withdraw, make me glance about hoping to spot a nurse, a doctor, anyone. Anyone but me. I'm afraid to hurt him but finally I get him up into a sitting position and begin to fix the pillows behind his back. He's not satisfied, shuffles about, fastidious, always fussy and short-tempered.

"Not like that," he says. I can hear the self-same rapprochement that had chastened me as a boy. "Not like that, move that pillow, no, not like that, come on, *ma cosa fai, cosa fai*, Sandro!" It takes a while. Finally, he finds a position of relative comfort. "Yes, is fine," he says dejectedly. "Leave it, leave it, *per favore, lascia stare.*"

I retreat to the hard-plastic chair. "How are you feeling?"

"I couldn't sleep last night," he replies, waving at the room. "They gave me something—" he gazes at me with eyes widening as he recalls suddenly— "they gave me something and next thing, next thing, you are here. I think it was," he drops his voice conspiratorially, "drugs. Do you think they *drugged* me?"

"Did you sleep?"

"Yes."

"Then that's good."

He sucks his lips unconvinced. "Where are you staying?"

"Usual place. In Vicenza."

"Why don't you stay at the flat?" He waits for a while before his lids lift and his eyes—vague, tired, buttery—stare at me until I blink away. What can I say? That I'm afraid? Old people's eyes all look the same, as if they're drowning in their own piss. "Have you checked my car lately?" he asks suddenly.

"What? No. No, I'll do it today."

"Okay. You know the battery goes flat if you don't start it up every now and again."

"I'll go today."

"Okay," he says. "It doesn't matter, I just ask."

Silence then. He has oxygen being pumped into his nostrils. Cannulae, they call it, those tube things that vanish into the nostrils. Two litres per minute. The things you learn ... the things you do, and there's no point, really, there's no point just being scared when something must be done.

"I spoke to the doctor," I tell him. "Dr Puccini. He was here last night, right?"

"Was he?"

"Yes. He spoke to you, he said, about the MRI. Do you remember what he said?"

"Not really," my father replies, his eyes fixed on a spot far away from ever meeting mine. "You know what doctors are like." And then, sharp as ever, "How do you know he was here?"

"He told you they found something. In your lungs. From the mines."

"What mines?"

"In South Africa."

"I don't remember ever going to mines, Sandro," he says dismissively.

"But didn't you work for mining companies?"

"Yes, but not *in* the mines," he says irritably. "Maybe once or twice. I remember in Sasolburg, but that was a dirty place. Your asthma came from there."

My asthma. Me in the back of his FIAT 1300 with the windows open trying to inhale air as he rushed me to the hospital through the night, my mom's voice shouting, "Sandro, Sandro, *Dio santo*, Sandro!" And me dying.

Scratching at the air that wouldn't come, watching the milky streetlights go blink-blink-blink. I blink this away and tell him, "They found something in your, you know, your—your lungs."

"Is serious?" he asks in English.

"It's a tumour," I tell him. The words flee my mouth. I didn't expect those words. They just come to my lips, and I'm horrified. I look up, expecting a reaction, but he just lies there, staring beyond me, at the dust dancing in the sunlight. "But no one knows, really, it's not—it is what it is," I blurt out, and this sounds reasonable to me even as I think, this man is so much more than I will ever be, and so I say it again, "it is what it is."

His eyes catch mine and hold them. "So what will they do?"

"There's nothing to do." I glance away. At the window. "It is what it is."

"But not serious?"

"They don't know. To find out they'd need to do an operation. And they don't think you're strong enough."

I listen to his breath. Raspy and wet. "But is serious?" he insists in English.

"At your age," I tell him, "waking up is serious."

He looks at me for a while. Then his fingers touch his chest, where the tumour is, he touches his chest and rubs it. "Will you check the car today?" he asks after a while. "The battery."

"I'll go through today, yes. Do you want me pick up some newspapers when I come back this afternoon?"

"No. They make too much noise. Always the same news anyway. Just some magazines. GENTE."

"Okay. Is that the magazine my mother used to read?" Read. She'd look at the photos, mostly. She'd left school at twelve. Functional illiterate—but they didn't have those terms back then. Back then she was just a person, not a profile with delimited expectations.

"Yes," he replies, and focuses in on the wall-shelf at the end of the bed, at a red-framed photograph of my mom. Monochrome, before she'd had kids, the woman he'd fallen in love with in Torino in the summer of '59. I'd brought it in a couple of weeks back—he'd asked me for that very one—she must be in her thirties in it, beautiful. So beautiful. And so kind. I picture my father waiting for her with his seven red carnations because in Italy, you only bring an even number of flowers to a funeral, waiting for my mom, dead on a fucking red chair in the winter sun not even able to remember his name, a life erased.

"And Sandro," he says. English again.

"Hey."

"Can you take that photo home? I no want it here no more."

## "Meraviglioso"—Domenico Modugno

My mother's keys on a long blue ribbon that she'd begun wearing around her neck when her memory started to fade—"Sandro, do you know I sometimes forget things?"—unlock the brown metal door to garage number five, down in the dank subway beneath their apartment building. It's as I lift the door and expose the insides—a white-washed cinder block cavity and there, dead-centre, is my dad's 1986 red FIAT Uno—that Messenger pings once more.

Sofia. Again.

I trash the circle icon and don't bother reading the message and focus in on the FIAT gleaming dust under the naked bulb on the ceiling. They used to call it a supermini. FIAT built nine million units of this chassis, the eighth-most produced automobile platform in history. I know this because I'd written a piece for *Cars Magazine* some years back, a retrospective of the turbocharged variant that'd been the sleeper of the summer of '92 in South Africa. My dad had bought it on the same day he'd bought the apartment. "La Vecchia" I'd christened it, even back then when it was but a few years old.

Hanging from rusted nails on the yellow-stained walls are old football pennants—an '83 Juve pennant, '82 Inter, and an Italy '82 World Cup-winning one with the names of boyhood heroes: Paolo Rossi, and the tiny mop-top wizard Bruno Conti, and big-old Dino Zoff. I'd played 'keeper on those yellow, razor-sharp winter fields in Joburg wearing a grey pullover to simulate his cup-winning jersey. Zoff was forty when he'd won that cup. His face reminded me of my father. His face will always remind me of my father.

It's odd because my dad had never liked football. He'd told me once about the early '50s when he was edging to get out of Italy and how it was *"quei cretini"* reading nothing but the football scores on the trams that'd pushed him on the slow-boat to São Paulo as a twenty-year-old immigrant. And yet I remember him in '82 taking me up to the deserted highlands in Yeoville, up on a ridge with Joburg stretched out below us in a warm golden glow, horizon-to-horizon with the distant gold-ash walls fortifying the city from the winter night. And his two friends—but I wonder now whether they were friends at all because I never did see them again—fostered a fire in an abandoned oil drum around which we gathered to listen to the World Cup Final on an old Telefunken radio with commentary by RAI. Up there was the only place we could get a signal, and the game wasn't on TV that'd only been launched in fascist South Africa in '75. I remember the bite of the Highveld winter, and the darkness and the crackle of the fire under that dark-dark sky, and the faces of my dad and his friends like liquid shapes shifting in the chiaroscuro of orange flames and feeling safe up there, a part of his life when he gave me a small shot of grappa as we listened to the game, and that strange smile that crossed my dad's lips when Marco Tardelli scored for Italy comes to me now, and if I listen hard enough, I can still catch the echo of the commentator's voice— *"Tardelli, Tardelli, gol, gol, gol, Tardelli, Tardelli..."*

I was ten years old the year Italy became champions of the world. Strange, these memories, just clips, like a highlight reel of a long-forgotten football match.

I climb into the FIAT. It weighs less than 900kgs, and I feel the suspension sag. The ignition key sits in the ashtray. I insert it and turn. The motor rolls over precisely once and promptly plays dead. Then the battery light comes on orange on the dashboard. I try again and the thing doesn't even roll over this time. I see the choke button. I'd forgotten about these things. I pull it back all the way and turn the key again. It does nothing much at all. I sit back on the seat and glance about. The scent in here is sweet, pine, and it reminds me of when they'd come pick me up in Venice when I'd fly in from New York with my daughter still a baby, a toddler.

My folks had driven down to Calabria in this thing, 1,200 kilometres, a decade ago. That was their last road trip, my mom and dad…the last of so many. I remember those road trips in Africa of my childhood when my father would wake us at 4AM and carry me down in my pyjamas to his Alfa Giulietta, and I'd be dozing when he'd cut into that African dark thick as syrup, arrowing to the wild-wild ocean in Natal. I'd wake on the backseat all sweaty in the mid-morning heat and my mom would turn in the passenger seat, a '70s-toned fading memory this, and she would smile back at me just so, and the scenery beyond the dirty finger-stained windows would be barren and the mountains blue-topped and the trees wide and short-limbed in the mayonnaise-dense light, and she would give me a biscuit and milk as she would for Natalie when she'd come to collect us from the airport in Venice forty years later. And her smile, my mother's smile, so open, and warmer than the air that would blow in from my dad's open window as he'd smoke with one hand guiding the steering wheel—I'd always thought the Mona Lisa was a mother's smile until someone had pointed out my ignorance.

They'd driven from the Copper Belt in Northern Zambia, north of Chingola, on the border with the Congo—up where Livingstone had died less than a hundred years before searching for the source of the Nile—all the way south to Joburg, this in early '62 when the shit was kicking off and Dag Hammarskjöld and Patrice Lumumba had just been executed, my dad refuelling the car with a jerrycan on roads that were nothing but dirt tracks yellow-washed in his FIAT 1300's tired lights, and nothing in the dark bush but the rustle of danger, my mom standing shotgun with an actual automatic aiming into the blackness. Two thousand kilometres they'd driven, these two Italians who spoke not a word of English, barely in their thirties then with my infant brother in the backseat. Two thousand kilometres through the fading colonies of Southern Africa with nothing to guide them but a wrinkled map and hope and the headlights splat on white-flecked silver birch trees whooshing on by. They'd done their road trips back in the '60s for sure—Zambia, Lourenço Marques—peri-peri prawns and

Gary Edwards on LM Radio—Vic' Falls and who knows, without her, who knows where else my father would've ended up. Who knows where I'd have been born if it'd been up to my dad and his need to what? Run from himself? Too easy. It's more than that—I should know because I'd run more than him from whatever it was that chased us.

I rub the tears away and abandon the FIAT and head out for the Porsche. My phone pings again. Messenger again. Sofia again.

*You're violating the law. I will take legal action if the image is not deleted. You don't know what you're doing, please, just do this.*

What the fuck. I trash the window and bury the phone in my jacket next to the photo. I can't anymore. I think, you're leaving me when I need you most.

## "La Nevicata del 56"—Mia Martini

"A man does not bleed on the frozen steppe, he falls like an angel, stiff already, and lies there dead. We know he is dead when the fleas bolt from his corpse a black river of blood, a sneering snake stretching for another host. At least the itch of life surrenders with death."

I see the quote on Pinterest, along with hundreds of photos of the vanished army—*l'armata scomparsa*—that went to war one hot day in the summer of '42 and disappeared. Ten divisions, including three new Alpini divisions—the 2 Alpini Division Tridentina, the 3 Alpini Division Julia, and the 4 Alpini Division Cuneense—all sent to protect the German VI Army's flank as they stumbled at the gates of Stalingrad. Boys, 255,000 of them. In the end, 100,000 came home—the rest just swallowed up forever by the ice of the Russian steppe west of the Don River.

The Julia was my uncle's division; he was with the artillery Gruppo Udine. One of the vanished. He'd had a dentist rip out all his top teeth when his call-up papers had come, had feigned illness and disease, but none of it mattered; in August of '42, nineteen years old, he'd climbed aboard a train with the rest of the class of '22 headed for Gorizia and whatever godforsaken fate Duce had planned for him.

I sit back from my laptop. Familiar now, the rich tapestry of walls in the hotel room. I've been here so many times, always this room, room 408 at the Villa Scacchi, an old Palladio-style villa dating back to the 1800s, plenty of ghosts and a hollowed-out church beside it where death-black crows nest, and in here, rustic furniture and a bed shaped like a sled in polished oak deflecting the warm, buttery lights.

My uncle's matriculation papers from the army that lost him between January 16th and January 30th, 1943, places him square-centre in the greatest military defeat in Italian history and—as is usually the case with these things—its greatest moment of sheer, insane heroism. He was declared dead in '48, five years after he'd gone missing, and given a medal of honour in '57. Got a medal for dying, I guess. Got a medal for never coming home, and neither had his body or his tags. All of it gone. It's a strange thing when you get down to it. To vanish off the face of the earth like that. Or maybe not—maybe it's that someone loved him enough to have noticed that he'd vanished. That's the real surprise.

On the desk is the photo I'd found in the apartment. I pick it up and hold it in the moist light of the desk lamp. Four men trapped off-guard in an instant that reveals nothing. My uncle stares out at me tragically, and I lean closer, wanting to see his eyes, but it's all so vague—and anyway, the dead always seem tragic to the living. But it's one of the men holding him up that attracts my interest. The man on the left. Something about that face, as if he's aware of a secret, as if he's mocking me through time. Something about that man, with his beard and that curious Che Guevara smile, staring at me through the years as if he realised that one day someone would appreciate the mystery of that smile.

I stand and slide down on the soft bed and grab my phone charging bedside. I open a browser and do a cursory search for Alpini, 1943, Don River, Julia. I select the images tab and run through the images. I don't find this image. This one seems never to have been published at all.

Beyond the leaded, thick-paned windows, the afternoon is underwater, heavy clouds staining the sapphire sky. Just gone four. I watch the night fold into the room. There aren't many photos of my uncle, not since my grandmother had consigned them all to fire one afternoon in '47, all his letters from the Eastern Front, all his photos, everything. My dad had once told me why, but now that I think of it, I really can't remember *when* he'd told me—it just seems to be something I know, this scene from my grandmother's life, of the day she'd come back home from her visit to the local council and set about burning every memento of her eldest son.

"What was your son doing in Russia, anyway? Did he think the Russians would welcome him with vodka and sausages?" the man from the council had replied that afternoon when she'd gone to ask, yet again, for news on her missing boy. "You're pretty enough, go make another fascist."

She'd never spoken of him again after that day, the nineteen-year-old boy who'd been sent to die in the Caucuses, that was the idea, to Baku to secure the oilfields, marching in the heat of a Ukrainian summer in fields of sunflowers before orders were reversed and the Italian 8th Army and the Alpine Divisions had been rerouted to the Don River. My uncle had died forever the day his mother had abandoned the relics of his memory.

From antiquity, from Ptolemy all the way until the 18th Century, the Don had been the border between Europe and Asia, and it'd become the western flank of the German VI Army, stalled at the gates of Stalingrad in '42. ARMIR—*Armata Italiana in Russia*—had marched one thousand kilometres to its banks to wait for the bone-crushing winter and the Russians to kill them.

I can't help wondering why my dad had left it there, this photo, why in the pouch that contained his will. His will—what a strange word—his will after death. But I can't ask him—I can't ask him this. Not now.

I lift my phone and dial.

"Yes?" says my wife's voice, exasperated.

"Hi."

Silence. My wife doesn't do conversation. You wouldn't be able to drown a fly in the shallows of her emotions.

"Can I speak with Natalie?" I ask.

More silence, for a minute or so, then my daughter's voice comes on the line. "Hi, Dad," she sighs.

"Hey. How you doin'?"

"Fine. You?"

"Not great. Wanted to hear a friendly voice." Silence. "So whatcha doin'?"

"Nothin'."

"Okay. Any plans for tomorrow?"

"Dunno."

"Okay. I'll be late tomorrow night, so we'll see each other Monday."

"Okay."

"I miss you."

"'kay. Bye."

"I love you," I tell the dead line before tossing the phone onto the bed and into the creeping dark. The rain is falling out there. I walk over to the window and stare out at the mist crawling over the flatlands toward the hotel like a tide. The phone buzzes. I grab it and notice I have a PM on Messenger. From Sofia with the pretty avatar.

*I know what happened to your uncle Alessandro. In Russia. Take down that image and I'll explain everything. Just take it down. This is urgent.*

I sigh and click the Facebook app, find the ARMIR page, locate my post, and think fuck it. It's been seen by thirty-nine people. No comments. No likes. They destroyed the world, the world I had grown up in. All this noise. I delete the photo, throw the phone aside, and stare into the indigo light until the phone auto-dies and leaves me listening to the rain clapping the gravel in the dark.

## "Sapore di Sale"—Gino Paoli

February

It's when I join up with a Swiss convoy headed onto the A1 motorway after the tollgates beyond Como and set the cruise to 180kmh that I see the impatient flash of lights in my mirror. There's a car back there homing in at some serious rate of knots. I shift onto the right lane and allow the car through—a Mercedes-AMG CLS63 S shooting brake with an immense 5.5-litre twin-turbo V8 and equipped with immunity-granting ZH plates. A bald man holds the wheel with one easy hand, his *apéro* in his other, on his way, I imagine, to Cortina. He looks like Vin fucking Diesel. I hit the throttle and cut back into his stream and watch my mirror as something quick closes in on me, unmistakably the xenon headlights of a Porsche 911. I chase the Merc' until, at 256kmh on my speedo, the flat-6 behind my head goes asthmatic and I can do nothing but move aside and let the 911 through—another bald prick, this one with a little smile as he raises his brow at me and then goes off to hunt the Merc' down into the night.

    There are messages on my phone when I step into room 408 at the Villa Scacchi just gone 2AM—my wife wants more love, my brother wants more info for the lawyer, and Messenger has a notification from Sofia. It takes me a moment before I remember who she is. I read the message.

    *I'm sorry it's taken so long to get back to you. Do you think you could meet me in Valdagno sometime tomorrow?*

    I type *sure* feeling anything but.

Doesn't take long. About thirty seconds.

*OK,* the message pings back, *meet me at the caffé garibaldi on the piazza del commune. 1.30.*

I give it twenty minutes before I type *yes* and climb into bed shivering.

## "Dio Come Ti Amo"—Gigliola Cinquetti

Last week my father was transferred to Malo, a neglected town some ten kilometres out of Schio that's clinging to life on the back of a renowned rehab centre where they'll try to get him onto his feet. The town sits at the head of a flat, dead-straight road that cuts north-south out of Schio through a sinister and haunting landscape. To the west, beyond dead, frost-crusted fields, squat the snow-flecked, craggy mountains of the Pasubio over which a nasty winter sun arcs obliquely; to the east, the unwelcome flats of the Veneto landscape and its dark earth pushing up naked-limbed trees from the ground-mist like tombstones. Like a moonscape, otherworldly.

Luigi Meneghello, Malo's only famous son who'd emigrated to England as soon as he could afford passage, wrote a book about this place entitled "Libera nos a Malo"—Deliver us from Malo—and I get where he was coming from when I follow the jarring cobbled roads through narrow alleys between ancient, rotting buildings, and come out right by the rehab building, a faded-white concrete edifice built in the '70s, hefty and brutal and full of shadow and weirdly deflected light. It's as forbidding as a prison, a prison for people who've been condemned for nothing but the crime of not yet dying.

I find a parking space near a desiccated lawn in the pale light where a couple of sickly plane trees seep pasty from between the trash on the patchy grass, and head toward the rehab clinic with its white concrete stained by rainwater like mascara tears on a face. I follow the signs down a hallway to the elevator bank and climb into a massive car with a smoked-glass mirror. I stare at myself long enough to realise I need a shave. I avoid my eyes. It's been a long time since I could look into my own eyes, and there's probably something in that, but I'm in no mood to reflect on it. Natalie would have enjoyed that pun. I step out of the elevator on the third floor. To my left are white double doors, both shut. Beside them is a notice with visiting hours on it. I'm early, but it's always wise to be prompt when you visit the dying. I push the doors open and step into the ward.

My dad is sitting right there in a wheelchair.

He sits next to the radiator on the yellow-tiled hallway with a window behind his head throwing up a vista of Monte Malo and the regiments of vine terraces rising up the sun-facing slope beyond the red terracotta tiled roofs of the old stone town. My father in a wheelchair. He wears a pair of tracksuit pants, bushy cotton ones that are speckled by lint, and a grey jersey with a sweatshirt beneath it. He has shaved—and nicked himself—and his eyes are fluid when they look up and clock me.

"Sandro," he says, something curious in his face, "you here?"

I don't trust my voice. I spot a chair and drag it over slowly, buying time that neither of us have anymore, and sit in front of him.

"I brought some stuff," I tell him, magazines from Zürich, English ones, politics and economics, which I place on the marble-tiled window ledge, and we sit there beside the warm radiator and cast around for things to say. Whatever they are, these things that men are meant to share with their fathers, they're not coming. We sit silent instead and watch the nurses pass and the patients with their wheelchairs and walkers and the shadows hurrying over the vineyards on Monte Malo from a sky uncertain.

"Everyone here," my father says after we watch a woman roll past with the wildest eyes I've ever seen, "is mad."

He has a point. I realise we've said not a word about my mom since that last night we'd eaten together at the apartment. I never did see him shed a single tear. I think perhaps he's shed all the tears he had in him a long time ago.

"You no say much," he says eventually. English. I shrug. "What you t'ink about, Sandro?"

"Nothing much," I tell him and accidentally catch his eyes full. He's watching me and I look away.

"Is funny," he says. "You never think it happen like this."

"What?"

"That it happen like this," he repeats, and then we fall into our silence and watch the shadows over Monte Malo until, at the end of visiting hours—12.30PM—I leave with the promise of returning for evening hours. I walk to my car in the cold. I feel like throwing up. I have a fine under my wiper. I grab the pink slip and tear it up. Swiss immunity.

The road up to Valdagno runs through a tunnel that shaves twenty minutes off a ride that'd once gone around and up a middling mountain pass. A short hop to Schio's twin-town. Twin, because where Schio was developed by Alessandro Rossi and his Lanerossi concern, Valdagno, on the banks of the rushing dark-waters of the river Agno, was created by textile-tycoon Count Marzotto. Both came into the 1900s saddled by an industrial miracle that employed tens of thousands of workers, and both were faced with the complexities of housing and caring for an increasingly unionised labour force. For Marzotto, that meant creating a city that seems weirdly out of time when I drive into it, a quiet, puzzling, bleak place of shaded arcades and rigid Liberty-style buildings ill at ease like cap-holding peasants in their Sunday best.

The town had been conceived between '28 to '44 by architect Francesco Bonfanti as a city of light and shadow and concrete, an efficient and contemporary fascist aesthetic for the workers of the colossal Marzotto factory. It's still there—an imposing boat-like edifice of faded, defiled concrete, hundreds of crenelated, filthy windows, and the pleasingly stylised *Marzotto* logo printed in giant flowing letters. They called it the Social City, *la Città Sociale,* built on the left bank of the Agno complete with houses and nurseries, orphanages and schools and nursing homes, sports fields, swimming pools and sports clubs, all the rewards for workers who were smart enough to shut the fuck up and do as they were told.

I pass the Casa del Balilla and the Casa del Fascio, epic fascist structures that throw long shadows over the roads built to follow the river's course and where the cool air was meant to calm nerves in the blistering summers of industrial action before the *squadristi* had come and broken skulls and hopes in the '30s. If a city could ever represent fascism and the ethic of work, Valdagno would be its poster child. I drive past the old Rivoli Theatre, once an 1,800-seat colossus that was stripped of its marble façade and converted into apartment blocks twenty years after Count Marzotto's statue had been razed from the centre of his planned town during the Years of Lead. But Marzotto had still won one over on his competition down in Schio: his company had bought the failed Lanerossi brand back in '87.

I drive up a skinny street that runs astride the river entombed in a deep channel of white stone walls and find a lot up the hill where I leave the Porsche and head into the pedestrian-only centre. I feel strangely disconnected to time and place when I walk past the pink- and blue-shuttered Palazzo Festari and its plaque dedicated to Valdagno that'd earned a Silver Medal for its partisan resistance during the war forever displayed alongside General Diaz's Victory Bulletin from 1918. Ahead is a cobblestone piazza and the fin de siècle Caffé Garibaldi on the mezzanine of a tobacco-coloured stucco palazzo with the Italian and EU flags dripping from a gabled balcony. There's a scent in the café that reminds me of mornings of my youth—Nutella on warm bread, caffè latte ... and my mom's smile.

I find a table inside—the smattering of tables on the *terrazza* are all abandoned in the chilled wind because here, unlike in Zürich, the chairs don't come with sheepskin blankets—and begin scrolling my phone like some weird rabbi, pretending to be busy, pretending to be someone else.

Doesn't take long, a minute or two, before a chair scrapes on the marble floor in front of me. I sluggishly lift my gaze as if in reverie to some crucial matters there on my phone screen.

A woman is standing over me. Thirties, I guess. Pretty as her avatar. She's gazing down at me, half-accusatory, half-sadistic and all woman, dirty blonde hair in flawless rich strands framing a face that shows just the briefest of smiles.

I stand up too quickly, my crotch hitting the table that bristles about as she holds out a hand.

"Signor Lago?" she asks, her face delightfully predatory.

"Yes," I agree, touching her hand and getting the jolt of an electric charge. "Alex, please. You're—"

"Sofia." She meets my gaze with sincere eyes, green and flecked like the cosmos. She's wearing a tight leather jacket, a silk scarf, blue jeans, and worn, tough leather boots that extend up to her knees. And she's beautiful, I think, because I'm too tired to pretend I don't notice. She sits and doesn't need to wait long for the waiter to appear at her shoulder. I imagine she doesn't need to wait long for service anywhere she goes. She orders an espresso and glances at me invitingly, but I wave it all away.

"Alex," she says. "Not Sandro?"

"Sandro to my parents," I tell her. "Alessandro to my mom when she was pissed at me. Alex to everyone else."

She smiles. "I'd like to thank you," she says in English with an inflection that sounds vaguely American, "for deleting that image. It was quite a shock seeing it there."

I glance away at the clean-tiled piazza beyond the towering windows when the waiter brings her espresso and a glass of dust-flecked water. I let the waiter hover near her, doing his thing. The wind is throwing shadow and light out there over the cobbles in a way that unsettles me. When the waiter scuttles away, I turn to her and lie. "I'm sorry it took me so long. I was busy with—things. Can I ask why?"

"I'm sorry?"

"Why you were shocked?"

She looks at me in a way that flusters my heartbeat. "Let me ask you something first. Where did you find it?"

"What, the photo? In my father's things."

She sips her espresso, just so on her lips. Then she downs it in one shot, swirls the little cup to get the sugar moist, and slides that down her throat like a dark oyster. I can't look away. "Your father," she says now, dabbing her lips with a napkin, her eyes making me feel deeply inadequate, because that's what beauty does in the end, it just reminds you of everything you aren't, everything you can never be, it just births resentment, "how's he doing in Malo?"

I'm about to reply when I realise, "How do you know my father's in Malo?"

"I have a friend there, at the rehab clinic."

Her smile makes me anxious. "I'm sorry," I clear my throat, "but I'm just curious—why did you want me to delete the image?"

She places the glass of water to her lips and sips. And says nothing for a while. Long enough to make me shift in my chair. "Photos are strange things," she says eventually, placing the empty glass onto the scarred table and shifts it about distractedly. "Now we snap thousands of them, don't we, without much thought, but back then, they were—like a metaphor, is that the word? Metaphor? We focus on the faces and things on the photo, but most of the time the real story is out of the frame, controlling our emotions. You follow?"

I sit back on the wooden chair and try hard not to look at her moist lips. In the airy, tall-ceilinged room with the black rafters and the checked marble floor, the wooden framed smoky mirrors and ancient espresso machine gasping and steaming like an old train behind the polished-wood bar, and the solemn faces of dead men of industry staring down at us from dark portraits on the golden walls, she takes on an unreal, almost spectral vision. I'm tired, I think. I'm tired.

"Is the person who took this photo the story then?" I ask.

"Oh no," she replies. "Quite the opposite in this case. In this case, the shit is right *on* that photo."

"The shit?"

"I could," she replies, smiling, and her eyes flash-freeze mine, "have found a better expression."

I look away, down at her hands on the table. Nails bit to the quick. "You seem to have me at a disadvantage, Sofia."

"I realise that." She slides her hands from the table and onto her lap. "And that's the way it has to be for now."

"Until what?"

"Until I'm sure of your intentions."

"My intentions?" I glance behind her. There's a group of kids sitting together around a small table staring down at their phones, laughing at shared memes or something. The sun comes through the windows in firm, dusty spires and then a shadow cuts across the marble floor, bringing me back. Her eyes keep staring at me and I glance away, ever the fucking coward.

"Alex, what's your interest in this photo?" she asks.

"Aside from my uncle? Nothing much. The—"

"Alessandro Lago, vanished in January 1943 in Russia."

"Yes. Exactly."

"Where did he get the photo?"

"Who, my father? I have no idea."

"Have you asked him?"

"No."

"Why not?"

I sip water, wipe my lips with a hard napkin and don't reply.

"Why did you post it? The photo? Why now?" she asks.

"Because I found it the morning I put it up."

"Where?"

"Where what?"

"Where did you find it?"

"In my father's things. As I said."

"No one gave it to you then?"

"What?"

"No one gave you this image, asked you to post it?"

I ball up the napkin and throw it onto the table. "Listen," my words come out angrier than I'd intended, "you know what?" I sit a little closer and fail to keep the edge from my voice. "I don't need to justify myself to you, okay? So why don't you just cut the crap and tell me what this is about?"

She smiles. Disarming. Beautiful. So far from the angry secretive snarl that I've become accustomed to. "Your family and mine, Alex, we're linked in a," she pauses, looking for a word, "a strange coincidence of history."

"A what now?"

"The Massacre of 1945."

It takes me a while, watching the shadows scuttle across the marble floor, to find words. "What are you talking about? What massacre?"

"So for me," she says, red lips moist and teeth expensive, American-white, "the question remains as it was when I walked in here."

"I was under the impression you'd asked me—"

"*Whether*," she interrupts, "I want to trust you with the truth."

"Why wouldn't you? What truth?"

"Because," she says, and her eyes crawl over me like a cockroach, "I might be afraid of what you'd do with it."

"Do with what?" I always get a sense of shame before I say something offensive and age has made the filter sharper, so I pause and suck up some oxygen. "Listen, why don't you spell this out for me. What is it that you think I'd do with—with whatever it is that we're talking about here?"

"Say," she sits forward with her elbows on the table, the leather tautening around her shoulders, "that I revealed some information to you that would expose—just say—people close to me to questions we'd rather not answer right now. What would you do with it?"

"I don't know."

"You're a writer, yes?"

"I write about cars," I tell her. "I'm an old white man who writes about cars. No one gives a shit."

"Cars?"

"Cars."

Wispy hair expensively cut and a face that has seen more than it wants to reveal and an expensive-skin smile. "You're not that old."

What's there to say?

"Do you know anything about the other men in that photo?" she asks.

"Not a thing."

"No idea who Russo was?"

"No. Who's Russo?"

"Alex," she says, and my name on her lips makes me sit up like a fucking dog, "those eleven days in Russia in January '43 changed everything for us. My family, yours, our country, it changed everything, and it changed nothing at all. Do you understand?"

I give it a moment. "Sure," I reply, wanting a cigarette.

"Sure," she echoes, but she's obviously not. "When we lost 100,000 boys in Russia in less than two weeks, it was the end—the end of Mussolini, the end of fascism, the end of the war, of, of—"

"Italy."

"Yes, I suppose that's true, in a way. But if you follow the political rise of any Italian in the '60s and '70s, you'll find links back to the war, you understand this, yes?"

"Of course."

"Any man here, in Italy, from back then, any man who rose to prominence, be it politics or business, they all wore the stain of war."

"The stain of fascism, sure."

She sits back. "But here's the thing, Alex." That name again. "Italy is not Germany. We didn't come to terms with our past, our history. We didn't have some great reckoning like they did in South Africa after the fall of that regime. We just went back to business because that's the way things have always been here."

South Africa. My phone number. Malo. She knows too much.

"But it's like an affair," she says. "You must respect your marriage enough not to flaunt your lover, your infidelity. Not to provoke, do you follow? There are things best left unsaid. Always. It's the core of kindness, yes? Except, perhaps, between people you trust, who share a common bond."

"All bonds are common."

"Not that common, Alex. I'm talking family."

"And that's us?"

"It could be." Her eyes look at my mouth and I swallow the promise dangling there between us. And then, just like that, she's on her feet and looking down at me, her hand hanging there over the table. "I'll contact you again, Alex."

"When?" I ask, standing too quickly and bump the table with my hip. Cups clatter and her glass wobbles about. Her hand shoots out and seizes it, rights it.

"When I decide," she says. Her hand, when she grabs mine, is firm and dry.

"Decide?"

She nods.

"Decide what exactly?"

"Whether we can be friends, Alex."

"Does that depend on me not publishing the photograph?"

Just a moment's pause with my hand in hers. "You'd be doing me a favour if you kept the image to yourself," she concedes, letting my skin go, "and you'd be doing yourself a favour too. I mean, I doubt you need any more complications in your life right now, either. Right?"

I watch her walk out and cross the piazza. Her back is ramrod straight, her walk confident, shoulders blunt, hair caught in the wind. I watch her jump onto a lime-green Vespa. She slides on a helmet, open-faced, then a pair of Ray Bans, and turns the ignition. A moment later and she's powering by me without even acknowledging my existence.

Behind her a black Maserati SUV follows, driven by a man in dark-dark shades whose face turns my way and somehow, I know he's looking straight-dead at me.

## "Mi Sono Innamorato Di Te"—Luigi Tenco

My father's sitting in his wheelchair just beyond the doors to the ward and I wonder whether he sits there because he's near the radiator or because he's waiting for me. He doesn't reveal anything, head bowed, shoulders drooped, liver-stalked hands on his lap as if he's sleeping. Beyond the windows, over the medieval, red-tiled roofs, Monte Malo is shrouded in a cold blue mist cut like ribs into the barren vineyards. It makes me shiver.

"Sandro," he says, raising his head.

I grab a chair from outside the dining room and sit before him. I've brought some magazines from the shop, *L'Espresso* and the *International*. My father's politics have always been weird—anti-apartheid but convinced the ANC would be the end of South Africa, a sometimes-socialist who read *The Economist* as if he were an American businessman. Political pessimism—and yet he spent the last twenty-five years of his retirement watching political shows on TV and hurling choice words at the screen while my mom napped beside him as they'd done back in South Africa.

We sit there by the doors in silence and watch people come and go, the old and the infirm rolling on by in their wheelchairs toward the TV-room in an all-glass alcove that my father says he'd rather blow up than ever sit in. We watch the children of the predestined—middle-aged men and women crisply dressed for winter with faces flush from the cold—walk in and out of the double doors as if this ward was a theatre of the absurd, and what's more absurd than death? Eventually, I ask, "So how was physio?"

"Okay," he says, gazing distractedly at the cover of the magazines. The rise of the new right, Italy's reckoning for a past never reconciled, and Schio's right-wing mayor refusing to allow the laying of stumbling stones to honour fourteen boys who'd been sent to the gas camps in '44. "I walked a little."

"You did?"

"A few steps."

"That's good. Maybe we can get you out of here."

"No maybe, Sandro. I run out of here."

I smile, averting my gaze, down at his slippers on the footrests of his wheelchair. We've never been able to look each other in the eye. I don't know why. Probably it's me. No, of course it's always been me. We'd never bonded because I'm unable to, I've always been terrified of this, of losing him. And my mom? Had it been different with her? I think of a hundred things I want to say to him right then. Instead, I stare silently out the window, up there at Monte Malo silent and bleak and shrouded in the icy mist while he browses the magazines. I wonder how he feels, here, in this place, where time comes to die in lazy afternoons injected by fentanyl and anxiety. I wonder whether he even realises that death is sitting here with him. I look around and know, somehow, that this is the place. This is where he will die, in this ward, in this place.

"Would you have done anything else," I ask him that evening when the day has faded and Monte Malo has vanished in the dark, and the nurse—with a tattoo on her arm, a root of a tree or some fungus growing on her, and who speaks to us in stock English phrases, laughing all the while—wheels him to his little room lit pale, and prepares him for bed, "would you have stayed in South Africa, if you knew?"

"Knew what, Sandro?" he asks, innocent as my corruption. Does he sense a meaning in my words now? "Can you check the temperature? Always so cold in here."

I turn the thermostat on the wall up to 28C and walk over to the radiators and touch them. Hot. He's waiting for me to leave, so too the nurse. She needs to clean him, and he has some bizarre plastic contraption hanging on the bed for him to piss in, it looks like a horn.

I hug him in his chair. It takes everything I have. I feel his razor-sharp bones through his sweatshirt, his stubble on my face, smell his sweat and something else—I smell *him*, and the nausea works its way up my throat. I can hear his breath this close, the way he labours, the stringy wetness of it, and I don't feel his arms around me when I move away. He holds out his hand instead, wraps his fingers about mine, and looks up at me.

"You a good boy, Sandro. Is funny," he says in English. "I am like you son now."

I don't cry until I get to the elevator. Down on the road in the cold empty streets, the Malo cops have given me another fine. I've overstayed my welcome. I take the summons, tear it into ribbons and throw it into the air.

Saturday night, eating dinner alone at the Villa Scacchi in what had once been the stables, strange ricotta-based gnocchi from the hills near Recoaro where they bottle the water. Dino, the night-manager, had told me there's no one in the hotel aside from me tonight, said it with a smile that reminds me of Jack Nicholson in *The Shining*. "Just you and me," he'd said, and I'd grinned and headed for dinner where I have my phone on the table and scroll around.

Stalking Sofia.

I stalk her Facebook profile but there's not much there except some photos of Caribbean-looking beaches and yachts and her name: Sofia Ballarin. Bikinis, suntans, cocktails, smiles. I stare at her bikini for a long while and then do a Google search and come up with a few hits and I'm down the rabbit hole now, hunting someone named Sofia Godin, granddaughter of Ettore Godin who, a couple of decades ago, had been mayor of Valdagno. During the boom years of the late '80s, he'd risen up the ranks of a small regional party—*La Lega Veneta Serenissima*—whose dreams of secession and their own homeland in the Tri-Veneto had assured them of political irrelevance right up until the scandal years of the '90s had gifted them a national platform. A coalition with neo-fascist parties out of Lombardy had swelled their ranks and together they'd all mushroomed into the majority party in the last election when the Lega Nord, who'd once run ads promising to send southern Italians back to Africa south of the Po, had dropped the Nord from their brand and suddenly those they despised became their biggest constituents.

Italy.

I scan articles linked to Godin's name, one from the *Il Vicentino* that suggested a position with a portfolio in the governing coalition, this from back in '97. But a stroke seems to have done it in for him. I find an image of Godin from the late '70s in an American magazine, posing with his wife and two granddaughters, Eva and Sofia—is that little Sofia?—all smiling under a Sardinian sky. I compare the image of Godin to the men in the photo. It could be the same man, the man on the edge of the photo, there on the right by himself, there's a passing resemblance. And it could also be someone else entirely.

My brother sends me a WhatsApp. He says he's struggling today. My mom's been on his mind. He tells me of a dream he had, of him on a train, late for a visit to my folks. I think he should be here now. I'm incapable, I want to tell him, of doing this. But it is what it is. My brother says the doctors are wrong; he says maybe my father's had the problem with his lungs for a while. I don't reply and it's late when I finally shut the lights in room 408 and see the silver glow of a full moon trace the parquet floor. I watch some football show on the television, *Tiki Taka*, just watching with a shut-down brain and Luigi Tenco playing on my phone—Tenco who'd either shot himself or had been shot in a hotel room in Sanremo in '67—trying to ensure the anxiety that courses through my blood doesn't seize me entirely.

*Ciao Amore, Ciao.*

I watch the end to a dubbed Denzel Washington movie from the '90s, and Denzel, playing some hard-assed soldier, sounds like an immigrant from Ghana in the dubbed version, speaking pidgin Italian because Italy, and it's just as sleep is coming that my phone pings.

Sofia on Messenger.

*Can you meet me at the bus station in Schio? Tomorrow, early, say around 7?*

## "Anonimo Veneziano"—Ornella Vanoni

I'm on the road early, drifting through the streets under a murky sky and streetlights pale and uncertain. A hard, dry wind has picked up like a premonition, blowing yesterday's trash about like confetti—they call it the bora—and it makes me uneasy, rootless. The flat-6 behind my head snarls keenly when I pull up on the lot outside the bus station half-an-hour early.

I sit in the Porsche and smoke, scrolling my phone: my Facebook feed, the results from the Premier League, Serie A, Formula One. I find a short profile article on Godin from the archive of a defunct magazine from the '70s. In an interview about *La Cassa per il Mezzogiorno*—the state-sponsored program that'd been created in the '50s to speed-up the industrialisation of the South and instead became a cash cow for the mafia-owned political class—Godin mentions his two granddaughters, Eva (4) and Sofia (1), and how raising them after the tragic death of his son and daughter-in-law in a boating accident off the coast of Sardinia in '77 had given him a new drive in his fight for secession.

Little orphan Sofia.

I watch a bus roll in, and the dim lights blink on rigid as the doors open, good people with honest things to do on a Sunday morning before dawn stepping out into the wind and cold. With five minutes left before the appointment, I hear the ping on my phone an instant before Sofia's avatar pops up.

*Change of plan. Can you meet me at the agip station on the piovene-schio road? 5 minutes?*

I know where it is. Five minutes is a stretch, but under a beat sky fired up by three-day-old welts, I cut across town and pull up onto the gas station apron in a little under six. I see a motorbike by the pumps, gleaming naked carbon under the anxious light of the awning. Sofia's sitting on the bike side-saddle, smoking a cigarette, and when she sees me roll in, she slides off with the bounce of youth and strides on over.

"Nice car," she says, leaning forward and glancing into the cockpit as I drop the window.

"She's old," I tell her with the cold coming in scented by her.

"I like old things." Her eyes meet mine. "Is this the one you did that trip up the Stelvio with?"

"What?"

"I read your article, for *Cars Magazine*. I love that run up the Stelvio. 'In the Footprints of Tazio'. You made me want to get up there again."

"Wheel tracks."

"What?"

"'In the Wheel Tracks of Tazio'," I tell her. "That was the title."

"Wheel tracks? Is that even English?"

"If I were any good at this," I reassure her, "I'd be writing about shit that actually matters."

"You got over a thousand likes on Facebook for that story."

Junk for likes, likes for cash. But there's also this. A beautiful girl who's been spying on my life. I guess I should be grateful, like an old man in Kansas discovering he's just inherited a few mil' from a dead Nigerian prince exiled to Abu Dhabi.

She ducks her head out of the window and says, "Come on, follow me," and flicks the cigarette over my car. I watch her walk to the Ducati Diavel, her black leather fluid in the dawn, and listen as she turns the engine and guns the throttle, smoke filling the cold air from the exhausts. That's a lot of bike, I think, that Ducati gleaming like something straight out of *The Transformers*. She has a full-face helmet today, shiny and neon green, a tribute to Rossi that she slides over her head and slaps down with three hard slaps of one palm.

I follow her toward Piovene and then onto the low road that leads past the abandoned Lanerossi factory and the baroque bridge over the Astico River wavering orange in the dawn. A friend of my mom's had jumped from here once. That's the thing about suicide; you spend years working out all the intricate details, like a sex fantasy, and then when the time comes, it's all irrelevant—you just jump or you don't. Suicide is a lot like writing that way. My mom always said this was where she'd do herself in, but the madness had got to her first.

We run up through Caltrano to the traffic circle and then take the first exit onto the SP349, the road up to Asiago. For readers of *Auto Reviews* from July 2008—I wonder now if that includes Sofia—this is one of Europe's classic mountain runs that starts off leisurely between crenelated stone-wall bends in the shadows of overhanging woods before, up about a kilometre, bunching into tense hairpins, about two dozen switchbacks that start off tight and then open up so you can feed the power in early with gobs of oversteer on the billiard-smooth surface on the exits.

Sofia takes it easy until she gets to the first hairpin, and then she opens the Ducati up. I do the same but there's no way I'm keeping up with the bike as it powers up the hill. Not until we get to the tight bits, and that's when I'm onto her fast, sliding inside as she leans over with more guts than I'd be ready to devote on a cold Sunday in February, and pull out ahead. There's a FIAT hobbling up the hill and I don't even slow to see what's coming, duck out and overtake with the flat-6 right on the cam and I'm back on my lane when I glance in my rear-view to see Sofia hammer by the FIAT and gain on me as the next hairpin approaches way too fast. I wait to hit the brakes, scaring myself and willing my right foot to be brave and then wait a breath longer before stomping on the middle pedal and go down three, four gears until I run out of road and lock it all up. I turn the wheel but the Porsche understeers toward the sky as the scraping tyres try to find some bite. By the time they do, she's slipped inside me and she's up and out of the turn with the front wheel rising off the road like a praying mantis. I avoid the outside Armco by inches, so close I can see the rivets and the rust. She goes up the gears with that motor wailing and by the time we get to the next hairpin, she's left me for dead and I lose heart and keep pushing but not so much anymore, my adrenaline tamed by my fear and my ego along with it. Old age, I guess, where pretend racing is fake sex. In my mirrors I spot a black SUV's cold white lights rising up the pass and wonder where the hell it'd come from—I'm sure I hadn't seen it down at the foot of the climb, and that means it's somehow not only following, it's actually gained on me.

Up at the summit, where the road gleams in a blood-red sunrise, a series of fast sweeping bends, with Swiss pine on the inside and on the outside a railing beyond which is nothing but sky and the distant peaks of the pink-tinged Dolomites, await the brave and the mad. The road leads on to Asiago and the Altopiano between walls of tall pine trees gouging rays that flicker pink across the glassy road, and there just past the rose-stone osteria where a single-track road leads off to the trenches and mountain fortifications—miles of tunnels where the Italians had fought the First War along with Hemingway and Rommel—she's pulled up on the shoulder, waiting for me. I follow her onto a hard-packed stone-and-dirt road that winds through a dense forest. It's as dark as death in here and I'm getting more nervous by the minute until we finally emerge into a clearing.

Before us is a red-stone farmhouse all aglow in the dawn light. The villa rises from a sparkling meadow in the thick shadow of a gnarly rock of a mountain that stretches up to a lemonade sky, and it reminds me of a cabin from a cowboy movie, up in Montana or something. I kill my engine and climb out into silence and think, if she kills me and buries me up here in the woods, ain't no one going to find my remains—not for a long time. They're still digging up the dead from the battles in '15 and burying them at the ossuary in Asiago from up in these mountains.

"This is yours?" I ask, my shoes crunching loudly on the gravel as I approach her.

She stands astride her bike with the helmet under one arm. I can hear the tick of the engine warmed between her legs. "It belongs to my family," she says, and I find I can't read anything in her face at all. The beautiful have an inscrutable mask—or maybe it's beauty itself that's the mask? It's cold up here, cold and desolate, and the rugged mountains always remind me of death. In Asia, I once read, white is the colour of death. I get it now, staring up at the snow-capped ridges that lean down over me. I zip up my loden Dolomieten coat and tell myself not to be an idiot.

"You nervous?" she asks, watching me step closer with her hand reaching for something in her jacket.

I blink and freeze. "What?"

"Do you have the photo on you?"

The silence around us is claustrophobic. I glance about, my senses heightened. And then her lips slit open into a slow smile, and she beckons me closer with something that sounds a lot like a laugh. "Come on, let's go inside, you'll catch your death out here."

She walks toward the door, flecked with paint and age, and unlocks it with a key card. Holding the door ajar, she waits for me to brush by her and into the villa. Cold. There's a parlour with leather couches and *sciccoso* rustic bric-à-brac and a wall of floor-to-ceiling windows beyond the blood-red cupboards of a can-only-have-been made-in-Italy kitchen. The walls are stone and inset white masonry. Elegant. Expensive. And the view beyond the windows is eternal—the distant steeples of Austrian onion-dome churches dotted about a flowing green valley where meadows fall away in a champagne of early morning dew beyond an ancient wood-stick fence that sweeps across the back of the house.

"That's—quite a view."

"We hire it out as an Airbnb during the summer. In the winter, when it snows, the road becomes pretty hairy, though. Not that it snows anymore. Not as much as when I was a kid."

"You grew up here?"

She shuts the door, and we stand there, separated by inches. "I spent my summers here, and sometimes we'd come up to the *Sette Communi* to ski during weekends in the winter. I hated it then—too secluded. It scared me. Especially when we found the dead writer in the pool out back."

I take a moment. "You have a pool?"

She laughs. It sounds genuine. "A long time ago. Anyway, why don't you sit, and I'll make us some coffee and explain things."

The parlour has a cavernous stone fireplace, and a steel-wire terrace wraps around the villa beyond the windows. The place has been modernised, the ceiling's recessed lights lasering down in *Star Trek* beams. I catch the sound of the Nespresso machine stream in the kitchen. There's a bookshelf and I can't help snooping. Italian books—the complete works of Rigoni Stern, who'd lived and died near Asiago, a hero from the war in Russia who'd somehow found his way back home before being sent to the camps after Italy's surrender in '43—lined up next to a row of German and English ones. There aren't any photos, nothing personal lying about. Anonymous. Isolated.

She's back with a tray and out of her leather jacket, replaced by a woollen turtleneck. Two cups and two glasses of water are on the tray that she places on the fabric-covered coffee table between the crisp made-in-Italy leather couches. She steps to the fireplace and with skilled hands has a wood-fire catching before the head of my espresso has sunk into the black.

She sits on the couch opposite me, and I watch the fire spurt and splutter. "Your father, how's he doing?" she asks.

I don't have words and drink the espresso in a shot, then twirl my wrist to mix the dregs with the sugar and slide the nectar down my throat like syrup.

"It must be so hard for you—to have lost your mom and now this." This. "May I—I don't," she smiles, uncertain, and it seems real to me, "I mean— how long—"

"Weeks," I tell her.

She looks away from me, finds fluff on the couch and flips it away. "He's lucky to have you."

I stare into the coffee cup.

"You have to be brave," she says.

"That's what they say."

"It's not for everyone, is it?"

"It's not for me."

"And yet—"

"And yet here we are," I tell her. "Mind telling me why?"

"What do you know about the *dopo-guerra* here in Italy?"

"Post-war Italy? I don't know. A little, I guess. Why?"

I watch her speak. She's had training, some business face-to-face coaching, I'd guess, and I sit back to listen. I could sit here and listen to the words that come from between those lips for a long time. "Depending on how you look at it," she tells me, "it was either a tragedy that ended in a farce or the other way around. There were two wars here," she says, "you understand? The Germans versus the Allies after Italy changed sides in '43, and while the heavyweights had their war, Italians fought Italians in the lightweight division."

I sip from a glass of chilled water.

"By July '45, with the Nazis back beyond the potato line, Italy moved on to the *resa dei conti*, the settling of scores. Tens of thousands of Italians were executed—Nazi sympathisers, fascists, collaborators, factory owners, businessmen, Duce and his whore in Milan, all *giustificati* by the partisans, right? The vacuum created by the defeat of fascism was filled by the broken labour unions and the socialists and communists from the '30s, and they'd waited a decade for revenge. But they also wanted to change the social fabric of the new republic. So you see where this is going?"

"I'm figuring a massacre?"

She takes a moment to study my face. "This is heading for '48, for the first post-fascist, post-war election when Togliatti's Communist Party would have led Italy—or so the Americans believed—straight behind the Iron Curtain in the same way as the coup in February of '48 had done for the Czechs. So the CIA, the mafia, and the church down in Rome got down to working out how to make sure that didn't happen."

"You studied in the US?" I ask.

"I did my MA at NYU, can you tell?"

"You have an accent," I tell her.

"Me? I have an accent?" She laughs. "Anyway, what the Americans did, they began a propaganda campaign, publishing forged letters to discredit the Communist Party, suggesting the communists were somehow responsible for the killing of Italian POWs in Russia, and tens of thousands of letters were sent to the electorate, warning them of the red peril. And they used the memory of the post-war massacres as exhibit A, you follow? The communists would seize power and anyone who'd had anything to do with fascism would be punished—and by punishment, they meant executions. And this being Italy, really, everyone was a fascist in 1939, right? The propaganda that was first used in Italy in the election of '48, you know, the CIA would use as the blueprint for subverting democracies in every corner of the globe for decades after. We were the test-tube. And it wasn't cheap—we're talking over twenty-million dollars, all diverted out of the Marshall Plan. Even *Time* magazine was recruited into the fold—"

"My daughter would enjoy that pun."

"What? Oh. Oh, I see. Anyway, *Time* gave Christian Democrat leader De Gasperi the cover in the build-up to the election. So what happened? The Communists lost, the Christian Democrats won, and the Americans had bought themselves their first client state. And they kept pumping millions into every single election in Italy for the next fifty years to keep the communists from power. You follow?"

"Sure."

*"La brava gente,"* she says. "That whole post-war American stitch-up would eventually lead to the violence of the late '70s and early '80s, the Years of Lead."

"I don't understand—"

"Because in their minds," she interrupts, "I'm talking about the left now—there was never a true accounting for the war. Up here, in '44, they had the Battle of Malga Fossetta, when students known as 'the little masters' and led by Luigi Meneghello, a writer from Malo—do you know him?"

"Yes."

"He fought the fascists—up there," she repeats, waving at the windows, at that rocky slab of mountain, "near the summit of the Isidoro, real battles, a real war, yes? So you see where all this is leading?"

I sit back on the couch. "The massacre?" I try again.

"The massacre. Exactly. In the months after the war, from the Veneto to Torino, tens of thousands of accused fascists were murdered, and the Americans were not happy. They wanted to rebuild Italy quickly and didn't have a lot of time for a brewing civil war. With Slovenia and Yugoslavia all going red, Italy became crucial to the Allies' post-war plans. If we turned red, that would bring the Soviets to the Mediterranean. So they needed to rebuild fast, and to do that, there had to be peace. And peace came from forgiveness. And forgiveness, you understand, comes from forgetting. It's like a relationship, no?"

I notice the wedding ring on her finger.

"So those partisan-led massacres went unreported and un-investigated by the occupying Allies. In reality, they didn't have much of a choice given the communist partisans were armed to the teeth, and it was either try to work the back channels to get them to ceasefire, or get into a shooting war with them, and no one could see any kind of win from that." She's seen my glance and rubs the ring around her finger for a moment. "So they needed a third way. They needed somehow to discredit the partisans. Because discrediting them was to discredit the communists, you follow? Problem was, making the killings unpalatable to the Italian public who were, in the months after the war, delighted to see justice meted out to those who'd been fascism's enforcers, needed something … well, let's just call it a set of unique circumstances. And in Schio, in July 1945, destiny gave the Americans a tailor-made gift."

"The massacre," I tell her. She gives me a glance and then stands and steps to an antique desk near the windows. On the desk is a lime green Bottega Veneta bag that she brings with her back to the couch. She sits down and draws out a paperback book from it, encased in a plastic zip lock.

"Thing is, Italy's still the same place," she tells me, "same old fascist versus commie derby. It goes into hibernation, and then one fine day it all comes back again, as it did during the Years of Lead. And then we got rich, and everyone forgot. And now we're poor again, and people are beginning to remember." I can't help but notice how beautiful she is in this light, and I glance away, out at the windows. "You can blame the immigrants for that," she says. "Even the communists hate them. Internationalism died with globalisation, it's one of those ironies."

"Is that a slogan?"

"No," she laughs, "no-no. Part of a speech, actually."

"I'm not sure I understand."

"Which part?"

"Any of it—what does this have to do with my uncle?"

"Your answers are in here," she says and places the paperback on the coffee table between us. The cover is white, the pages deep yellow, the spine cracked and ribbed. It sits there with its title in bold red and it occurs to me that touching it would be to give her a victory—and I'm not even sure what the battle is. Or the price of defeat. I lift it anyway. Soothingly light, a weight of words. I decline my first instinct to smell the paper. Inside, the pages are scripted tidily, a pro job in an old-school serif font—Perpetua?—though the lack of copyright and publishing date makes me believe this is a vanity publication.

"The only proviso here," she tells me as I flip through the pages carefully, the glue flaking, cracking audibly, "is that you're not to take any notes or photos, okay?"

"Why?"

"Because forgetting—"

"Brings peace?"

"You see," she says encouragingly, "you *do* understand more than you think."

# TWO
## *CREDERE, OBBEDIRE, COMBATTERE*

*By the time of the cease-fire in Italy, the U.S. Fifth Army had been in continuous combat for 602 days, well over twenty months, far longer than any U.S. field army during World War II. During the entire Italian campaign, Allied losses had exceeded 312,000, of which 60 percent, or about 189,000, were sustained by Fifth Army units.*
—Thomas A. Popa, "Po Valley"

# THE LOLLER REPORT
## BY LT. JOHN CASANOVA

FOR MY SON, STAFF SERGEANT JOHN CASANOVA JR.

# CHAPTER ONE

JULY 13, 1945

Let's start with me aiming my jeep through rubble-strewn roads under a concussive sun with my off-white linen jacket streaked by dust and my tongue candied by the dirt that'd been running shotgun since I'd set out from Bologna just after breakfast, sweating an exhaustion that can come only to a man who'd survived what should've killed him straight and true.

The drive out had been slow and butt-blisteringly painful. Italy was like one of those whores tottering about on the Corso Umberto in Naples on a muggy Sunday morning after working all night for a can of C rations, and from what my pops told about the old country—not that he'd ever had have much to say except that he'd been happier'n a dead pig in summer the day he'd got to Ellis Island—I guess it'd always been a shithole. We'd just flushed the turlet, us and the Nazis who didn't leave much behind but a floater in Europe's latrine. All morning I drove through towns and valleys blackened by war, kids on bomb-cratered streets with nothing but rags chasing fat bluebottle flies up-under a merciless sun festering their goddamn diseases until finally I found the gates leading to the Villa Scacchi. The long driveway was shaded by two distinct and perfectly running rows of plane trees that brought cool to my skin, and it was only a couple of seconds after I pulled up under the stretched white-stucco villa that the whirlwind of dust that'd been tailing me from Bologna buried me in a warm shower of smut.

I lit a Lucky and looked at my linen suit and wondered what the hell I'd been thinking. I rubbed the dirt off the jacket and succeeded only in smearing it worse, so I left well enough alone and trotted up a wide, short staircase to where a GI stood guarding the double glass doors to the villa that'd been sectioned as provisional HQ for CID Veneto. He had all the enthusiasm of a fighting Joe delighted to be in Italy in July and not getting his ass shot off by some gook on an island in the Pacific, and his salute was even more eager when I showed him my credentials. We shared the top step in the shade of the villa and smoked in silence and gazed out at the fields that spread out into a shimmering dreariness, a melting world that smelt of cowshit, and I couldn't get in that villa fast enough.

"Where can I find Colonel Loller?" I asked him, and a couple of minutes later I was out through the rear of the villa onto a flagstone terrace where a moss-layered marble statue of a woman with one missing tit baked in the heated oven. Beyond that was a jaundiced lawn and a kidney-shaped pool the colour of a faded wet dream beside which, on a wooden chaise longue, was spread a man as brown as a side of bacon on a griddle.

Colonel Loller had one of those faces that gave away no age at all under a tan as dark as whatever it was that'd wobbled his brain around when he'd led his regiment to frontpage victory down at Monte Cassino. He lay on his chaise longue in nothing but white swim trunks, Ray Bans, and a toothy grin so white it gave me an instant migraine.

"Colonel Loller, sir," I said when my shadow fell over his ripped muscles, "John Casanova, CID Bologna, reporting for duty."

Loller was living high in the cotton, and I guess that's what comes to a man with three Purple Hearts and more brass than a band in Biloxi. The sun was fat in his face when he said, "Sand's man." I scanned the Ray Bans but couldn't see his eyes back there in the shadows. "What time do you make it, Casanova?"

"Sir, it's," I dropped my salute to glance down at the Rolex I'd bought in Naples from a *scugnizzo* for a pack of Luckys, and for some reason I recalled a conversation I'd had with a writer named Malaparte on the Piazza Umberto where he'd taken me to see the high-class whores and who'd told me the Neapolitans were the only people in the world who celebrated getting invaded because no one'd ever left Naples richer than when they came, "just gone noon, sir."

"Just gone noon, sir," Loller repeated, and his imitation was accurate enough to shame me. He tilted his head, and I felt his eyes watching me from behind the murky shadows of his aviator shades. "I thought I told Sand to have you here by eleven thirty."

"Yes, sir." Colonel Sand was my commanding officer back at CID Bologna, and he'd already briefed me on Loller's eccentricities: "He's fucking nuts, Casanova. Just say yes sir and do whatever he tells you". I said, "The roads, sir, they—"

"The roads," he said, and waved one hand around limply, "the roads," making it sound girlish, feminine. "Goddamn Romans conquered the world on these roads, boy."

"Yes sir."

He sat up on both elbows with his six-pack tightening, lowered his shades a tad with a strange screw of his neck, and two hard-won blue eyes, solid as marbles, stared out at me from the top of his head. "You about to bust an aneurism, Casanova? Take a sit-down, son."

Around us was nothing but the water, the lawn, and the chaise longue. Loller's six-pack tautened further as he stood with the smoothness of a predator. His back was wrinkled by a series of jagged white gashes, deep scars that grinned at me like shark teeth when he took a couple of steps toward the lip of the blue-blue-water pool, arms extended heavenwards, pecs and shoulders flexing, and suddenly he held everything in position. The day paused. And then, as slow as a summer storm, he toppled forward and belly-flopped the water so damn hard it sounded as if someone had shot him square with a pistol. I watched him glide off to the opposite end of the pool under water, his legs kicking like *Aquaman*, water crashing over the lip and onto my moccasins. He twisted and broke the surface to breaststroke his way back toward me like a hippo. I felt a tear of sweat drip off my nose and onto my tongue, and it tasted like tears. Loller rested his elbows on the lip of the pool and gazed up at me, hair gelled back by the water that ran down his broad face in tearful rainbow streaks.

"Am I gonna have a problem with you, Casanova?"

"Sir?"

"What'd I just say?"

"Sir?"

*"Sit the fuck down, boy!"*

I looked down at the chaise longue and his white cotton towel and sat the fuck down and it took no time at all for the damp from the wet towel to spread between my ass cheeks.

"Better now?"

"Yes sir."

"Yes sir. Bet you wish I'd invite you to strip and jump into this pool, 'm'I right?"

I swallowed desire and sweat.

"You know why, Casanova?"

"Sir?"

"Why I'm in this here pool cool as a cucumber in a virgin's ass and you're up there sweating like a fucking water buffalo?" Loller's teeth were as white as the marble in the Vatican and whiter than his towel that was already giving my ass a rash so bad I couldn't think of anything but digging my nails in and scratching the shit outta it. He was waiting for a reply, so I set my mind to thinking but I guess he forgot his question after a while because he said, "I gotta tell you the truth, Casanova, ain't nothing out here but dirt and heat." He laughed—it sounded girlish and came on the intake—and ducked his head under the water and came back up shaking his hair about and a few droplets fell on my face. As cool as paradise.

"What did you do in the real world, Casanova?"

"I was called up when I was eighteen, sir."

"So that makes you what?"

"Twenty, sir. Last week."

"Sand tells me you've had yourself a good war, that right?"

"I don't rightly know there's any such thing, sir."

"Commie bullshit, son. We fucking won, didn't we?"

"Yes sir."

"Goddamned right we did. That there's a good war, pal. Ask the fucking wops what a bad war looks like." He tilted his head and studied my face curiously. "You came all the way with the Fifth from Naples, that right?"

"All the way sir, yes sir. From Salerno, sir."

"I know men like you. Men who shat their pants from Salerno to Salò."
I blinked.
"How d'ya feel about killing your kin at Cassino?" he asked.
"Sir?"
"You always this slow, son?"
"No, sir."
"'cause Sand tells me you're the best interrogator he's got. 's'at right?"
"Sir, I don't—"
"So how'd you feel killing your kin. *Wops*, Casanova. Killing fucking wops. Dagos. Eye-fucking-talians."
"I'm American, sir."
"Everyone's American now that we brought out a can of whup-ass. We fucking levelled Cassino, didn't we?"
"Yessir."
"Fucking *levelled* it." He pushed away from the wall with one powerful thrust of his legs and floated away. "I need a man I can trust and who can speak monkey," he told me as he floated like an island there in his oasis under that Italian sky that was frying my brain. "Sand tells me you're fluent in *capisch*, that right?"
"Yessir."
"Where'd you learn to speak monkey, soldier?"
"At home, sir. My parents were—from here. Down south, I mean."
"That's what I figured. You got any problems pledging your allegiance to these you-nited-states, soldier?"
"No, sir."
"No, sir. Because there's gonna come a time in the next week or two, Casanova, when you're gonna have to make a decision about where your loyalties run. You get what I'm saying to you, buddy?"
"I ain't ever had no problem whupping wop ass, sir, I—"
"Make the right call for your country and you'll be leaving this man's army with my gratitude and a medal up your ass. Make the wrong one and I'll have you shooting fucking gooks with nothing up your ass but my boot." He tilted his head and plugged an ear and slapped at his temple for a while

and shook his brain around. "Did that make sense to you?" he asked after a while.

"Yessir."

With elbows on the side of the pool, he studied my face like a killer, like those crocs they have out on the Nile. "There's a fella named Snyder waiting for you in there." He nodded at the villa. "He ain't the sharpest blade in the drawer, but he's got a memory like an encyclopaedia. He'll fill you in."

I stood up and saluted, my damp ass on fire. He took a last look as a man does when leaving a whore and then pushed himself through the water as I walked away.

"And Casanova."

"Sir?"

"This is the part where I stop you and say something profound."

I stood at attention with the sweat slick on my face like oil and watched him drift about. He crucified himself in the water, nipples brown as the soil and his face grilling under that faded blue summer sky and I stood there until my brain started itching worse'n my ass and I realised he'd forgotten all about me and I walked back to the shade of the villa.

Snyder I found by the marble staircase that circled up into the villa. He was tall, dark, and had probably been handsome too, right up until he'd wound up with a scar that cut down from behind his ear to his lips and made him look like a grinning clown that'd been stitched together by a ten-year-old with blunt scissors. He wore a woollen charcoal suit and white shirt without a tie and the sonofabitch didn't have a bead of sweat on him. He looked like a wop, but it didn't take nothing but for him to open his mouth and release a low-ball twang with the whacky after-effects of a childhood soaked in corn and milk in the heartland somewhere no one had ever heard of to dispel that fallacy—one of them places that comes with a town name followed by state, a nothing life in a nowhere town and now living la dolce fucking vita in Italy. I offered him my hand to shake.

"Staff Sergeant Snyder, sir, seconded to your investigation by Corporal Loller," he told me, and I noticed he was carrying two sealed manila folders with TOP SECRET—CID EYES ONLY edged on them under an elbow.

We stood in the peculiar marble cool I only ever felt in Italy, and I told him, "I'm afraid you're gonna have to give me a bit more, Snyder."

"Yes, sir. Mind if we do that in the car, we have an appointment in Schio that won't hold."

"Schio?"

"Yes, sir." Snyder led me out into the heat that flushed up my neck and face, and I followed him down the stairs toward a waiting black Buick Super with its torpedo C-body cracking skin in the heat like a month-old onion. I slid into the sedan before he joined me behind the wheel and watched him place his two dossiers between us. It took about five seconds before we were both smelting into the leather upholstery, my damp ass burning the itch of syphilis.

"Do I need to brief you on what happened in Schio last week?" he asked, firing up the fat Straight-8 Fireball that bubbled beneath us as he grated in a gear.

I rolled down my window as he pulled onto the long pebble drive, but the air that wafted in was as hot as my uncle Lou's chili coming outta my a-hole the morning after. "I read about it down in Bologna, another of them mass shootings." I waited until he got through the rusty metal gates and turned left and then right onto the Vicenza Road before lifting my ass from the seat. Ain't nothing as good as scratching your ass, that's what my pop used to say, and Jesus my nails digging in felt good. When Snyder looked over at me, I grabbed one of the dossiers resentfully and got busy unsealing it and shuffled about on the blistering leather.

"Another mass shooting, but this time it's different, sir," he told me.

"It's Casanova, Snyder. Sir ended with the war."

"Thanks."

"So why different?"

"Because we got called in on this one," he said. "And this time they want the guilty brought to book."

"Brought to what?"

He blinked. "Book," he said, changing into third gear.

"So what do we have?"

"Ninety-nine Scledensi were being held—"

"Scle-what?"

"That's what they're called—I mean, people from Schio—they're called Scledensi. I heard Hemingway loved that town. He was stationed there when he came to drive the ambulances before he got shot."

I gazed down at the neatly typed report burning words in the sunshine. "They shot Hemingway?"

"What? No-no," said Snyder, rolling the Buick through the village of Lanzè and zigzagging through the rubble and hollowed-out, carbonised brick buildings, before we hit the badlands where sunflowers watched us pass with heads bowed in shame. "What we got here, we got ninety-nine men, women, and children held in the local jailhouse in Schio, all rounded up as fascists and collaborators by the local partisans when the town was liberated back in April. On the night of July sixth and early morning July seventh, a group of partisans broke into the jail, filed the prisoners out onto two floors—women and children upstairs, men downstairs—lined them up against the walls and machine-gunned them. We got forty-three dead *in situ*, eight dead at the hospital, four without much hope of recovery, and nine expected to make a full recovery."

"*In situ*?"

"At the scene."

"You speak Latin, Snyder?"

"Don't even speak wop, sir."

"So do me a favour, pal, let's drop the Latin and the sir and focus in on the math."

"The what?"

"Forty-three and eight dead make fifty-one. Add the nine and you get sixty. What happened to the rest?"

"They got uninjured."

"They got what?"

"Small space," said Snyder. "Bodies on top of bodies. The top bodies were shot dozens of times, one had over eighty holes in him. Sonofabitch was still alive when they got him to the hospital."

"He's alive?"

Snyder shook his head. "Nah, died that same night."

The dead have been well photographed, and I glanced at a few stills in the files. Death has a look. After a while you just learn to flip the page 'cause they're all the same. A stiff's a stiff. It's gonna happen to all of us sometime, what was that Shakespeare thing, 'We owe God a death and let it go which way it will'? For sure, if this war had taught me anything at all—and it'd taught me more'n I ever wanted to know about men and fucking Shakespeare, because I'd carried a compendium of his works all the way up from Salerno—it's that those who fight hardest to survive are usually the first fuckers to get a shell land dead on their head.

In those early days, though, back with the shit-inducing fear of '43, right off the boat and into the action, I got to thinking a man could learn something from the dead. But that was before I got to figuring they're dead and I'm not and there ain't much to learn from some sonofabitch feeding the bluebottles in a ditch in some shithole country where the mules don't even crap right. And when you see the serenity of a boy with a fistful of his maggot-infested guts in his hands, you get to figuring neither the dead nor the living got much to say about anything at all. The stench though, the stench always made the saliva run in my mouth, you never forget the smell of the dead, that sweet rot of fresh dirt-potato, and I dropped the photos and stared out at the road, swallowing hard to keep the vomit in my guts.

"So why do we care about this, Snyder? We got what, five, six thousand fascists killed since April?"

"That we know of," said Snyder, the big wheel in his hand. "Probably closer to ten thousand killed by the partisans now. But yeah, we don't give a shit. Problem for us is, Loller does. Seems there's a pipe that runs direct from General Dunlop at HQ to Loller's pool and he was swimming in it when this deal went down." He took a quick peek at the folder, glanced back at the road, then down again to finally peel off a sheet of paper that he edged my way.

*From: Allied Governor of the Veneto Region, General Dunlop*
*IMMEDIATE RELEASE*

*It is my duty to tell you that never before has the good name of Italy fallen so low in my esteem. It is necessary that all you Italians look reality in the face. You ask that Italy should be considered as an ally and friend of the United*

*States of America and of Great Britain. I tell you openly that you cannot win such a friendship while foul acts such as this are committed. You must realise that our countries are free and that our people hear of this and will speak of it ... It is not liberty, nor civility when women are lined up and machine-gunned at close range. Such things have been unheard of in my country for centuries. What happens to Italy is her business, but I tell you frankly that if you wish for the friendship of the Allies these things must cease.*

"That ran in most of the papers last week, even on the *Trib* and the *Times*," Snyder said, rubbing close to a mule and a cart on the road. In the cart was nothing but dust.

"And Dunlop—"

"Wants us to bring some justice to the wild west. And when Dunlop gets an itch, Loller does the scratching. 'Get me some wops hanging on a pole, son'." Snyder's rendition was pretty good, and I cracked a smile when he checked to gauge my reaction. "This civil war benefits only the commies. They're the biggest party in town these days—mostly on the back of the partisans. But now we gotta show the locals that our way matters—justice, democracy, and the good ol' American values that saved the world."

"Was that Loller?"

Snyder's head turned. "No," he said, frowning, and returned his attention to the dirt road. "That's gotta stand for something, right? If they had an election here today, them goddamn commies would be a shoo-in; that'd bring Moscow all the way to the French border. We don't want that."

"We don't?"

"No, sir."

"You care about any of this shit, Snyder?"

"About what?"

"About whether the surrender monkeys in France turn red?"

"I care about getting home," he said, looking at me. "And between you and me, I don't fancy going home via Japan, if you see where I'm going with this."

"I do, Snyder. But you might wanna look and see where we're going *right now*."

He steered quickly 'round a woman in a black shawl, her head covered in a black kerchief, leading a black mule that seemed dead on its feet. Fucking wops, I thought—mourning their dead for life.

"Problem for us," Snyder was saying, taking a quick peek back at me again, but this time I just kept my eyes focused on the road and did the driving for him, "is them partisans, they're heroes batting for the home team who haven't had a win all season. Them wops got no one to believe in no more, not since they hung old douche in Milan. So we're gonna have to go in and bring some heroes to book, Casanova," he tried the name in his mouth, "and that's not gonna make us a lotta buddies with the locals. You comprende?"

"I capisch, Snyder."

He nodded and settled his sight on the road, rounding a series of mud-filled craters until, "You and me, we gotta get someone hanging for this. We got one of them already, a guy by the name of Balbo, Renzo Balbo, a partisan ID'd by some of the survivors. It's like he didn't give a crap, he was waiting at his farm when we picked him up, he'd even packed a little bag."

"Where's he being held?"

"At a jail in Schio. Well, it's an elementary school with a cellar, and we got him down there. Got a few MPs securing the place. Can't trust these monkeys as far as you can throw 'em. Which reminds me, this shit-show was being run by a group of partisans, call themselves the CLN, and they're made of the PDA, the DC, and the PCI."

"Slowly," I said. "*Langsam.*"

"That German?"

"It's a useful word," I told him, "when you're shoving your fist up a Nazi's ass."

"The CLN are the commies, mostly partisans, and they're the big honchos now. They were running Schio on behest of General Dunlop. We don't have enough manpower, so we've let the partisans take the lead on security and police work. Not that we had much of a choice—they liberated Schio before we even got there. So the shit-stain here is long and wide and we're gonna have to clean it up for them. You hungry?"

We were rolling through a one-horse village named Piovene Rocchette, its main road shaded by a row of gnarly oak trees. We pulled up outside a café with a few tables and chairs outside in the heat that branded my ass when I sat down, and we ordered polenta and *soppressata* and a couple of beers. Across from us was a fine old stone monument of an *Alpino* standing tall and firm on a concrete platform, one palm raised toward the mountains that rose about us as if we were in a bowl of warm soup. "You do not pass here," it said to the regiments of Austrians that had, after Caporetto, come within a few miles of this place. Or so said Snyder, who'd read a book by Hemingway whose title I can't rightly recall.

"So, what's the background here, Snyder?" I asked, my plate clean and a warm glass of beer in my hand and the breeze coming down the green-tree hills dense as cough medicine. "How d'we get to a mass murder?"

Snyder nodded at the Buick. "It's all in the files."

"*In nuce*, Snyder."

"In what?"

"I thought you were fluent in Latin."

Snyder grinned, took a deep drag of beer, and dried his lips with his knuckles. "Between us, what you've been reading in the papers is a load of horseshit. Everyone's covering their own ass on this one 'cause everyone saw it coming."

"Saw what coming?"

"Go back to May of '44. Fourteen kids were arrested in Schio and sent off to Mauthausen concentration camp. Guilty of subversion against the Republic of Salò. They joined dozens who were disappeared after the general strike in late February and early March of '44. Kids, yeah? We're talking kids. End of last month, one of them kids comes home—sonofabitch *walked* back from Mauthausen. That same night him and his dad go visit the families of the other thirteen kids, and the kid tells them all what's happened. They're all dead. They all died in the camps and they're never coming home. This was a week after the local cinema showed footage of the liberation of Auschwitz. So now the piazza is swarming with wops wanting vendetta, right? And they got a jail full of fascists, been in there since April, arrested by the partisans when they came down the mountains to liberate the town—wait," he stood and walked across to the Buick and came back with his files, a cigarette dangling from his lips, and slipped a sheet of paper in front of me.

*On Thursday 28th June 1945 while at VALDAGNO I was telephoned from SCHIO and given information that there was a demonstration. I returned immediately to find about five thousand people gathered together in the PIAZZA. I discovered that their intention had been to go to the prison and take and kill an equal number of prisoners as had been killed or had died in the concentration camp in Germany.*

"This is from?"

"Captain Paget—AG at Schio. Acting Governor. English."

I sat back in my chair.

"So this was at the end of June. That night, Paget drags his ass to the piazza and tries to settle the natives down. At two in the morning."

I found a Lucky and waited for Snyder to light me up.

"'course, being a Limey, he totally misread the scene and instead of calming shit down, he gave the crowd some red meat—the CLN, he said, had precisely five days to charge the prisoners in the jail for *actual* crimes, not just being fascists or assholes, after which he was gonna personally release anyone and everyone who hadn't had a formal charge laid against them."

"Played out well, did it?"

"Went down colder than a mother-in-law's love," said Snyder.

I finished off the beer and watched foam slowly slide down the glass.

"It gets worse. This memo," Snyder rifled through his files and handed over a cable dated July 2nd, "was sent to Loller, Paget, regional HQ, *and* General Dunlop by the local carabiniere, a guy named Svavi."

*It is further stated that, due to the fact that information has been received in the town that a number (14) of former residents of Schio have been murdered in Germany, reprisals have been threatened against certain inmates of the gaol by Communist elements of the patriot band.*

"Where are you going with this, Snyder?"

"So we got Paget trying to calm the savages down while they're headed for the jail with their pitchforks, we got the local cop sending Paget and

Loller a cable, warning them the shit was about to hit the fan, and what did they all do? Absolutely nada. Two days later, we got fifty-one dead splashed across the papers and Dunlop's left holding his dick—"

"And Loller's being asked to suck it."

Snyder grinned. "Between us? I figure Loller is getting it hard from General Dunlop. This whole fascist witch-hunt is not going down too well in DC. The *Times* is calling this the triangle of death."

I gave it a minute, wondering where the triangle was, before I killed my cigarette under my shoe. Snyder checked his wristwatch and called for the check.

"We're going into a nest of vipers here," he said, watching the waiter watching us from beneath the awning. "As far as these commies are concerned, we're taking a shit on their doorstep. We're the enemy, Casanova."

"They ain't wrong," I told him.

He pumped the rest of the beer down his throat and threw a few coins onto the table. "Wrong or right," he said, nodding distastefully at the waiter coming toward us, "these monkeys fucking *hate* us."

## CHAPTER TWO

I was halfway asleep, lolling about on the big hot seat, when Snyder pointed the Buick through the gates of a driveway that meandered up between a nest of pine trees pitching down shadows like threats, and pulled up beneath an airy red-brick villa with rows of white-trim crenelated windows glinting the afternoon light. A sign out front, on the patchy lawn, read *Ospedale Baratto*. From one of the windows, I could see a man smoking, his eyes gazing down at us.

"We got forty-something survivors," Snyder said and glanced at me to see if I was paying attention when we click-clacked up the red-stone stairs into the hospital and down a shaded ward that smelt of ammonia and piss. We walked past a couple of nurses who gave us the usual look I'd become accustomed to, something this side of fear and the wrong side of hate, "and nine of 'em are here and they're all telling the same story. It's in the files I gave you—"

"Did you see me read 'em?" I asked, following him down the long ward where curtains danced in the dry breeze.

"So yeah, okay, they're all saying the same thing except for two."

"Two what?"

"And here's one," said Snyder, pushing at a door that opened into a sun-swept room where a lethargic fan on the ceiling stirred porridge-like heat and dust. A single, metal-framed bed below a crucifix on a cracked, cream-and-white wall extended out to welcome us. In the bed, under a white sheet, a woman lay with a bandaged arm strung up to a bar and one eye hidden beneath a bandage that oozed blood and puss and nothing good. A fly buzzed about, drunk and fat on the seeping wound.

"Signora Della Valle?" said Snyder. The woman opened one moist, drowsy eye. "Signora," he said, waving at me, "*questo,* Casanova, CID."

"Bondì," I said and glanced at Snyder who had a roll of sweat above his lip from speaking foreign or maybe he just needed a cold shower. "*Come si sente, Signora?*" I asked her.

I got a bit of background. She was the wife of a banker who'd strayed too close to the fascists during the early years of the war and who'd walked into a bullet on his way to the Todt factory in April '44. She'd been arrested in May '45 by the CLN for conspiring with the enemy. "Without any charges," she told me, insistent, "they held me without any charges. All of us, they caged us like animals. *Disgraziati.*" She said there were a dozen men who'd broken into the jail, all with handkerchiefs over their faces. Red handkerchiefs. "Except for the leader, he was wearing an old gas mask," she said with her hand showing me, masking her mouth like she was in the midst of a plague. "Like from the trenches back in '18." When the shooting started, she'd feinted and ended up buried alive under a pile of the dead.

"Mr Snyder," I told her, "says you recognised one of the men, is that right?"

"You mean Renzo Balbo?" she asked.

I glanced at Snyder. "Does she mean Renzo Balbo?"

"No, ask her about the other one."

I gave Snyder a look that my ma would give as warning that I'd be getting an ass-whipping when we got home. "Not Renzo Balbo," I told her. "The other one, did you recognise him too?"

"No. Not recognised. It's more something I overheard." Her one eye was bothering me, it was like that Shakespeare line about hate not seeing with the eyes but the soul—or was it love? "Before they started shooting, they were arguing, all of them, like they couldn't make their minds up, then one said, 'orders are orders', and another one said, 'if Pianov wanted this done, he should have been here himself'."

"Pianov?" I asked and saw the name resonated with Snyder.

"Pianov," she said.

"Pianov. Is that a name?"

The woman shrugged. I glanced at Snyder. "Could be a battle-name," he said to me.

"And do you know, Signora? Is Pianov some sort of battle-name?"

"*No sò*," she said, "but I know those *disgraziati* were commies."

Out on the corridor, Snyder and I took turns drinking water from a metal fountain, cold and fresh in my cupped hands. I placed my palm on the back of my neck and felt the cool run down my spine.

"You ready for number two?" Snyder asked, swatting his fingers of water, and drying it all up on his slacks. I followed him up a flight of creaking wooden stairs to the second floor and down a corridor where green-speckled flies came at us in glinting squadrons. A couple of nurses were wheeling a body out of a room, white sheets pulled up over the face. The patient's name on one blue toe, written on a piece of cardboard, read Antonio Martini. The nurses paused as we shuffled by, and I tried hard not to touch the bed. Snyder opened the door to a room further down the hallway and we walked on in. A man sat on a ribbed-back chair by the window, staring out into the bright afternoon. His arm was in a sling, the bandage running around the inside of an opened pyjama shirt. He had a good Olympic-sized head on him and a fine nose that reminded me of old Douche himself. His feet, crossed on the wooden floor, were naked and blackened by gangrene or some disease or another. I watched the flies feed on his ankles.

"They shot me alright, those sonsofbitches," he said after Snyder had introduced me and I'd felt his firm, no-nonsense, sandpaper-rough handshake.

"Do you know who they were, Signor Godin?" I asked, sitting on his bed and crossing my legs while Snyder leaned up against the cool white wall by the door.

Godin stared at me with his tight green eyes. "You got a smoke?" he asked.

Snyder offered him one from his pack and the three of us lit up. Godin licked his top lip and nodded his chin at me. "I know exactly who shot me," he said, picking tobacco off his tongue and inspecting it on his fingertip. "The rest of the killers, they had," he showed me with his one hand, hiding his mouth and nose behind his splayed fingers, "but the bastard who shot me, that was Renzo. Renzo Balbo." I watched Godin's blue smoke trace patterns in the dust. "And you know how I know?" he asked, flipping the tobacco off his finger.

I shut up and smoked.

"I gave him a fucking job," he said, "that ungrateful worm. *That's* how I know. Renzo Balbo," he repeated. "That's who shot me. Sonofabitch," he added, aiming his cigarette at me between two fingers like a smoking gun. "Put a goddamned bullet in me. Can you believe it?"

I glanced over at Snyder. "Ask him about the signal," Snyder said to me.

Godin looked back at him, then at me. *"Cosa?"*

"Signor Snyder," I said, "wanted to understand a little more about the signal."

"The signal?" Godin glanced around for an ashtray before flicking ash onto the bare-wood floor and scraped the ash under one bare foot. I got up and found a saucer from his abandoned breakfast and placed it onto the windowsill. "It was a whistle," he said, ashing into the saucer.

"What kind?"

"What kind what?"

"A man's whistle? Football whistle? Train fucking whistle?"

He took a couple of drags before replying. "A man," he said, his brows coming together in a knot and his eyes finding mine through the curtain of smoke. "A man's whistle."

"Not a woman?"

"What?"

"Maybe it was a woman," I repeated.

His green eyes pierced into mine. Not a man to be fucked with, I thought. "A *human* whistle, will that do?"

"Maybe," I said. "When was this?"

"A second before they started shooting."

"A second?"

He stared at me, and I got to figuring that in a different world, this one wouldn't be taking shit off no one.

"Look, we were innocent men, all of us in that jail. I'm a fucking Russia veteran for Christ's sake." He waved his hand around. "These boys here, they get wind of some commie shit and a gut-full of wine and they're all fucking Gramsci, right, ready to usher in the goddamn worker's paradise, and usually all they need is a slap or two, but these bastards—they were arguing amongst themselves and then, then," he took a last drag of the smoke and blew it all out at me, "then the whistle came and they just," again with the smoking finger, this time with sound effects, "just opened up on us," he said, and he seemed surprised by this. "Machine guns, can you imagine? The room was no bigger than this, and they just—"

"So you figure that's what they were doing? Waiting for the signal, for the whistle?"

"Doesn't make sense otherwise," said Godin, flipping the cigarette through the window to an impressive distance. "They started shooting downstairs at the same time, didn't they." It's not a question. "Shooting the women. And the children. Waiting for orders, they were, I heard them say Russo, they kept saying Russo."

"Russo?"

"Russo."

"Is that a name?"

Godin shrugged, his eyes wavering, looking at Snyder, then up at the crucifix above his unmade bed, the sheets smeared crimson with blood. And then his eyes, green and as dead as the void, fixed in on mine and it made me blink. "The fucking partisans," he said, "were all called Russo."

"Were they?" I looked over at Snyder who seemed to understand enough to nod imperceptibly. "So how did you recognise this Balbo? If he was wearing a handkerchief?"

"I told you. He was my employee. You see a man day-in-day-out for a year, you get to know them. It was him alright. I could smell the bastard. Sonofabitch eats cats, doesn't he?"

"Does he? Cats? Really?"

"*Magnagatti*. Those people—*Dio can'*—they'll eat anything with legs aside from the kitchen table. They were waiting, like I said." His eyes drifted from me to Snyder. "They were waiting for Russo. And then the whistle came, and that was that."

I followed Snyder out into the afternoon and paused to light a smoke under the shade of a couple of pine trees. The hospital, built up on a ridge, held out a good view of the town, withered terracotta roofs all stuck together around a few open piazzas. There was a castle up the hill from us, dark stone and broken brick and looking haunted and crooked in a tangle of trees and brush, and on the west side, a factory splayed itself out in an industrial field beside a road that meandered off into the mountains squat beneath a sky milk-white with heat.

"What's a Gramsci?" I asked Snyder.

"A what?"

"A Gramsci."

"Oh, Gramsci. He's a dwarf, a hunchback commie." He nodded his head up at the mountains. "Up there in the Pasubio, from late '43 to the end of April '45, that's where the partisans were based."

"You're well informed, Snyder."

He did something with his mouth, like he was shucking an oyster. "I got here at the beginning of May," he said, "came in with the first wave under Captain Talon. This is all in—"

"The files, yeah." I scratched at an itch behind my ear. The heat was making me sweat in places I couldn't reach. "So we have the killers waiting for orders," I said, counting with my fingers, "and we have a whistle that told the shooters to open fire, and we have a guy named Pianov who wasn't there—right?—but he was obviously in charge somehow, and then we have this Russo guy."

"Can we assume the whistle was Russo giving the orders to shoot?"

"I don't see any reason why we can't," I said. "So where do we find him?" I pointed my cigarette at the granite peaks of the Pasubio. "Up there? Fucking Russo and Pianov. Sound like some shyster lawyers from New York."

Snyder thought about it for a while. Then he pointed down at the town. "Down there," he said, "is where we'll find them."

There was a room for me at the Miramonti Hotel in the town centre, up on the third floor, a tiny room with a washbasin and a window that stared out at a cobbled road headed up to a piazza. In the evening gloom, I sat on the bed smoking my way through Snyder's files, fresh from a wash with a bucket of soapy water down in the courtyard like a goddamned dog. But the water was clean and cold, and it was good.

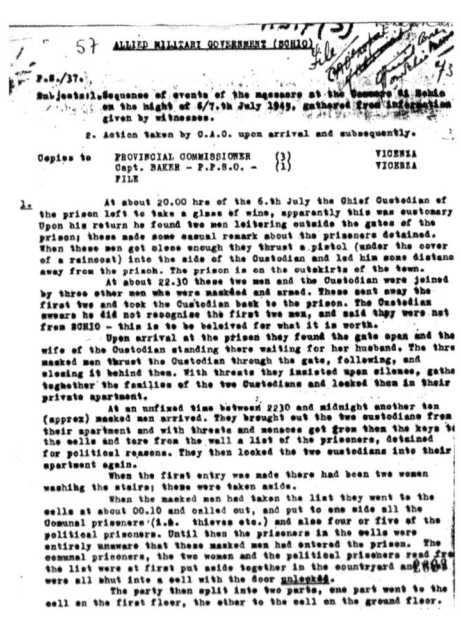

```
                ALLIED MILITARY GOVERNMENT (SCHIO)
    F.S./37.
        Subject: 1. Sequence of events of the massacre at the Commune di Schio
                    on the night of 6/7th July 1945, gathered from information
                    given by witnesses.
                 2. Action taken by C.A.O. upon arrival and subsequently.

        Copies to    PROVINCIAL COMMISSIONER      (3)          VICENZA
                     Capt. BAKER - P.P.S.O. -     (1)          VICENZA
                     FILE

        1.        At about 20.00 hrs of the 6.th July the Chief Custodian of
                the prison left to take a glass of wine, apparently this was customary
                Upon his return he found two men loitering outside the gates of the
                prison; these made some casual remark about the prisoners detained.
                When these men got close enough they thrust a pistol (under the cover
                of a raincoat) into the side of the Custodian and led him some distance
                away from the prison. The prison is on the outskirts of the town.
                    At about 22.30 these two men and the Custodian were joined
                by three other men who were masked and armed. These sent away the
                first two and took the Custodian back to the prison. The Custodian
                swears he did not recognise the first two men, and said they were not
                from SCHIO - this is to be believed for what it is worth.
                    Upon arrival at the prison they found the gate open and the
                wife of the Custodian standing there waiting for her husband. The three
                masked men thrust the Custodian through the gate, following, and
                closing it behind them. With threats they insisted upon silence, gathe
                together the families of the two Custodians and locked them in their
                private apartment.
                    At an unfixed time between 2230 and midnight another ten
                (approx) masked men arrived. They brought out the two custodians from
                their apartment and with threats and menaces got from them the keys to
                the cells and tore from the wall a list of the prisoners, detained
                for political reasons. They then locked the two custodians into their
                apartment again.
                    When the first entry was made there had been two women
                washing the stairs; these were taken aside.
                    When the masked men had taken the list they went to the
                cells at about 00.10 and called out, and put to one side all the
                Communal prisoners (i.e. thieves etc.) and also four or five of the
                political prisoners. Until then the prisoners in the cells were
                entirely unaware that these masked men had entered the prison. The
                communal prisoners, the two women and the political prisoners read from
                the list were at first put aside together in the countryard and then
                were all shut into a cell with the door unlocked.
                    The party then split into two parts, one part went to the
                cell on the first floor, the other to the cell on the ground floor.

                The following is a list of the dead or wounded as of Sunday
                at 2000 hrs.

                    30 men   }
                    13 women }    died in prison              43

                    7 men    }
                    1 woman  }    died in hospital            8

                    7 men    }
                    4 women  }    detained                    11

                    8 men         treated and discharged      8

                    16 men   }
                    5 women  }    unharmed                    21
                                                              ──
                                                              91

                                        S.W. CHAMBERS Capt. R.A.
        SCHIO                           C.A.O. Schio (Vicenza)
        9.JULI45
```

```
        In the house of the arrested man were found the following expl
    9 German flat-shaped mines - type 34 -
    1 Italian anti-tank mine - type 34 - (prolonged)
    1 round-shaped blasting charge of 3 Kilos
    1 rectangular-shaped blasting charge of 1 Kilo
    2    "         "         blasting charges of 1 Kilo each
  160 explosive gelatine tubes (Nobel) of 100 grammes each
  135    "        "      "     of 200      "      "
   20    "        "      "     of   1 Kilo each       (808)
  550 Ammunition for machine-gun "Breda" cal. 8 mm.
   36     "       for Rifle cal. 6,5
   22 Capsules for explosive mines
    About 50 meters of slow combustion fuse.
```

# CHAPTER THREE

JULY 14

It was 5AM when I sat up in bed in the pasty dark and realised I'd missed the obvious. I sat there for a good hour with Snyder's files spread on the bed around me and slowly worked it all out. Sonofabitch, I thought. I dressed and left the room to meet Snyder at the Bar Excelsior up from the Miramonti on the Piazza Rossi where I slid in across from him behind a small rickety table.

"Sonofabitch," I said.

Snyder had bloodshot eyes and was nursing a cappuccino and a couple of brioches and the moment I leaned on the table it began to tipple, and Snyder whispered with genuine sadness, "These people can't even stick four legs upright."

"I read your files." My voice seemed to make him recoil, and something like a groan escaped his lips as he held his head in his hands.

"We got a meet with Balbo this afternoon, at three," he whispered.

"Heavy night?" I asked. He groaned. "Those weapons they found—when they arrested Balbo. At his farm."

"What about them?"

"Those gelatine tubes they found—they're British stock, right?"

"Sure."

"Balbo's whole cache was mostly British, right?"

I waited for Snyder to catch up. "Oh," he said eventually, red eyes blinking at me. "Sure. The Brits were running the partisan units up here, it was their show. Balbo's farm was one of their safehouses." He watched me for a moment, blank like an ape until the obvious hit him. "Wait, so you're thinking—" I waited. "If it was their show, they probably—they probably know who Russo is."

I grinned and Snyder glanced down at his carryall on the floor next to him. I helped myself to his two brioches—there was jelly inside, sweet apricot—while he burrowed about down there like a rat until he came up with a typed sheet of paper. "Knew I had it here someplace," he said, laying the sheet of paper with a photo clipped to it onto the table. "Coke," he said, glancing sadly at his brioche in my chewing mouth. "Captain Christopher Coke was the British liaison with the partisans in the Veneto."

"Good work, Snyder. So where do we find our Captain Crunch?"

Snyder smirked, held out his finger at me like a witch, and beckoned me closer. Then he jabbed his chin somewhere behind me. I turned in my chair and glanced back into the café. There was a slim man sitting on his own by the window with the morning light crisp over the pages of the local Vicenza newspaper he was reading. I peeked down at the photo and back at him and couldn't help but share Snyder's grin.

"You're fucking kidding me," I said when I got up to follow Snyder across the check-tiled floor.

Snyder got there first and said, "Captain Coke?"

The man slid his *Il Gazzettino* paper down from his face and gazed over the top of it. Twenty-something, floppy hair, watery eyes, soft lips. I'd recognise his mother, I thought, those blue eyes and long lashes. Ladylike hands lowered the paper further still to expose a baby-blue cotton shirt and silk handkerchief around a long neck. Red.

"Captain Coke, my name's Snyder, this is Lieutenant Casanova, we're from CID."

"It's pronounced," he said with an accent that made me instantly dislike him and his ancestors, "Cook."

"Not Cock, then," I said.

Coke took turns with our faces like a hooker deciding who'd be the least trouble. "Did you say CID?"

"US Army Criminal Investigation Command," I told him. "You need to see some ID?"

He raised his brow, just one. "Depends, you keen on showing me?"

"Can I get you another?" I nodded at the empty glass on the table before him.

"You can do whatever you want," he said, "freedom's free these days, isn't it?"

"We sure fought for it, yessir," said Snyder, and I signalled the barman for three more of whatever Coke was having and grabbed a chair from a neighbouring table and spun it around and sat with my elbows resting on the wooden spine-back. Snyder did likewise, and we were now crowding in close around the small table when the waiter delivered three shot glasses.

"Cheers," said Coke, holding out a glass. Snyder and I offered him a silent toast and downed the liquid, and I came up the other side coughing as the grappa charred its way down from my throat to my guts.

"First time I landed here," Coke said, smacking his lips, the paper now folded neatly at his elbow, "on Monte Pau, so it was, on the southern edge of the Asiago plateau, the partisans gave me a shot of grappa and a slice of polenta. Welcome to bloody Italy. It was like eating sawdust washed down with petrol. Still," he said, and placed his empty glass thoughtfully on the table, "it beats a slap across the face with a wet fish."

He found a Dunhill and lit up. I offered Snyder a Lucky and we smoked until Snyder said, "We understand that you oversaw Mission Ruina. Is that correct?"

"Riuna? Whatever gave you that impression, chum?"

"He has files," I said, nodding at Snyder, and I noticed the grappa had brought a polished sheen to his face.

Coke tipped ash into a plate. "Your files may have overstated things a bit, I'm afraid. Oversaw is a bit of a stretch. Major John Wilkinson was the man who ran that show."

"And where can we find Major Wilkinson?" I asked.

"Finding him won't be a problem," said Coke with a smile that needed slapping. "Speaking to him might prove a challenge though."

"How's that?"

"He's dead."

I took a good look at the sneer on his face and imagined what I could do to it with a knife.

"But you *were* in charge of ground ops for the partisans around here, right? With battle-name Salvaggio?" insisted Snyder.

"Was I?"

"Yessir. Your action zone was in the Western Veneto," said Snyder, and as I watched him speak, I saw something of this man I hadn't quite expected, some freaky photographic memory, "between Vicenza and Trento and between the rivers Brenta and Adige to the east of Lake Garda."

"That's in your files?"

Snyder nodded.

"Fascinating. I'm kind of sad to have to disappoint you chaps, though—truth is, I inherited the show from Wilkinson. I was the twelfth man, really, if you follow my drift. Now what's this about?"

"How about another drink?" I suggested.

Coke folded brown brogues under the table. "I have an engagement this AM, I'm afraid. With the AG," he added, his stare dead. "Now why don't we—what is it you chaps say—cut to the chase?"

I'd like to cut you for real I thought, touching a small flick-knife in my pocket. I gave Snyder the lead with a quick nod.

"We're here investigating the massacre," Snyder said.

"The what?"

"The massacre," repeated Snyder.

"Is that what you people are calling it?"

"You see it as anything else, buddy?" I asked.

Coke fixed his eyes on my face.

"We got over fifty dead," I told him. "Sounds like a massacre to me. What do you chaps call it? A fucking tea party?"

Coke rolled his cigarette in the ashtray for a while, sharpening the end of it like a spear. He took a long unhurried drag and vanished behind a plume of smoke. When he reappeared, the smile was still there, but the eyes were staring straight down into my gut where the grappa was rotting. "Fifty dead fascists," he said, "sounds more like a good day's work from where I'm sitting."

He had a point. "Listen, I ain't here to defend no fascists," I told him. "I fought my way up through Monte. I got no skin in this game. But what happened here was a crime."

"Crime and punishment," Coke agreed.

I was getting on my own nerves now. "What we need is to find a man named Russo."

"Russo?"

"Russo."

"There's a graveyard full of Russos," said Coke, gazing at me. "I worked with a dozen or more. Every lad with a Russian parabellum that came back half-dead from the Eastern Front figured himself to be a Russo."

"Any that had a connection with Renzo Balbo?" asked Snyder.

"Schneider is it?"

"Snyder."

"I'm really not sure where you're going with this, Schneider. But it sounds like you're about to take out the Klieg lights, mate."

"We're American," said Snyder, "we don't do torture."

God give me and Di Matta five minutes with this prick, I thought, and he'll know about fucking Klieg lights alright. I said, "We have reason to believe Russo was one of the killers."

"What reason would that be?"

"That's none of your business," I told him.

"Isn't it?"

"No." I placed my elbows on the table and removed them fast when the whole thing began toppling like the Titanic. "It really ain't."

Coke sighed out a last stream of smoke and killed his cigarette in his plate. His wet eyes looked at me for a while. "Scores are being settled, gentlemen," he said eventually. "The Italians, they call this the *resa dei conti*. Those people in the jail, the people who were being held there, you know who they were?"

"I don't give a crap," I told him.

"They were fascists, Casanova."

"None were charged."

"None were charged because the *Commissione d'Epurazione*, who were *meant* to have brought the charges, have been conveniently losing evidence since the beginning of June."

"The *Commissione d'Epurazione* is run by the partisans," said Snyder. "If they can't keep their shop in order, it's not our problem."

"The *Commissione* was run by Captain Paget and your Corporal Loller from July second, *before* the shooting. The CLN was cut out of the loop," said Coke.

"So what?" asked Snyder.

"Nothing to do with you chaps?"

"Nothing to do with us," I told him, unsure of who was doing what.

"The case files," Coke said, "vanished."

I glanced at Snyder. "You know about this?"

He shook his head.

"Remember what your killers did, when they broke into the jail, the first thing they did?" Coke waited, but I wasn't in the mood to reply, and Snyder was studying the table, trying to find the cause of its fragility. "They ransacked the office, didn't they, searching for the files. They wanted to separate the prisoners; they wanted to know who was and who wasn't a political. Do you know why?"

"Because they wanted to kill anyone they decided was guilty," I said. "And that doesn't change a fucking thing. They're still killers. Fucking wops, they're the same back in the States, buddy, peasants, fucking vendettas and cannoli—this one's a commie, that one's a fascist, that one a collaborator. Old scores, all of it bullshit and none of our business. We got a crime, we got the guilty, the guilty swing and we all go home and have a fucking beer."

Coke was watching my lips with that uppity look the Brits get from birth, some entitled superiority that left them the unenviable task of having to tolerate the lesser species. "Done?" he asked.

"Not until I see some wops swinging, pal."

"Casanova," he said, tasting it. "Is that a," he nodded his chin at the walls of the café and came in closer as if he had some shameful secret to share. "You one of these chaps?"

I looked him square in the eye.

"Casanova and Schneider," he said, chewing on the names. "You guys sound like you'd have been batting for the wrong side given a small change of fate. You ever think about that? Casanova?"

I could feel my sweat build. "Lieutenant," I said. "It's *Lieutenant* Casanova. And the only thing I'm gonna bat right-side the fucking head is a dozen wops on their way to the gallows where they'll fucking hang high for the world to see that this shit won't stand."

Coke seemed on the verge of saying something before he looked into my eyes and thought better of it. He lifted his newspaper. "If I come across anything, *Loo-tenant* Casanova," he said, folding his newspaper under an elbow and standing up, "I'll be sure to send it your way. But if you ask me, I'd encourage you to use this time for a bit of R&R. The girls here are keen, and the wine is bitter. Let the wops sort out their own mess. That's what freedom's all about—*ain-it*?"

"They ain't free to murder each other," said Snyder. "Jesus, a hundred people were machine-gunned like animals! *Women*!"

"You should have seen," said Coke, looking down at us, "what the fascists did—"

"We don't need no lecture about fascists," I told him.

"You know what the code was? For every dead Nazi, ten dead Italians. And those fascists in the jail, they were doing the rounding-up. And the torturing. So you'll have to excuse me if I don't—what's that you Yanks say? Cry me a river?"

We watched Coke walk away, languidly waving his folded paper at the barman as he stepped out of the café into the daylight.

"Prick." Snyder sat back in his chair, and it almost toppled over backward as the waiter deposited the check on a saucer. "He fucking stiffed us as well," he said, throwing down a handful of coins and getting off the chair. "So now what?"

"I guess we pay," I replied and watched Coke walk past the windows like the King of Italy.

# CHAPTER FOUR

Snyder and I took a walk on the cobbled streets of Schio, there amongst the arcades adjacent the Piazza Rossi with the Duomo Cathedral—an imposing granite hulk on a small hill facing the piazza—clanging its bells as we headed downhill toward the station and the Miramonti Hotel.

"*Omertà*," I told Snyder.

"What?"

"I never thought the Limeys would be in for that action."

After a nap that came in fits and sweats, Snyder and I took a long boozy lunch in a trattoria on the via Cavour, spaghetti that Snyder slurped up like he was inhaling straws, and he had me walking toward the school where Balbo was being held right on 3PM with the heat a hammer behind my eyelids and the streets empty and silent, the rotting wooden shutters on the pink-and-cream buildings shut up tight as the good people of this dismal town had their *pennichella*.

The school was a neat and pleasingly concentric blond box hidden beyond a weedy piazza down near the bone-dry river. A big old weeping willow spread its dense gloom over a couple of MPs who were guarding the place and inside a sergeant with a slow eye and whose name I forgot the minute Snyder introduced me, led us down a narrow, dark-brick corridor to a door at the head of the passage. It was damp down there, cool, and I shivered when he slid a deadbolt and unlocked a rusty metal door. He was about to accompany me into the room when I placed a palm on his chest.

"I'll take it from here, fella," I told him, and he took a breath that was probably meant to come back as a sound, but whatever he saw in my face shut him up fast and he saluted and returned to his office where Snyder was waiting for him.

When you gotta break a man, you break a man by method.

Balbo, Renzo. Twenty-three-years-old, born in Torrebelvicino, a village not seven clicks from Schio. Sent to Russia with the rest of his class in the summer of '42, returned injured and unfit for further active duty in the spring of '43. In '44, after the labour strikes, he joined up with the partisans of the Garibaldi Battalion. The file Snyder had given me was not exhaustive, but Balbo had been recognised, and it wasn't surprising, I thought, seeing him now, all six feet of peasant, square and solid and hard-baked by the mud and toil of his ancestors. He sat across from me now, in a wobbly chair that seemed to want to fold under his weight. Between us was a scarred schoolroom desk with an ashtray, Snyder's file, my Zippo lighter, and a pack of Luckys. And his hands. Big and heavy and gnarly.

"Renzo Balbo," I said. "Battle-name: Apache."

He had a cigarette in that one hand with the chunky peasant fingers and there was a tenderness in his eyes when he smiled, almost a longing. It was the kind of weakness I would shove up his ass.

"A man about to be executed for the murder of fifty-five men and women," I said, and I shut the file on the table between us. "How's that strike ya?"

"Fifty-five?"

"Signora Della Valle and three others expired this morning," I told him.

"Your Italian is excellent," he said. "How did you learn it?"

"I was born here. Down in Brindisi. My parents immigrated to America when I was three."

"Brindisi?" I stared at him. "Brindisi," he repeated and smoked and shook his head. Just under the vaulted ceiling was a slit of a window, filthy panes protected by rusted bars allowing sunlight filtered in shit to fall about in bushy, ugly shadows that had me glancing about into the corners on the hunt for more vermin. It was a sizable room, the floor hardwood and dark and a single low-watt bulb dangled above us, burning tired.

"*Da dove sito?* In America?"

"Altoona," I told him. "Altoona, Pennsylvania."

"Il tuna? *Porco can'*."

I scratched an itch just under my nose and settled my gaze on his face. Square jaw, square everything, an honest face, open like a happy ape, strands of hair curling about beneath a stretched and stained white vest.

"So why 'Apache'?" I asked.

"Because America," he said. "Such a beautiful Italian name, America."

"Yeah, they should write a song about it."

"I fell in love with America watching those Tom Mix movies when I was a boy."

"Never saw the attraction," I told him.

"Of America?"

"Tom Mix. Horses and shit."

"Did you ever watch *Scapegoat*?"

I lent him a smile and leaned back on the chair and entwined my fingers behind my head. "So how we gonna play this, buddy? You pretending to be innocent?"

"I am innocent," he said.

"Mind if I call you Renzo?"

"What do I call you?"

"You can call me John."

"John. That sounds very American. John." He tasted the word on his tongue and liked it. "Not Giovanni?"

"Not anything," I told him. "Just John. That's the first thing we do when we come to America, Renzo. We strip off the shit of the old country."

"There's a lot of shit in Brindisi," he agreed.

I stared at him for a while, leaning back on my chair so the front feet lifted off the ground and I balanced it there before returning to earth with a bang. "Renzo, let me explain the situation to you. Fifty-five people are dead. And you, buddy, are the only dumb fuck we got to hang right now, you following me? There were twelve killers in that prison. I need the other eleven. And I need the leader. Give me that, give me eleven names and tell me who planned it, who gave you the signal to shoot, and I'll see what I can do so's you avoid the noose." I grabbed my throat with the web between index and thumb and squeezed, marbling out my eyes. "They did a lot of hangin' in them Tom Mix movies, right?"

"You're offering me a deal?"

"The best one you're gonna get, Renzo. I figure that's better'n swinging from a rope. What do you figure?"

"Why would you do that?"

"Do what? Hang you?"

"Give me a deal."

"Because I like your face," I told him. And it was true—he looked an honest man, and I kind of hoped he'd be smart enough not to keep bullshitting until we both ran out of options. "You remind me of a friend of my old man, he used to coach our basketball team—we were called the Savoia Boys, go figure—but he was a bit soft, you know," I showed him where, "up there."

"You wouldn't be looking for me if you hadn't already found me," he said.

"What?"

"John," he said, as sincere as an alcoholic hooker, "I can't tell you what I don't know. I wasn't there."

"Come on, pal, make this easy on me. When you told your comrades to follow orders, in the prison, you remember? I'm curious—whose orders?"

He showed me two chunky palms. "John, what orders can I possibly be under, the war is over."

"Those were innocent people you killed. Don't you have any regret?"

"If I was guilty, I'd be weeping for them," he said, and met my eyes. "But I feel no burden. These people who saw me, they're simply settling old scores, you know what it's like. I wasn't there."

"You know what I'm thinking, Renzo?" Renzo sat forward as if genuinely interested. And who knows, perhaps he was. "I'm thinking you saw all your monkey friends in the piazza, all *uga-uga* for revenge, fucking bunch of baboons, you all had a goddamned hard-on for vendetta, that's what I'm thinking. And I'm thinking you felt it was your duty to do something, to be the big gorilla, you and your partisan friends, fucking heroes, right? You figured no one would give a shit—that everyone would just shrug their shoulders and move on like we always do. Well, buddy, this time that ain't the way this shit is gonna go down, okay? You and your pals, you went too far—a child, Renzo, you shot a goddamn kid. Not even the Nazis."

"What do you think you know about Nazis?"

"Not much," I said. "Only ones I ever got to know were either dying or begging me to kill 'em."

He swallowed some nicotine and maybe didn't like the taste of it because he killed the Lucky, and we watched the tendrils of smoke rise like jellyfish from the ashtray for a while. "Do you know," he said, "I heard that when they buried them, those fascists that were killed in the jail, the coffins went right past the funfair, and everyone turned their backs. Is that true?"

I showed him my sad face. "Haven't a clue, buddy. I was in Bologna, balls-deep in your sister's ass. But I gotta ask—you figuring they'll look at your coffin, give you a hero's parade when you come back from the gallows in a box?"

"They were fascists," he said. "Everybody here would be guilty of murder if hating them was a crime. Of course I wanted them dead—*everyone* wanted them dead. What else do you do with fascists?"

I offered him another smoke and lit him up. "Just tell me who the other eleven men were."

"John," he said, "you understand, if I tell you I'm guilty, I spend the rest of my days in prison."

"I told you, pal, we hang killers in this man's army."

"I don't think I'm in your army."

"You're all in my army now, Renzo, from the day I had to come here to save your sorry asses."

He nodded sombrely. "That was a bad day for all of us, John. But maybe you enjoy the wine and pussy before you go home?"

"I'd enjoy working a deal with you, Renzo, I'd enjoy that more. I got nothing against you."

"I like you too, John. You have a girl there? In il tuna?" I shook my head. "I had a girl here. Luisa. So beautiful, I would make love to her twice, once with her and then once with her memory."

"Is she waiting for you, Renzo?"

"I want you tell me all about il tuna. What's it like?"

"Like anywhere else. People get up tired, they go to work tired, come home tired, raise a couple of kids and if they're lucky, their wives drink too much and spread their legs once in a while. Oh, and yeah, we don't go around shooting kids. We got a thing called the law."

Renzo considered this. "The Germans also believed in the law. For every one of them, ten of us."

"Seems fair," I said, "ten of you is worth less than one Nazi."

He sat back.

"I saw good men die for you worthless sonsofbitches," I reminded him.

"Then you understand."

"I understand the dead deserved a chance to have their day in court."

"Court? Come on, John—they would never have been charged, much less prosecuted. You heard what Paget said, they were all going to be released, he'd already let—" he slowed, and something swept across his face in that pause that made my senses prick up. "It's always the same old shit."

"So you decided to kill them first, the women and the kids, is that it?"

"Why are you so obsessed with the women and children? You think men dying, that's nothing?"

I let it hang there and grabbed my Zippo and smokes. "In my book," I told him, "those who did this thing, they're the fascists. You, Renzo. You're the fascist."

His face darkened, and I knew I was gonna have a piece of him. You keep probing, you make a man start to look around him, here in this cell, just the two of us, and he starts sizing it all up, starts thinking maybe he can be a tough guy. And it's when he doesn't, when he understands he needs to sit there and shut the fuck up and take it like a good boy, that's when you start breaking a man.

"You go back to il tuna and forget all about it."

"Only after I see you with a rope around your neck, Renzo." I lifted the file from the table and stood up. I stuck the web of my hand on my throat and showed him how he was going to die, one more time.

## CHAPTER FIVE

Snyder was chatting with the two MPs when I walked out into the afternoon. He followed me into the shade of the willow tree where a dry wind made me cup my hands around the flame of the Zippo.

"Break him?" Snyder asked.

"Yeah."

Snyder took a second to make sure. "So what are you thinking?"

"Take the day off," I told him.

"And you?"

I headed into town and got myself lost in the washed glow of the late afternoon on those weird, cobbled streets that led nowhere in circles of ever-decreasing misery so that you kept unexpectedly re-entering streets just abandoned. I did the rounds of the cafés and bars after the whistle from the factories let out the workers, listening in to conversations, and it didn't take long for me to be reminded of Altoona and my pop and his buddies at the Bird Head Bar round the corner from our house. I spoke English loudly when I ordered my drinks, but it didn't matter much—anyone within listening range either spoke in local dialect that sounded like a primate trying to speak French, or they walked away from me as if they could smell my disease.

It was almost midnight when I called it quits and left the Caffè Carrari on the via Veneto with the last of the drunks and headed for the Miramonti with nothing gained aside from a gut-full of bitter wine and a vague sense of being followed.

There was drizzle in the air, pasty and spicy on my skin, the sky as dark as the shadows that I sensed were tailing me when a voice, so close to my neck that I could smell fried peppers and polenta, whispered, "*Sigaretta?*"

I turned quickly to confront a face that peered at me from less than a foot away, a short man with a shock of blond hair and a pair of the greenest eyes I'd ever seen staring at me wet and feral.

"I'm sorry," I said. "You speak 'murcan, li'l buddy?"

"*Dammi tre*," he said.

"Non capisch, buddy. Cigarette? Is that right?" I fumbled for my pack of Luckys and took two steps back and away from him. We stood on a narrow, cobbled street, and I realised, with anticipation rushing over my skin, that they'd picked this spot well. I held the pack of smokes toward him, and he calmly slid three out and slipped one between thin lips and two behind his ears. Cocky little fucker, I thought, and I could see all the way into his dirty little soul down those green pebbles of his that stared at me from a few inches away.

"*Acendino?*" he asked, his breath warm on my face.

I took another step back from the haze of garlic. "Sorry," I said, "non capisch." He snapped his thumb up and down impatiently. "Oh, of course." I put my hand into my pocket and dug around for the Zippo, making sure the knife was there. He watched me carefully, watched my hand appear with the Zippo, and I handed it over to him in my open palm.

"Casanova," he said, lighting up his face and cigarette. "Da Brindisi?"

"What?"

"*Pàrlitu Venesian?*" he asked, speaking Venetian. "*Na lengua sola no la xé mai bastansa.*" He was a good-looking kid, I thought. A good fit for my fist.

"Joe," said a voice behind me. I turned. Two men—tall guys under an awning that spelt out Ottica Barroni—smoked behind a curtain of darkness not six feet from me. I watched their faces light up as they sucked on cigarettes. The way they stood there, like coiled springs, I figured these fellas had seen action and I felt that beautiful jolt of fear weaken my knees. "You go home, Joe."

"Listen, fellas," I showed them palms. "I—"

"*Parla Italiano*," said the man smoking my Lucky. He was holding the Zippo in his palm as if assessing its weight. "We know who you are, Casanova from Brindisi. So cut the shit. This isn't il tuna."

"Altoona? Si," I said, pleased. "Si, Altoona."

"*Te si furbo come na quaja.*"

"Listen, *non* capisch."

"You say that one more time," said one of the guys behind me, "and you'll capisch my fucking boot up your ass. *Gheto capio?*"

The blond laughed. "Casanova," he said, titling his head as if he was about to kiss me, "take some advice—quit walking around sniffing ass like a bitch. You capisch?" He came in closer. "This isn't il tuna. This isn't your home."

"Altoona," I said.

"You want to see il tuna again," he took one more step forward, one that he would regret, "you back off. Go fuck some whores, GI Joe, okay? Otherwise, you'll end up needing a priest."

"To read you your last rites," said the guy behind me. There was a silence then, as if they were all considering whether that last line was needed.

"Fellas," I held my hands up, "I'm going to sleep." I nodded at the blond. "Keep the Zippo." I started to cross the street. I took maybe four steps before the two men cut out of the shadows, shoulders squared, to crowd and edge me back toward the blond. There's always a moment when a confrontation becomes inevitable and a man can lose a lot more than a few teeth if he backs down—a man can lose his dignity, and I wasn't that kind of man.

"We don't want to see you here tomorrow," Zippo said as I stepped toward him meekly, my head bowed. "You want—" I guess he thought I was about to slow and listen to whatever crap he had on his mind. One of the things my pop taught me—if you're gonna hit a man, make it fast and make it first. I swung my fist with hardly any backswing and connected with his face. He tried to block but way too late and I felt my knuckles hit bone and flesh and something snapped when his head went back twice, once when he tried to avoid the punch, the second when my knuckles split his eye open. He stumbled, and as he fell onto one knee, I swivelled around, my fingers grabbing for the blade in my jacket pocket. The two men were coming in fast but the blade flicking silver in my fist made them have a little think. I curled my body tight, sideways to give them less of a target, and waited for them to circle with the flick-knife nice and loose at my side.

"I'm gonna fucking stick you," I whispered, crouched, waiting for them, knowing I was going to take a beating and worse if I managed to get the blade sunk into some soft flesh. "I'm gonna stick yous both."

"Casanova!" came a voice suddenly through the dark, and all of us looked up the street. At Snyder, walking quickly toward us with the two MPs from the jail fanned out around him. "No *Americani*, no party!" he shouted.

The two men froze but for an instant, and then they were running into an alley leading back down toward the Lanerossi factory and a warren of streets toward the river.

"After them!" I shouted. I spun round and saw the blond running in the opposite direction.

Snyder and the MPs went after the two men, and I went after the blond. He was quick on his little legs that pounded like pistons, way too quick for me. It took less than a minute before I came running out of a narrow alley and onto the wet cobblestones of a little piazza and slid to a halt, looking about me. Nothing but shadows and night. Stucco buildings, three alleys leading out of the piazza, a stone fountain that had been turned off, and silence. I listened hard but there were no running shoes, no nothing but a set of shutters that clanged shut resentfully. I snapped the blade back into its metal sheath and shoved it into my pocket. On the soggy cobblestone by my foot was a damp cigarette, a Lucky. I crunched it to grains under my shoe. The rage had me shivering as I walked back to the street, thudding in my temples. Snyder was standing on his own waiting for me, his hair gelled by the champagne sprinkle of warm drizzle.

"Get them?" I asked.

"They vanished faster than fucking rats," he said, lighting a cigarette and handing it to me.

"Sonsofbitches." I sucked the nicotine so hard I got dizzy. "Sons of fucking bitches."

"Come on," he placed an arm around my shoulders, and the booze wafted off him.

"This lousy town," I told him, shaking his arm off. "These lousy fucking people."

"Wops," he agreed, and we began walking toward the Miramonti.

"Where your people from, Snyder?" I asked, scrubbing the blood from my knuckles onto my pants.

"Don't rightly know," he replied. "My grandpop was from Kansas. Me, I was born and raised outside Bloomington, Indiana."

"You got wops in Indiana, Snyder?"

"None that would admit to it," he said when we arrived at the Miramonti. "We ain't got no niggers neither, come to think of it."

## CHAPTER SIX

JULY 15

I sweated it out at the Miramonti. The heat reminded me of that one time we'd gone down to Florida with my pops, the kinda heat that felt as if someone'd squeezed the sky like a lemon, and it was dripping bitter out there in the night when I heard the soft rap on the door. I already had my hand on the doorhandle when I figured *uh-uh* and stepped back to grab my Colt from the holster over the chair. I stood to the left of the door, grabbed the knob, took a gulp of air, and swung it open. Light from the hallway came spilling in like my ma's tears, unexpected and vengeful, and it took a moment before I worked up the courage to plunge round the door with the Colt extended from my arms.

The hallway, narrow and dim with shoes abandoned on the threshold of shut doors, was deserted. On the floor, under my foot, was an envelope with my name on it. "Casinova." In the envelope was a sheet of hotel stationary and a simple instruction written in green ink. "Come to the military cematry. 4AM."

I checked my wristwatch. 3.35AM. I was dressed and outside Snyder's door in four minutes, and the two of us were rushing to his Buick in a soaking thunderstorm that came at us from the flank like tracer bullets in less than ten. Lightning flashed up over the Pasubio, and we could hear the thunder roll on down through the valleys toward us. There was something about them mountains, something bleak and death-like about those silent fists of rock crackling under the lightning that gave neither life nor shelter, just sitting there like my pops when he'd had too much beer and you knew for sure he was gonna give you a taste of whatever was souring in him sooner rather'n later.

The Buick was sweating hard in the night, the wipers about as useful as a back-pocket on a shirt, but Snyder was a solid driver, running the Buick over the puddles on the empty, dark streets with no fuss and a light touch, and we were pulling up at the entrance to the military cemetery on the road to Piovene dead on schedule.

The cemetery lay beyond a six-foot stone wall, and I could make out a stone tower of a church scraping the wet black sky.

"You got a flashlight?" I asked.

Snyder nodded at the cubbyhole, and I slid it out, tested it for a moment inside the car, the light shielded in my palm. Hot as a lighthouse. The car doors sounded like explosions when we stepped out into the rain.

"Umbrella?"

Snyder smiled moist white teeth in the night. "It'd spoil the effect," he told me, heading for the wall that wrapped around the cemetery. No way I was climbing over that. The entrance gates were shut tight with a padlock and bulky chain, but they were a lot shorter than the walls. I grabbed onto the top of the metal gates, slippery smooth and cool to the touch, and clambered up and over. I'd hardly hit the sodden ground when I grabbed for my Colt.

"You fixing on shooting ghosts?" asked Snyder on the opposite side of the gates.

"Fixing on shooting anything that fucking moves, Snyder," I told him when he'd vaulted over with an athleticism that surprised me. Together, we walked cautiously toward the silhouette of the church rising there before us, a shadow nested within the night. A campanile was drowning in the downpour, sheets of water waterfalling like a curtain, and cuts of lightning like a distant battle led us on to the narthex. To the right of the church, about twenty meters away, ran a raised platform with a red-tiled roof and one back wall. The structure ran about a hundred feet into the dark, then twisted at a ninety-degree angle and ran back toward the church to shape a central quad and an inner cloister where fresh-dug graves and bone-like gravestones seeped. There were flowers lying dead-still and drowning beyond my trailing flashlight.

"Well ain't this charming," said Snyder.

"Stop whispering," I told him. "You're making me nervous."

The church doors were locked up tight. Snyder nodded at the raised platform, and I followed him on, our shoes shucked deep into the sodden soil like a premonition. We got up onto the platform where the rain sounded like rats running on the roof. I aimed my flashlight on the tiles on the back wall: names, names of the dead and dates, birth and death. So many of those poor sonsofbitches honoured by my flashlight and the random slash of lightning, each one dead before his time. I knew them all, one way or the other, because there were a thousand ways of getting killed in war but only one way of dying.

"What's in a name, Snyder?"

"Don't know," he replied, "but we got a live one." He pointed his flashlight to the quad beyond the waterfall that gushed down from the roof above us. Took me a moment to focus in on it—a dim red light winking on the muddy ground in the inner cloister. I had to squint to make sure I was seeing it right.

A flame in a bottle abandoned on the ground near a tombstone.

"You gotta be fucking kidding me," I said as we stepped out into the quad, the rain pouring over our faces and our footfalls squelching in the mud. The flame twinkled in a bottle abandoned there on a freshly covered grave marked-out by jagged white stones as if it were a new foundation for a house. Rising from the mud at the top of the grave was a marble tombstone.

"Never figured that," said Snyder as we got closer, "why they want you to know where the head of the corpse is."

"That's deep, Snyder," I whispered and noticed that he had a revolver in his fist. I squatted by the grave and Snyder aimed his flashlight and lit up the tombstone in the falling rain. I could see a photo sheathed within a frame wedged to the marble. The glass was weeping rainwater, and I wiped at it with a finger to get a better look at a man's face with a wild beard and hair that fell down way past his shoulders. Not a portrait, this photo, it was taken, I thought, when he hadn't even been aware of the photographer.

"Looks like Jesus," said Snyder, squatting beside me now.
Beneath the photo was a name, carved skilfully in the marble.

*Giuliano Moro 'Russo'*

And below that, two dates. The second one made me stand up with a start.

10/10/22—7/7/45

# CHAPTER SEVEN

We walked back to the Buick under the rain and the lightning and Snyder steered the big black sedan through the sodden streets like a boat. We stank in there with the sweat and the damp, and Snyder used the back of his hand to smear steam from the windscreen.

"So now what?" he asked when we pulled up on the cobbles outside the Miramonti and sat with the wipers sweeping water aside to clear up the view of the murky street instants at a time. We watched a man stumble through the rain, his hair wet and his clothes stuck to his skin.

"Now we get some fucking whisky," I said, and we sat in my room in our underpants with towels around our shoulders and two dirty glasses in our hands and shared a bottle of whisky in the cloying filth.

"The massacre happened on the night of the sixth and early morning of the seventh," Snyder said.

"And Russo died on the seventh."

"So we're not figuring that's a coincidence?"

I gave it some thought a long time after Snyder had gone back to his room carrying his wet clothes. I lay under the blankets, chilled by the damp. The moment I shut my eyes I began to get dizzy—my eyes that remained gaping under the flesh, that's what my pop had told me once when I was a boy, and I'd never forgotten that, that my eyes were always gaping and staring under my lids, and all you had to do was slit the soft palpebrae with a razor to never see the dark again.

I lay on the bed smoking and staring into the hotel room thinking, this is how men end up deep-throating the barrel of a .45.

I dressed in a fresh suit, grabbed my Colt, and headed out into the dawn.

The ozone smelt of cat piss as I walked up the hill to the Piazza Rossi and passed the granite certitude of the Duomo on my right. The cobblestone was slick, but the rain had rushed away, and I could see the knuckles of the mountains up north pierce a sour-cream sky. Days before the massacre, thousands had turned up on this square, I thought, gazing at the empty piazza and the cafés under the arcades in the dawn with their pale lights already on. It must have been a zoo. I could smell fresh bread and brioche and my stomach gurgled. They'd wanted justice their way—justice that looked a lot like vengeance, that looked a lot like a dozen men with machine guns and almost sixty dead assholes in the morgue. I kept walking down the hill on the via Fusinato, past a yellow stucco villa on my left and the Farmacia Marchesini on the right, just on from the Palazzo Gasparini, and in less than a minute I was standing outside the jail.

It'd been a hospital once, built here on the crossroads of four small roads back in the 17th Century. I knew this because Snyder had written it down in his files. I stood there in the gathering light and stared at the triple lancet windows on the faded façade of the burgundy jailhouse, and the six quatrefoil windows, and it all looked vaguely Moorish to me, like those whorehouses in Cairo, and I recalled from Snyder's notes that the blood had flooded out of those narrow doors before me and had run down this hill like water after a storm. The Due Spade hotel was behind me, and I leaned back on the wall beside the entrance and smoked a cigarette.

A dozen men had walked in through those jailhouse doors, the leader wearing a trench-issue gas mask, the others with their faces hidden behind red handkerchiefs. They'd ambushed the guard on his way back from his nightly drink 'round the corner at the osteria Tre Morari on the via Baratto. Everyone knew his ritual, and it was a simple thing to stick a gun in his face and force him to open the doors. Then they'd cut the phone wires and rounded up the prisoners: women on the first floor, men downstairs.

Up there, I thought, walking to the side of the building to gaze up at the solid wall before me. On this side it was just stucco all the way up to the pink terracotta roof. It was at 10.30PM when they'd gone in, the killers. They'd ordered the guard to hand over the evidence files, but the dossiers weren't there anymore, and then they'd ordered him to write out a list of the political prisoners. When he wouldn't do that, they'd told him to show them who they were. The guard had refused. "I won't write the execution list for you," he'd said. He'd said it loud enough to be overheard on the main floor. The men had slapped him about but that was the end of it and then they'd locked him into his office, and the twelve killers had split up into two teams. Six had gone to the first floor. Six had taken care of the men on the ground floor. One of the women was a child. Sixteen. I tried to imagine her dread, and it wasn't difficult. That first time you saw the endless void of a barrel aimed at your face, it's quite the turn-on. After a while though, a man gets used to it—a man gets used to death like he does sickness, like he does disease. After a while you don't much mind the idea of dying or killing, and I got to figuring it was like that for the killers. It wasn't a big thing and really, it ain't all that bad, dying hard like that, it's all over in an instant, and the only miserable sonsofbitches I ever saw were the live ones trying to magnify the inevitable.

Snyder's report had been thorough—I recalled the witnesses all agreeing that the killers had seemed confused, arguing amongst themselves. "We can't kill them all, that's not why we're here," one had said. The man with the gas mask had been called for. He'd walked in and said, "Orders are orders."

Orders. Pianov. Russo.

And then, at around 12.15AM, July 7th, Godin had heard a whistle from outside. Here, I guessed, where I was standing. Ninety-nine people, twelve killers, and a guard locked in a room downstairs. And then a whistle. From out here. And then what? A dozen men had aimed their machine-guns and fired into ninety-nine human beings at point-blank range. First from downstairs, and then upstairs. Six men up, six men down. I tried to picture that scene. They'd emptied their guns, reloaded, and emptied them once more on bodies already ripped apart and lying on the floor in that abattoir. Close to a thousand rounds had been fired in less than two minutes. And then the blood had run down the stairs and flooded through the door and down this road.

They'd been efficient, I thought. Well-disciplined. Shooting unarmed prisoners takes a bit of getting used to—I'd learnt that in Aquila with Di Matta—but eventually you figure you didn't start this shitshow, you're just there to finish it off. And there ain't nothing more finished than a dead fascist with a face-full of lead.

I tossed my cigarette onto the ground and minced it under my shoe. The dead had been carted through this miserable town a week later and interred in a mass burial, and the bereaved had been smart enough to stay home while the rest had not even paused to watch them pass—it was, I thought, exactly as Balbo had said. They'd wanted these people dead; they'd wanted this, and they'd turned their backs even as the funeral procession had hurried the dead to their place in the mud. What kind of people, I thought, what kind of fucking animals are these people?

It'd taken over an hour for the doctors and nurses to arrive from the hospital. Over an hour. The hospital, I figured, was a ten-minute walk away, no more. And then they'd had to climb those stairs on hands and knees, as if they were climbing a mountain in the winter so slick were the stairs with blood.

I stared down the hill and saw two kids coming toward me. They walked by with an indolent stare, and one coughed up some phlegm and spit on the ground. The other laughed, glancing back at me. I followed them through the piazza and smiled when I saw one nod his head back toward me before they scampered down an alley. It was no longer quiet. Horses and men and bikes and women and the Bar Excelsior was serving *correttos* and wine in the rising day for the workers on their way to the factories.

The receptionist at the Miramonti watched me walk past her banco in silence and I paused outside Snyder's room and clacked my knuckles on the door. I saw that livid scar that ran up his stomach to his chest, red like a whiplash, when he opened-up.

"I never asked," I said.

He glanced down and ran a finger up the scar. "From the circus: when I was a Lion tamer," he said. He turned, and I stepped into his room. Bigger than mine. With a fan on the ceiling slowly spinning. "What's happened?"

"I want to smash this town up," I told him.

"Oh," he said, nodding groggily and grabbed a shirt from his closet.

"I fucking hate these people, Snyder."

"Which people?"

"They don't have the guts to kill but they find joy in the dead."

"I gotcha, Casanova. Wops, pal. They're all the same."

I had an espresso down in the bar while I waited for him. Then I had two more. Fucking wops and their mean little coffees. I was down to my last linen shirt, and I could smell the stink of sweat. It clung on my chest, and I wanted to rip it off. I wanted to rip it off and my skin with it.

Once Snyder came down, we walked back toward the Duomo and past the statue that stood in front of it, a man holding a loom or something, and I was reminded that this was a textile town, an industrious town like Altoona, but a town that needed smashing all the same.

Acting Governor Captain Paget, Snyder briefed me as we headed into the morning clean on our faces, was a Brit and a dipsomaniac.

"No need to repeat yourself," I told him.

Snyder didn't get it. "Every night," he said, aiming a thumb at his mouth. "He keeps a room at the Due Spade but he's usually up in Valdagno where he cavorts with women."

"Cavorts?"

"Whores," said Snyder. "He gets shitfaced and then he fucks whores. Pretty much every night."

"They're all fucking whores, Snyder."

Just beyond the Duomo, in the Palazzo Gasparini that'd seen better days and better people, Snyder and I found Paget in his gloomy office, sitting sterile behind a dark wood desk from where he nurtured a cup of tea and what seemed to be either malaria or a serious hangover. The room was murky, the shutters half-closed, the walls wood-panelled, and his eyes yellow piss-holes. He nodded drowsily at a couple of chairs in the shadows before his desk. The chairs were antique and creaked and wobbled when we sat on them. Paget was an old guy, thirty or more, with a rustle of ginger hair and a long sad face and the kind of ashen white skin that makes a man always look dirty.

"So, you're the gents from CID," he said, clearing some papers from his desk and setting his elbows on it. He was a pretty-boy, Paget, had that aura of someone who'd be your best chum and wouldn't ask that much of you except to stiff him a couple of rounds and lie to his wife. "Any progress worth noting?"

"The locals," I told him, "are not exactly forthcoming."

"Hardly surprising," he said, and he watched Snyder trying to keep his balance on the chair as if he were observing an animal at the circus. "They're either commies or fascists."

"Or whores," I said and grabbed a pack of Luckys from my jacket and slid one between my lips.

"I would rather you didn't," said Paget. I sighed. He waited for me to insert the Lucky back into its pack before, "I wouldn't go hoping for any help from these peasants. This place—they're like the mafia, Al Capone," he said, and looked pleased, as if he'd found some way of engaging with us. "Far as these people are concerned, the dead are better off dead and better yet forgotten. Which they were," Paget said, folding his legs under the desk, and considered the tea leaves in his cup, "until you chaps came along."

"Guess we won the lottery. Tell me, were you actually going to release the prisoners?" I asked, distracted by Snyder who was looking over his chair as if on a sinking raft in shark-infested waters.

"I visited the jail a few times, the last time the day before the massacre, if that's what you're referring to. It was inhumane, almost a hundred people in a space that couldn't even hold thirty, no windows, no air, smelt like a cesspit—it *was* a cesspit, come to think of it. A rat hole. They were living like animals. Not that they know any different, filthy buggers, but if I'd left them to it, we'd have ended up with a bloody cholera outbreak."

"What was your intent?"

"I beg your pardon?"

"You were just going to release them?"

He eased back in his chair and considered the murk for a while. The cavernous room seemed to hide secrets there in its dingy corners where the spiderwebs collected up near the ceiling. "When we got here," he said eventually, and his face seemed pained by the exertion of having to explain, "on May third, the partisans had already arrested a number of these people—those they hadn't marched off into the woods and shot—and we accepted that the local partisans would be responsible for the prisoners. The partisans set themselves up as the local constabulary, and we were happy for them to do so. We didn't come here to rule," he added, "we came here to free them. Most of those they arrested, however, were non-politicals, rounded up on spurious charges. Old scores being settled. These were old bosses, you understand? Old bosses and landowners and managers, and there was no real evidence of any *actual* crimes. Unless being a fascist is a crime. In which case, most of this damn country would now be behind bars."

"Rumour has it you released prisoners on the day of the massacre?" I asked, running on a hunch.

Paget frowned. I made sure to ignore Snyder's glance. "Where did you get that from?"

"Is it true?"

"Are we batting for the same team here, chaps?"

"I would jolly-well hope so, chum," I replied.

"No," he said. "No, I didn't release any prisoners before the shooting. Wish I'd released them all, but hindsight and all that, what? Who told you I did?"

"So you saw the files?" I asked.

"What files?"

"The files," I repeated, and I felt Snyder's eyes on me. "The dockets, on the prisoners. The killers were searching for them at the jail when they broke in. They weren't there. Do you have them?"

Paget sighed and looked at me like a man does trouble. "I don't like what you're inferring, Lieutenant Casanova." His languid voice had sharpened a bit. I gave his tone a while to echo through the room. Long enough for it to circle back to him as I stared at his face with my hands playing with the knife in my pocket.

"I just need to understand what happened to the files," I said. "They seem to have vanished."

"Have they now," said Paget, sitting forward. "Have they indeed. You know what else has vanished? The victims. Because they're bloody dead." He seemed to develop an itch under his top lip. "And whether they were fascists is hardly the point," he added, his voice a whisper, aiming for conciliation. "We know they were fascists. This is Italy. Everyone was a bloody fascist. Fascists and peasants and commies. The irony, eh? They went to Russia as fascists and came home communists, the lot of 'em." He glanced at Snyder who was now moving one of the chair's legs back and forth, and then at me, gauging our reactions to the irony. I guess he wasn't happy with what he saw because he frowned as if he were about to take a dump. "But whatever the prisoners were, they deserved to be charged, and they deserved to have their day in court. Not so?"

"I don't give a fuck," I said. "They were wops, they got whacked. I'm here to find me a few to hang. And you can help me do that by telling me where the files are."

"I haven't a bloody clue, chap. I didn't pay them much mind, no need to. The charges and allegations were being dealt with via the CLO rep and Marshal Svavi, the carabiniere—they were responsible for having a docket created on each prisoner. That's when my office would have taken a serious look. They were ostensibly doing just that when the killings transpired. You should go down and speak to Marshall Svavi, he would know about the files."

I stood up and Snyder, surprised, did the same. On the way to the door, I paused and turned around. "There's a name that keeps coming up, a Giulio Moro, alias Russo."

Paget sipped his tea.

"Know him?" asked Snyder.

"Russo? Of course. Who hasn't? They had a big funeral the day he died, the procession was a mile bloody long, right down here," he jabbed a thumb behind him at the window defending the light behind the paint-flecked shutters. "Hundreds of partisans. Half the town turned up."

"Half?"

"The other half was too busy taking a wee on the graves of the dead. Died the day after the massacre as I recall."

"You find that strange?"

"That they needed to take a wee?" he asked. I stared at him, and his chuckle turned serious as he considered things for a while. He turned his tea mug around on the desk dolefully until finally he leaned sideways and opened a drawer to his desk and rifled around in there. He came up from the fishing trip with a manila folder that he spun onto his desk. He opened the file and pushed papers about while we stood watching. "Your chum got into a bike accident," he said, reading a report in the folder. "Russo, I mean. We checked it out, see? He was up in Trento; part of the provisional police forces up there. On the night of the sixth of July, while his chums were executing people down here, he was run over by a car. Here," Paget slid the file toward the edge of the desk. I walked over and grabbed the file and browsed through the documents.

"Very thorough," I told him, noting Russo had had his accident at 7PM on the night of July 6th. I slid pages across the desk until I found his death certificate. And frowned.

"He died in Schio?" I asked.

Paget nodded. "They brought him here, after his accident."

"They brought him down here from Trento? Why?"

Paget shrugged. "He was an important man," he said, watching me from his chair.

"Important how?"

Paget sipped his tea and frowned at me. "I'm sorry?"

"Don't be."

"You mean," Paget said, "you don't know?"

"Don't know what?" I looked at his face and he let out a laugh that had me want to make him eat his teeth.

"Russo was the leader of the Garibaldi Battalion. Renzo Balbo's battalion." Something must have gone across my face because Paget paused. "You really didn't know?" He seemed to delight in my surprise. "It was Russo who negotiated for the Nazis to leave Schio without any bloodshed. Think General Patton, if Patton was an ape leading a pack of baboons."

There was a photo of the funeral procession. I glanced at it absently and was about to throw it back onto the file when something caught my eye. I held it up to the light to make sure and then called Snyder over. There was a hearse on the photo, and on either side of it, extending back down a narrow road, a phalanx of resistance fighters, all armed and marching astride their dead leader with commie flags flying red like fresh blood.

"Sonofabitch," said Snyder, staring at the photo over my shoulder.

"Mind if we hold on to this photo for a while?" I asked.

"By all means," said Paget, waving it all away with one hand. "But the file, I'm afraid, stays here."

I looked down at him. "I also want his body exhumed."

"Whose?"

"Russo's."

"Oh dear. Really?"

"Really."

He sighed. "That means paperwork," he said. "*Loads* of paperwork."

"And one last thing," I said. Paget raised his brows. "Your man Coke."

"Captain Coke? Hardly my man, chum. Hardly *anyone's* man outside London."

"We need him to open up."

"Open up?"

"Like a dollar whore," I said.

Paget smiled. It seemed to hurt because he flinched and grabbed his tea mug for support. "I have no authority over Coke, I'm afraid. Between us, I have a sense he went a bit native up in those mountains. You know he was parachuted in when things were getting a bit peppery up there. He was supposedly here to help one of our agents who was already in place. A man they called Freccia."

"Arrow."

"What?"

"Freccia. Means arrow," I told him.

"Is that right?" Paget took a sip of the tea and swallowed loudly, mewling with a long "ahh."

"Why supposedly?" asked Snyder, and I glanced at him along with Paget.

"What? Oh, oh yes." Paget spun his tea mug about. "Yes, quite. Look, none of this is to leave this room, you understand?"

I said nothing.

"Wilkinson was his name. Freccia, I mean. Good chap: had a wife and a couple of kids, we were somewhat friendly before the war, we both came down from Oxford together, as a matter of fact. He was our liaison with the partisans—"

"The Garibaldi Battalion?"

"Indeed. Anyway, seems he was ambushed in January '45 near the Laghi, on the road up to Tonezza. They say he was tortured for days—disembowelled in the end, poor bugger. After that, Coke took command, became London's man with the resistance, running ops and what not. But the way Wilkinson told it the last time we met—"

"When was that?"

"Oh, goodness, this was sometime in, in November, December? We were both down in Siena for some R&R. Anyway, the way he had it, London's new man wasn't coming to run the partisans as much as to report on their strength and exact number, you follow?"

"Not really."

"No," said Paget, "I don't suppose you do. Well, let's put it this way—Wilkinson came to fight the Nazis. Coke came to figure out what to do with the commie partisans when we were done spanking the Krauts." He looked at me and raised his brows. "You're aware that Coke was with them—with the partisans—when they came down the mountains, right?"

"With Russo?" asked Snyder.

"Him and Russo negotiated the Nazi surrender together. A big bouquet for his bosses in Baker Street by all accounts, seeing one of their boys freeing the world from tyranny and all that. Not that anyone would openly give him credit. All hush-hush and in the shadows. But given you boys were still a couple of days south—"

"Baker Street?" asked Snyder. "Like Sherlock Holmes?"

"SOE," Paget said. "Special Operations Executive. The boys in the shadows. Our little spy shop, gentlemen, for whom Coke is like a spring rose."

"He'll always be a fucking cock to me," I said, and we left him chortling into his teacup.

"So now what?" asked Snyder when we came to stand on the cobbled street to smoke. Rain was coming in from the massif of piled black clouds over the Pasubio.

"He died here, in Schio." I told him. "How far's Trento from here, you figure?"

"An hour's drive, maybe more."

"So Russo, he's badly injured, about to die, and they drive him down here? Just so that he can die in the hospital? That make sense to you, Snyder?"

Snyder gave it some thought.

"Go speak to the survivors again," I told him, staring up the hill at the Piazza Rossi.

"I don't speak capisch."

"Nothing a few slaps and a couple of grunts won't sort out, Snyder."

"And you?"

"I'm gonna see if I can find me one sonofabitch in this town who's not busy covering his own ass."

# CHAPTER EIGHT

Menacing clouds raced me all the way down toward the river and it'd started raining by the time I'd walked past the two MPs and into the old schoolhouse. The sergeant led me under the vaulted red bricks of the passageway to the heavy metal door to the cell and was kind enough to shut it behind me with a thud.

Balbo was lying on a field cot, feet dangling over the edge, arms folded under his head. His face turned to me when I stepped in. "John," he said. "*Pasa na bona xornada*?"

"Stand up." He shifted his feet onto the floor. "Tell me about Giulio Moro."

"Who?"

This one, I thought, lies like a virgin in a whorehouse. "Russo," I said.

"Russo?" Balbo stood before me now, a big man in his bare feet, and I could smell his sweat. I got to figuring what would happen if he came at me and I could sense he was thinking the same thing. I smiled and came in even closer, my hand on my knife, and let him smell my breath.

"You were with the Garibaldi Battalion, right?"

"Sure."

"So you're going to pretend you don't know who your own fucking leader was?"

"Oh," he said. "*That* Russo." We stood there separated by a foot and a lifetime and I waited until he dropped his stare. "Russo's in Trento," he said, turning from me. "Working for the council for the provisional—"

"Russo's in a box," I told him. He spun back around, and something crossed his face. I sensed his surprise was genuine. "Did they forget to tell you? He died at the hospital the same night you murdered fifty-six women and men."

The news hit him hard, I thought. Then he said, with a tight smile, "Fifty-six? Does one die every time you come here?"

"Seems death follows you around, pal. Tell me about Russo."

"Who killed him?"

"Who says he was killed?"

"You."

"Said he was dead, Renzo. Fell off his bike." Balbo's brows came together. "What?" I asked him. "Tell me."

He shook his head dismissively. "Nothing. Just that Giu—Russo, he never had a license. He didn't know how to ride."

"Who says he was on his own on the bike?"

"You—"

"This isn't how it works," I told him. "That night at the jail, you were waiting for a signal and then there was a whistle from the street before you began shooting. Was that his signal? Was it Russo's signal you were waiting for?"

"What whistle?"

"Did I tell you this isn't how this works?"

He checked himself. With his palms open at his sides, massive palms of a man accustomed to manual labour, Renzo stood back from me and said, "John, I wasn't there. But even if—if—"

"Even if what?"

He swallowed something that was either bile or emotion and I thought his eyes looked as if they were tearing up. "Russo was done with the war—he was done with all of it. He was up in Trento, far away from here, from *this*."

I stood there and stared at his face until he looked up at me and I thought I saw the truth there in his damp eyes. The truth, I thought, but also a question. I turned from him and walked toward the door. "Renzo."

"John?"

"Tell me what I need to know," I said, facing the door. "Don't take the fall, pal. The war's over, like you said. You don't owe anyone your life."

"John, why don't you sit down? I can tell you about Hemingway, about how he lived at the Due Spade—"

I swung the door open and stepped out without a backward glance and slammed it shut. The metal bolt slid on its track smoothly and I stood there behind the door in the cool corridor for a long time smoking a cigarette. I'd hoped I was done with this. I looked down the dark corridor. Empty. I stubbed the cigarette out on my palm, wriggled it about and heard it sizzle before I made a fist and let it die in my flesh.

I shut my eyes and welcomed the pain.

I found the sergeant in his office reading a week-old copy of the *Herald Trib*.

"I want everything removed from the cell."

"Sir?"

I stared at him until he dropped his paper and stood up. "Everything," I repeated.

"Yes sir." A moment and then his one sloppy eye took a quick look at me. "Including the bed?"

"I don't know, what does *everything* mean to you? And that includes all personal belongings. And before you ask, that includes his clothes."

"Sir, that's—that's in contravention—"

His words stuck there in his throat when I looked at his face. I let him have all the time he needed, but all he managed to scratch out was a grunt. I stepped closer. "Maybe we should call Colonel Loller," I suggested, nodding at the phone on the desk. "Ask him if *he* knows the code we're violating here. I'm torn actually, between questioning a direct order from a superior officer or insubordination. Which do you figure you're guilty of, Sergeant?"

He looked at the phone. And stood at attention.

"He's not to be fed, you *comprende*? No one goes in there for any reason."

"Until when?"

"Until I fucking tell you otherwise," I snapped and let him listen to my voice echo a bit before coming in even closer. "Are we having a moment here, boy?"

"Yes sir. No sir."

"And no one includes *you*," I told him, and shoved my finger into his face as he stood there at attention, and I looked up at him from under his chin and gave him a whiff of my bowels through my mouth. He was smart enough to keep his eyes staring past my head at the wall behind me.

The storm had broken when I stepped out into the piazza. A hard summer rain, packed with pellet-like drops that stung like pop's coat-hanger as I hustled round the station abandoned to the wind and the trash kiting about. I was drenched by the time I got to the Miramonti and went in search of the girl from reception. I found her coming down the stairs doing up buttons on her dress, and I got her to place a call to Milan.

"Di Matta? This is Casanova," I yelled into the receiver an hour later when the call finally went through. "I'm gonna—yeah, I'm fine, brother, out here in a two-bit town with a bunch of filthy commies—what? You're kidding me? Well, that sonofabitch had it coming—listen, we can talk about it in—in person, yeah—I'm—I'm gonna need you down here for a few days—Schio—yeah, near Vicenza. Don't worry—no, don't hassle about that, I'll have you—yeah, I'll sort that out, I'll have you and your men cleared in an hour with HQ—I'll tell you when you get here. Yeah, it'll be good to see you too, Di Matta. You and the boys. We got some work to do, brother, so bring some fresh clothes, it's gonna get messy." I hung the receiver up and looked over at the girl. She was busy inserting mail into pigeonholes behind the reception bar.

"Do you know Captain Cock?" I asked her.

"Captain Cock? Yes, of course," she said, glancing back at me. Took her a second to see the direction of my gaze before she quickly buttoned up a last button around her tits.

"Any idea where I can find him?"

She glanced behind her at an old, stained clock on the wall. "At this time, he's usually at the Due Spade, having lunch. He says he doesn't like to eat where he sleeps," she added and gave me a chilled smile.

"And where does he sleep?" I asked.

"Here," she replied, frowning.

"At this hotel?"

"Two doors from yours."

Well at least I knew Coke wasn't who she'd been swapping her juicy bits with in the afternoon, I thought. I told her to find me an umbrella with which I headed out into the rain and walked quickly past the piazza and the Duomo. The prick was at the Due Spade alright, happy as fucking Larry, sitting on his own near the rear of the stone and wood-panelled restaurant, a folded-up newspaper wedged up against a tall empty glass with a saltshaker. He glanced up when my shadow fell over the news.

"Well-well," he said, returning his gaze to his paper, "if it isn't Dick Tracy."

"More like Sherlock Holmes," I told him. "Didn't he work out of Baker Street?" On his plate was polenta and a slice of Asiago cheese and a small salad. I grabbed a chair and sat down opposite him, and I could smell myself now, damp and sweaty.

"Did it just grow darker in here?" he asked, nostrils flaring.

I was on the verge of replying when a waiter appeared beside me.

"I'll have the same." I waved at Coke's plate. The waiter didn't budge. I looked up at him. He was staring at Coke. "You don't understand Italian?" I asked the waiter. "I'll have that." I pointed at Coke's plate again. "Pronto," I said, and clapped my hands loudly. "Chop-fucking-chop."

Coke gave the waiter a glance and a weary, knowing smile.

"I get the sense," Coke said, piercing a tomato and drawing it to his lips, "you're not much of a people person." I watched the tomato slide between his lips, his tongue blood-red like pastrami.

"Which are you?" I asked.

"What?"

"A person or a people?"

"What *are* you on about, chap?" he asked, and I watched him sniff the air with a look of revulsion on his face. He glanced down at the *Times*. "And what's this about you robbing graves? Is that another of your charming 'murcan customs?"

"We have him down in Vicenza," I said and realised, when his gaze shot up to meet mine, that he'd meant something else entirely, and I grinned big enough to hurt my lips. "Oh, were you referring to that little amusing jaunt you sent me on to the graveyard? No-no, Coke—I'm talking about Russo's exhumation—did Paget forget to tell you?"

Coke took a sip of red wine from a small dusty glass. I had his attention now. "Digging up bodies of war heroes," he said, swallowing. "You really do know how to make friends, squirt."

"I ain't looking for friends, *squirt*," I said. "Not in this fucking place. I'm looking for killers. Cold-blooded fucking murderers who killed innocent men and women and shot a child."

Coke gave a shudder. "*Ooer*," he said, "how unpleasant."

"And it's Cas*a*nova, not Cas*i*nova."

"You wops are all the same to me, sport. But tell me, Cas*a*nova, do you really care about those people? Or is there something," he levelled out his stare, "a little darker that's driving you on your quest for vengeance?"

"I'm after justice," I told him, and ignored the truth in his eyes. "And we have our man. Now we need to find eleven more. And their leader. The man who whistled."

"That's a good title for a book."

"And I'm pretty sure I'll have them by the end of the week."

"How jolly exciting," he said, cutting a piece of grilled polenta that still had brand marks like barbed wire on its flaky and mildly greasy yellow flesh. "What kind of whistle?"

"A human whistle."

He popped the polenta in his mouth and chewed for a while. "That's what we all love about you chaps," he said, swallowing everything down with wine, "that can-do pioneering spirit of the wild west." His index finger circled a few times as if were rounding up a posse, his dead-fish eyes wide and staring at me.

I slid my hand into my pocket and took out the photo I'd taken from Paget's file and placed it onto the table as if it were a winning hand of poker.

"Do you know Hemingway used to eat at this very table," he said, waving a fork behind his head at the wall. There was a photo of old Papa up there alright, young and trim with a fine moustache spread black like a crow. "A real American," he added. "Came to drive ambulances before he got himself blown up not twenty miles from here. Though I figure he didn't have a moustache back then."

"I've been told. I've also been told you and Giulio Moro, AKA Russo the Red, ate at this table. Did you forget that when I asked you if you knew Russo?"

Coke starting giggling and had to wash down the polenta with a long sip of the wine before he could laugh for real. "Russo the Red?" He laughed some more, shaking his head. "Dear oh dear. I know fifty Russos, squirt." He focused in on me, avoiding the photo that lay on the table between us like a ripe turd he was too polite to mention. "You should have been more specific."

"The Garibaldi Battalion was under your command, is that right?"

"No," he said, sliding a piece of Asiago into his mouth and chewing. "We've been through this before, remember? With your German mate Schneider. These men were their own command, they fought this war way before I came onto the scene. I merely helped where I could once Wilkinson was murdered."

"And who was Russo?"

"Russo was one of the most inspiring men I've ever met."

"Like him a lot, did ya?" I licked my lips and showed him some tongue action. "'cause he's now seducing some morgue technician down in Vicenza with a scalpel up his ass."

Coke used his finger to draw a ripe vine tomato to his lips. "The morgue technician has a scalpel up his arse?" he asked, chewing down and I saw the tomato leak out the side of his mouth.

"I want their names."

"Whose?"

"The Garibaldi Battalion. I want *all* their names. Every single one. That specific enough for you?"

The waiter appeared beside me and lowered a plate between my elbows. I wondered if I could see his spit on the food. Coke, as if reading my mind, sat back in his chair, and let out a laugh.

He seemed genuinely amused, so I pushed the photo across the table toward him. "You recognise any of the men in this photo?"

Coke lay down his fork and lifted the photo, scratching at an itch over his eyebrow and held it at an angle to the soft lights on the wooden ceiling. "Russo's funeral," he said.

"Recognise anyone?"

"Sure," said Coke, and glanced closer at the photo. I knew the precise moment when he recognised himself.

"Did you have a jolly good time," I asked him, "marching with your fucking commie friends? With your right fist raised. Your fucking fist raised like some sort of—you a commie, Coke? Is that what's happening here?"

Coke took a lingering look at the photo and then brushed it back my way. "What I am, squirt, is above your pay grade."

"*Fuck* you, Coke. Tell me their names."

"They're good men, Casanova."

"They're fucking killers."

"Killing fascists is like killing cockroaches."

"The war is *over*."

"So why are you still here?"

"Why are *you* still here?"

"Because I'm not going back to il tuna to spend the rest of my life scratching my arse and playing the banjo."

I took a moment over that. "You know what I'm thinking, Coke?"

"Truthfully, mate, I don't even want to try."

"I'm thinking that your *mate* Russo was the brains behind this operation."

"The brains?"

"I'm thinking you're protecting these sonsofbitches."

"Now what would give you that idea?"

I tasted the polenta. "You're right," I said, pushing the plate away, "it does taste like shit." I got up and threw a couple of coins onto the table.

"Don't forget your photograph."

"Keep it," I said. "Frame it. It'll bring back some good memories of the time you helped the commies kill fifty-fucking-six innocent people."

"Fifty-six?"

"They shot a child."

"The fascists buried children alive. And what do you care, anyway?"

"What happened to Freccia?"

"Freccia?"

"Wilkinson. What happened to him, Coke?"

"Got his guts ripped from his arse and fed down his throat," he said, looking up at me with disdain. "And just maybe one of those grease-sticks that got themselves killed at the jail was responsible for that. What do you think?"

I leaned over the table and showed him a finger. "I think I'm gonna find your boys," I said, jabbing the finger at him. "And when I do, I'm gonna smash them. And if I—" there were faces staring at me now, and I saw the waiter coming in hot.

"And if you what?" Coke asked my finger.

"I'm gonna smash this place up," I said to him. "And if you're in the way, *squirt*, I'm gonna fucking smash you right along with it. And you know what, *mate*? I fucking *hope* you're in the way. *I fucking hope*." And just to make sure, I shoulder barged the waiter hard on my way out.

## "Domani È Un Altro Giorno"
## —Ornella Vanoni

She's marooned on the couch as if on a boat with her woollen-socked feet softly kicking over one side and her index finger scrolling her cell phone. I reach for the glass of water. The afternoon is pale and the lights in the villa soft and warm, the logs in the fire crackling. I could stay here for a long time, I think, sipping the water now warm on my throat. I could stay here forever. She looks over at me when I place the paperback book onto the couch beside me.

"I guess Russo is one of the men in the photo with my uncle?"

She watches me slide a cigarette out. "Yes," she says, placing the phone down beside her and swinging her feet onto the wooden floor. "He's the one with the strange gaze. The Che Guevara-like bearded one. He's buried in the cemetery, the military one, in Schio. Right by the bus station where you were this morning. Have you ever been?"

"My uncle is there," I tell her.

"Oh," she says, frowning, as if this is something she should have known.

"He's on the wall in the church. His name, I mean, not his—his body."

"I can show you," she says, "who he was. Russo, I mean. You have the photo with you?"

"I don't," I lie. "I left it at the hotel." I have all my gear in the car, I'll be driving straight back to Zürich tonight, and the photo is in my carryall. I get up and wait for her to lead me out onto the deck, a metal and wire affair as modern as the world falling behind the curtain of night is ancient. I light the cigarette out there in the cold.

"Who are the other two men?" I ask. "In the photo. One I presume is Balbo, yes?"

"Yes. Renzo Balbo. He's on the other side of your uncle, holding him up. Him and Russo."

We both watch the smoke from my cigarette vanish into the cold. "And the fourth man?"

"You don't know?"

"Why don't you tell me."

She watches me smoke. "That's the shit I was telling you about."

It's cold out here. She nods at a dead potted plant at my feet, and I kill the smoke in the frozen soil before we walk back into the warmth.

"Do you want anything? Coffee?"

I sit on the couch and lift the book. "I'm alright."

"I need to make a couple of calls," she says, and heads toward the kitchen. "If you need anything, just holler."

# THREE
# THE SCHIO COUNTRY CLUB

*To those who no longer have a homeland, writing becomes home.*
—Theodor W. Adorno

# CHAPTER NINE

The storm was a distant rumbling when I stepped out into a haze of that filthy afternoon, the air damp and humid like an infected wound. I walked past the Duomo and turned right and speared down the hill toward the river. I must have had a look about me because people seemed eager to get off the sidewalk as I barged on by and turned right again, down a narrow street lined with buildings so close together that their shadows coalesced in a deep pool of dirt that smelt of open sewers, and there at the end of the street loomed the Lanerossi factory, a red-brick edifice that rose from the mud as if it were an ancient Egyptian temple. The building stood immense beyond a shoulder-tall stone wall, seven stories of blood-red brick with hundreds and hundreds of windows blinking industry.

I asked a couple of rag-thin women where I could find the carabinieri barracks, but they were as fucking useless as a dog with two tails, and I wandered about lost until a kid led me to a building with rusted bars over cracked windows and bullet scars on the brick in return for a smoke and a slap across his face.

The bell for lunch at the factory had begun ringing when I stepped into the barracks and found Marshall Svavi sitting in a dusty office beyond an open door with a cigarette smoking in an ashtray while he pecked at letters on an Olivetti typewriter like a canary. He had an open bottle of beer quenching a fly's thirst next to him and a small electric fan blew lukewarm air and nicotine in his face. He looked up when I tapped on his door.

"Lieutenant Casanova," he said, *"finalmente*! You've slighted me, sir." He hobbled around his desk with an extended arm and open hand. "Two days now that I've been expecting you." His handshake was firm, his smile open, hair thinning over a sweating brow and peeping like maggots from under his grimy collar. "The bell means lunch," he said, "are you hungry?"

I was.

"Come," he led me out onto the street and locked the barracks with a thick key. "I'm the lone cop these days," he explained, fiddling with the lock, "until the local authority sorts its shit out. Kind of like a sheriff in the Far West."

"Christ," I said, "don't tell me—Tom Mix?"

"Yes!" He laughed and slipped the key into the pocket of his dusty jacket. "To be Tom Mix now—out on the range, just me and my horse, Tonto."

"That was the Lone Ranger."

"Really? Was it?" He thought about that for a while and then, "So how are you liking our little town?"

"It needs rearranging."

"Hemingway found it beautiful. He called it his country club."

"Hemingway's a drunk."

He turned to me searching, I suppose, for a smile. I stared at him until his dark eyes, like fresh turds in the shitter, looked away. Out of the factory gates men, chatty and grim, walked past us in a file of bodies, unwashed and unhurried and carrying the stamp of the boot on their asses. "You've met the wrong kinds of people then, Lieutenant Casanova," Svavi said.

"I sleep with a Colt under my pillow," I told him.

"You make me feel—" he searched for a word, down there on his black shoes, and I realised one had a thick rubber high-heal, "terribly inadequate." He limped on down the hill in the shadow of the factory wall, and I couldn't but try to figure out what was wrong with his gimp leg. "We're honest, hardworking people," he said and nodded at the factory. "Built it in the style of Manchester, all time and motion and Protestant zeal. But with that factory came all our problems—the workers and the unions and the communists and of course the money. It split us down in the middle. And then in the '20s, the fascists came and smashed our heads."

"I can see how that would happen," I said.

"A lot of broken skulls."

"Not nearly enough."

Svavi's walk was a kind of shuffle, a limp that favoured his left leg and I had to focus hard on not developing a sudden limp of my own. "Fascism was the best thing to happen to that factory, I'll tell you that for free. But these guys," he nodded at the men about us, "they got nothing out of it. Nothing but poverty and misery."

"The working stiffs," I told him, "are the same everywhere."

"Yes, but you never had Russia," he said. "Things changed when the boys came back—the few who made it back, poor bastards—and found everything exactly as they'd left it, as if Russia had never happened. You can imagine the resentment. And then when we changed sides in September '43, that's when the boys marched up into the mountains with their Russian guns. And they were fierce," said Svavi, "make no mistake about that. The partisans up here, they learnt everything from Tito. They took no prisoners."

The sweat was beginning to run down my forehead and tickled my nose.

"Over there is the old carabinieri station," he said, waving at a stucco building that'd been clearly ransacked, the front door hanging crooked from one hinge, windows smashed, "and down there is the old Firenze barracks. And just down there, if you walk down and turn left, is the Marconi school. That's where the Black Shirts did most of their torturing. I'll be honest with you, it was bad before September '43, but after that, when the Germans decided we were the enemy, things got really nasty: hundreds and hundreds of men and women, even girls, they would go into those places and not many came out."

"War's ugly," I told him, "and torture ain't the worst thing that can happen to a man."

We walked past the bombed-out remains of the Lanificio Rossi on via Pasubio. No one had cleaned it up, and it lay there in piles of debris, brick and wood and masonry along with rusting metal pipes and broken guts. "You guys bombed this in February," he said to me, looking at the rubble.

"Pity we stopped there." I watched bare-chested kids with ribs like welts playing in the debris and wondered how long before they tripped over unexploded ordinance. Not soon enough. I needed a drink.

"When they came down those mountains, the boys were convinced they'd get to change things. Those who'd made their nest with the fascists would be punished and there'd be a reckoning for the past. And you can't blame them. A man here gets fired by one *azienda*, he can forget about getting work anywhere else. Back in the late '20s, we had twenty-five percent of the population emigrate. A whisper about being a union man, a communist, and a man was done for. And nothing's changed. Nothing's ever gonna change. They have a book they share, the bosses—a man gets his name in that book, he's finished. Him and his family. So you see, the resentment and what happened during the Nazi occupation—"

"I need a drink," I told him.

"We're almost there. When they had the strikes, the big strikes in February last year, the Black Shirts were under serious pressure from Salò, and the punishments went on for months. They were still raping girls up at the Cazzolla factory in October, the boys from the Tagliamento. So when the end came, when the partisans came down from the Pasubio," he showed me the mountains with a finger, "you can just imagine ... they'd fought for two years, seen their friends die in Russia, their lovers and family tortured, others sent to the camps, and now it was payback time. The partisans liberated this town days before you guys got here, so they had a lot of time to *giustiziare* a few arch-fascists like the members of the Brigata Nera, the Black Shirts who they shot up in the Valletta dei Frati along with their leader, Grosso, AKA *il Tartaro*. But really, if you understood only a fraction of the things those bastards did, you'd spit on their graves."

"Where are they?"

"Who?"

"Their graves?"

"Well hidden," said Svavi, "and with good reason."

"So what are you saying?" I asked, the sweat dripping off my nose. "That the prisoners got what they deserved?"

He paused mid-limp and waited for me to come to a standstill beside him. "What I'm saying," he said, and his eyes measured me, "is the war didn't start any of this. And now that it's over, it won't end it either. Many of those killed in the jail, that was just to settle old scores. This is a civil war that's been going on for decades, Lieutenant Casanova, and it'll be going on long after you're back in il tuna. You see, really, the problem," I started walking, and he limped after me, "the real problem is the partisan leaders gave us vengeance when we had no one else to give us justice."

"There's no difference, pal."

"You're right. For many of us, seeing Duce swinging, that was justice. To see that bastard hanging with his cock in his mouth, that was a sort of vengeance too."

"I don't care about any of this shit," I said. "I just want a drink and a dozen wops hanging from a rope. In that order."

"So do the bosses," said Svavi. "They want the killers too, and they want them to be partisans, they want the communist heroes to be the killers just as bad as you. And that's why they hate you. Because just when they finally got the upper hand, along you come to fight for the bad guys."

"Fucking Tom Mix," I said and wondered how much of that speech he'd prepared when he led me through the narrow doorway of an ancient stone-and-brick building and down a flagstone staircase that wound into a cellar, all shadow and dank, and with a scent of food—garlic, fried polenta, and beef—that had me salivating halfway down. Svavi pushed through a couple of communal tables that went quiet when we stepped past and found us a scarred table up against the rear brick wall. I listened to stolen fragments of words from men bent over tables with shot glasses of wine, and through the gloom, white-capped eyes glistened out at me and blinked away when I stared back, vanishing into the shadows of dulled voices.

Svavi sat across from me and drew his chair closer toward the table. "So you see, in a civil war, you're either on one side or the wrong side."

"And whose side was Russo on?"

"Russo?"

"Giulio Moro."

Svavi watched me light a Lucky. "American?" he asked, nodding at my cigarette.

"Lucky Strike."

He grinned. I threw him the pack and watched him sniff a cigarette under his nose and then light it up, savouring it. "The best," he said.

"So tell me about Giulio Moro."

He looked at the cigarette between two stubby fingers, and I noticed the nails had been chewed so badly the fingers had become disfigured. "What's there to say? The boy was an eccentric. Came from serious money. Loaded. He was one of the leaders of the strikes in '44. *The* leader. Did you know that?"

I shook my head. "What strikes?"

"Oh," he laughed, "they'll be talking about those strikes for generations. Right as the Nazis were sticking their boot in, Giulio Moro decides to organise a general strike. Madness. But here's the thing: Everyone—*everyone*—went on strike, it was unbelievable. A strike right in the middle of an occupation." Svavi laughed and shook his head. "But that's the kind of man he was. Big fucking balls. Right after the strikes were crushed, he vanished up into mountains, and hundreds of men followed him up there. His battalion liberated this town, you know. The Garibaldi Battalion. A true working-class hero, that was Giulio Moro. But why do you ask?"

"His name came up."

"In what way?"

"A way that makes me think he led the entire massacre."

"*Russo?*"

I looked at his face. "You sound surprised."

"Who told you, about Russo being involved?"

I gave it a moment. "One of the survivors."

"They saw him there? At the jail?"

"They heard his name mentioned."

"*Who* heard his name?"

"I told you. One of the—"

"Who? Give me a name."

"You're being a cop," I told him.

"So?"

"Guy by the name of Godin."

"Godin?"

I waited but Svavi had clammed up, staring at his cigarette. "What?" I asked. Svavi shrugged. "Tell me."

He considered his reply for a while. "I wouldn't hinge your whole case," he said, and I realised he'd found a way out from the trap he'd built for himself, "around what one man says he overheard."

"Is it true Paget released a bunch of prisoners days before the massacre?" I asked.

Svavi's eyes, at least, didn't back away from meeting mine. "Who told you that?"

"Come on," I replied, "I've met you halfway already."

Svavi studied me for a while as if trying to work out what I knew—which was less than nothing. And yet, I thought, I'd stumbled onto something here. Something I just couldn't quite place. "More like *on* the day of the massacre," he said eventually, and licked his lips and tasted American-roasted nicotine.

I ran my palm over my neck, smooth with the sweat, and rubbed them dry on my pants. "Do you have the files?"

"What files?"

"The files of the people held in the jail, their accusation sheets, is that what you call them?"

"No. Paget ordered all the files seized from our authority when they had that demonstration in the piazza. I was told the investigation was now in Allied hands and he had orders to expedite either the filing of charges or the release of the prisoners. Captain Cock came round and picked them up."

"Cook."

"What?"

"It's pronounced cook."

"What did I say?"

A waiter came with two carafes of wine and water and two dusty glasses and a familiar greeting for Svavi. Svavi poured for the two of us, water mixed with wine, and offered a silent toast. "Coke is one of those shadows that come with war, Lieutenant Casanova."

"It's John," I said.

"John, to you," he raised his glass. I did the same. "You have family in America?"

"I have family everywhere," I replied, the wine tasting like poverty on my tongue. "Even, I'm told, in Brindisi."

"Let's drink to those poor bastards then." Svavi raised his glass again, and I noticed a hole in his dusty jacket beneath his armpit as he downed his drink and poured us another round. "Did you know he was spotted by the Germans when he parachuted in and had to hide out in a safehouse for a week?"

"Who, Coke?"

Svavi nodded. "Do you remember where we found Balbo—the day after the massacre, I mean?"

"He was at his farmhouse," I replied, recalling Snyder's file.

"Would you be surprised," Svavi placed the glass to his lips, "to learn that the shed at that farmhouse is where Coke hid out after he landed?"

I blew smoke up to the ceiling that run close to my head, the charcoal-black cross beams sagging and veined.

"On the night of the massacre," Svavi pushed a newly topped glass toward me, "Paget arrived at the jail at around two in the morning. Guess," Svavi sipped his wine, "who drove him down from Valdagno?"

"Coke?"

"Coke. He did all the first witness interrogations."

"And where were you?"

"At home. I only heard about it the next day when I came into work."

I sipped wine. Without the water, it was tart, acidic, like the soul of this place. "So where are you going with this?"

"Going with this?" Svavi smiled. "I'm not going anywhere, Lieutenant—John. I'm staying here, this is my home. It's you who'll be going home soon, no? To *il tuna*."

"Al," I said, "Altoona. *Al*-fucking-toona."

"But I'll tell you something else," Svavi waited for me to edge closer to his whispered voice. "I warned Captain Paget."

"Of what?"

"Two days before the massacre, there were rumours. It's a small town, people here drink too much and swear too much and sure as hell they talk too much."

"Not to me they don't. Anyway, old news."

"Yes. And yet," Svavi spotted the waiter and sat back. The waiter came at us through the cigarette smoke carrying two plates of paste-like broken-up pasta and fagioli and we waited for him walk away before Svavi said, "And yet the jail was left without protection except for the old jailer, a man everyone knew was a strong arm-lifter."

I watched Svavi lift his glass and drink. "I'm not sure I like where you're going with this," I told him, looking down at the muddy pasta.

"I'm not going anywhere," he replied, sliding food onto his tongue. The pasta was syrupy and went down fine with the wine. "I told you."

We ate in silence for a while until I'd picked my plate clean. The waiter returned with two plates of steak cut into ribbons with polenta and grilled mushrooms.

"So what do we have, John? We have the commies less than two hours from here, right, on Trieste's doorstep, we got commie Togliatti down in Rome with the best funded political party in Italy courtesy of his friends in Moscow, and we have the communist partisans all armed to the teeth, thanks to the Brits and you guys."

I ate slowly. "So?"

"So, nothing," he said. "I'm just talking, John. It's a good time to be a communist these days is what I'm saying—to dream of sticking it to the bosses, to the rich. It would be a pity if that was all ruined by a massacre."

"Were you a fascist?" I asked him and saw him smile.

"I'm a cop, John. My dad used to say I should become a priest, I hated injustice, even as a boy. Tom Mix, I told you."

"And your mom?"

"She said only pedos become priests." He laughed. Perhaps it was the wine and the food, but I couldn't help mirror that laugh. "But here's a strange thing. Three days before the killing," he said as if picking up a thread from a faraway conversation, "I got word that an old revolutionary had come back to town. A man by the name of Ivo Pranjic."

I asked him to spell it out and he did better; he wrote it out for me on a matchbook.

"Pranjic. Pianov."

"What?"

"Nothing," I said, folding the matchbook into my jacket. "Did you tell anyone?"

He watched me chew for a while. "I filed a report and sent it to Paget and Coke."

"You said revolutionary?"

"I did."

"What kind of revolutionary?"

"Do they come in flavours in America?" he replied, smiling. "Here in Schio, we have a rich history of exporting Marxists. Pranjic was just one more of our more exotic exports. He left for Russia back in the '30s with the rest of the exiles, then turned up in South America, a real-life revolutionary, trained by the Russians, did some," he waved a fork around, "soldiering out Mexico-way and Venezuela or something, maybe Argentina, not sure, but for men like that, this war was a blessing. He came back to Europe sometime in the early '40s, fought for a partisan brigade near Milan and then headed east. And then he came back here, came home, suffering from some sort of liver complaint. He's not a young man anymore, forty-five or -six."

"And? Where is he now?"

Svavi placed his fork on his plate. "Would you be surprised to learn he vanished the day of the shooting? He arrived here in early June, and then," Svavi blew into his palms like a magician. "Gone." He sipped wine. "Perhaps our fine wine cleared up his liver?" I watched him mop up his plate with bread. "Beautiful," he said. "During the war, John, my God, we dreamt of food more than freedom." He laughed and wiped his lips with the back of his hand. "Not all of us, mind you. The *Nobili*, the Lanerossis of this world, they never felt a day of hunger, I can tell you that as Jesus was a virgin. I remember back in '42, I was at the Osteria Cantarana, and at the table opposite was Signora Della Valle having lunch, and a woman came to her saying she had no food, only caffè latte for her kids, and *la Signora*, you know what she said?"

I shrugged, breaking bread.

"'Tell them to eat the coffee with forks then, it will last longer'."

"She's dead."

"Who?"

"Della Valle."

"Is she." Svavi dunked bread into his wine and slipped it into his mouth. I stared into his chewing face for a while. "You're aware, of course, about the boy they found buried alive, yes?"

I sat back from the plate before me, stuffed. People and their justifications, I'd heard it all before, and it didn't change a thing. "I don't give a shit," I told him.

"You shouldn't dismiss it out of hand." Svavi burped silently. "Because I believe that boy, more than anything else, was the trigger that set this all off."

"Ain't no trigger for mass-murder, pal, except for the fucking obvious. And I'll leave the why for God after I see them hang."

"That's very Tom Mix," he said. "But listen to me. The boy was accused of being a partisan, but there wasn't much to it—I mean, sure, he probably ran a few messages and what not, but he was a boy playing at soldier when the local Black Shirts caught him back in February, up near Magrè, going home to eat at his mother's, stupid bastard. Sixteen he was. Sixteen, John. They dragged him to the Marconi school—it's just here," Svavi pointed behind him, "just here on the corner. Everyone knew he was there of course, and his mother came to beg for his release, she brought him lunch in a fucking hamper, can you imagine? They fucked her up on the street like an animal and no one's seen her since. She left her teeth on that road, I can tell you. Her teeth and her boy. They had him in there for a week, they ripped his nails out one at a time, then they took out his eyes. They used a spoon," he showed me, "they gouged them out with a spoon. And then they shoved him in a hole in the cellar just for laughs and dumped a rock on top of him so he couldn't move and buried him alive."

I sipped my wine. "I'm still not giving a shit," I said, and looked down at my palm. The blister was nice and puffy, floating in a sea of puss, and I dug a nail into the fishlike peel and dug in deep until it burst with sweet pain and pus.

"When the partisans found him, April 29, the day they liberated us, they invited the whole town to come see what they found in that school. We all walked through there, it was like a funfair attraction, and it was a real house of horrors, John. They'd left behind their tools, household gadgets—scissors, spoons, irons, garlic crushers, cheese graters—but let's not go there, it would spoil your appetite. And there he was, that poor boy. Still had that stone on his belly. I'll never forget his face." Svavi blinked. "None of us will ever forget, John. One of the guys, one of the torturers, they found him in early June. Man by the name of Fosilli."

I lit a cigarette. "Sounds familiar."

"It should," he said. "He was one of your victims, shot in the jail."

I agreed to coffee and grappa.

"You know," Svavi said when I paid for the meal and we were standing outside in the late afternoon feeling boozy and tired, "three weeks ago—a week or so before the massacre—four men broke into the prison and wanted to take a group of prisoners including Fosilli and a few others out to the fields."

"The fields?"

"That's what they call it, the partisans, that's what they call," he aimed a finger gun at my face and pulled the trigger. "It was Russo who came down from Trento and managed to talk them down."

"Russo?"

"Russo."

"He drove down?" I asked.

"God no, I don't think he ever had a license. Had something of a phobia about driving, I believe. He had someone drive him down."

"Any idea who?"

Svavi tossed his cigarette onto the sidewalk. "Not a clue," he said. "The last time I saw him—Russo, I mean—was the day before the massacre. He was with Coke; I saw them at the Due Spade. Like old friends," Svavi said. "Like old friends just passing the time together. Like us, John, today."

# CHAPTER TEN

The walk back to the Miramonti did little to settle the food or the drink. I was reminded of those boozy Saturday afternoons behind the high school back before I'd been signed up for this lousy war. Reminded of Millie who I'd left behind on a spring afternoon that was as blue as the sky was tall, Millie standing there on the porch appraising my uniform, her hair as yellow as the cornfield on her poppy's farm. Last I'd heard, she'd gone off to California to become an actress—there was always, I thought, something too small about Altoona for Mildred Steenhausen.

I found Snyder in the lobby sitting on a leather couch sipping on some apéritif the colour of blood. I stood behind him and said, "Enjoying your vacation?" He turned and watched me round the couch to sit across from him on a spartan red chair. "What the fuck are you drinking?"

"Cinzano and soda," he said. "How was your day?"

"Fruitful." I watched him sip his drink, so cold the sweat was running down the glass. "Yours?"

His glass clattered delicately down onto the coffee table. "If any of the survivors know anything, they're not telling me about it. One of them thinks they're trying to kill him."

"Who?"

"Godin," he said, licking his lips. "Remember you met him?"

"Godin is trying to kill him?"

"What?" Snyder blinked at me.

"How many of those fucking things have you had, Snyder?"

"Two," he replied defensively.

"Okay, so why don't you take it from the top."

"It's all a bit vague. Godin claims the nurses haven't even bathed him, says one of the survivors died because they refused to give her antibiotics."

"Is that true?"

"It was that woman, Della Valle. I spoke to the doctor in charge, man by the name of Marcon, he tells me there ain't any antibiotics for no one."

I lit a smoke and sighed out smoke. "What do you think, Snyder?"

"About?"

"This fucking town."

Snyder glanced at his drink as if he'd betrayed me somehow. "One more thing, though, from the doctor, about our friend Russo."

I glanced about for the woman at reception. I needed a drink.

"Seems two weeks before the shooting, a group of partisans decided to settle some accounts in a field just up the road here."

"Let me guess, Russo came down from Trento to save the day."

Snyder stared at me. "Right. I also got the accident report," he said, "from Trento, from the night Russo had his accident. It was written up by one of Russo's men, one of the local cops up there. Here," he slid sheets of paper across the coffee table at me.

I lifted the report and scanned it quickly. Thorough. Even a rough drawing of the accident, tiny stick men and a stick bike and the names of the two roads and an arrow demonstrating the point of impact. "Very thorough."

"You say it as if it's a problem."

"I'm always suspicious when a whore offers pussy for free. Speaking of, where's the girl from reception, Snyder?" I watched his reaction and then sunk my head down and read the report. "So who was riding Russo down that night?" I asked.

"No one knows."

Russo was travelling as a passenger on a Moto Guzzi motorbike toward the mountain pass road that led down to Schio when he was hit by a dark sedan. One witness said the car had run a stop street. The impact threw Russo and the unknown rider off the bike. The driver of the car fled the scene, leaving Russo unconscious on the street. The rider was seemingly uninjured and fled the scene on foot.

"Strange," I said, reading.

"What?"

"The rider of the bike—he didn't help Russo."

"No," said Snyder. "He ran away."

"Why would he do that?"

One witness saw a man matching the description of the bike rider get into a black sedan about half a kilometre down the road. The witness didn't see the accident, so he couldn't identify the car as the same make and model that hit the bike. But he did see a scuffle before the man was forced into the car.

"Forced," I said, and glanced up at Snyder. "Forced."

"Yeah."

"So what happened to Russo?"

"It's all in there."

"You have something else to do, Snyder?"

Snyder nodded his chin at the papers in my hand. "Page five. Russo was taken to the local hospital in Trento. He had a concussion but asked to be driven down to Schio that very night." I flipped through the folios of paper and followed along to Snyder's voice.

"Anyone ask why?"

"Yeah. Apparently, he was a bit confused, acting strangely, insisting he had to get down to Schio no matter what, so they put him in a car and drove him down. Funny thing, though?" Snyder took a sip of his chilled drink, and I could taste it. "They took the road down from Tonezza, not the main pass. That added probably two hours to the journey."

"What time was this?"

"He got in the accident at around six. Left Trento, from what I can work out, around eight or nine."

"So he could have been at the prison around eleven that night," I said.

"In time to give the signal," said Snyder. "Sure, plenty of time."

I looked around but the girl from reception was nowhere to be seen. "Did you find the driver?"

"Which driver?"

I sighed. "The guy who drove Russo down to Schio, to the hospital."

"Oh, yeah, I did. Not a guy, a gal. With legs," he showed me, "up to here."

"Really?"

"Jesus, Casanova, the girls here," he started blushing and I couldn't help but laugh.

"Did you happen to ask why Russo asked her to drive down to Schio by way of Tonezza."

"I did."

"And?"

"She said Russo was convinced someone was waiting for them on the pass down to Schio, insisted they should take the long road down. Which is what they did—and then she delivered Russo to the hospital."

"No pitstop at the jail then?"

"Not that she would confess to."

"Do you believe her?"

Snyder shrugged.

I threw the file onto the coffee table. "It's only her word, right?"

Snyder took a while before he shook his head. "I sense she was telling me the truth," he said. "Do you want to go up? Ask her yourself?"

"No. No, I trust you've seen enough of her legs, Snyder. Or do you want to go up and see if you can force a confession out of her?"

Snyder looked at me and I thought maybe he was having a moment. "You know what's even stranger?" he asked after shaking the ice in his cool, long glass. "The doctor down at the hospital in Schio ordered an x-ray of his leg."

"Whose leg? Russo's?"

"Yeah."

"His leg?"

"Yeah."

"I thought he was concussed?"

"Yeah, exactly. I spoke to the doctor—Marcon—at the hospital. He managed to find the x-ray for me, it was forgotten down in the radiology department—but wanna know something really weird?" I waited. "He told me there's a rumour that Russo had been seen at the hospital hours after the massacre with a bandage on his head. Still had his clothes and boots on."

"What do you mean, a rumour? He wasn't there?"

"Who, Russo?"

"The doctor, Snyder, Jesus."

"Oh. No. No, it wasn't his turn of duty."

I frowned.

"Something's not right," Snyder said, "right? I mean, Russo gets run over in Trento and the rider, instead of helping him, runs away. No one knows who the rider was. Then the rider's seen being forced into a car that may be the same one that ran him down. Which doesn't make any goddamn sense. Then they check Russo in at the local hospital in Trento with a concussion and he asks to be taken down to Schio. So they drive him down the longest route possible and he gets to the hospital in Schio around when the first of the injured from the jail shootings are being dragged in, and then he's seen with a bandage on his head, gets an x-ray for his leg, they never even took off his boots in the hours from when he was run over to when he's seen at around 4AM—"

"And then—"

"And then," Snyder said, "he winds up dead. In the hospital. Cause unknown."

I rubbed my temples and watched Snyder finish his drink with a long sigh. "He died at the hospital?"

"Yeah. He died in the hospital."

"What's the doctor say about this?"

"Who, Marcon? He doesn't know anything—was up in Valdagno with his girl. It checks out."

"So who was in charge? That night?"

"A Dr Trulli."

"Drag him in," I said.

"Not gonna happen."

"Why not?"

"He died two days after the shooting. A climbing accident, up near Trento."

I looked at Snyder's scar for a while. "He must have left behind some, some files or notes or—"

"That's what Marcon thought. Except ..."

"Lemme guess—they're gone?"

"Into thin air," said Snyder. "All he found was that x-ray. Without that, I swear we wouldn't even have known Russo was really there. So," he said, gulping down his drink and crunching on some ice, "what now?"

# CHAPTER ELEVEN

## JULY 16

I went down to welcome Di Matta and his men at the schoolhouse mid-morning and found them looking about as happy as tornados in a trailer park. Di Matta hadn't changed much since the last time I'd seen him in Imola a couple of months back—perfectly symmetrical bald head, lizard-like eyes that shifted only when he moved that Olympian-sized skull of his, and those massive hairy hands that always reminded me of tarantulas. There were men still alive who'd spend their lives trying to forget those puffy hairy hands. But not many. I'd heard he was a concert pianist back East once, but he always said that people had him mistaken for *di* Matta, who was no relation at all. He, Di Matta, was the first-born son of a coal miner from Pittsburgh, from a family of refugees—Albanians or Romanians—and without, he'd insisted from Salerno all the way to Milan, a drop of dago blood in him. But he spoke Italian like a wop, German like a Nazi, and it was pretty clear there was little to be gained in trying to get to the truth. Not that I cared anyway; when you got to fight in another man's war, you got to be whoever the hell you wanted to be so long as you got out alive.

His two men, Jack and Shirl, were from out West somewhere. They looked similar, and I always got to figuring them as brothers, but who knows, they spoke less than Di Matta and I couldn't help thinking the war was probably the best thing that'd ever happened to the pair of them. They were like those old batteries you kept lying around in a drawer and then one day when you needed them, they came in low and weak, but they did the job until they died, and you got some fresh ones from the store come Monday morning.

"So how was your drive?" I asked, leading Di Matta and his men into the school.

"Dirtier'n your momma's ass," he said, chewing gum. "Where's the turlet? Shirl's holding a log the size of Texas."

Jack and Shirl headed off to the head, and I took Di Matta past the office where the sergeant sprang to his feet and saluted, and down the cool corridor.

"So," he said, when we slowed outside the metal door, "what's this about, Casanova?"

"Usual," I replied, and left Di Matta and his men outside Balbo's cell with a short brief on what I needed. I went back to the office and told the sergeant to go take a long shit somewhere, and sat there all morning behind his desk smoking his cigarettes and reading the *Trib* outta Paris that Di Matta had brought for me, trying hard not to listen to the screams coming from down the brick hallway. It takes a bit of getting used, listening to a man cry. It's an unnatural thing, but I figured it would do the sonofabitch Balbo some good. Di Matta had a rhythm, and the screams came in like air-raid sirens, winding up to a wail and then the crescendo wound down before starting up again.

Eventually I tired of the screams and got the operator to patch me through to Paget, and while I waited, I stepped over to the office door and kicked it shut.

"Lieutenant Casanova," said Paget in my ear. "What a pleasant surprise. Was just talking about you with Captain Coke last night. You seem to have made an impression."

"I make friends fast," I said.

He chuckled. "So what can I do for the United States today?" he asked.

"I got a question."

"Shoot," he said. "Is that the expression?"

"That's a solution," I told him. "The file on the prisoners."

"What about them?"

"You said Svavi had them."

"Did I?"

"You did."

"Righty-o."

"He says you have them."

"Does he now? Well, that's a bit of a, erm—"

"Sticky wicky?" I tried.

"Oh, very good, Lieutenant. Very good."

"*Do* you have them?"

"I do not. But that doesn't mean we—as in, you understand, the United Kingdom—don't have them somewhere. What we need is your man Schneider to come file for us—we keep losing things."

"Losing's a habit," I told him. "Like fucking hookers."

"Is that a verb or an adjective, Lieutenant Casanova?"

"When you find them," I told him as he chuckled away, "leave a message at the Miramonti. It's important."

Di Matta had started his work at 11AM. By 3PM, the screams had stopped and Di Matta, his hands and hair slick with water from his bathroom break, stepped into the office. "Stubborn as a mule with a fucking carrot up its ass," he said, sitting down heavily across the desk from me and grabbing one of my smokes. I'd seen that look on his face before, plenty of times. It seemed to take a toll on him, this work, on those eyes of his, those black eyes that reflected nothing at all, that seemed to absorb light and souls and offered not a glimpse of what he was thinking. They were, I remembered suddenly, the scariest fucking eyes I'd ever looked into. "Anywhere we can get some food?" he asked, and I watched him light up and blow an arrow of smoke at my face from across the desk.

"Did you get any names?"

Di Matta shook his head, lifted his blood-freckled boots onto the desk and picked at something on one knuckle, eyes squinting. "Not yet. But we're done for the day."

"Wait here," I said and walked down the brick passage toward the cell. I paused outside the door and stared at the rusted-out deadbolt and took a long breath. Walking in after Di Matta had been at a man was always an experience—you were never quite prepared for whatever he'd left behind for you to work with. I felt a stare and looked back down the head of the hallway. In a pool of light stood Shirl drying his hands on a bloody towel, watching me with a vague, inscrutable look. I nodded at him. He just stared back and watched me draw back the deadbolt.

Insipid light collapsed weak from the barred window up near the ceiling, blue and ambiguous. The smell hit me first. It's how a man smells in war, redolent with fear and shit and piss and the sweet cologne of drying blood. Balbo was in a corner, away from the light, lying there in the shadows, doubled like a big rat. Naked. I looked at him for a while, stared at his big hairy sweaty ass. He knew I was there, and I waited for him. It took a while, stubborn as he was, but he was always going to look-see what was about to happen next. That's the thing—you gotta make a man *want* to know what happens next, because that's the fear right there. It's like a suspense novel. You make them bring their own fear—like at a picnic. It's not just about the pain. You hurt a man long and hard enough and he'll say anything to make it all stop. That was Di Matta's job. Mine was to make sure the anything was the truth.

Eventually his face rose and all he saw was me. He was crying. I could see the tears like mascara down his cheeks. But I saw no surprise in his broken face.

"Why, John?" he asked. *"Ma perché?"*

I didn't have an answer for him. Or maybe I did, but he knew the answer as well I did: because when you get here, the only regret you ever have is to draw it out too long. Because there's a point when a man slips away from you and his psyche becomes fractured like the truth. I'd seen that a few times in the early days—the truth is fluid for men on the verge of breaking. I slid a Moleskin notebook from my jacket and tossed it down onto the floor. Then I threw a pen next to it.

"My friends will be back tomorrow," I told him. "You like Hemingway? You write me the best confession I ever read about how you killed fifty-six people. You tell me who your accomplices were. You do that for me, Renzo, you do that for me, and I'll get my friends to go back to where they came from."

"Still fifty-six?" he whispered.

I turned from him and walked out, stinging my palm when I thrust the deadbolt to lock. I took Di Matta and Jack and Shirl out past the MPs. Di Matta's men wanted to get back to the hotel, and I dropped them at the Miramonti before taking Di Matta up to the Piazza Rossi and the Bar Excelsior where we ordered beer and *soppressata* panini in fresh, still-crumbly bread.

"He ain't innocent, I'll tell you that much, Casanova." Di Matta's jaws masticated furiously on the bread as he added as an afterthought, "I'll bring the 'roaches tomorrow, that'll move us along." I placed my sandwich down on a plate and switched to the beer. "Ain't no man ever gonna resist the 'roaches," he said and swallowed dry and washed down beer. "You know why?"

"I can't say I've spent a lot of time on that one, Di Matta."

Di Matta stuck a fingernail between his teeth and flipped away a slice of salami skin. "We all got fears," he said, looking around the bar and settling his gaze on a guy sitting on his own in the corner whose eyes immediately met his, "but all men got the same fear for the 'roaches, brother."

I pushed my plate away and lit a cigarette. "You looking forward to getting home?"

"Sure," he said, laying his head over on one side and eating from the bottom of the sandwich like a man trying to get at a cow's tits. "Why not, ain't nothing for me here, even if the whores are half the price and twice the fun. They don't," he elaborated after swallowing a big gulp of his beer, "get to thinking they need to talk."

"I heard there's something big planned," I told him. "Something over Japan."

"Yeah?"

"Gonna end this war once and for all, that's what I heard."

He wiped his fingers on a napkin with the kind of thoroughness I'd seen from our surgeons on the field. "Always gonna be war, Casanova. It's like disease."

"So whatcha gonna do when you get back?"

"Pick up where I left off, I guess." Di Matta considered the remains of the sandwich. "Third year psychiatry at Duke. You?"

"I was right outta high school," I said, my half-eaten panino on the plate saddening me. "They recruited me 'cause I spoke Italian, shipped me out with the Fifth to Salerno in '43 after a month training in counter-ops in Egypt."

Di Matta burped. Looked at me for a while. And found a yet longer burp, this one coming from deep and wafting across at me. "Funny that," he said.

"What?"

"Known you for almost two years and that's the most you ever said about yourself."

I smiled.

"Relax soldier," he said, picking at his teeth with a blackened fingernail, "I'll break that commie prick for you tomorrow or my name ain't Salvatore."

"That's your name?"

He wiped his still-chewing mouth with the back of his hand and glanced over at the guy in the corner. "Are you nuts? Name's Brian. Brian Tex for Texeria Di Matta. My dad wanted to make sure no one ever got the idea we came from this fucking place." He nodded his big head at something vague beyond the flecked windows. "I get why."

# CHAPTER TWELVE

I left Di Matta in the bar and found Snyder waiting for me at the Miramonti, sitting cosy on the couch with a long cool drink on the coffee table before him. Outside the sky had gone pallid, dirty-yellow light splayed over the lobby like a fading disease.

"Any news?" he asked when I sat down on the chair opposite him.

"Not a nada," I said. "What's that?"

He looked at the black fluid in his highball glass and picked it up. "Chinotto," he said, "some apéritif."

"Apéritif?" I glanced around for the receptionist.

"We got the report back. The exhumation report."

"And?"

"Russo's dead."

I looked at him and his drink.

"Died of septic shock," he added quickly. "Nothing that would suggest he didn't fall from a bike, though. Nothing to suggest anything much."

I sat back on the chair and shut my lids. "Septic shock? Really? In what, four hours?"

"There was one other anomaly," I heard him say.

"What?"

"There was a needle mark."

"So?"

"So nothing. Except the needle mark was at the base of his skull, they found it when they shaved his head otherwise—"

"Otherwise what?"

"No one would have seen it."

"Could be anything," I said. "Did you ask?

"Ask what?"

"Ask them if it could have been the cause of death."

"I did."

"And?"

"They said there's no way of telling. Too late, but—"

"But?"

"But," said Snyder, and he leaned forward to read his notes. "But his death would, they said, be consistent with someone who'd died of hypoglycaemia."

"He was diabetic?"

"Nope."

I thought about it and put a few more pieces together.

"So I guess we just gonna have to wait for your men to finish their job then," said Snyder after a while.

"My men?"

"The guys who arrived today."

"Di Matta," I said, keeping my eyes shut. Just a thin layer of skin, no thicker than a razor blade.

"How long's that gonna take?"

"Long as it takes."

"Sure. But how long, usually, does it take to torture a man 'til he breaks?"

There was something in his voice, and when I opened my eyes, he was staring at me like my mom used to stare at pops when he came home a little too late at night. But at least she knew better'n to open her stupid mouth. "Who said anything about torture?"

"Did I get that wrong?"

"You got that wrong, Snyder. Ain't no torture. Di Matta's a trained psychologist."

"Is that right?"

"That's exactly right." But I could see he wasn't done with this bone.

"It's not what we do," he said eventually, weighing his words as if he'd been sitting here all-day sipping his apéritif, practicing. "We're Americans. This isn't who we are."

"We got a job to do."

"Torture ain't part of it."

"It ain't torture."

"So what is it?"

"It's a fucking massage—the *fuck* are you on about, Snyder?"

He touched his apéritif. Thought better than to lift it. "Loller—"

"Loller wants results."

"Loller wouldn't approve."

"You fucking kidding me? *Loller?*"

"The war's over, John."

"It *was* over," I reminded him, "when your buddy Renzo Balbo walked into a prison and shot ninety-nine innocent men, women, and children. Why the fuck do you figure Loller brought me down from Bologna? If he needed someone to blow wop cock, buddy, he'd have sent you along on your own." I felt a headache coming on, right behind my right eye, like a needle trying to get out.

"You want to go home with this?"

"With what?"

"With this, this—" he waved at the air.

"I ain't taking shit home with me, Snyder. All of this—this whole fucking war, these fucking people, *you*—there ain't a damned thing I'm taking home with me. You fought your way up here, you were at Monte, this ain't nothing, what are you getting your panties in a twist for?"

"That was war."

"And this is *what?*" I asked and my voice was louder than I'd intended, and I saw him flinch and I went in hard. "People died, Snyder. Fifty-fucking-six people were killed like fucking rats. And we got a fucking job to do. *This* is what we do, pal. Now do me a favour, you got nothing better to do than sit here and worry about your fucking conscience and drinking your fucking *apéritif*, I'll give you something to do." I grabbed the matchbook from my jacket and threw it onto the table. It sailed and missed and ended on the floor. I waited for Snyder to bend over to pick it up and walked in close so he could see my shoes there by his face. "Go find that sonofabitch. Name of Ivo Pranjic. A revolutionary communist, Snyder, who just happened to be here when this massacre went down. A commie from downtown fucking *Mos*-cow. You go find that sonofabitch and get off my fucking case."

## CHAPTER THIRTEEN

JULY 17

I spent the night in the company of Gordon & Mc-never-Phail. Outside the rain kept falling, teardrops as big as rats oozing down the windows that refracted the sick liquid light from the street onto the walls. I listened to the occasional car thread through the water and the act of wondering who it may be out there, what life they were returning to through a stormy night like this, reminded me of Altoona, of home. I thought of my pop and my ma and my sisters and most of all I thought of Monday night football under the lights, and the girls on Main Street in the late fall with hearts as chilled as beer, and the cornfields prickling in the dying embers of spent summer evenings, and I was drawn away into a halfway world where dreams felt real and sleep was just a jumble of ejected mirrored images of a past filled by screams and blood and Millie's moans.

The screams continued all that morning as I sat in the office with the paper and warm beer. It's a satisfying but unnatural sound, a man screaming. It's like his soul's coming out. Some men are screamers, some men take it silently. For a while anyway. The instant screamers are the ones you want—they always break without much fuss. But it did take a bit of getting used to, and I recalled the first time I broke a man, and that was sure the hardest thing I'd ever done. Harder than killing a man. It was like kicking a puppy, but I was good at it. You gotta stay detached, that's the thing—you can't make it something it ain't. That kind of power, though, over another man, that kind of power can corrupt a man, ain't no doubting.

The clock on the wall had just clipped 2PM when I heard the deadbolt slap-shut hard and footsteps approaching down the brick hallway. Di Matta glanced into the office. He had blood on his cheek, like freckles on the face of a boy on the first warm day of May in Altoona.

"All yours," he said, stepping away toward the head.

I guess it's different for men like Di Matta.

I stood and waited for Jack and Shirl to brush past the office, shoulders drooped. It ain't nothing, but it takes it out of a man. It makes a man want to hurt—makes a man want to smash it all up good. I lit a Lucky and walked down the hallway into the darkening shadows and stood outside the door and listened to the silence. Silence that was broken by the deadbolt sliding metallically in the palm of my hand before I pushed the door open.

The stench hit me first. He'd emptied his bowels, the dirty little wop. That's what they do, like puppies, that's what they do when they're near breaking, they take a shit for you, and there was the cloying stink of sick when I took a step in and a cockroach scuttled by my foot, rushing for the door. I stepped on it. It cracked like a bone. On the floor, close to Balbo, who lay naked in the foetal position by the wall, was the notebook and the pen, and beside it an upturned glass. Trapped in the glass, thousands of 'roaches scurried and scaled, a fist of sweltering copper-coloured filth, porous and lustrous like organs scurrying about with wild probes searching and probing and silently shrieking.

It always ended this way. He should have known that.

I stepped closer and the scent of him made me gag even with the cigarette between my lips blowing smoke into my nostrils. I lifted the notebook from the floor and cracked it open. Balbo had been a busy boy— dozens of pages filled with a neat hand and the first words read, "Dear John". That kind of shit could make a man cry.

I used my thumb to scroll through to the last entry. "What the fuck is this?" I asked, and ash fell from my Lucky onto my shoe. Balbo lay silent. "I don't see any names. Where are my names?"

"I've done as you asked," he whispered. "I've written the truth."

I waited for him. Took a while but eventually his eyes, wet in the gloom, blinked my way. He saw me, he saw my foot resting on top of the glass with the 'roaches, tenderly swaying it back and forth, and I heard him groan.

"Did we have a misunderstanding, Renzo?"

"I couldn't finish in time," he whispered. He was looking for excuses now. Justifying himself. Which meant he accepted my dominance. Back with Di Matta on our way up from Salerno, we'd take men like this and have our fun, break them so completely not even their mommas would ever put 'em back together again. But I felt for Balbo, I felt for this poor sonofabitch.

"Doesn't take that long to write eleven names, Renzo."

"You asked for the truth."

"I asked for the names."

"You asked for the truth," he insisted, and his voice broke when I let a couple of 'roaches scurry from under the glass.

"I think you misunderstood," I told him. "Did you misunderstand me?"

"Yes," he whispered, watching the 'roaches quickly scuttle toward him.

"Did you?"

"Yes."

"Yes?"

"Yes."

"And are you sorry?"

A slight hesitation. "...yes."

"Yes?"

"Yes."

"Tell me."

"I'm sorry."

"For what."

"For, for misunderstanding you."

"Yes, yes you did, Renzo. You understand me now?"

"Yes."

"Yes?"

"Yes."

"I'll be back tomorrow." I placed the notebook in my jacket, found a fresh one and threw it at him. It hit him full in the face and it cut him. He moved like a beat dog, and I saw between his legs, and it took me a moment and then I laughed. "The Apaches," I told him, "always lost. You should have remembered that, from those Tom Mix movies."

"Why do you do this, John?" he whispered.

If they ask, they haven't quite accepted. He should have shut up. "Tomorrow," I told him. "Eleven names. And the man who organised this. *Gheto capio?*"

I tippled the glass and watched the 'roaches ooze out a wet moist fist scurrying like a rash and heard him moan when I let him alone with them for the night.

## CHAPTER FOURTEEN

In the office, Di Matta was holding the phone out at me. "It's Loller," he said. "He sounds ... miffed."

I took the phone from him. Miffed? "Colonel Loller, sir?" Silence. "Sir?" Silence. Di Matta gave me a consoling glance. "Hullo?"

"Casanova. That you?" came the voice in my ear suddenly.

"Yessir."

"Is that you, Casanova?"

"Yessir, this is—"

"Can you hear me?"

"Loud and clear, sir."

"You sure you can hear me, Casanova?"

"Yessir, you're coming over loud and clear. Good copy, sir."

"Loud and clear?"

"Yes sir."

"You're sure now, Casanova?"

"Yessir."

"I'm just asking, 'cause I'm figuring the last time we spoke, you didn't hear a goddamn fucking *word I said to you*."

"Sir?"

"Sir? Sir? What the fuck have you and Snyder been doing up there, boy?"

"I—"

"I'm gonna ask you two questions, Casanova."

"—sir?"

"One: Are you aware of the Eighth Amendment to our Jesus-given Constitution, Casanova?"

"The—"

"I'll take that as a no, you goddamn wetback sonofabitch. Let me quote: 'Excessive bail shall not be required, nor excessive fines imposed, nor cruel and unusual punishments inflicted'. You got all that? You sonofabitch."

"Sir, I—"

"*Two!* Do you know anyone *stupid* enough to torture civilians in peacetime in a goddamn *school*?"

"Sir—"

"In a *goddamn elementary school? A*re you fucking *shitting me*, you stupid dago sonofafuckingbitch, are you *fucking shitting me*?"

"Sir—"

"Shut the fuck up, Casanova. Does it sound like I want your fucking opinion right now? Listen to me! *Anyone* caught using cruel and excessive punishment under my command is gonna get my boot up their ass. And then they're gonna get court martialled. In that order—"

"Sir, there's no punishment—"

"*Shut up, Casanova.* We're Americans. You need to get what that means. You ain't no goddamn wop no more, not in my army, boy."

"Bu—"

"Now listen to me. And listen good, you dumb sonofabitch. I'm sending a battalion to Schio tomorrow. Thirteen hundred hours. Colonel Jenson'll be running that show. The battalion will—Jared, *Jared*! Where the fuck did you say they're gonna meet him?" I heard a voice faintly on the line before, "Piovene-Schio road, marker 125. *Casanova*? You got that?"

"I can find it, sir."

"You can find it?"

"Yes sir."

"You fucking better find it, boy. You best meet Colonel Jenson at Thirteen hundred hours. You with me?"

"Yessir."

"Are you with me!"

"Yessir!"

"And Casanova."

"Sir?"

"You get me those names, boy, because if you've gone down the rabbit hole and come up with nothing more than air, I'm gonna get busier'n a one-legged man at a butt-kicking convention on your wop ass."

"Yessir," I said wondering if he meant hair or air, but the line was already cut, and Di Matta was smiling at me.

"He sounded happier'n a fat dog with fleas," he said.

"Like a tornado in a trailer park," I said.

"What? No, Casanova, no, that's not what that means—" but he shut up fast when I looked at his face.

## CHAPTER FIFTEEN

I spent the afternoon at the Miramonti reading the papers—yesterday's edition of the Paris *Trib* had found its way to the lobby—waiting for Snyder who finally walked in with the evening birds in full song. The wound on my palm was exquisitely painful as I scratched and prodded into the meat, but in its depth, I could feel the gelatine of infection. I was sitting on his couch, and he walked over to the chair, and he'd hardly reached it when the receptionist appeared with a Cinzano and soda which she placed directly into his hand, her tits hanging out like goddamn melons. I ordered a whisky and waited for her to bring it while Snyder spread his files and notes out on the coffee table.

"How's your day been?" I asked him when she'd brought my drink along with a happy big smile for Snyder. Women are easy in war—and even easier when they gotta make peace. I made sure Snyder saw me watch her ass walk away.

"Rewarding," Snyder replied.

"Yeah, I'll bet." I looked at him. His scar was deep, like a welt from a whupping my pop would give me out back in the summers when he'd a few too many by the BBQ. Puffy and pink. "What do you know about the Eighth Amendment?" I asked him when he placed his apéritif to his lips. He blinked and our gaze met there over the coffee table, and I was in no doubt then. No doubt about what this grinning clown had done. "You're fucking kidding me, Snyder."

"Listen—"

"You're fucking kidding me."

He was smart enough to shut the fuck up. But not for long enough. "What did you expect me to do?" he asked.

"What did I *expect*? I expect fucking loyalty."

"That ain't fair," he said, meeting my stare. "You didn't have to do this."

"Didn't have to do *what?*"

"You know what."

"No, Snyder, I don't. Why don't you spell it out for me?"

"It ain't right."

"What ain't right?"

"It just ain't right."

*"You* get to decide that do you?"

"No, the *United States* decided that for us—"

*"You* get to decide that?"

"I told you—"

"You think you're more fucking American than me, Snyder, is that it?"

"No—what? No. Jesus, Casanova, this—"

"Maybe you figure you're whiter than me, Snyder, is that what this is about? Me being some sorta fucking wop—is that what's happening here?"

"What's happening here is wrong," he said. "It's just plain wrong."

"And so you thought you'd try to fuck me by going behind my back to Loller?"

Snyder shook his head, searching for words from his stupid clown face, his mouth like a fish drowning in oxygen.

"You thought you'd go behind my back," I whispered, "and try to *destroy* me?"

"That's not—"

"You fucking ever pull that shit again, Snyder, and I'll fucking cut you."

"Hold up—"

"I'll fucking *cut* you, Snyder, I'll fucking cut your ear off, you sonofabitch."

He sat back in his chair and sucked in air. "Look—"

"Loller's sending in the troops tomorrow," I interrupted. "They're gonna smash this place up, pal. They're gonna smash it all up and all your fucking wop friends with it. And if you and me, if we don't have some names for Loller by tomorrow, we'll be playing 'where's my cock' with some squinty-eyed gook shoving bamboo rats up our asses. You little …"

Snyder stared at me and thought about it. "Tomorrow?" he whispered eventually.

"Tomorrow."

"Jesus," he said, and his head fell forward. I let him consider the consequences of his treachery for a while.

"Don't sweat it," I told him, throwing the *Trib* onto the coffee table and grabbing the whisky. "I got it covered."

"Covered how?"

"You know *exactly* how, pal," I told him. "Now how 'bout you? You got anything to share?"

"Pranjic."

"What about him?" I tasted the whisky. Watered down.

"He's gone. Best I can figure, he made a run for Yugoslavia. He had mates in Czechoslovakia, Prague, old guard, that's where a lot of the old Italian commies hid out during the war. Strange thing though?"

"What?"

"He left everything behind. In the apartment he was renting."

"How do you know?"

"I went for a visit today. Place looked like he'd gone out for a coffee."

"That's what people do when they leave in a hurry," I told him.

"Yeah except for this." Snyder burrowed through his carryall and threw four passports onto the coffee table. "Found them taped-up under the slats of his bed."

I lifted the passports. Pranjic had collected names and citizenships like he had revolutions. He had a face that reminded me of the pope.

"Strange to leave those behind, right?" asked Snyder.

I threw the books back down and shrugged. "Don't matter none anyways, he wasn't one of the shooters, way I figure it."

"There's more. I spoke to Pranjic's brother—works at Lanemoro, the big textile factory, tame old guy, you wouldn't imagine they shared a mother. Anyway, he told me a strange story."

"What strange story?"

"Told me Pranjic was arrested back in '44. Near Verona. He was in prison there for about two, three weeks as far as I can make out."

"Arrested?"

"And then he was released."

"Yeah. That's what happens, you get arrested and then," I said before the pieces connected with a snap. "Wait. *Who* arrested him?"

"That's what I was saying. Pranjic was worked over by the Gestapo."

"In '44?"

"Yeah."

"The Gestapo?"

"Yeah."

"In Verona."

"Yeah."

"Why would they do that?"

Snyder watched my face.

"You figuring," I said, working it out, "you figuring he was turned?"

"I'm not coming up with a lotta other alternatives," Snyder said. "In '44, in Verona, might as well been in Salò, the Nazis get themselves a bone fide commie revolutionary and they let him walk right out?"

"Bone fide?"

"I got something else, too."

"You *have* been busy."

"So remember Freccia, the guy who got ambushed on the road to the Laghi?"

"Wilkinson?"

"Wilkinson, yeah. Freccia. So guess who he met the morning before he got ambushed?" I could've smashed his little smiling mouth. "Russo," he said, and I watched him take a sip of the blood-red drink.

I finished off the whisky and lay the glass on the coffee table and spread my arms over the back of the sofa like a vulture and tried to focus. "How do you know this?"

"Because Russo's sister told Pranjic's brother who told me."

I gave that one a bit of thought and my head hurt. Small towns, I thought, and everyone living in everyone else's pocket. "So let's go through that *langsam*, Snyder. Russo and Freccia—"

"They were up near the Laghi. Russo was bringing Freccia down from the Garibaldi Battalion's camp when they were ambushed by a squad of Black Shirts. Seems someone informed on them. Russo got away. Freccia didn't."

"And got his guts taken out from his a-hole," I said. "So how does Russo's sister know Pranjic?"

"She doesn't. She knows his brother. Because Russo," said Snyder with a grin, "AKA Giulio Moro, is scion of Baron Moro, who happens to own Lanemoro, Schio's third-biggest textile concern."

I rubbed my eyes and sighed. "Okay, let's—take this slow."

"So Pranjic has a brother who works at Lanemoro."

"Right."

"And his boss is Russo's sister."

My head hurt more. "I'm gonna need a diagram," I told him and let it all sink in for a while. "Scion?" I asked eventually, trying to connect the pieces.

"It means—"

"Don't smell right, Snyder."

"Smells like shit," Snyder agreed. "So now what?"

"Now," I said, "I'm gonna get dinner and read a little book someone wrote for me. And then tomorrow, you and me, we're going to smash this fucking lousy town. We're gonna smash it like a piñata."

"A what?"

"What the spicks do," I said. "And what I'll do to your face if you ever try and fuck me over again, pal."

# CHAPTER SIXTEEN

JULY 18

The morning had come in sticky, and I'd come in early, just gone 7AM, and the screams lasted until just after eleven when Di Matta walked toward the office, and I glanced up at the clock on the wall one more time.

"Your boy is ready for his consultation," he told me.

I scraped my chair back and headed down the cool corridor. The blister on my palm was stinging good now, an open sore into which I dug the moon-nail of my index finger and scraped deep inside until tears came to my eyes.

Balbo was lying in the corner in a pool of his own piss. His naked body was discoloured in the darkness, the sweat on his flesh like a rash. The notebook lay on the floor. I bent down and picked it up and eagerly clipped to the last written page. There were seven names.

"I know nothing else," he whispered. "I told your men. I know nothing more."

"It's worse than that," I told him. "You know nothing at all." I slid the notebook into my jacket. "Who was the chump with the gas mask?"

"Mitra," he whispered.

"Is that a battle-name?"

"Yes."

"What's his real name?"

"He came from up near Posina, we never got his name."

"There are seven names here. With you, that makes eight. Who are the other four?"

"I don't—"

"Not part of the Garibaldi Battalion?"

"No."

"You know why, Renzo?"

Silence.

"Because you got played, buddy. You're going to hang for no reason at all. Where do I find him? Mitra."

"There's a—there's a rest-house for partisans—up near Lavarone. At the Albergo Astoria. Last time I heard, Mitra was up there. The others, maybe they're there too, I don't know. *I don't know.*"

"I'll get the sergeant to come for your confession," I told him and walked out the door with the notebook in hand. Before I shut it, I turned to him and asked, "All of this for one man?"

"You don't understand."

"He left the hospital yesterday. Gonna live a long life, my friend. Gonna live long after he watches you hang, you stupid sonofabitch."

"Who," he whispered. "Buonfuoco? But—he died—"

"Buonfuoco?" I asked. "No, not, no—what?" His eyes met mine in the gloom and the last piece connected in my brain like the bolt to the door. Sonofabitch, I thought. Son. Of. A. Bitch.

# CHAPTER SEVENTEEN

From the office I called Snyder at the Miramonti and told him to come fetch me and waited for him outside on the little piazza where I shared a smoke with Di Matta under the willow tree.

"Fancy a ride?" I asked him.

"Where to?"

I blew smoke toward the mountains. "And get your men," I said.

"We expecting trouble?" he asked.

"We gonna make us some," I replied.

The Buick arrived in less than five minutes, and Snyder and I, with Di Matta and Jack and Shirl in the back, rolled out of town on the Piovene-Schio road.

We met Loller's battalion just south of Piovene, on a ridge overhanging the Astico River running white caps under the sun. I could see a couple of boys down there on the golden-pebbled verge, shirts off and fishing rods extended into the glacial green water, and it reminded me of home. Colonel Jenson was standing at the head of a column of Jeeps and trucks with canvas tops shielding about a hundred men. He stood there smoking, one boot on the Jeep's front tyre like a boss, gazing out at the world like a cowboy on the range from behind aviator shades. I climbed out of the Buick and walked over to him, saluting.

"I have the list, sir." I tore out the page from the notebook with the names and handed it over.

Jenson stared at me from behind his shades. "Follow us," he said.

"With your permission, sir, there's one more lead I need to track down."

He looked at the list, shrugged, and climbed into his jeep. "You're on thin ice with Loller," he told me. "Try not to drown, son."

"Yes sir." He started up the engine. "And sir, there's just—" He looked at me. "Smash 'em up, sir. Smash 'em up good for me."

Jenson smiled. "Loller told me the same thing."

I walked back to the Buick and stood there smoking as the convoy slowly swept by me in a tunnel of dust with dead-eyed soldiers watching idly from the deep shadows of the truck beds. When the last camion had vanished into the copper-stained grime, I climbed back into the Buick and showed Snyder the way as he powered the sedan across the old bridge over the Astico and began to climb the dirt road up toward Trento.

"You bring the weapons?" I asked.

"In the trunk," Snyder replied and glanced at me. "We expecting trouble?"

"No," said Di Matta at the back, "we gonna make us some."

Jack and Shirl grunted something at the same time.

We rolled up through small villages where kids watched us like *Cocui*. I liked that word. Balbo was on my mind on that run up the mountain. He was a good man. He was also, like all good men, stupid. Stupid because good men can't conceive of the rottenness of the world. There ain't nothing sadder than a good dog and a decent man, I thought. The dust followed us up, up to where the Swiss pine trees ran in thick clusters up the mountainsides and the coolness was a breeze that whistled through our open windows.

The hotel was precisely where Balbo had said it would be, just beyond the town of Lavarone, a grand, faded, vaguely Victorian pile sprouting from a parched meadow surrounded by a forest and a lake as green as the football field in Altoona in May.

"Lovely," said Snyder as he pulled the Buick up into the small lot. "Wanna tell me what this is about?"

"This," I climbed from the Buick and took off the safety on the Colt, "is a rehab clinic for resistance fighters. An actual, bone fide fucking commie den, Snyder. And we're gonna get the God-given chance of smashing it all up."

Di Matta, Snyder, and Jack and Shirl began grabbing guns and ammo from the trunk. Snyder walked back to the front of the car with a Thompson pointing at my feet and stared at the hotel.

"We ready?" I asked.

Di Matta locked and loaded a shotgun and smiled. "Fuck yeah," he said.

I led them across the meadow. Up on the metal-trellis verandas, men were sitting about, and I made sure they saw us coming. I waved my Colt and told Di Matta to go through the front door with his men. "Shoot whatever runs," I told him.

"*Awwww yeah*," he said, running toward the door with Jack and Shirl on his six. With Snyder on mine, I circled round the back.

The men up on the verandas ducked into the hotel. We were just getting to the rear when a door burst open and a man with a shock of blond hair ran by us in nothing but white shorts.

"*Mitra*!" I yelled.

The man kept running. I aimed and fired over his head. The explosion echoed, and it was still back-chatting when the bastard slowed and paused, his back to me.

"The next one's in your fat fucking head," I told him. "On your knees, *paesan*."

He hesitated, head darting about, probably figuring the distance to the nearby trees and his chances of making it. Then he looked back at me and the big hole of my Colt aimed at his face. His eye was still bruised. Sonofabitch. I walked toward him. "You're gonna hang anyway," I told him, "so you might as well make a run for it."

Mitra raised his hands.

"Run," I said. "It's a better death than the rope."

He fell onto his knees and placed his hands on his head. I walked closer, Snyder covering me and the rear door. From inside the hotel, I heard a few gunshots and then the boom of a shotgun.

"How did you find me?" the blond asked, on his knees there before me.

"Your friend Balbo. He was upset you stole my fucking Zippo," I told him, my crotch in his face. "Now get on your belly."

He went down slow until I shoved my shoe into the small of his back and forced his face down on the ground. I stuck my shoe on his head and crunched it about as if his head were a cockroach and then I aimed the Colt and felt my finger tighten on the trigger.

"Casanova," whispered Snyder. I turned to him. I couldn't read his face, but his Thompson rose in his hands.

"You think," I said to him with my shoe grinding Mitra's face like a cigarette butt, "he wouldn't have killed you if he had a chance?"

"It's not who we are," said Snyder and then he shut up when I pointed the Colt at his face.

"You think he wouldn't have put a bullet in your face?"

"Put the gun down," he whispered, and I could sense the fear. I could see the sweat, damp over his thick lips. I smiled and lowered the Colt.

"Just fucking with you, Snyder," I said, and jumped to land on Mitra's head and heard a satisfying crunch. "Just fucking with ya, pal. Couldn't hit a barn door with this Colt if I tried."

# CHAPTER EIGHTEEN

The ride back to Schio was slow. Snyder drove into the twilight with an arm leaning out of the window, his fingers testing the resistance of air. Mitra was on the back seat, tied and lolling about between Di Matta and his men as the sedan took the turns like a sponge bath. Beyond the dirt of the windscreen, the fading light burst out wild over the fertile valley of the Veneto, and in that blue haze I could make out the Lanemoro factory down there on the plain, the Astico a white wound on that boiling, flat, red-rich earth. I lit a Lucky and looked back at Mitra. His face was swollen, and a stream of blood ran down his cheek from the cut above his eye. It made me want to get back there and hurt him some more.

"Tell me," I said, "do you know Captain Coke?"

He shrugged.

Di Matta raised his eyes, and I shook my head no. Not yet. "Make it easier on yourself, pal," I told Mitra.

"*Fanculo*," he said.

"You know what I think?"

He stared out of the window.

"I think you got played. You and your crew of killers. Y'all got played."

"*A morir e a pagar se fa sempre in tempo*," he replied in his monkey dialect. You're always on time when it's time to pay and die.

Snyder glanced at me, and I smiled at him too.

# CHAPTER NINETEEN

That night, Snyder and I had a meal at the Due Spade with Jenson's report that'd been sent to the Miramonti on the table between us. The roundup had been successful; dozens of partisans had been swept up and five men from Balbo's list had been arrested. They were all having a chat with CID down in Vicenza. The others had all already crossed the border into Yugoslavia. Rumour, according to Jenson's report, was that they'd first headed down to Rome where they'd attempted to get an audience with commie party leader Togliatti, who'd had the good sense to hide in his office until the men left on a train bound for Trieste from where they'd skipped the border and vanished into the mountains.

"Not a good look for Togliatti to have a bunch of killers hanging out in his office," I told Snyder. I found a note Paget had left for me at the Miramonti and splayed it on the table for Snyder to read.

*Seems the files were taken to the hospital the night of the massacre to help ID the victims, and in the confusion, they never found their way back.*

Snyder read the note and then looked up at me. "So?"

"So why did the files vanish?"

He gave it a minute and came up empty. "Why?"

I grabbed the note and folded it into my pocket. "You figure that out, Snyder, and you figure out what happened here. This whole fucking thing was a set up."

"What do you mean?"

I poured him some wine and said nothing.

"So now what?" he asked.

"Now we go home, Snyder. It's over. This whole filthy war is over."

"You figure the Japs have had enough?"

"Everyone's had enough. It's just the quitting that's hard. Like puppies," I said. "They got them a taste for blood. But you kick 'em hard and long enough, they get to figuring eating shit is better than being dead."

Snyder considered his plate. "What did you mean Mitra got played?"

"What?"

"You said Mitra got played."

"Did I?"

"Yeah, in the car."

"I thought you didn't speak monkey, Snyder?"

"Di Matta told me, when I asked him."

I chewed on a tough piece of steak. "Does it matter to you?"

He thought about it and said nothing more until we'd had our fill of meat and polenta. "I just don't get it," he said eventually.

"Let's get going." I called for the waiter. "Loller wants our report by tomorrow noon, sharp. I'll work on it tonight. I got me a little diary to read too."

## CHAPTER TWENTY

JULY 19

Loller was lying poolside on the chaise longue, out there amidst the fields that smelt of ripe shit. A copy of *The New York Times* was lying by his feet, the headline—*49 ITALIANS SEIZED IN RAID; Group Linked to Massacre of Political Prisoners in Schio*—flecked by water, and there was a drinks trolley and two chairs under the shade of a yellow-striped beach umbrella.

"Grab a seat, boys," said Loller, head under one elbow and body glistening from what smelt like baby oil. "Help yourselves to a drink. I even got some Cinzano for you, Snyder."

Snyder stepped over to the trolley and got on with mixing two highballs and brought them over. Ice. Clinking. The Cinzano and soda tasted bitter, and I set it aside, sucking up a golf-ball chunk of ice instead that froze my tongue.

Loller sat up with his stomach muscles tautening and gave us a smile so white it seemed to suck in the sun itself, sat up like a mummy from one of those Boris Karloff movies and gazed at us for a while. "Paget tells me you boys did a fine job," he said. "We got us a full confession from Mitra last night." He placed his shades on and glanced at the pool water. "And your man Di Matta is on his way back to Milan, Casanova, I thought you'd like to know. I sent him a copy of the Bill of Rights to keep him company. You might want to read it one day. Still, the man deserves a medal. And you too, when you get down to it." He nodded at the manila folder in my hand. "Is that my report, son?"

"Yes sir."

"Good man. What's it say?"

"Sir?"

"Why did this whole shitstorm go down, Casanova? Why don't you—condense it for me?"

I swallowed the ice down in one gulp wondering if I could choke on it. "It's war, sir," I said, and as I spoke, he folded one leg onto the other and began to scrape at a toenail. "They call it the *resa dei conti*, settling of debts, and I figure it was all set off by that boy who came back from Mauthausen, and then the local cinema played the first reels from the death camps in Poland and then there was the kid who'd been buried alive..." I slowed when Loller stuck his big toe into his mouth and began ripping at a nail with his teeth. "You put all that together and throw partisans who were essentially left free to run the place into the mix, and then you add Captain Paget wanting to release the prisoners, and the years of animosity and hate and—"

"Snyder?" interrupted Loller.

"Sir?"

Loller spit a sliver of toenail toward me. "You agree with this?" he asked, turning his face from me and I felt like Jesus on the cross.

"It's as," Snyder lowered the glass from his lips, "as Lieutenant Casanova says, sir. Revenge."

"Revenge against what? Innocent women and children?"

"Sir, some were—"

Loller's gaze whipped out at me like a belt. "If I want to be interrupted, boy, I'll ask."

"Yes sir."

He gave me a look that melted the ice in my blood-red Cinzano. I dug my nail into the wound on my palm and went in as deep as I could, feeling the pain in all its sweetness. "These people who died," Loller said, and satisfied with his toenail, returned his foot solidly onto the ground, "were innocent." He looked at me and then Snyder in turn. "Innocent. They were killed by wild-eyed fucking commies wanting to start a worker's revolution in Italy. Run by a Moscow agent, gentlemen. These killers, these cold-blooded animals, these communist bastards, these, these," he searched the air for inspiration and came up hot and empty. "I'm gonna tell you straight-up that the death penalty will be applied to this case, fellas. These men are gonna hang. You boys ever see a man hang? Weirdest shit you ever gonna see. You know why?"

Snyder wasn't sure whether to remain silent or speak, so he tried to nod and shake his head at the same time, and he was like a marionette whose strings had been cut.

"Because the moment they're given even an ounce of power, this is what the communist does." Loller seemed to like the sound of that. "The communist," he repeated, tasting it. "The international, global, revolutionary communist. And we, gentlemen, we Americans, we ain't gonna sit by and let that go down on our watch. Are we, boys?"

"No sir," said Snyder, sitting there with his red drink.

Loller's eyes turned toward me. "So, tell me again, Casanova, what does your report say?"

Snyder stared at me along with Loller's shades. Sweat ran down my back like a little stream and made me shiver. "They used the end of the war to get even with their bosses," I said. Loller shook his head. "To get even for supposed crimes that were never proven against any of the men and women in the prison." Loller shook his head. "They wanted to start a communist revolution?" I tried.

Loller showed me his white teeth. "Atta boy, Casanova. They killed children," he said. "They killed women and children. And you know why them sonsofbitches did that?"

"It's what, what the communist does?" said Snyder and flashed me a look that was both conspiratorial and not a little apologetic.

"The communist," said Loller. "Damn straight, Snyder." He looked at me. "So your report doesn't mention anything about Mauthausen?"

"No sir," I said, thinking how easy it would be to cut the paragraph out.

"Nothing about goddamn kids being buried alive?"

"No sir."

"No sir," Loller said, and he placed his palms on his knees and sighed. He stood up drowsily and stepped toward the lip of the pool, raised his arms up to the sky, met them together in prayer above his head, roused one foot and balanced the ball of it on his calf, and ever so slowly toppled into the rippling water. The waves flooded over the pool and the newspaper was swept away in the tsunami, and we watched him swim for a while before he came back toward us and said, "I want the Loller Report on my desk by tomorrow, eleven sharp, so best you fellas get that fuck out of here and back to work."

We watched him dive under the water. I stood and began to walk toward the villa with Snyder in my tracks. We were just about to file through the doors when Loller's voice cut across the lawn.

"Casanova!"

I slowed.

"Your boy Balbo, CID Vicenza paid him a visit yesterday, to lay out formal charges." I turned and stared into the deep blue of the pool. "He was asked about his condition. He told them he'd fallen off his bed. Now you boys make sure you have your bags packed when you get here tomorrow, you get me?"

It was only when Snyder and I were back in the Buick that Snyder said, "Old Renzo must've really taken a shine to you."

## CHAPTER TWENTY-ONE

That afternoon, after Snyder had driven us back to the Miramonti and left me in the lobby to go pack in his room, I took a walk down past the Duomo toward the castle. On a narrow, cobbled road just beyond a shaded piazza that sat isolated and alone at a crossroads, I found the optometrist Barroni. It was a small store, hemmed-in between a haberdashery and a butcher, and beyond the fly-curtain and bell that tingled unhappily when I walked in, I found a man reading *Il Gazzettino* behind a long glass-topped table.

"*Buongiorno.*"

"*Bondì,*" he said, laying the paper on the glass counter and watched me come in closer. "Americano?" he asked.

"*Si. Mi chiamo* Casanova. John Casanova."

"*Ma allora lei è Italiano?*"

"*In modo da dire,*" I told him. "I was wondering if your son was here?"

"My son? Which one?"

"Your son who was in Russia."

"Benedetto?" He gave me a strange look. "Benedetto never came home from Russia," he said. "Why are you—"

I shook my head. "I didn't realise. I'm sorry to have wasted your time."

"Please," the man came around the counter quickly. He was a small man with the whitest of beards, untrimmed and a little wild. Dark eyes looked up at me with something on the wrong side of anguish. "Why are you looking for Benedetto?"

"He was a journalist, right?"

"Yes, yes he was."

"I was looking for some of his work. During the retreat."

"His work?"

"Photos."

"From the retreat?"

I nodded. "In Russia."

"I don't understand. How do you know about my son?"

"I read it somewhere but it's not something I can discuss with you."

"Why?"

"Because I'm from CID—criminal investigation. I was told your son took some photos during the retreat and I thought those photos could help with a case I'm working on."

"The massacre?"

I shrugged noncommittally.

The man stared at me as if trying to find the truth in my face. "Come with me. His camera," he explained as he shuffled behind the counter and led me back into a windowless storeroom, "they sent—well, that's not true, they kept the camera, but they sent me his photographs, the film, you understand, that was still in the camera, they sent that back with his dog tags. I have Don Gnocchi to thank for that." I watched him open a chest of drawers. "I had them developed—there were," he found an envelope and took it out, "here, you see? There were about a dozen photos on that roll." He slit open the envelope and drew out the photos and placed them on a small table and clicked on a bijou lamp. "Here," he said as if he were inviting me to buy something valuable, "come look. He was talented, Benedetto. Come, look. His mother, she always said he was going to make something of his life. She'd have been happy to find an American come to look at his work."

I peeled through the photos. I don't know much about journalism, but the images were fine. The image I was after was the fourth from the bottom. I lifted it and held it to the light. Four men trapped there by the mechanical eyes of a dead man's trigger. Two of the faces I recognised immediately. I brought the photo closer to the light and smiled when I recognised the third man. That sonofabitch, I thought. That sonofabitch.

"Would I be able to make a copy of this?" I asked.

"I suppose." He hesitated, looking at the photo in my fingers. "This is important? For you?"

"In a way, yes, but not for me."

"It will make a difference?"

"Yes."

"Then take it."

"Are you sure?"

He looked at the photo. "What good does it do," he asked, "just sitting here in a drawer?"

# CHAPTER TWENTY-TWO

I ate in my room alone that night, gnocchi washed down with the dregs of McPhail, and retyped the whole Loller report under the yellow glare of the desk lamp. Typing a short memo that explained how twelve men, former communist partisans and led by a known Marxist revolutionary named Ivo Pranjic and labour organiser and communist Giulio "Russo" Moro, had perpetrated a heinous crime on innocent Italians held without charges in a goal in Schio, VI. The motive was a communist plot by Pranjic and Russo to begin—and what Togliatti in Rome and his handlers in Moscow had hoped—would be an armed rebellion by communist resistance fighters throughout northern Italy to create a de facto Marxist state out of the chaos of post-war Italy. Whether Mitra, Apache, or any of the partisans had any idea that they were pawns in a Soviet game of destabilising Italy was unclear and likely never to be discovered.

It was bullshit. All of it. The truth? The truth would be the only damn thing I would be taking back to Altoona with me from this goddamned war.

## CHAPTER TWENTY-THREE

JULY 20

Snyder rolled the Buick out of Schio under a grim flat-dead sky that promised little but rain, our bags packed in the trunk along with his stockpile of guns and ammo. On Piazza Rossi I saw Coke standing outside the Bar Excelsior sipping from a long-stemmed glass of white wine. Beside him stood a young woman. I kept the window down on the Buick, my elbow out. I watched Coke pass on by with a longing that hurt as much as my memories of Millie. Suddenly his head rose, and he clocked me and raised his glass in a silent toast. I could sense his sneer from a hundred yards.

"I got to figuring last night," said Snyder.

"It's not what we're here for," I said, distracted by Coke, by my vision of having ten minutes alone with him, just him and my knife, just ten minutes. It was the rot of his soul that made the world stink the way it did. And my finger found the wound in my palm and twisted in and kept digging into the soft, wobbly meat.

"I think we missed something."

I watched Coke slowly vanish beyond the rear windscreen. "I missed nothing, buddy. Except one thing."

"What's that?"

"How did you get all that info—I mean from up in Trento, with the woman with the legs up to here, and the doctor, and Pranjic's brother, and Russo's sister—I thought you didn't speak Italian."

"I don't," he said, and a flush rose from his neck.

"So?"

"You know the girl at the Miramonti, Maria?"

"Not as well as you, pal."

He glanced at me quickly. "Her sister's an English teacher, so she came with me as a, you know, translator."

He couldn't keep the blush from his face, the scar like a white tentacle, and I laughed. "Both of them, Snyder? Really?"

He stared out at the road with grim determination, but he was blushing so hard he'd started sweating.

"She was upset with you," he said after a while.

"What? Who?"

"Maria. You stole her umbrella."

I laughed when I remembered where I'd left it. "Jesus. At least you got some free pussy out of this, Snyder. Me, I just got fucked dry and ain't that the truth, brother."

We were driving slowly by the Lanerossi factory walls when he asked, "You know what's been bugging me. That Pranjic guy—"

"What about him?"

"Why—"

"Commie revolution."

"Yeah but—"

"He was turned, Snyder."

"Sure—"

I pointed to the curb. "Stop here."

Snyder pulled the Buick to the side of the road, and he'd hardly come to a halt when a group of kids ran out of an alley. They were touching the scorching steel and stroking it with dirty palms when I walked past and left them to it.

"No *tocca*!" I heard Snyder shout, "no fucking *tocca the car*!"

I walked into the office and found Svavi sitting behind his fan pecking at his Olivetti typewriter. He smiled when he saw me and there was genuine delight, I thought, when he said, "John!"

"I came to say goodbye." I threw a brown-paper-wrapped package onto his desk. "And to leave you this."

"What is it?" he stood and limped toward me.

"Your insurance policy," I told him when we shook hands. "You may need it one day."

He lifted the package. "Insurance?"

"Did he ask you?"

"What?"

"To arrest Godin. Did he ask you?"

Svavi met my gaze. Took him a couple of moments before he said, "Ah," as he bounced the package in his hand and felt the weight. "Not asked. Ordered. But like I told you, John—my job is to arrest and sometimes—"

"—to release," I interrupted and nodded at the package. "I figure it was this or your funeral."

He gave me a lingering look that one day I hoped a woman would give me and said, "You're a kind man, John—what they say about you, about what you did—"

"I got this for you too," I said, and found the photo in the inside pocket of my jacket and handed it to him.

He stared at it for a minute and then turned it over and read the words I'd written there for him. "Why me?"

"Because after I leave, you're the only decent man in this whole fucking shithole of a town," I said. "And by the way, Tonto was the Indian. The horse was called Silver."

Svavi laughed and gave me a hug and a couple of air kisses and I slapped the top of his arm a couple of times and promised I'd write from Altoona, and he promised to learn enough English to one day come to America and visit. I smiled at his decency and walked back to the Buick.

"So Pranjic was turned, right?" Snyder asked when he bucked the Buick away and I noticed the kids were counting coins on the corner in their money-grubby hands. "But I don't get—"

"The question you *should* be asking, Snyder, is who else knew he'd been turned?"

"What do you mean?"

"What about his mates in Prague, his commie friends? Did they know?"

Snyder turned onto the road for Vicenza, arrowing out into the flatlands and I could see the lightning cut across the dark sky up there on the Pasubio as we rode into the heart of the storm. "How would they know he was turned?" he asked.

"They wouldn't. Unless someone told them. And that would have been it for that sonofabitch. Finished in Italy, finished in Prague, finished in Moscow."

Snyder gave it a while. "So we was coerced, is that what you're saying?"

"To do what?"

"To organise the—the massacre—but—why?"

"Wrong question."

"What?"

"Who, Snyder. Who profited from the massacre?"

"Who?"

"You," I said.

Snyder glanced at me. "What?"

"You, me, Loller, Paget, we all profit, pal. All of us. We fucked the commies over and now we get to disarm them and save the peace."

Snyder engaged top gear and gave that a long thought. Eventually, he said, "Why d'you hate these people so much, Casanova? They're your people, man." I gave him a look, and he shifted in his seat, and it took a while before he said, "I still don't get it," and I saw him glance at my hand and when I looked down, I saw I had gouged so deeply that blood was trickling over my palm and onto my trousers.

"Better that way," I said, shifting my hand from his line of sight and grabbing a handkerchief.

"Why don't you explain it to me?"

"When I was a boy," I said, watching the sky and earth come together in a narrow band of dark-silver fog, "I used to lie out in our yard and watch the clouds drift across the sky. You ever do that, Snyder?"

"Guess so," he replied.

"I'd see shapes up there, faces and dragons and snowmen and shit, you know?"

"Sure."

"And then, if my sisters were around, I'd point them out—point out those shapes up there, but I don't think anyone, ever once, saw what I saw in them clouds."

Snyder waited, but I had nothing more to say, and he piled on the speed as the rain began to fall on the windscreen, first a couple of sluicy drops and then the world vanished in the downpour, and we rushed through the little twisters of steam that came up off the road, rushed west toward Vicenza, toward Bologna. Keep going, I thought, keep going and eventually we'll get home.

# EPILOGUE

APRIL 2003

I write this now out on the porch of our home in Altoona. I write this for you, son, knowing that you'll soon be joining up with your men in Aviano to fight a new war that's come our way. It's been almost fifty years since that afternoon when last I saw the Villa Scacchi. I was driven back to Bologna that very afternoon, and that's where I got to sit out the rest of the war, in a fine stone villa on a hill out of which I worked as a translator for the Army's press department. That day I left the Villa Scacchi, Loller told me it wouldn't be long—any day now, he told me in his office where he stood and stared longingly out of the dirt-stained windows at the rain that rippled on his pool, any day now the Japs were gonna get an ass-whooping they weren't ever gonna forget.

Guess he got that right, son.

Snyder had already left for Rome by then. I remember Snyder now, out on the stairs leading to the villa that morning, I remember how we shook hands by his Buick with the rain cool on my skin and him asking me, "You figure we'll ever meet again, Casanova?" and me replying, "Sure, Snyder, sure, why the hell not?"

But we both knew that neither of us was ever gonna go out of our way to make that happen. And so it proved—I haven't heard a thing from him since 1945. Better that way, I guess. But today, out here as I finish typing this with the night falling about me and the cicadas so impossibly loud and the lights from the football field white over yonder because it's Monday night, son, it's Monday night, I wonder what ever did happen to old Staff

Sergeant Snyder. I wonder if he ever got his face retread when he got back—that sure was an ugly scar he brought home with him. But I guess we all came home with our scars, one way or the other. War seemed such a big thing for Snyder, but it's nothing like that, son. It's just little grunts fighting and dying, and it's all personal in the end. All of it. The big ideas, they exist beyond us. For Russo, for Balbo, for me and Snyder, it was all personal. You ain't gonna get a man to kill unless you get a man to hate. It's that simple, but Snyder couldn't deal with that. He was too busy seeing the big things to connect the small shit, couldn't see that it ain't the dying, it's the living with the wrong that eats away at a man. It ain't the grunts pulling the trigger that makes a wrong. It ain't the killing, son. Always remember that. It ain't never about the killing.

# FOUR
## CHE TI DICE LA PATRIA?

*Guess if you can: the whale is not a fish, the bat is not a bird; and some people, who knows why, are human but they're not.*
—Gianni Rodari

## "Dimmi Che Non Vuoi Morire"—Patty Pravo

Sofia's sitting on the couch, idly scrolling on her phone when I gently drop the book beside me on the couch with a mild sense of loss.

She glances over at me. "Done?"

I nod. "I need to get back." I stand slowly and head for the deck with a smoke between my lips. She follows me out into the cold. "Where did you get it?" I ask.

"The book?" Her eyes gaze out into the valley that falls away from us beyond the fence. The silence up here is overwhelming. The mountain peaks are ablaze in crimson and pink, like roses in bloom, and I can see the moon, a disc hovering up there in that satin sky and I think how alien it is that I'm here standing on this rock able to conceive of it all. So clean, and so distant from the filth of life. Down in the valley the lights blink, distant villages and lives, and I glance at my watch. Just gone 4.30PM.

"Casanova's grandkids," she tells me. "He had a few copies printed before he died. When his son went to war in Iraq, for some reason he decided to write it. I flew over to Altoona."

"Il tuna. That's a long way to go. Why?"

She stares out at what I'm seeing and lets it all hang there.

"What happened to him?" I ask.

"Casanova? He died about fifteen years back. Went back to Altoona in November '45. Never left again, never left America, not even for a vacation. Became an insurance investigator in Philly."

"Philly?"

"Philadelphia," she says and smiles at me. "Philly, no?"

"Yes. Philly."

"He had a three kids and a dozen grandkids. Happy life, they say—managed to get himself elected to the school board, the American Dream—really active in the Italian-American community. His one grandkid was living in his house, broken down place in the centre of a dying little town. Church on Sundays and spent his retirement doing crossword puzzles and walking his dog, that's what they said."

"And Snyder?"

"A little more obscure, our Snyder. From what I gather, he died in '86. He lost his only son to suicide in '81. A wasted life, I guess, in a nowhere town."

I look at her face, so close to me, so beautiful in that light, so soft, Vaseline-lens male-gaze, and she doesn't step back. I swallow nicotine. "And Coke?"

"Became a cold war spy. Chief of Station in Rome for a while. He died four years ago. Long, active life."

I dig the cigarette butt into the hard-frozen soil of the ceramic plant pot. "I need to get going."

"I understand." She holds the door open for me to step back into the yellow warmth of the house.

"Thank you," I tell her.

"Why don't you ask," she says as we walk together toward the front door.

Is it an invitation? I've never known with women—mostly because I couldn't ever conceive of a reason why anyone would care to get close to me, so I ask, "What happened to Balbo?"

She watches me draw my coat on. "He was sentenced to death in September '45. Funny thing? When I spoke to Casanova's grandkids, they told me he'd never said a word about any of that to them. Nothing about the war. Just that book. None of them had ever read it. I wonder if he even knew Balbo was never executed."

"He wasn't?"

"No. You don't know? They retried the case in the '50s and by then the Togliatti Law had passed, giving immunity—well amnesty—to those who'd perpetrated war-related crimes in '45. He was released in '56 or '57. Him and all the killers, even Mitra. Lived his life out in Schio, Balbo, spent his days working at the factory and his nights writing poetry that no one ever published, never married, no kids, and one day he died," she says, "and that was that."

I step out into the cold. One day he died. And all of it went with him? The Porsche sits there in the dark that has come so fast I get disorientated. "And his confession? The one he wrote for Casanova?"

"The missing piece, yes. Took you a while to ask."

"Is this a game we're playing?"

"I don't know," she says. "Is trust a game?"

"Mine or yours?"

"You tell me."

"That confession—"

"What about it?"

"Do you have it?"

"No." She watches me draw out my car keys. "But I know where it is," she says.

"And my uncle—"

"It explains everything."

"What is everything?"

"What happened to him. What happened to Russo. And Renzo. And your uncle. What it doesn't explain is how your father came to possess that photo."

"I won't ask him," I tell her.

"I understand."

"Is there a way I could read it?"

"Renzo's confession? Of course," she says. "I'll see if I can arrange it for you."

I find another cigarette and light it up, blowing the smoke cold into the night. "I don't really understand what we're playing at here."

"We're not playing," she says, and turns from me. "It just matters to me that you don't publish that photo. Okay? You keep that photo to yourself, and I'll try to get you access to the confession. It's not as simple as you might imagine. There are—sensitivities."

"Whose?"

She's still smiling when she shuts the door in my face. Out here in the cold and the dark, I sense I'm being watched and walk quickly toward the Porsche. The woods close in, and my senses are on alert, anxiously scanning the dark woods when I click open the door locks and slide into the car and lock it all up. I slide the key into the ignition and the engine bubbles to life. The engine temp' is cold, and I let it idle for a while, click open Spotify and find my playlists. There's nothing much I want to listen to. Instead, I open Radio Box and select a livestream of Springbok Radio, old-time radio plays from the '70s and the voices of childhood coming to me from the grave.

The road down from the Altopiano is dark. I start out slow, caressing my way on the tarmac, notoriously slippery up here in the Veneto, and then I open her up. The flat-6 lives at 5,000RPM, and I'm getting into a beautiful rhythm down the mountain, downshifting and heel-and-toeing until a campervan from the Netherlands, slowly descending like volcanic ash, ruins it all. I sit there trapped in its wake as we corkscrew down the mountain. I guess they don't have mountains in the Netherlands. I recall those days in Joburg, in our apartment in Yeoville with my dad's wooden Telefunken radio with its rope-like antennae sticky-taped to the wall tuned to Springbok Radio. I think of myself then, this fragment of memory, but I'm not there—not in any form or shape, just me, sick in my bed in the yellow room, always sick, my bedroom door open and my mom going about doing her daily things and those sounds were so soothing, and I remember her checking in on me with her soft hand on my forehead, and the radio plays personating in the mid-morning sun, and the white linen curtains rising and falling like breath as drafts of air cut across my skin cold. Drifting to sleep with the sky so blue out there beyond the windows where the world echoed the sounds of life and a man's voice shouting, *Mielies! Mielies! Mielies!*"

The World of Hammond Innes.

*"Non ti senti bene, eh? Non va?"*

My mother's voice. I can hear her voice tonight. The things she said, like "Hey Rambo," when my brother would call, and "Hullo, is me you looky for?" when I would call. Eventually the face and the voice must fade, I guess, like those spent voices from the radio, she'll go silent and forgotten and with that perhaps the pain. My mom. To still it, to still the pain and the tears that refract the night and the road like rain on my sclera, I drop the Cayman into second, gun the throttle with the clutch in and pull everything out onto the opposite side of the road and commit to a blind overtake. *Il Sorpasso*. I can't see what's coming out of the bend ahead and I'm halfway around the campervan when lights pop-out of the night headed straight at me, white and bright. I keep my boot on the gas and dive ahead of the van with the oncoming car whooshing past so close I can hear the driver shouting. Or is it just me? The campervan flashes its lights. I give it a wave and focus on the road ahead, skiing into the turns, the car pushing and pulling me down, ever down toward the plains, the g-forces giving my neck a workout. That's the thing about a mid-engine car—you really need to commit to the entry and there's a freedom there on that edge, a beautiful freedom because it's either going to grip or you're going to come off fast and hard. In my rearview, I spot lights chasing me, and I slow down thinking it's the cops until the lights come closer and I focus in through the mirrors. A dark SUV. No markings, no sirens. Still, I slow it all down and light a smoke and keep to the limits, and I'm running late by the time I get into Malo and park the Porsche. Late, but I still find myself walking slowly toward the entrance to the rehab clinic with its lights white and just too bright in the quiet dark.

My father is waiting just beyond the white double doors. He sits by the radiator, alone, the night beyond the window an inky mess. He doesn't look up when I walk in. It's so quiet now. It's too much. I think, I need you now, I need someone to touch me, tell me it's going to be okay because tonight my mom is tearing at my soul, and I say "Hullo" instead because he's leaving me too and I can sense it so badly tonight on this ward as quiet as a graveyard.

"Sandro." A smile crosses his lips as he watches me grab the usual chair and drag it on over. "You make me worry," he says in English. And so you *have* been waiting for me. It makes me feel useful, and I think, you're my father, we lived together for eighteen years, and you'll always be a stranger.

The lights on the ward have already been dimmed, the hallways trailing off into dark spaces where nothing shifts. The last person in the world who cares if I make it home alive, the last person who has a spare thought for me and my life. I sit before him, this old man in his wheelchair, my father, and the nurse with the tattoo steps by and shares a smile with me.

"How arrrr *you* doin'?" she asks in English.

I smile. My dad says, "Where you be that nice, Sandro?"

I shrug. "I just had to sort something out. How you feeling?"

"My chest," he says, touching, showing me. "Closed."

"Okay."

We fall into a silence that we'd practiced over too many decades. It lasts a long time. I stare out into the night, and he down at his hands on his lap, but his echo is there in the windows, and I look at his ghostly face half-unseen in that reflected night, a dark mirror into our lives, and all I see is me and my father yellow and tired and faded. There isn't an understanding, not until you have a child yourself. And then you recognise the sacrifices willingly taken for no reason other than love. My wife has friends—scientists—who tell me this is all just part of our survival mechanism, handed down over millennia, protecting the young, protecting the species. I suppose that kind of rational learning is useful when one has no actual soul, when one's heart is incapable of love, but I've no idea, really. I realise now, with his cold-cold image in the window, that I have no idea what he's like—my father—what kind of man he had once been. I guess he'd never thought his life was worth sharing—perhaps because he'd been afraid that one day I'd settle for what he'd had to settle for, this man who'd lost his dreams in the war that'd consumed his youth and taught him life isn't worth a damn to those who decide who should live and who should die.

"Sandro, you should go," he says. "Is getting late. What time is it?"

"Just gone eight," I tell him. And yes, I should leave, Sunday night and a six-hour drive back to Zürich. At this time, I can probably cut it down to five, probably less. I watch him wheel himself back toward his room through the silent, empty ward. He's getting good at rolling the wheelchair. There's a short corridor that leads to the doctor's station, a squared all-glass cabin, and then it's left and down another corridor with doors on either side, cavities leading into darkened rooms. Sunday night. So quiet. The patients are all in their pilot-lit rooms, warmed by the flickering light-and-shadow of TVs on the walls set to variety shows, old people waiting for the drugs to kick in and sleep to come. My father would rather be dead than this.

"These people," he says, wheeling his way on. "They go to sleep at seven. *Pazzi*, Sandro."

I smile. "They're old," I tell him.

"*Pazzi*," he insists.

I follow him into his room. There's a French window on the far side, the metal venetian blinds already drawn, and I catch myself in its reflection, me standing and my father below me like a child.

"Can you check the temperature?"

I check and turn the thermostat up to 28C. He's always suffered the cold.

The nurse walks past on the hallway and slows. "*Meesster* Lago, you ready?" she asks in English. My father has his back turned to her. "I'll be back now to help," she says, and smiles at me.

"She's nice," he says. "Her name is Julie."

I squat by his chair. "Time to go," I say, looking at his face. "Do you need anything else?"

He sits there in his wheelchair staring down at his blue slippers. His hair is silver, his face sallow, yellowing as his metabolism slowly shuts down. So small now, my father. Feather-thin. Waiting to die.

My father.

"What you t'ink?" he asks me and lifts his sallow face with something unreadable in his gaze. "What you busy t'ink about, Sandro?"

"I was thinking about rugby," I tell him.

"Is there a game?"

"South Africa play the All Blacks next Saturday."

He nods at this.

"You remember," I ask, "you remember when we would wake up at, like, four in the morning, you and me, in South Africa, you remember? And you would make spaghetti and we would watch the All Blacks in New Zealand on the TV? Against the Springboks? And we would cheer for the All Blacks?"

He looks at me now with a frown and I make sure I'm smiling. "No, I don't remember this, Sandro," he says, distracted by something.

I keep my smile frozen. "I'll see you on Friday night, or Saturday," I tell him, steadying my voice. Those memories of the two of us sharing the dawn with the rugby and him making a *spaghettata* in the mid '80s, just the two of us, it meant so much to me. Is it possible that he remembers none of that?

"Okay, Sandro. Just be careful, drive slow."

"Always." I lean down and hug him in the chair. I feel his bones and I feel my shame. I walk to the doorway and pause, glance back at him. He turns in his wheelchair. I look beyond him, at the window that reflects the room in a yellow stain like an old photograph exposed too long to the African sun. I see us as we are now. He watches me stall at the door. I want to say I love you. But I guess I won't even do that. "I'll call tomorrow," I tell him.

"Just let me know you home."

"I will."

"Okay, Sandro."

"Okay."

On the autostrada, I open the Porsche up, all the way to 7,200RPM through the gears, and I'm hitting 250kmh by the time I pass the Schio turnoff, the windows open and my tears turning to ice on my cheeks. I turn the volume right up on Spotify playing over Bluetooth when Oasis's *Cigarettes & Alcohol* comes on and the noise of the wind and the music and the engine is enough to drown out my screams.

Rushing the night, running from death to the eternal loneliness of my life, my marriage. I think English women are like fruit that seem so full of sweet but never ripen, it just turns sour and spoils on the vine. I think of my shrink that'd come with my New York life who asked me once, which would you choose, a decade of the same life you're living now or a quick death in your sleep, and the answer to that is haunting me when I get to the dark apartment and tiptoe my way into the spare bedroom that'd somehow become my home in middle age. To a bed without sheets, just a blanket and a couple of pillows that haven't been washed since I left New York a year ago, and a suitcase I'd never unpacked. Lying in the dark, dizzy and deaf from the Porsche and the speed, I send my dad a WhatsApp message telling him I'm home safe, neither of which is technically true, and I think middle age is when you pay for the mistakes of youth. Youth is credit. And now it's time to pay.

He's awake, my dad, and he writes back, *Okay, now relax.*

Just before I fall asleep, an email pings on my phone. It's from Villa Scacchi.

*Saluti, Sig., Lago. This is Dino from reception. I am obliged to write and inform you about an incident here at the hotel this afternoon. One of the cleaning staff believes there was an attempt at a break-in to one of the rooms and, after a few enquiries, we believe room 408 may have, in fact, been broken into.*

*Given you checked out in the morning, we're confident that your belongings etc. were not in any way compromised. However, because there was also a gentleman here asking questions about you this afternoon—details of your stay etc.—I thought it prudent to inform you. I suggested the gentleman refer all his queries directly to you. As a valued guest of the hotel, we appreciate your custom, and of course your privacy. If there's anything more we can help with, we are, as ever, at your disposal, and I look forward to welcoming you again in the near future.*

*Distinti saluti,*
*Dino Balbo.*

## "Una Rotonda Sul Mare"—Fred Bongusto

I'd spoken to my father every day during the week. Physio, he tells me, has gone okay. He even managed to walk a few paces again. And then, on the Friday, there'd been no reply to my calls. My brother sends me messages asking what's going on. Finally, at just gone six in the afternoon, with the Zürich sky dark and snow dusting the roads promising all sorts of hell up in the mountains toward which I will soon race, he answers my call.

"Hey!"

"Sandro."

His breathing sounds laboured. "What's wrong?" I ask.

He tells me he's been running a mild temperature all day and is now resting in bed.

"I'll see you tomorrow then," I tell him.

"Sandro, is such a long way, why you come for?"

Because I love you. Because there's so much I want to say. And because I'll never say anything at all. But I'll watch you die. I'll watch you die because that's the only way I can show you I love you. "Because I want to," I tell him. "Do you need anything?"

"We discuss when you come," he says.

And so I come on the Piovene-Schio road in the dawn and sense the echoes of the soldiers that'd once marched on these roads and my father who'd lived through it all. He never said much about the war—sometimes he'd mention those days, working at the Todt factory in '44 as a 14-year-old boy. And the cold. But not much else. As if there was a shame, somehow. But for what?

The cold is rigid now, late February in the lowlands with the sterile fields ice-white on that malevolent road to Malo. I take an espresso at the café near the clinic and then walk slowly toward the building in the early-morning sunlight. It's flaking, the white of the concrete stained, I can see it now, the hallways tired and old. But it's clean, and it's where we are.

My father isn't waiting beyond the double doors. I stand there and glance down the hallway both ways with nausea etching up my throat. Then I walk down the hallway deeper into the ward and look inside his room. He's lying on the bed, hooked up to an IV drip, eyes shut, face unshaven. Gaunt. I walk in and stand over the bed. His eyelids rise and his groggy eyes stare with a vagueness that scares me. I want to save you, I think. I want to save you.

"Sandro," he whispers, "how long you here?"

"Just arrived."

"I think I fell asleep."

His cheeks are sinking. My mother had looked like this. My mother, she'd died eight weeks ago today. I'd like to speak to him about my mother. Instead, I hear myself say, "I brought some magazines." I place them on his bedside counter with the other magazines, a stack of them now. "So how you feeling?"

"Bad," he says to me.

"Okay. Temperature?"

"A little."

"Okay." I gaze at the *flebo*. "Antibiotics?"

He coughs. Wet. Thick with fluid. He coughs again, trying to bring something up. "I can't," he wheezes. "Closed."

"Okay."

"Why Sandro?"

Because you're dying. "You remember what the doctor found?" I ask, my heart quickening as I stand over him like a plague doctor.

"Emphysema?"

I blink and take three steps back. "No. No. You remember, I told you, Dr Puccini?"

His lids shut. They seem so heavy. "Is bad," he says. "What is it?"

"Do you remember?"

"No."

I grab a chair from the wall and drag it closer to the bed. "It is what it is," I tell him. "Do you want to go home?"

"What you t'ink, Sandro?"

"Okay."

"Here," he tells me, showing me his chest with a finger. And his eyes stare at me. Wide. Fear.

"I'll go past the apartment, start the car. Is there anything else you need?"

He coughs. A rattle. I put it out of my mind and look at the plastic tray hanging off the bed by its hinge. He hasn't eaten, the remains of his breakfast untouched.

"I have no appetite. What's wrong with me, Sandro?"

"You have to eat something," I tell him. "Force yourself."

"Is easy to say," he admonishes me. "Is easy to say."

"I know. I'll get a cake," I smile, "from Ale and Sandro." Ale and Sandro, two gay guys—or at least my mom always had it they were gay—who run a bakery down in Piovene, my mother loved those guys, loved their cakes. That was all she ate, their fruit tarts, that was all she could eat near the end. That and ice-cream. I recall my daughter feeding her fruit cake on the couch, and my mom's strange smile, that last time Natalie saw my mom alive. Somehow, my mother had willed herself to die. Even then, destroyed by her own mind, unable even to stand or talk anymore, unable even to recognise herself, she'd managed to make herself die.

"Help me up," my father says.

I stand and place both arms behind him. I can smell him. Like flowers. He's hot to the touch. That strange heat of fevered flesh that makes you feel ill the moment you sense it near you. His bones are hard on my fingers, they're wanting to push through the flesh now, his shoulder blunt swords when I lift him up. He weighs so little. I slide him up afraid to hurt him so that's he's half-sitting on the bed when I begin fixing the pillows behind his head.

"Not like that," he says exasperated, "come on, Sandro. *Ma cosa fai?*"

Always not good enough, I think, shuffling pillows about this way and that until he gives up and resigns himself to a job half-done. Six months ago, I'd have got pissed. But six months ago was a different life, and I was not a man. "It's okay, is okay like this, Sandro, *lascia stare*." Sitting now, he draws the tray over his lap and checks for messages on his iPhone.

"You brother send a message," he says, reading.

"Oh, yes?"

He nibbles on a piece of toast. And then he begins to cough. That wet cough that sounds as if he's drowning. "Every time I try to eat," he says, and that cough is wet and cruel, and I can see it hurts.

We say hardly a word as I sit with him in the strange serenity that comes with the morning, scanning my phone. My wife is pissed that I woke her up at 1AM when I'd left. She sounds angry. But then she's always angry. My father monitors his phone. My brother calls him at around ten. They have an easy way with each other. They'd bonded somewhere along the line, I guess. He's six years older. My father was still young. That's what I tell myself. But I know it's me.

At noon, the nurses begin their rounds with lunch, and it's time to clear out the guests.

"I'll be back at three," I tell him, standing on legs that are worryingly weak.

"Okay, Sandro."

"You sure you don't want anything?"

He looks at me and I can't make out what he's thinking right then. On my way out, the nurse—what was her name? I check her nametag—Julie—catches me just as I'm about to get into the elevator.

"Do you have a minute?" she asks. "Dr Marcon would like a word."

"Of course."

I follow her back into the ward and to the doctor's station, a glass box office made entirely of windows with white blinds drawn tight. Dr Marcon welcomes me in with a face that shows nothing and a handshake as dry as sand. She offers me a chair across from her white lacquered desk. Behind me, a nurse is opening a layered cupboard stacked with brightly coloured med' boxes.

"You got in early today," Marcon says to me.

"I left Zürich at one," I reply.

"You come every weekend, I'm told?"

I look at her hands on the desk. What's there to say?

"It's a long drive," she says.

"I suppose."

She glances down at the desk, at her hands, and slides them away. "My brother lives in Horgen," she says. "Near Zürich."

"Oh. I'm in Thalwil. Just up the road."

She nods. A question answered, perhaps. She watches the nurse leave the room, assiduously waits for the door to shut, and looks at me. "We're concerned about your father."

"Right—"

"We've placed him onto an antibiotic regimen," she interrupts, "but," she looks at me with one eye, I notice, slightly lower than the other, "he's not responding anymore."

"What does that mean?"

"I had the provincial medical examiner come in on Thursday, and I received her report this morning. They align with my findings."

"And that is?"

"We believe it's time to consider our options."

"I'm sorry?"

"Hospice care," she says. I try to focus on her words, on her lips.

"Because, sorry, hospice means …"

She doesn't say anything to that, and her silence is my answer.

"There are two options," she says when she senses I've understood, "two options that we're able to suggest. There's the Immaculate Conception in Thiene. And then there's here."

"Here?"

"We're of course not a hospice, but we're able to facilitate the transition. And here, of course, he's familiar with the way things are, with the staff. The hospice would be a new place for him. But this—naturally, the decision is yours."

"How long are we—"

"We have accepted that a decision needs to be made soon."

"Soon—"

"Maybe in a day or two—at the outside."

I stare into her face. The sleepy eye blinks once.

"I'll drive by the Immaculate Conception today," I tell her. "Just, you know—but here, I—"

"I can make an appointment for you if you'd like to tour the—"

"I'll drive by today and see what it looks like."

She stands with me and offers a hand. I take it. She holds onto it for longer than is necessary.

By the doors, heading out for the elevator, I step around a woman in a wheelchair. The one with the wild eyes. "They're not coming," she says to me when I walk by her. "They never come anymore. They just don't come anymore."

*"Buongiorno,"* I tell her with my voice sounding as wild as her eyes.

# "Torpedo Blu"—Giorgio Gaber

Downstairs, making an espresso last so it gets bitter and having a cigarette out on the bench by the shrub garden, I send my wife a message on WhatsApp. Loneliness knows no pride and even less shame.

*My father is close now*

I'm already in the car on the road to Piovene when she replies. *That's sad.* Then, a minute later: *Can you buy coffee in Italy before you come back. I'm so tired, can't believe you woke me up. So selfish.*

I eat a plate of gnocchi in a café in Piovene. Flo's Bar. The gnocchi are melt-in-your-mouth and I find I have an appetite halfway through. On the walls are hundreds of old monochrome photos dating back to the turn of the 20th Century. I stare at those faces, finding solace in things that have passed. No one left to mourn those faces now. They've gone, and the pain has gone with them, and from those they left behind.

Google Maps leads me down to Thiene through an industrial swampland, concrete and glass factories pushed up aside crumbling stone barns and dead-flat farmland in rich browns and reds and finally vomits me out into a warren of narrow streets between derelict stores and decaying buildings. The town centre, with its washed-out villas and absurd palm trees shivering in the cold, reminds me how much I've always hated this place. There's something forlorn and sad about it all, like a half-finished project that some kid had abandoned before moving on to something better, the peeled-stucco villas behind graffiti-strewn walls a reminder of an Italy that had long-since been chewed raw by its nasty passions.

The Immaculate Conception Hospice sits on a quiet cul-de-sac where new suburban villas rise behind mean little yards, its main structure concealed beyond a short driveway snaking away between two well-manicured hedges. I don't know what I'm expecting, but what materialises in the sloppy sunshine before me isn't it. This is just an anonymous structure of concrete and glass that reminds me of an American hotel, some sad seaside hotel with chewy muffins and weak coffee and cling-wrapped, flower-patterned chairs, and it all fills me with a sense of dread. Like a hotel on the Jersey Shore in a town no one ever wants to die in, I think, slowing the Porsche and staring out at the building rising from a green-green lawn like a tombstone. The glass refracts the cold afternoon, and I slide down my window to light a smoke and realise I haven't a clue what the fuck to do and I'm the only one here who's meant to do *something*.

And what do I tell him? My father? I've decided to move you to the Jersey Shore to die? This is the decision that I must make? Me, a fuckwit who spends twenty minutes deciding what brioche to have with his breakfast buffet, I'm meant to decide where it is that my father should die?

I sit and smoke and stare at the building as a motorbike rolls down the drive toward me. The rider is down on it, belly on the fuel tank, helmet glinting. I watch it pass like an arrow into the future, and it takes a little longer than it should before my brain connects the spaces.

I punch the Porsche down the driveway, take a left beyond the entry gates and slide onto the road with way too much exuberance. I gather it all up and rush toward the roundabout. I get a glimpse of the bike taking the Schio exit, the rider down low, one knee inches off the tarmac. I follow it out toward the Hyper Co-op and the Campo Romano shopping mall with its arcades where my daughter had once lost her little teddy bear and where my mom and I had spent a frantic afternoon searching for that old blue friend whose bunny-like ears had been softened to velvet through the years by my daughter's anxious fingers. My mom had understood—she'd have done the same for me, I guess. But we never did find dear Captain Camembert, and Natalie had cried and cried while my mom stroked her hair on the backseat of my rental FIAT when we'd given up the search and driven to the apartment in the twilight of a day that felt a lot like loss. "I can't believe you'd be so stupid to lose that thing," my wife had told me over the phone that night.

The bike is four, five cars ahead in the traffic. I settle down to follow. Just then I hear the bike's throaty clatter rise and I see it twist out of the stream of traffic and make a run toward the oncoming traffic, the rider's body falling this way and that, in full command of the bike, before it dives back into the stream a dozen cars ahead.

*Fuck.*

I drop two gears and do the same, the Porsche grenading with a hostile whine behind my head. I keep it on the left lane and watch the traffic coming at me fast. I'm doing 120kmh when I run out of road and force my way back onto the right lane inches ahead of a campervan. I wave apologies in my mirror as the campervan blares its odd-sounding horn. I pass the Norris Hotel on the right, round the traffic circle, and now the road splits into two lanes headed up a steep hill with a series of open turns where the bike screams away and I'm on it, cutting across the traffic left and right, and in my mirror I see a Giulietta gamely try to keep with me, but he's on his door handles when we get to the top of the hill and the sharp right down toward the pool and the basketball stadium where the local all-winning Schio women's team play.

The bike doesn't take the turn, keeps powering straight onto the road past the railway line and I hit the tracks so hard I smack the roof of the car with my head. The bike takes the right, past the Nico and Brico superstore strip mall, and heads toward the old town. The bike has slowed now, and I follow it nice-and-easy down to the via XXIV Aprile. On the left is via Cimatori, my dad's home after the war, and I follow the bike past the eerie Lanerossi factory, now a skeleton of red brick buildings and vines and ghosts behind a moss-covered stone wall. I follow into a maze of narrow cobbled streets to finally slip out into the Piazza Almerico da Schio hemmed-in by colourless concrete blocks of flats that'd been built in the '70s and left to rot. It always reminds me of *Mitteleuropa*, this square, Belgrade or something, all that stained concrete and sallow tree stumps of winter and the insurance logos gleaming bleached-blue neon, and the shadows beneath the windsheered porticos a reminder of the first wave of heroin that'd come and swept away a generation in the bleak '80s.

The bike pulls up in the parking lot next to the arcades that run across the southside of the piazza. There's a slot available further on and I park the Porsche, grab phone, cigarettes, lighter, and slide out into the chill with a sudden realisation that I've no idea what the fuck I'm actually doing, and it's as I'm about to give this a little more thought that a voice behind me says, "Why are you following me?"

I turn around. A green helmet is staring at me like the *Antman*, body shielded by tight-fitting leather.

"Why are you running?" I ask.

"'Cause you're following me," she says, stripping off her helmet.

"*The French Connection?*"

"*To Live and Die in LA*," Sofia says with a smile that feels awfully like an embrace.

"Oh, yes, of course, I remember now." That's the best I have. *I remember.* Fucking old. But then I'd always been pathetic around beautiful people.

Sofia places the helmet under the crook of her arm and juts her chin at the bar behind us. "Coffee?"

We order two cappuccinos outside the Bounty Bar and sit on cold wicker chairs. No blankets here—this isn't Zürich, even if there's a resemblance. It's cold in the shadows of those brutalist palazzi that surround us, but we can smoke out here on the sidewalk under the apartment buildings that swallow the warmth, all those lives behind the yellow-lit windows.

"That was quite a coincidence," she says. "Right?"

"No," I reply, "it seriously was." I watch the waitress place two *capuccios* on the table. I do up the top button of my coat, raise my collar and sink into its warmth. She looks at me with those eyes of hers and I ask, "Why were you there?"

"Where?"

"At—" I sip my cappuccino and watch my breath turn to mist. "We playing games again?"

"You first."

"I don't think I need to explain."

She looks down at her steaming cappuccino. "I'm sorry," she says.

I shrug. But I don't trust myself to speak. Not for a long while. "Your turn."

Cigarette between her fingers and a thumbnail between her teeth, she gazes at me as if searching for something that I know she'll never find. It's a strange sensation, to be seen. Then she crushes the cigarette into the ashtray, and I watch the smoke rise nervously into the cold. "Do you believe in destiny?" she asks me.

"Maybe, yes," I tell her. "Maybe now more than ever."

"Why?"

"Because I need it to make sense," I reply before I can self-censor and glance down at the ring on her finger. "You're married."

"Yes," she glances down at her wedding band and then my naked fingers. "Happily married. You?"

"Married," I reply, but my mind is distracted by a thought that has just occurred to me. I'm about to ask when she says, "Come. Let's take a walk," and standing, she slips a five euro note under the ashtray and leads me up toward the Duomo casting its pompous shadow over the ornate Piazza Rossi. She turns left, down the hill past the Benetton store and the Palladio-designed façade of the Palazzo Schio. The shadows here, between the buildings, are dense, and the cold penetrates my coat.

"I was hoping you'd call," I tell her.

"Really?"

"Sure."

"I was going to send you a message tomorrow, actually."

"Really?"

"Really, yes."

"About?"

"The confession."

"Yours?"

She smiles. I can almost picture my father as a young man walking these streets. He was born in the house down there on the left, just past the Due Spade. Nothing has changed much since back then; even the house, he'd told me once, still has the same front door. *"Il freddo,"* my father would say, as if it were a monster, "the cold, Sandro, always the cold." Just there by the Due Spade, he told me, before the Nazis had left that April morning in 1945, he'd come across a dead German soldier in an alley with a set of binoculars around his neck and he'd had the desire to steal them.

I can't understand why he'd come back here.

Sofia slows in front of a tiny piazza laid-out before a red stucco building.

"The library," she says. "This is where it happened."

It takes me a moment. "Wait, this was—this was the jail?"

"Once a hospital, then a jail, and now a library," she says. "Life compressed, no?"

There's a tree that stands sentry before the building, a lone tree that rises in a stump from a vague round hole cut into the cobbles of the piazzetta. Circling the tree are two concentric, curved metal benches aiming at one another but never quite meeting. The tree stands fragile and cold, custodian to voices that have shared forgotten secrets on those benches, but I suspect that's not our destiny, Sofia's and mine.

"Come on." Sofia leads me through a narrow door and into the yellow-lit library and down a long hallway flanked on one side by broad windows beyond which is a murky courtyard. I think of my father in Malo. I should be with him now, not here, not doing this. Whatever this is.

"Here and upstairs," she says, "is where the shooting happened. Offices now." There's a reading room to our right, and behind the long communal tables, kids flick through pages under lights invisible in the sun, and people shuffle about in the silence of heavy carpets. There's no link with this place and the past. It's just bricks. And a place where things have always come to die—people first and now their words. History is memory and objects deflect memory. Who'd told me that?

Sofia slows and her face turns to me with eyes probing. I stare back with the innocence of the ignorant and it seems to please her. "Stay here," she says and steps away. I watch her put a phone to her ear and walk on a few metres, her back to me. I can hear her speak, but the words are lost. The conversation takes a while, long enough for me to want a cigarette as I stare down at the courtyard. There's a plaque down there, and I try to make out the words. I can just make out the final paragraph: "Not in memory of hatred, but as a sign of pity ..."

"It took them sixty years to erect that plaque," her voice says, and I spin around. She's standing right behind me with the phone dead in her hand. "Sixty years to agree to the text that commemorates the massacre. The family of the victims had one idea, the liberals another, the mayor a different one altogether. The compromise pleased no one. Not even the truth. And every year the neo-fascists come here to remind everyone that they were martyrs once, too."

"Are they?"

"Sacrificing for a cause, right or wrong, deserves our respect," she says offhandedly. "I have something to show you. Do you have a few hours? Two, maybe three, depending?"

"Yes," I reply, glancing at my TAG. "I guess. What is it?"

She leads me further into the library, through a door and up a murky staircase of dark tiles on which her boots squelch, and then through a series of glass doors until we come out onto a hallway lit by strict white lights on a low ceiling. A woman is waiting for us at on the hallway, standing with her arms crossed and watching us approach like a matron at a death camp.

"Luisa," says Sofia as she hugs the woman and the two swap kisses. "Thank you so much. This is Signor Lago," she steps aside to give the matron a clean field of view.

"Alex." I hold out my hand. The woman considers it, then takes it into hers. Soft. Her eyes, behind a trendy set of red spectacles that reflect the row of lights overhead, measure me with a care that seems somehow misplaced in this provincial library.

She glances at Sofia and the two share an impenetrable look before the woman says, "Okay, come on," and Sofia and I follow her down the hallway lined with office doors adorned by nameplates. The woman uses a fob on her keyring to open a door down near the head of the hallway and beckons us into a windowless room: one white desk, one white chair, and one clock on the white wall. There's a desk lamp that clicks on automatically, white-white light, then the ceiling lights blink to life, even brighter and whiter, and suddenly there isn't a shadow anywhere in that sterile room. On the desk are two Ziplock-type bags with zippers sealed and name tags on the outside. Inside the bags I can see two moleskin notebooks.

I glance at Sofia.

"Sign this." The matron has an iPad in her palm. It has words on it. And a box where I can free-write my name. "You will not be permitted to take photos, videos, or notes of any sort," she tells me, but she's staring at Sofia, and I sense the orders are as much for her as they are for me. "Your signature here signifies that you understand what I just said. *Do* you understand?" she asks. I nod. "I want to be clear," she waits for her gaze to be met, and the lenses of her specs are like two landing strips in the night, "we reserve the right to inspect you on your way out. That includes your person and your belongings, including your phone. You will be accessing an official document belonging to and protected by the Italian State." She pauses so it can sink in for me. "It's not our library that insists on this—I want you to understand this carefully because this is very unusual," she gives Sofia a glance that I can't read, "very unusual but okay, I need you to be clear in your mind about this—you will be under state sanction if you make any sort of copies or notes of what you are granted access to today." She looks at me, then at Sofia, and she doesn't seem convinced. "Do you understand what that means?"

"Sure," I tell her.

"You will remain under observation at all times," she says, and shows me a camera up on the wall above the door, and I sense she'll be the one doing the observing. "Do you consent?"

"Sure."

She nods at a wall clock. Just gone three. "You have until five-thirty." She nods at the iPad, and I sign it digitally and jab my chin at the two notebooks. "This is—"

Sofia nods.

"How did they end up here?"

"I'll be back at five-thirty," she tells me and walks out of the door.

"Five-thirty," the matron repeats and shuts the door on me with a final glance that seems a lot more sombre than I'd expect and abandons me to the notebooks. I slide one out. Ribbed and cracked and on the first page, desiccated blood that has taken on the shape of some Rorschach test that reminds me of my father's insides.

# FIVE
## THE WAY OF THE DAVAI

*A little bit mine, a little bit yours, a little bit of all the people of the world: everyone did or didn't do something, in due course, to get to war. And now we settle the bill. Amen. And the others? We hope that our example will at least serve for those who are yet to come.*
—Giulio Bedeschi

Dear John,

If empires were built on desire, the kids who stood here with me in this school with hands cupping hearts belting out the words to *Giovinezza* in our neat little rows like mini legionaries would have forged an empire worthy a thousand Roman years. Instead, we left our generation frozen to the Russian ice. It was in this room that I dreamt once of being a writer—until my teacher beat that notion from me. A boy with those hands, he would tell me, whipping them with his ruler, is good only for planting turnips.

How right he was.

But I suppose I should begin not with the pithy, but with death.

Captain Bianco died. That's where it began for me, the moment I understood that destiny is bigger than a man. He was killed after ordering us to abandon our heavy pieces on a frozen hill we'd captured the day before—our metal band that included 75/38s, 105/28s, and 105/11s—and to join the infantry down on the valley floor where the Russians had emerged out the pre-dawn dark white like ghosts.

We'd been pinned on that hilltop by Katushas and artillery for hours, and down on the ice-covered steppe below us, the Russian T-34 tanks were enthusiastically crushing our lines. That's when Captain Bianco decided it was his time to be a hero. And being the man he was, he decided we should all go die with him. Those tanks were savage machines, John, which wedged men down as if they were toy soldiers—toy soldiers who never bled out because the cold would freeze their blood in their broken bodies. They'd just lie there, contorted and frozen and dead like plastic figurines below the tank tracks, and when Bianco died that morning after he'd jumped onto a T-34 and tried to throw a grenade down its throat—a grenade that never went off, they never did, not in that cold—and he'd earned himself a face full of lead, it was then that it'd all became so clear to me. It was as if a veil had been lifted when I found myself on that ice-field and recognised my fate as a man does a beautiful girl he'll never be good enough to sleep with—the instant I watched Bianco fall from the tank with a jet of blood gushing out of what had once been his neck, I understood it all, in that moment when his body was minced beneath the tracks of a tank.

A sacrifice of shit, John, just like this was a war of shit.

Bianco died, and we found ourselves fighting simply to prolong our death. Ten thousand men from the Julia Division, all ordered to die in place, in *this* place, in a meadow of ice surrounded by woods and Mongols in white with knee-high Valenki boots who rose from the snow like supernatural beings. We were there to die. That was all that was expected of us. The point was to fight long enough for the rest of the Italian Army and whatever was left of our German allies to pick their way out of the sack in which the Russians had bagged us with their December offensive. Bianco had about a hundred men under his command, and I know only of seven who came home. I'm one, John, because when Bianco died, I ran. I dropped my rifle—useless as it was, jammed and good only as a club anyway—I dropped my rifle and ran for the woods, and I kept running until the night came for me.

A coward, I suppose you'd call me. I'm guilty of that—but a coward knows more about heroism than a brave man, isn't that so? Through the trees I ran until my legs could carry me no further and then I staggered on into the darkness with my every sense tuned to the surrounding silence. An unimaginable silence magnified by my fear. I knew they were hunting me, those Mongols, men who had no compassion—really, they had no compassion, and who could blame them? We Italians had come two-thousand kilometres to invade Russia. *Russia*, John! We'd come to invade Russia with our little fucking leather boots and flimsy coats and summer socks. Can you imagine it? Peasants, that's who we were, and that's who we came to kill, peasants half-way around the world in the ice, wearing our leather boots that turned to newspaper in the snow and in coats that wouldn't have warmed us in Rimini in October, and armed with weapons that hadn't been useful even at Caporetto in '17, shooting our anti-tank missiles that bounced off the T-34s like rubber balls and grenades that either exploded in our faces the moment we pulled the pin, or never worked at all. That was us, John, Mussolini's Army that came to invade the endless ice-steppes of Russia. You can laugh. But for us, us Italians, the comedy wasn't really that funny at all.

In that darkness, alone and hunted and so far from home that the distance was inconceivable, I experienced a dread so deep that when I think back on it now, it's as if I think of another man, as if my own self was erased by the horror of knowing this was where I was to die, on this night, in this place, alone and lost and nameless, hunted like an animal and left without a grave, without honour, without ever being considered a man.

I stumbled on through that night hearing nothing but my blood and my breath until a sublime dawn that knew nothing of my shame appeared before me—a powder-blue sky so flawless I imagined it would shatter if I shouted at it, and a sun so round and so red smearing its blood on that infinitely smooth carpet of snow. I sank down just within the tree line and found the last of my rations—a tin of frozen biscuits. My spit and snot had frozen on my face, and it felt as if I'd grown a bone from my lips. My feet had congealed, but the pain had long since turned into a numb blunt needle, and in that sparse cold light and in the cotton-silence of thick-packed snow with not an animal or a bird or an insect to break it, in that wasteland of silence, I watched a small black object appear on the distant horizon, there beyond that flat expanse of white. I squatted behind a tree chewing my biscuit and watched that speck come toward me, steadily taking on a shape that, bit by bit, became a sled pulled by a mule whose breath spurt billowing tusks of steam from its nostrils like a train. I watched it edge ever closer, that black mule and the long wooden sled that it hauled, skimming benignly upon the snow, ever closer as I hid behind the stand of trees.

I had to stifle a groan when suddenly it came to rest not a dozen metres from me.

Had I been seen?

I watched in horror as a man climbed from the rear of the sled. He wore a blanket that fell from his neck down to his knees, and his head and face were covered by yet another grey blanket. He was like a Bedouin of the desert, a figure from one of those Salgari novels of my youth. His legs sank knee-deep into the snow as he took sluggish steps to the front of the sled, to the mule, as if he were wading through a swamp.

On his back he carried a Beretta M1935.

*Italian?*

The man found something in one of his pockets and began feeding the mule from the palm of one gloved hand, speaking to it, murmuring words I could not make out. It was madness, I suppose, that made me stand and step from out of the woods and into the open to shout, *"El me scuxa,"* with my voice sounding ridiculously loud.

The man feeding the mule turned to me alarmed and clumsily grabbed for the rifle hanging over his shoulder and I wondered suddenly if I'd got it all wrong.

*"Italiano,"* I said, raising my arms. *"Italianski."*

Something glinted to my left. I glanced toward the wooden sled where the long barrel of a Beretta 38 rifle was aimed at my face. I lifted my arms in the air and shook my head. "Please," I said, "please, I'm unarmed. *Italiano. Italianski!"*

"We're going to Portofino," the man behind the rifle in the sled shouted in Italian. "Where are you going?"

I stared at the rifle as it slowly lowered, then glanced at the man by the mule. *"A baia,"* I said. "Home."

The man in the sled rose. Blankets and a fur hat and a scarf covered his face. *"Ma mi ti conosco,"* he said. "I know you."

I stood dead-still when he jumped out of the sled. His legs vanished up to the waist in the snow and the blanket he wore was a long mantel that raked the blood-red sunrise behind him. *"Ma non sei Balbo?"* the man cutting a path toward me through the snow asked. "Aren't you Balbo? Renzo Balbo?"

I peered at this man coming toward him but there was little to recognise beneath the layers he wore until he began peeling off his scarf and now I saw a beard encrusted by an ice bone, his snot like elephant tusks falling to his chaffed lips, but the face trudging through the snow toward me I recognised as it said, "Balbo," his rifle now at his side, "don't you recognise me? Giulio. Giulio Moro."

*"Dio can'.* Giulio?"

Giulio Moro. We'd been at school together, John, here in this very school, we'd been here together in '29 until the summer of '32 when I'd left to work my father's field and he'd gone off to some private *liceo*. He lived not that very far from our farm, in a vast stone villa on a hill shaded by palms where, in the summers, wisteria and parties as wild as our fantasies had given it a secret, mystical life of its own, and we'd come to Russia together, Giulio and I, we'd walked those endless hot plains of Ukraine to the river Don with nothing but heat and thirst and sunflowers but six months before.

Giulio now stood before me, and his swollen gloved hands grabbed me by the shoulders and pulled me close. "Renzo Balbo," he said, hugging me and then, when he pushed me back playfully to slap my face, "Renzo fucking Balbo." He laughed, holding me by my shoulders, and I remembered that laugh then, I remembered Giulio Moro and the way he made you feel when you were in his presence. "What the hell are you doing here?"

"Invading Russia," I replied, looking at his face, at the ice that was like garish makeup on his eyelashes.

*"Sempre lo spiritoso,"* he said and slapped me again. Then he turned and nodded his head at the man by the mule. "That's Godin. I don't think you know him. From Schio also. But he attended private school." Giulio began trudging back toward the sled with his arm pushing me on alongside. "Godin!" he shouted. "I've found a proletariat—the working classes, Godin! A live one!"

Godin ignored us, feeding the mule a rotten apple in his palm as Giulio and I came to the sled. I stopped suddenly and sucked in my breath when I glanced into the sled. Beneath a pile of icy blankets rigid as steel, a face stared back at me from the strange violence of the dissolved. A desiccated face with a set of gaping black eyes and snow-crusted eyelashes, two bullet-hole eyes staring back at me from the wrong side of madness. Giulio glanced at me as if gauging my reaction and I turned from those haunted eyes and stared into Giulio's instead.

"What's this?" I asked.

"That's Lago," said Giulio. I thought the name familiar, but I couldn't place him. "His mother is the hairdresser—on via Pasini. You remember?"

I recalled him then. He'd been in our class, he'd been in this very room with me, John, a quiet boy who'd slipped through the years and my memories like water.

"I know your sister," I said, forcing myself to look into those eyes that stared back at me like marbles from the sled. Lago said not a word from lips that were as translucent as the flesh of a fish.

"I'm sure you do," said Godin, walking toward us through the snow as if he were dragging his ancestors behind him. "She's a fucking whore. And that one," he nodded at Lago, "is a fucking coward."

"Don't mind him," said Giulio. "He's just in a bad mood from losing the war."

"How did you get here?" I asked.

"We got caught up in a firefight when we were withdrawing," Giulio said.

"Weren't you with the Verona Battalion?" I asked.

"We still are," Godin said, close to me now so that I could see his green eyes, the colour of a burnt summer field. "We got separated from our command."

"We were left behind when the Eighth withdrew to Podgornje." Giulio climbed up into the wooden sled and discarded his Beretta onto the side, enveloping it meticulously within a blanket. Those Berettas had cost a thousand lire on the black market when we were on the Don. That's how we were going to invade Russia, John, with guns filtered through the black market and Breda 30s that would fire only when the sky was blue and the temperature was perfectly stable at 23C and anti-tank canons that could pierce 40mm of armour, useful against the Russian tanks that were 45mm thick. They offered us the Beretta at a thousand lire each, and then they sold us bullets at ten lire apiece—courtesy of the mafia collaborating with their mates from Sicily on the rear lines. And then they told us to go kill the

Russians, peasants like us, at ten lire a bullet. It was cheaper to fucking die. *Guerra a l'Italiana.* With radios whose range were shorter than our screams.

"We're headed for Podgornje now," Giulio told me, holding out his gloved hand. "Hop in."

"Hop in?" said Godin. "What, are we a taxi service now for all your deserter chums?"

*"La vaca de to mare,"* said Giulio and helped me up onto the sled as Godin climbed in behind me and took the reins and spanked the mule. Reluctantly, the old beast trudged forward. Giulio asked, "Did you really desert? You? I never thought you'd have the courage."

"I got—separated," I said.

"Podgornje's beyond the sack," said Godin. "Once there we'll regroup." He looked back at me. "We'll regroup and then we'll fight. So get used to it—"

"Fight who?" said Giulio dismissively. "With what? Jesus. Fight," he repeated and laughed, looking at me as if I were meant to share in the joke.

The clarity and the silence and the cold and the sled grinding on the snow and Lago lying there beside me, his head lolling to the strange rhythm of the mule's gait—a strange netherworld, John, and a man could lose himself in those eyes just as you could in that endless wasteland of the Russian steppe.

"Something broke," was Giulio's whimsical explanation when his palm touched Lago's forehead. "He left something behind back there."

"He left his guts behind," said Godin. "And we should have left him behind right along with them."

We would continue to Podgornje and find a medic, Giulio said, but looking at Lago, I didn't think he'd ever get anywhere near a medic, and what good, I thought, would it do anyway? The kid seemed all but dead already, drifting in and out of consciousness, and whatever pieces had broken, they'd been scattered on the steppe, and I doubted anyone was ever going back to find them. Good men break, John—the good shatter and the brave die and only the cowards have a hope in hell of walking out alive, isn't that the way of it?

The mule dragged us along into an eternal, purple-tinged twilight. There were no real days here, just that fragile sky and the ice and the flatness of this world, this strange ice-world where the sun skimmed but never rose over the horizon, like a cripple, frigid and distant. It was in the late afternoon when the darkness crept about us in sick shadow and we had limped up a plateau of a small hill, that we saw, stretched out there below us, the full horror of our destiny.

It was perhaps because we'd not been expecting it that it made such an impression. We'd seen nothing, John, all that day, nothing but the vast expanse of the steppe, that softly undulating eternity of snow and ice—and then we climbed that hill and Giulio slowed the mule and Godin and I stood on the sled beside him and the three of us gazed as if in a trance at a black stain on the ice that extended westwards ten, twenty kilometres deep. A phalanx of men and sleds and mules and trucks and motorised tanks and camions and men, men and men and thousands and thousands of men in a meandering line within a cloud of ice-dust, all of it trudging into a blood-red sun, a column of men and machines and animals like foam on that clean boundless ocean of ice, and it was its silence that throttled our voices, the silence of that column, the silence of a quarter of a million men winding lost and broken into the waiting night.

"*Porco Dio,*" I said and stared out at the coiling convoy of defeat that had once been our army.

"Our great Italian people who fight with the courage of lions on land, sea and air fronts," said Giulio. "But Duce never did mention the ice, did he? Godin! What did Duce have to say about the ice?"

I don't know now what Godin was thinking because he said not a word. I guess he, like me, could only share Giulio's sentiment. We were fucked. This was no longer the army that'd come to share in the spoils of Russia's defeat. Not the army that'd been sent to secure the German VI Army's flanks in Stalingrad. This was no army at all, this was just a rabble of fractured men heaving their corpses into an abyss of ice as far as the eye could see, an invasion of the ejected, a converse invasion of the damned.

It was January 18th, late in the night, when we made our way into the chaos of the small town they called Podgornje. Fires burnt in every izba, buildings overflowing with men fighting for every scrap of space and food in the serrated orange light, the silence of the steppe that froze its secrets like the rich suddenly shattered by the voices of the mad, and we were with the stragglers, the hunchbacks, we were the last of the column forcing our way through that town in search of warmth and food that had all long-since been taken by the strong.

I'm not a man of words, John—for men like me, words have always been denied—but how to describe -45C to you? Until you stand in it, in that cold, wet from the snow, congealed and hungry, your flesh rotting and your skin slipping off your bones, until you have seen men die with their blood turned to ice in their veins, until you see a man die that way, men of crystal standing up frozen from the inside with veins like glass rupturing inside their flesh ...

Orders were simple: We were to avoid all roads and villages and to abandon all motorised chainless vehicles. The big pieces of artillery were to be abandoned as well. We were, John, disarmed, hungry, and walking. Four German tanks, five canons of 152s, a rocket launcher battery transported on mule-led sleds, and a few small artillery pieces and mortars, that was all the heavy metal that would be coming with us; everything else was to be left behind in Podgornje—anything that could not be carried was to be gutted in fired-up oil barrels that lined the main road out into the steppe, oil barrels that singed with the diesel fuel that was no longer needed.

That night in Podgornje men drank the last of the cognac and ate the last of the food that could not be carted and threw away their possessions and their weapons. Threw them on the snow and walked away because we were no longer an army fighting a war, we were men fighting for survival, fighting to go home and with no taste for the kill. Just to live. Just to live one more day. We understood what was expected of us and it didn't matter what Signorini, the commander of the 6th Alpine Regiment said, or General Reverberi—old *Gasosa* himself, in command of the Tridentina Division— or anyone else said. It was each man for himself now, and the only mission was the one that would take us home.

At dawn we began to follow the column out of Podgornje. Our destination was Postojali, some forty kilometres west of us. Radio Scarpa—

word of mouth from one soldier to the next that'd been, throughout our stay on the Don, the most reliable source of news—reported Postojali was already in Russian hands. We knew this because the Russians had been signalling our last remaining radio all night.

"Attention! Attention! Stalin announces that the entire Italian Alpine Corps has been surrounded and not a man will be able to escape. Stalin has offered you all a new uniform, a uniform of peace and work. Those who choose not to surrender will die here. Do not fight and give yourselves up."

Radio Scarpa told us Reverberi, Signorini and the German, General Eidl, had made the decision not to surrender on our behalf. That was kind of them.

The column was to split in two beyond Podgornje; the left column to follow the Camonica Battalion, the right the Vicenza and Bergamo Corps, the fighting battalions of the 2$^{nd}$ Alpine Division Tridentina, men who carried their big Breda guns over their shoulders with arms spread wide and ammo-belts around their necks. They seemed to me like your Indians, John, like your Indians in those Tom Mix movies I'd watched as a boy with their blankets and rifles swinging on their backs. They were, to me, like your Apaches, and their arms like the arms of Jesus on the cross.

In the sled I could smell Lago—his shit and his piss and his gangrene. His and mine, too, our frozen, frost-bitten flesh reeking, and as we sluggishly left Podgornje into a cold that felt as if we'd been enveloped by a block of blue-white ice, we saw men on the sides of the road lying dead and unbending, covered in a light dusting of snow like marble statues. Men who'd drank too much in the night, men who'd fallen asleep to never see another dawn. They died where they lay, dead of the cold, dead of blocked intestines, dead from knife-wounds, dead of fear, their coats and boots stolen, their frozen toes turnips in the snow. It was, thinking back now, John—in this room where once I was a boy pledging my allegiance to *libro e moschetto, fascista perfetto*—not altogether a bad way to go: the death of men who'd guessed what was waiting for us out there in the steppe and had decided life wasn't worth the sacrifice needed for survival.

Podgornje was burning black behind us, our supply depots, our ammunition, our fuel, our trucks, our lives, and the smoke was a curtain that, once breached, revealed our chaplain, Don Gnocchi, standing on a mound of filthy snow that led to the steppe with his raised arms holding a wooden crucifix aloft to that brittle blue sky, and we could hear him long after he'd vanished behind us chanting, *"Dio è con gli Alpini. Dio è con gli Alpini."*

God was with us he said, but for the four of us in our sled, it was our mule, that black mule wading listlessly through the snow and who asked for nothing but a handful of food, that was worth more than an eternity of Don Gnocchi's prayers.

"If God is with us," Giulio said after a while and winked at me on that quiet steppe where we pushed between thousands of hunchbacks bent-double in the cold, "then why would he want to save us from where he put us? Godin? Thoughts?"

Godin looked back at him. "So what, now you're a fucking communist *and* an atheist?"

Giulio laughed. "The one presupposes the other. But perhaps God is testing us," he waved at the steppe, "perhaps out there he's going to test us to see which of us can endure the most and go home. I got my money on you, Godin."

Giulio. He understood before any of us, I guess.

The wind was beginning to pick up and whatever Godin said was lost to us. All that morning the storm built up, and it was a strange sound, one that seemed to belch from the vast snowpack over which streams of snow scurried like serpents as a front of clouds raced fast over us, dense gunmetal clouds full of snow and malice. Before us lay the steppe in a vastness that extended in an aching forever and then, just like that, it was all swallowed up into a world so heavy with snow and cloud that we simply vanished. In the sled, with our heads lowered to the cane of the wind and ice, blinded and deafened, we found ourselves alone in a gale that carried the sound of a thousand motorbikes, and it was only in the afternoon when the storm broke that we found ourselves on an incline falling gently into the village of Postojali.

The little pin thermometer on my hat showed -43C. We'd heard the fighting from a way off—grenades and machine guns mostly, and the occasional low quake from pieces of artillery—and now we could see that the Verona Battalion was already on the assault. The snow ahead of us was clotted with what seemed to be rocks but that we soon recognised as men, broken soldiers, John, who'd been destroyed by the mortars and shelling from the town heaving with Russian and partisan fighters.

From the hill above Postojali we watched Major Bongiovanni's Verona Battalion fight down in the valley, and from a brick building we could see a machine-gun spill its venomous bullets tracing like deadly fireflies to cut men down where they stood. Several of our battalions that had arrived through the afternoon joined the battle, and once two of the German light tanks arrived and sunk a hole into the brick building, the Russians and partisans were out on the streets and men fought hand-to-hand until the 6th Battalion rushed down the hill to mop it all up. By then, the Verona had long-since ceased to exist.

They were toying with us, the Russians, and they would destroy us in the same way that a man eats an elephant—bite by bite.

With the rabble slowly descending the hill, we threaded our way down into Postojali, men without orders who'd long-since lost their units, mule drivers without mules, soldiers without weapons and without fight, men without hope other than putting one foot in front of the other and finding somewhere to sleep for the night and maybe food in one of those sinister holes we knew we'd find in the abandoned izbas. On the sled we passed a boy from the Verona on his knees, an Alpino and a man and a soldier and I guess a hero, John, if you were American and not Italian, because to us he was just a chump who'd given everything to open this road for us. He'd get nothing from us, not even gratitude, because no one'd asked him to be a hero, and as we passed, we could see him swaying on his knees, swaying without a sound falling from his open screaming mouth in a face congealed in iced-blood and eyes so wide, wider than the world, John, as if he'd swallowed the whole world and nothing was coming out of his congealed wounds and we left him there to die in his own flash-frozen hell. In the end, no one asked him to fight. Those who fought did so because it was who they were. And the rest of us? Us hunchbacks? We found there in the faces of the hundreds of dead lying about the streets of Postojali every reason not to fight, so many reasons and impossible to know who was ours and who wasn't even if Don Gnocchi, when finally he came with the lateness of the afternoon and crept from corpse to corpse with a flashlight to retrieve dog tags and set them into a leather pouch he carried on his belt, tried his best to sort them out before God.

Giulio had found us space in a large two-storied green building that stood beside a brick factory blackened by fire, and he'd returned to the sled to help drag Lago toward it. He was a heavy man, Lago, tall and gangly, and he tried to walk as Giulio and I carried him toward the building with Godin carrying our weapons, and I remember—a strange thought that comes to me now—that we were taken by surprise by a man standing on the icy road who appeared like an apparition. He carried a Bencini camera held to his eye—a journalist with a red band around his arm who was embedded with our central command that'd set up their temporary HQ upstairs in the green building—and Giulio said, "Smile, Renzo, so they'll think we're having as good time back home." I knew the man—his father owned the optometrist in Schio, Barroni was his name, and we stood there holding Lago between us as he took his photo.

Radio Scarpa reported that Postojali was where we would wait to regroup before we continued our march, but I knew there would be no regrouping now. We'd ceased being an army the moment we'd fled because an army is not built to retreat, it's built to fight. We were men, not soldiers, and not fighting meant not dying.

Near the heat of those porcelain ovens the Russian peasants kept in their izbas, we rested, knowing the door would be ajar all night as the last of the stragglers tried to force their way into the building, pushing and shoving because outside was nothing but -50C and certain death and it would take nothing for a man to die now. Just a small ache, enough to slow you down so that you fell back to the rear of the column—that was all, death was a simple thing. A column of twenty kilometres, and who knew what happened to the men at the rear, John, how many were simply killed by small squads of partisans and spies and friends needing a coat or a blanket or a pair of fucking socks.

I remembered my mother telling me before I left, *"Fa' il bono,* Renzo." Be a good boy, she'd told me the night before I'd headed out for Gorizia and that train that would take us east, always east, my father in his bed with the fever that'd consumed him since the spring shaking my hand weak and infirm and my sisters handing me salami and wine for the trip. I thought of my mother that night in that green building when Giulio had me remove my boots in the dim light of the fires. He told me they were no good, frozen solid, and he had me wrap a blanket around my feet and tied them down with telegraph wire. I thought of Luisa waiting for me at home, and my sisters and our farm, and watched Giulio throw my boots off into the corner and thought, That's that then.

My makeshift Valenkis would wear off frostbite, Giulio said.

I thought of Lago's mother, a woman I'd known from when my sister worked at her salon in the summer of '41, I remembered her when Giulio brought us some of the soup they were dishing out in the building in our frozen tin bowls, our *gavette,* some sort of meat stew, they called us the *magnagatti* in the Veneto, the cat-eaters, but the meat wasn't even that, and Giulio slid the meat into Lago's mouth with his fingers and then he smeared honey on the man's blue lips from where his tongue licked and licked at the sweetness like a lizard in the summer.

Godin, his Beretta rifle resting on his lap, said, "Why do you bother with him?"

"Because I'm taking him home," replied Giulio.

"What's he to you? Were you even friends?"

Giulio shrugged.

"He's never going to make it."

"He's going to make it," said Giulio, and his hand stroked Lago's forehead. "Because if he doesn't, none of us will."

Be good, I thought. Be good. In this place.

It was late that night with the fires dwindling and the smoke dense in our izba when General Reverberi came to us. He came to us from out of the shadows, his boots clapping down the stairs, his eyes gleaming from the soft lamps, and it was strange, John, how his descent electrified that room of weary, cold men. We were maybe a thousand down there, perhaps even more, and Reverberi—this little man in his uniform that seemed pressed to his skin—stood there on the third-to-last stair and looked down at us in the doubtful glow and I understood then that there are men who lead because they were born to it and there are men who lead because destiny has fated it. Reverberi was a man who inspired simply by being, and in the hush his voice rose to speak to every one of us.

"The situation," he told us, not raising his voice, and yet we could make out his words so flawlessly, this short silver-haired man who they called *Generale dieci lire* because he'd always slip a ten lire note for his men on parade to drink to his health, this man with the lively smile and black-black eyes and deep-dimpled smile and *bello*, John, he could have been a movie actor, this man who was but days away from facing his phantastic destiny, "is becoming as clear as it is serious. These are not times for half-truths. If we're to find our way back to Italy—all of us—we must understand what we face. So tell your bothers outside this room that we are in a sack. Behind us is a mass of Russian forces of imprecise strength. They are closing in from the Don and there's nothing that will slow them. The Julia Division is now lost." He gave us a moment to recognise what that meant for us—what it meant that 20,000 men had vanished somewhere behind us. "Ahead of us," he said, slowly now, so that we could understand, "ahead of us is a mass of Russian units of imprecise, but considerable strength. We are therefore in an ever-tightening sack, and the only way we're getting out is to fight our way out. To fight and to move quickly is all that's left to us. The slower we march, the more the Russians will be able to strengthen their positions ahead and close in on us from behind. Behind us is Russia. Ahead of us is Italy. We go home. Tomorrow, we march for Seljakino. The enemy is pushing us west. They want us to weaken on the steppe, and they will wait for us to weaken. And they, not us, will decide when they will engage us for one last battle. We're cut off. Our last signal has us some three hundred kilometres from our new lines, but that will be fluid. We have no communications with our lines. Men, we walk with God. And God walks with you. We will walk and we will fight, and we *will* go home. All of us together. We *all* go home."

We all go home. Except that now the gathering rumble of tanks broke the spell like a first tremor of sickness and in that half-life of hunger and exhaustion men began to move, falling over themselves as they fought their way out of the building.

"Stay here with him," Giulio told me as he and Godin joined the men running out of the building. I looked down at Lago and thought fuck him, destiny was what it was, and followed Giulio and Godin into the night.

To my right, tanks—five lumbering T34s and *Betushkas*—rolled clumsily through the narrow street toward us. From behind me, the 45th Battery opened fire with their Pak 36 anti-tank gun, first at 90 degrees—I could hear the men shout—then 60 degrees, and then, "Zero, zero degrees dead-ahead and fire, fire! *Al fogo!*" The 37mm shells hit the lead tank square and our bombs fall away like bars of soap. The tanks kept moving, crushing forward with impunity as the Vicenza Battalion kept firing, and hundreds of white ghosts crouching behind those metal machines came toward us, waiting for the order to engage.

I hid behind the wall of the izba as a bomb hit the lead T34 on the wheel arches and the tank slowed, stumbled and came to a halt, and suddenly silhouettes bled out of the dark, *guastatori* from the XXX Battalion, running and then rolling under the tanks and throwing grenades into the wheel arches and as their bombs detonated, we saw two German tanks appear to our left. The *guastatori* attacked those Russian tanks with everything they had—flamethrowers, magnetic mines, hand grenades, even muskets, and it was then that I saw him. Giulio. He was running toward the tanks as the 45th Battery opened up again and suddenly the tanks were shuddering and recoiling and men were clambering out of their hatches as the tanks caught fire and Giulio was firing at them with his Beretta, firing at them from his waist as the Russians tried to flee and were cut apart by Giulio's bullets, and then he was up on one of the tanks just as the Russian infantry began to charge and Giulio jumped over the tanks and now he was sprinting toward me and it seemed as if he were being chased by the entire Russian army as a man beside me, lying on his belly, opened up with his Breda M37 fixed on a tripod and I watched bullets slash about him until one shot from a T34 pulverised him.

"*Avanti Savoia!*" I heard dimly, deafened now by the battle. "*Avanti!*"

I turned to see Signorini leading a charge of the Vestone and Val Chiesa Battalions straight into the surging Russian infantry just as two the German *Sturmgeschütz* tanks sealed the Russians in to their fate and I saw Giulio race to the Breda M37 and slide behind it and his head was reverberating as he squeezed his finger on the trigger until the gun overheated and stumbled and died and how we cheered, John, when the Russians turned and fled into the night. How we roared.

"If they only knew," I said to Giulio when he came to sit beside me and Lago later than night, his hands burnt from the violence of that M37.

"What?"

"The Russians," I said. "If they only knew."

"Knew what?"

"Who we are," I replied.

"It's okay," he said, but he didn't look at me, he had eyes only for Lago, "it's okay to be afraid, Renzo." He placed a blanket over Lago and then ran a hand over the boy's face. "We're going to make it. All of us."

I could feel Lago's fever, feel the warmth radiating off him. Giulio fed him water and now came the calls to get moving and when we reached the sled in that darkness of the pre-dawn hour, Godin was already in it, preparing to leave. As I was about to climb into it, I saw, standing disconsolately outside the burnt factory across from me, a medic named Boero who I'd become friendly with on the Don Front. He and I had liked to play *scopa* together, and he still owed me twenty lire from our last game. I stepped to him quickly.

"Renzo," he said, recognising me. He told me he'd been chosen to remain behind with the injured. Besides him stood a chaplain from the Tridentina I didn't recognise. He had, Boero told me, no morphine left, no antibiotics, and had been operating out in the open that night because the cold could stop a haemorrhage and frozen flesh was its own analgesic.

"There are no more orders," I told him. "Come with us."

"It ends the same for everyone," Boero said, and I remember his eyes, John, the blue of his eyes like a winter sky in the Dolomites and I could see he'd been crying. "And besides, I have my own priest here." And then he showed me his hand, four syrettes of morphine in his palm, and invited me to take them. "I owe you," he told me, "but I'd consult God before you use them." We shook hands there outside the building, and then he turned and walked inside to tend to the damned. Priests and doctors meant the same out there on the steppe.

On a small hill lit by fires in oil barrels, chaplains in the chiaroscuro chanted and absolved us of our sins as we fled Postojali and I watched as men knelt before those chaplains, genuflecting in the blaze of fires, knees in the snow, and then slowly they stood and stumbled west into the endless steppe.

"At least," said Giulio, watching me genuflect with an inscrutable look as we trudged on by, "we get to attend our own funerals."

In that brittle dawn we saw men dead on the steppe, and we realised there were Russians amongst us, in that column that stretched back into history, joining Italians who'd had nowhere to run but east when the *squadristi* had roamed the Po Valley in the '20s, and they were with us now, they were with us and they killed us as we marched in that silence—men who walked alone because to talk was to do something other than drag one leaden foot before the next and who knew, anyway, what to say now. Men hauled themselves on into that wall of cold, rifles now the crutches of the frostbitten hunchbacks, and those who were too weak and too tired collapsed, and others would just sit on the snow and we'd walk past them as if they were already dead, dead as those who we'd find frozen like effigies on the side of that highway we shaped beneath our feet and sleds, this ditch in the ice ploughed by the desperate steps of this parade marching to its own funeral.

Death was suspended by the cold as if it were a virus, as if it needed to linger, and I saw men without legs and arms and still the blood refused to flow, blocked by the cold and in the end it just prolonged the agony, those bastards staring at their amputated limbs wondering how long it would take, how long before they died and the last thing they felt, I suppose, was the hope that they would somehow live. And the hunger, John. I remembered the plenty of the steppe in the summer—food and peasant wine that stung the throat, the honey and milk and the bread, and the woman who would take us one by one, silent and accepting. Now there was nothing, and we would pass through villages frozen in their own sinister isolation, and when we raided the izbas, we found only the old and the children, submissive and resigned as we took what we needed, what we wanted, who we wanted, and they'd say not a word knowing they too were watching their own deaths along with ours.

We'd eat anything except for the vultures. The Cocui. Those birds we'd never eat. We'd pass them so close as they fed on the men who'd fallen and who'd yet to stiffen into dolls and they scared us, those massive-winged black birds that seemed to me some mutated giant bats that cared less for us, the living, than we cared for the dead, they scared us because they were like Dante's birds of hell, oil-smeared birds pecking at eyes and faces, and their indifference was as immense as the steppe. They feasted on us, the dead. Ripping through flesh and organs slick like earthworms in their blood stained beaks, opaque eyes forever watching. They understood death. They could sense it and to be looked at by those birds was to recognise that death had seen you, and we'd not eat those vultures because they reminded us of ourselves, because we too cared for the dead only for what they could still provide—a coat, a blanket—and Don Gnocchi, always Don Gnocchi who we'd see clapping his hands to scare the Cocui before kneeling to collect dog tags from corpses frayed to pieces by those animals, and whatever we left there on the ice, the Russians would take and it was them, not us, it was the Russians in the end who would bury our dead—those they could. For the earth was as rigid as our dead and the ice impenetrable and the Russians would use their flamethrowers on gasoline-doused corpses and burn it all and the smoke would rise behind us in the crystal-blue skies, smoke-signals that foretold our own coming end.

But we would not eat the vultures.

Our survival depended on the sacrifice of others. Those who were strong would fight and die for the weak. They were our only hope—and they would die for the thousands of cowards threaded across the Russian steppe. But a man fought because it was who he was, John. In the rabble on the march to Seljakino were thousands of men who could have chosen to fight and who chose, instead, to hide, to throw their weapons into the snow and to vanish into that mass of faceless zeros. We were bandits, fugitives, we spoke not a word to those strangers beside us, and worse—worse, because we were our own enemies now. We cared nothing for those who fell except for what their corpses could provide. We cared nothing even for those who would fight and die for us, we cared nothing for them just as we willed them on and they despised us, those fighters, those Apaches—the rabble they despised more than the enemy because in the eyes of the white ghosts they saw reflected themselves, warriors, but in us they saw the worst of themselves and they would have killed us with more ease and satisfaction than they'd have slaughtered an animal for survival. But the horde provided the fighters up-front with excellent cannon fodder, and we were useful at least in that way.

In the evening when we rose atop a hill, we could see our dead littered across the steppe for miles behind us. We marched with the column shedding waste on the steppe, our broken sleds abandoned along with the dead, limbs hanging out, our rifles with ammunition too heavy to carry for men whose jelly-legs could no longer shift the snow before them, we abandoned anything that slowed us, and for us it was always the same emotion, John, with every crest of every hill, those of us still able to move, we would gaze into a new vista in the hope of seeing there our new lines and find, instead, the old, cold eternity of the steppe. That hope kept us marching with our feet gangrenous and eyelids frozen and our feet and faces frostbitten, a column of 100,000 men by that third day, with bodies doubled-over like hunchbacks, *gobbi*, whipped and deafened by a wind that tore at our flesh as we dragged our hungry bodies on into the white, stumbling and falling and standing, one step, one step and falling, and those who did not stand once more would die where they fell and only the Cocui cared for their fate. The Cocui and Don Gnocchi who carried the dog tags in his satchel like souls.

In the sled, Lago was lying beneath a blanket that was as hard as metal and covered by ice. We shit and pissed in our pants, John, because exposing anything, even for a moment, would lead to frostbite. I learnt that lesson. Survival depended on keeping close to the fighting men spearing at the front of the column because in their shadow was the light of survival, and Godin and Giulio and I would take turns pulling the recalcitrant mule over the ice. The crown of the column cut a trail set by Reverberi who had formed an advanced unit of the XXIV Panzer Korps of General Eidl and two battalions of the 6th along with a hastily put-together and nameless fighting battalion composed of men who were ready to fight their way back home. They pierced ahead, creating a hard-packed road on the snow headed southwest for us, and as we marched, we could hear the distant sounds of battle.

"That's our artillery," said Godin.

"Russian," Giulio said.

In the night we saw the lights of a town we believed was Charkovka, and we learned that Reverberi had overwhelmed two Russians battalions and a dozen tanks that afternoon. The second barrier of Russians blocking our retreat, Radio Scarpa reported, had been broken, and the road to Seljakino was now open.

Giulio and Godin had found an izba, and I helped them carry Lago into the shelter. Being as close as you could to the head of the column was life and death now because those who would come later would find no protection. They would die out there in the cold. The talk in the izba, lit by a porcelain oven in one corner, was of Reverberi's words that afternoon after the battle for Charkovka. That we were now only to march with the night. "They're waiting for us," Reverberi had told his fighting men, his Apaches, a race apart now. "Good. We will meet them. And God will show us the way."

That night I saw a man by the stove warming his feet—it was the only way to soften the leather of our boots and to get them off—but somehow the heat had softened his flesh too because when he removed a boot, his foot came off with it, and he just sat there with the meat stew in his boot and I don't know whether he wanted us to help him or kill him because all he said, over and over, was, "How am I meant to die now? How am I meant to die now?" Eventually someone managed to get morphine into him and that shut him up so we could sleep without his whining and dawn came with a storm of such cruelty that I carry its sound and fury still with me now. Thunder and lightning that first made us believe we were under assault and the snow was like nothing I'd ever before seen, a white wall that hurtled down before us and left us deaf and silent. The town was small and the men many, packed into those izbas like rats, and we were ready to protect our space now no matter what. Life depended on it. The stragglers who came with the day and in that blizzard were told to move on, to keep moving to Lymarev, a kilometre west. God alone knows how many died on that road, in that blizzard, God alone knows what was lying in wait for them out there in the white nothing.

From Giulio we learnt that the schoolhouse opposite our izba, a brick building peppered by bullet-holes and semi-collapsed from that afternoon's battle, was now an operating theatre where medics, he said, were working on the injured with penknives and candlelight. He'd gone over and found some morphine for Lago. The building was being protected by Reverberi's men, and we could see from our window how more and more men were attempting to push their way in, desperate for shelter as the storm worsened. The guards did what they could but eventually the sheer weight of men drunk on despair had shoved and pushed and fought their way into the school, spilling in and standing and walking over the injured and the dying who'd fought for that little building. We could hear screams and fighting and even gunshots that sounded a lot like thunder, and Giulio and Godin had their weapons on their laps as the door to our izba was kicked open and men began shoving their way in, and they spoke an alien language, they were Hungarians, or Romanians.

"*Fuori!*" Godin stood up and walked toward the door. "*Out!*" he shouted. "*Raus!*"

"*Baszd meg,*" said one of the men driving in through the door.

Godin lifted his Beretta, aimed, and fired. The bullet hit the man in the face and his head flew out of the izba before his body collapsed onto the threshold. Godin fired another round, two, and then kicked at the body and three men came to help him shove at it with their feet until it rolled away from the door that they smashed shut.

No one tried to get in after that.

That day an izba went up in flames and we watched it burn and not even one man managed to get out and when the night came, it was still smouldering orange, and through Radio Scarpa we learned that Command Group ARMIR had managed to relay a message over General Eidl's radio that Valiuki to our west was now in Russian hands and that we were to turn southwest and head for a town called Nikolayevka. We waited for the night and, in the dark, we walked out of the izba leaving the boy who'd lost his foot to die in the spent heat of the fire, and carried Lago to the sled and followed the column into the ice where men lay dead, shot and stabbed, naked and killed for a blanket, a biscuit, and as we sliced past mutely, on the way of the Davai, it was as if we were passing a cemetery. There was to be no mercy, John, we knew this, not from the Russians and least of all from ourselves.

It was just before dawn with the moon indifferent as the slicked-silver snow that we arrived on the steep banks of a river frozen like a vein. The storm had passed and in moonshine we could see General Eidl crossing the river in the lead tank. The river was solid, and the tank was halfway across when we heard the whistle of artillery. The ice rumbled, the tank growled, and then suddenly the ice gave way and the tank, ever so gently, tipped nose-first into the mouth of a crevasse. We watched a dozen German soldiers jump into that ice water, first running like skaters and then they fell into the water and in minutes they were scraping Eidl onto the riverbank while the tank gurgled away beneath the silvery surface. Our remaining tanks fired blindly into the night but as ever the Russian artillery just melted away like spring water in the steppe.

I know he was alive, John, but I learnt that Eidl died some days later of gangrene, and from that day on, another German took his place—Heidkamper. Those Germans were a brave lot, brave and determined, but they never came anywhere near us. We disgusted them more than a man does a rat in the winter rain.

It was still dark when we arrived in Kravzoulka. We were able to keep close to the 152 German artillery and Panzer Korps and we watched them cleanup a small division of partisans. So much cold, John, so much cold and hunger and fear and so few izbas that night, and the Germans took them all shouting *raus! raus!* if anyone got anywhere near them, and they were not above opening up with their machine guns, and I remember Godin, chortling as we watched a group of Hungarians sprayed by German bullets after they'd failed to *raus* fast enough, saying, "This is how a nation finds greatness."

The difference that day was an hour out of the cold, the difference between living and dying, and it was Godin and his rifle who secured an izba for us to huddle in at the far end of the village. The underground cellar had already been ransacked, but we found jam and honey and ate it with our fingers. And it was Giulio who fed honey to Lago, using his index finger to smear it on his lips.

"Waste of food," said Godin.

"Food's always a waste," replied Giulio.

All around us, Godin said, was the enemy—the Germans, the Russians, the partisans. "But the worst enemy we have," said Godin, "is us. Not enough discipline. Duce was right."

"Still?" asked Giulio. "Even now?"

That day I will always remember as the day of the suicides. I think it was the fourth, maybe the fifth day of our retreat—it's difficult to be precise, John, but I remember that day as the day of the suicides. A day that came beneath a crystal-glass dome of such purity that our eyes were blinded by the glare. I wonder now whether it was that light that made men suddenly stir like lice. They would begin to laugh and then they'd stand and strip down naked and run out into the snow, and men began having visions—shouting at ghosts and lovers and mothers and God and they'd rush out of izbas to charge down the streets firing their pistols until someone would put a bullet in their face. We would watch them from our izba, falling and dying out there on the snow and then men would secret out into the light like wolves to gather forsaken gloves and boots and food and blankets and watches and whatever they could find, the corpses stripped and prepped naked for the Cocui that circled black like lice in the sky, and we'd watch them land with such serenity and begin to strip the dead even of their organs while we sat in the warmth of the izba waiting for the night, waiting for our turn with the beak.

There were so many ways to suicide that day. The fastest was sticking a pistol in your mouth but that was the strong man's exit—I came to see that a man who shot himself was a strong man, John, because it required that one thing none of us had anymore—it required motion. And at -40C, who had the strength to do even that? The impulse was to do nothing. Just to sit. And die. And that was the easiest way of all—just to step outside into the snow, sit and shut your eyes because dying was that easy, and we undertood then that there's a limit to what a man will endure just to live another day.

That day in our izba I watched a father and his son, Alpini the both of them, a father and son whose feet were black with frostbite—men from up in Magrè—say goodbye to each other, and I saw the father take a pistol and aim it at the boy's face and the boy shut his eyes and the father, too, shut his eyes, and I wonder now if I heard him say "Mama" or if it was me who said it or whether the father spoke at all when he pulled the trigger and then stuck the barrel into his own mouth and without ever seeing his boy's face splattered onto the wall of that izba in a town none of us could ever find again, he swallowed barrel and bullet.

We ate a tin of biscuits that we found in the father's jacket after we dumped both the corpses out into the cold for Don Gnocchi and the Cocui, and then we slept in turns, armed, Godin and I, while Giulio headed out to find food. In every izba the peasants kept their winter provisions in underground holes—honey, flour, dried meats, smoked sunflowers seeds, potatoes, and sometimes even Tre Stelle cigarettes, and if you were really lucky, a warm body ready to bend to your desires. Much of the food was poisoned by the partisans, and after a few hours it was worthwhile to search the izbas to find thirty, forty dead men, poisoned, and rummage through the stores to see what was left once you'd figured out what it was that'd killed them.

"I was told we're about two-hundred kilometres from the German lines," said Godin when the call to march came with the dark.

"Might as well be two million," said Giulio, and he and I lifted Lago by fastening his arms around our shoulders and dragged him out to the sled. "We aren't retreating, we're in a backward advance."

"Because of cowards," said Godin, jutting his chin at the rabble scraping past us in the orange flicker of firelight. "Because of these fucking peasants."

How many men we left behind in the izbas that night, John, men who'd come that far and could go no further? Men who'd found their limit. And we were dead anyway, weren't we, in that cold eternal dark through which our mule pulled us, out of Krozodvka with the Vestone, Bergamo, and

Vicenza battalions creating a corridor for us stragglers, us *ardenti*, us hunchbacks, those fighting men with their big Breda guns on their shoulders and their arms wrapped around the steel as if crucified, walking tall in twin columns between the three remaining German tanks, challenging destiny, those men, John, with a bravery that awed and disgusted in equal measure.

## "Roberta"—Peppino Di Capri

I glance up from the notebook. The words end here. I touch the dried blood on those pages, and it makes me feel unclean, ashamed somehow. As if the crime were somehow mine, too.

I grab the second notebook and slowly draw it from its plastic wrapper. I leave it there for a moment and reach for my phone that's been strangely silent. This place is strangely silent. And that makes me wonder about something Casanova had said.

The 4G network is unavailable. I stare at the face of my phone; it may as well be bricked, and the sense of alarm at being in here, alone, with nothing but someone else's memories and no way of being reached makes me glance longingly at the camera. Is there, I wonder, at least someone on the other side of that dead, black eye?

The clock on the wall shows it's just gone 4.20PM. My father will be waiting.

I should care—I should care about my uncle because he'd changed my father's life, had made him into the man he was, and that had made me the man I was. As a baby, an infant, it was his anxiety, I suppose, that fed mine: we're all just products of those moments beyond our memory, when we were just crying little bundles of flesh being moulded by the thoughts and desires and fears of our parents, and my uncle had surely always been there, his death had always been there for my father, his big brother who'd just been swallowed up by the earth, a memory that must have influenced my life in ways that I don't and won't ever understand.

But still, I feel nothing for this man—he's but a name on the pages of a fractured notebook written in the summer of 1945. A man without a face, without a sound. I wonder if my father remembers his voice. I wonder why he'd never told me a thing about my uncle Alessandro. Perhaps he'd forgotten, and all that remains for him too is just a faint memory of a boy who'd disappeared into the Russian steppe so very long ago.

# SIX
# THE AMPUTATION FACTORY

*In my work with the defendants, I was searching for the nature of evil and I now think I have come close to defining it. A lack of empathy. It's the one characteristic that connects all the defendants, a genuine incapacity to feel with their fellow men. Evil, I think, is the absence of empathy.*
—Captain G. M. Gilbert, US Army psychologist to the defendants at the Nuremberg Trials, 1945–1949

Dear John,

    I understand now. Your men let it slip that this is what you have done for many months—lead interrogator for your unit. You must be a far more important man than I thought. But I wonder why you're not here? Why is it not you who lowers the cockroach in my mouth and forces my jaw shut so that I can do nothing but accept the crawl of it down my throat? Is it because you have a conscience that you don't want to leave behind? I can understand that. It's what I did. I left my conscience in Russia, with a boy on the steppe, and like you, all we wanted was to come home—a *baia*—even Lago I guess, even those who we left to die in Charkovka, those men whose toes and noses and fingers had been cleaved off with plyers, gangrenous and frostbitten, and one man, I will never forget, inching on the ice on his belly in chase of the column, on his belly for he no longer had feet but he had arms and he was crawling home, John, one arm-length after the next, and in the sled Godin laughed as we passed him and shouted, "Sonofabitch is gonna swim home, look at him! Swim, you bastard, swim!"

    We left Charkovka on a spitefully serene night on our way to Seljakino. On the road out, Don Gnocchi waited with his sack full of dog tags. He was on his knees holding a glinting crucifix to the sky and he said to us, "Alpini are worthy of God. *In questa campagna del dolore*," he told us, "in this land of pain, God will find us, God will save us, God will deliver us." I'm not sure the swimming man ever got close enough to Don Gnocchi to learn that God loved him too.

"Bless you father," Godin said, and I prayed and genuflected as Giulio watched me with a smile that I couldn't quite place—a knowing that I was yet to discover for myself. Giulio, I believe now, had a presentiment of what was about to happen that night on the steppe—a night that would reveal to me the full horror of my soul. Whipped by that wind and dominated by that velvet sky and that earth of endless shadow that wanted nothing more than my life, what frightened me most, John, was my insignificance. I felt nothing but my hunger, my cold, my exhaustion, and if there were a hundred thousand men around me, all were dead to me already. And it was that night—three, four hours out of Charkovka—that the sled suddenly slowed, and I raised my head as the mule's familiar gait shifted below me, to see Giulio pausing astride the mule.

"What's happened?" asked Godin, sitting up beside me in the sled.

I watched the mule slacken as if lame. And then, with a grace that was never his in life, one foreleg buckled, and the mule began to collapse, first its forelegs giving way and then its hind legs until, ever so gently, it toppled and fell onto its flank like a snowflake at Giulio's feet, quite, quite dead.

Godin jumped out of the sled and was onto Giulio in a second.

"What the fuck have you done!?" he shouted. His anger was bizarre—to be capable of such fury, such energy—and he had his fist raised when suddenly silhouettes peeled from the skin of night and I saw knives and bayonets glint in the moonshine as men fall upon the carcass of our mule and began cutting and carving through flesh and cleaving out organs, bowels white-hot and simmering in the freeze, and men on their haunches began to feed on the flesh, steaming hot between their flashing teeth as more men fell upon that mule like those massive-winged vultures and just as suddenly they were gone and all they'd left behind were the mule's entrails sizzling pink on the snow and that head that never even bled with two gaping holes where once had been its kind, stupid eyes.

The horror of the soul, John, is to not care anymore. But for that mule I had cared. For that mule I shed tears.

Giulio and Godin were arguing by the time I got near enough to gather what they were saying.

"We leave him," said Godin.

"We can push it," said Giulio.

"We can't push that sled. Don't be a fucking moron. We've done enough for him, *porca troia!*"

"It's only enough when I bring him home."

"You're as stubborn as a fucking mule," said Godin. "And you'll end up dead just like it." His boot kicked at the mule's head in disgust.

Giulio turned to me. "And you?" he asked.

"And me what?"

The three of us stood there, the cold eating into our flesh.

"We did what we could," Godin said.

Giulio shrugged. "I won't leave him here."

Around us the snow swirled, and through it all the hunchbacks shuffled, indifferent and immune to our suffering, one foot beyond the next, stained silhouettes like ink letters of a story no one cared to read.

"Then you stay. And you die with him."

"We can take turns," I said. "We take turns pulling the sled, two men at a time, the third rests—"

"I'm not your fucking mule," said Godin. "And I'm not dying for you. Or that prick." He took three steps forward and stood in front of Giulio and the steam from their lungs met. "We leave him here or we die with him. It's that simple. He's a fucking coward. Did you see his teeth? He fucking pulled them out before he even got here."

"Then we die," said Giulio. "We die like men."

"You call pulling a fucking sled with some deserter through Russia dying like a man? Fuck off." Godin pushed past Giulio, using his shoulder to dislodge the other man's balance, and walked to the sled. He reached into it and pulled out a canvas sack with our food and supplies and his rifle.

"What are you doing?" I asked.

"Stay out of this," he said. "You're a fucking leech." He spat into the sled and then shuffled back toward me, a pistol in his gloved hand. "Do you want to die?" he asked me, and I shook my head and looked down at the snow. "And you, Giulio?"

Giulio said not a word.

"Then you won't be needing this," Godin waved the sack about. "Of all the people to die for *patria*," he laughed as he wrapped his scarf tightly around his face. "You, Giulio? You fucking idiot. And for what? You'll leave him anyway. Do it now, do it later, makes no difference. *Gheto capio o no*?"

Giulio watched him.

"Give me your blanket," Godin said suddenly, as if this mattered, as if he needed even this. "You too," he said to me, "you won't be needing those where you're going."

"Don't do this," said Giulio. "Just walk away."

Godin lifted his pistol and aimed it square at Giulio's face. "Makes no difference out here. Makes no difference to me."

Giulio and I unfurled our blankets onto the snow and Godin bent and lifted them. "Always the same fucking Giulio," he said. "You think your shit don't stink? I'll make sure they know how you died, mate. Giulio Moro, the martyr for Duce. Mussolini's bitch. They'll laugh for days back home."

In a moment he'd vanished into the darkness, just another shadow bent-double against the icy wind, just one more of the damned, just another silhouette of the snow.

Giulio looked at me then and said, "And you?"

"And me what?"

Giulio raised the collar to his great coat. "You should go."

"No." The wind cut through my coat now, and I shivered.

"Then help me."

Together we hauled Lago from the sled and placed his arms about our shoulders, propping him like some sort of marionette.

"We're gonna make you walk a little," Giulio said. "Can you move your legs?"

"I try," he said, but he did nothing at all except pull us down like an anchor, and when we began to lumber forward, it felt as if we were walking through glue. I could smell death on my face as his head went limp on my shoulder and it made me want to puke. Giulio it was who did most of the carrying as I tried to keep pace in that cold with my eyes stinging, and I'm sure he pulled me along too until we were back amid the hunchbacks at the tail of the column. The sun was already a sliver on the ice when we saw

Seljakino sitting in a narrow, nervous valley with izbas dotted up the steep sides of a ridgeback mountain, jagged and silent. All of us who were there that day, John, those of us who came home, we'll never forget the bridge to Seljakino, that frail, slender wooden bridge that extended over a deep gorge that looked as if this world had once split like an egg.

Reverberi was standing beside the remaining three German tanks, his fisted gloves holding a pair of field-glasses through which he scanned the town. The Russians had left that bridge standing for us, but if this was to be our graveyard, they'd chosen poorly because in those coarse hills that surrounded Seljakino we saw home, we saw our childhood haunts in the foothills of the Dolomites, in the rocky cliffs of Posina and the *Sette Communi*. Out on the steppe we were sheep running from the wolves, but here, in the mountains, here is where we'd always fought and played as boys. In mountains like these our fathers had defeated the Austrians and bought Trieste and Trento with their blood, our Alpini, our mountain troops, this was our world, and if this was the place that the Russians had chosen to bury us, they had chosen poorly.

"*Avanti l'artiglieria!*" came the order from Reverberi, and the 32nd Battery of the Bergamo rolled up and began to shell the town. This day, I thought, will not be the day we die. I thought this when Signorini assembled the 255 Company of the Val Chiesa Battalion, and in the chaos of the shelling artillery, led them up toward the icy cliffs glinting in the dawn.

It was after we'd shelled the town for twenty minutes that the Russians decided they'd had enough and gave us their welcome. It started with a dozen Katushas—dear God, John, the sound of those Katushas shot from their trucks, those sounds were the sounds of hell—and then canons and artillery and mortars joined the choir, and then suddenly machine-gun-needles up in the cliffs opened up, and it all hit the rabble square. There was nowhere to hide, and men just threw themselves down into the snow and prayed as the fire rained down on us like blood and bone, and the blessed died and the wretched died a little slower.

The Russians were careful not to hit the bridge, and with our mortars firing, the first of our battalions ran across it toward the road that cut through between the brick izbas and into the town. We watched them run,

Giulio and I, with Lago abandoned on the snow between us, those men in their blankets with musket rifles slung around their necks, Lugers and Berettas and Russian parabellums and grenades in hand, running because all that mattered to them was to be able to shoot without stopping, to have something deadly in hand for fighting man-to-man. The moment the men crossed the bridge, the Russians in their white uniforms materialised, machine-guns and grenades and rockets firing and the machine-gun-nests up in the cliffs joined in and now the German tanks were bouncing and shredding over the dead on the bridge, and the tank tracks were crimson with the blood of broken men thrown into the gorge in silent and strange ballets of twisted, weightless limbs.

And then we saw them. The men from the 255 Company Val Chiesa who'd managed to flank the town and were now rushing down the jagged face of the ridges above the machine-gun-needles and three, four of those needles went up almost simultaneously to OTO grenades and suddenly the 255 Company were flowing down the cliffsides like an avalanche as the three German *semoventi* were over the bridge, the remains of the Verona Battalion rushing behind them, and the Russians were already retreating into the steppe by the time the 255 outflanked their defensive positions and the rabble was free to march into Seljakino.

Giulio carried Lago over that bridge into Seljakino on his back. The Russians and the tanks had done their work well—that bridge was a mortuary. The hunchbacks pushed us aside, hobbling as fast as they could to find their shelter, and Don Gnocchi was already on the bridge blessing the dead and collecting dog tags from mounds of steaming flesh that had once been our brothers. It was then that Giulio said, "Those poor fuckers will make heroes of us all." Those boys from the battalions with *patria* still gleaming in their dead staring eyes, hundreds of them, John, we walked over them and around them and slipped and fell into the abattoir of their sacrifice, and once over that bridge we searched for food on the streets as if we were dogs, our nostrils flaring, and the injured were abandoned in an izba on the edge of town near the ravine where they would be left for the Russians.

We made our way through the streets trying to force our way into izbas already seized by the fighting men and by the stragglers who'd come right in after them—they were like lice, those men. We saw a Russian sitting with his back to the wall of an izba, sitting there with a knife in his hand, his left leg nothing more than a frozen stump and he was cutting the veins on his wrist with such abject determination but the blood wouldn't flow, it was all frozen in place and he kept cutting and cutting, deeper and deeper, the wounds viscous and open, flabby like a woman's parts, and his face fully concentrated on his task but the blood just wouldn't flow and Don Gnocchi came to kneel beside him without any fear and said to him, "What are you afraid of, what more can we do to you?" and from behind Don Gnocchi a man came and shot the boy in the face and we just kept walking until we found, some way out of town, in a little izba, shelter for the day.

Seljakino was our Shangri-La, John. Perhaps the Russians has underestimated us because in those izbas the food was plentiful, cheese and milk and honey, and we found even our own rations that'd been taken when the Russians had smashed Rossoch, once our central command on the Don. Goats, John. Goats, all slaughtered and cooked in BBQs that lit the fading embers of day.

Radio Scarpa reported that the Vestone Battalion, running about ten kilometres behind us, had wandered off course and were now headed for a trap in Valjuiki, told to do so by a pair of Italian men on horseback. The men were Italians, communist spies, or so Radio Scarpa reported, and later that evening a horse came over the bridge carrying two dead men frozen solid. The horses were slaughtered and eaten, and the men were left there on the streets, and in death they joined our heroes in Don Gnocchi's dog-tag-sack.

It was late when the sudden order came for us to move. We were to walk to Vervorovka with the Morbegno Battalion running point alongside the three remaining German tanks. The order ran through the izbas and there was panic now, men shouting, *"Forza! Forza!"*

The Russians were coming! *Moskalenko* was coming!

In the izba, Lago lay under his blanket pale as the whiteness that waited for us out there on the steppe, shivering with fever, and Giulio said to me, "You should go."

"We go together."

"He's nothing to you."

"What is he to you?" I asked.

Giulio seemed about to say something but instead he grinned and laughed that laugh of his.

I helped Giulio lift Lago and together we shuffled out into a chill that felt as if needles were puncturing us. The snow was falling hard, the wind picking up, and Lago was of no use at all. I helped Giulio place the kid on his back and, hunched over carrying his load like a mule, I followed him into the razor-cold night.

Inertia. That was all. Once I began to walk, one step after the next, I forgot the cold. Walk. Giulio carried Lago on his back for hours, then I took a turn and fell on the snow. And stood up and Giulio helped settle the man on my back and I walked. I walked and fell and stumbled and fell and walked and stumbled and kept walking, one step after the next, inertia, that was all, the snow up to my knees and every step felt as if I'd marched a thousand and finally we arrived at Degtyarnoye in the midst of a blizzard, and that was hard, that walk that day, that walk killed the weak, John, it killed the weak with such disdain, and in that horizon that curved endlessly ahead of us, the order was given that we would not slow this night, we had to keep moving, *forza, forza!* Moskalenko was coming! And on we hobbled in the suffering silence with Lago the weight of sin on our backs, and I wished Lago dead then, I wished him dead even when, just before sunrise, we slowly made our way into a depression on the steppe and saw before us Malakeyevo.

The battle had been long underway by the time we arrived, and we could hear the artillery and the guns from a long way off. Thinking back, John, how strange it was that we walked toward those terrible sounds. But where else were we to go, us peasants of the snow? Death was everywhere, and the only way to survive was to walk through the doors the fighting battalions would open for us with their lives. Giulio was right—the dead would make heroes of us all because it was those who survived who would write this history.

The Russian artillery had been accurate that day in Malakeyevo, where izbas were spread about a few main roads and a handsome brick church blessed a modest piazza, and two German tanks lay smouldering and broken. Around the tanks were dozens of *sbadanti*, the rabble who'd been caught too close to the spearhead, too desperate to get to shelter first, and they lay there as if they were on the beach on the Lido, twisted and smashed and carbonised too.

The Val Chiesa Battalion was on the offensive from the south, pushing the Russians to the north where the men from the Vestone Battalion were waiting and behind us came Signorini with what remained of our heavy pieces carried in sleds by ribbed mules. We could see the Vestone break the Russian line and rush the church. The machine-gun up in the tower tore them away in ranks, and they fell like children playing Ring a Ring o' Roses. The battle continued through the morning, and with the sunlight came faith as the Russians retreated into the ice and the woods beyond Malakeyevo, and it was past noon when slowly we made our way onto the icy streets. In the church, over two hundred Italian prisoners had been found. We freed them. And now we would abandon those too weak to leave. It made no difference—they'd have died anyway with the Russians, on the walk to the camps, on the way of the Davai.

Reverberi's order came via Radio Scarpa soon after we'd stumbled into that godforsaken town.

"Those who can, will," he said, and those who can't were to be left behind. We would continue our march, there would be no rest today. The sleds were full, there was no more time, and the injured were to be abandoned in the church with nothing but Don Gnocchi's blessing.

"We'll send for you when we get to the new lines," they were told, but no one believed it, the silent and much less those who begged to be taken, and as Don Gnocchi celebrated mass in that church, on his knees with his steel *gavetta* splayed up to the heavens, a boy kept shouting, "This is our funeral, this is our funeral."

We walked. Giulio carried Lago on his back and we walked through Malakeyevo alongside the frostbitten and the decayed, a train of refugees, and we were the strong, John, those who had survived this far were the strong and death did not take a man without a fight now, not these men, and when a man fell now, he would try to get a grip of a passing sled and those on the sled would kick and stab and hack at hands and arms and faces and those poor bastards would fight to cling on with scratching fingernails until they fell and watched their lives inch away, and when the stragglers would find them dead, they would strip them of anything useful, blankets for Giulio and me and Lago too, and we'd pass those dead naked creatures about to have their time with the beak, and their open-mouthed screams none of us would ever hear—not until we came home, John, because I hear them now, I hear those screams. But perhaps they're just echoes of mine, here, in this room tonight.

But we were the strong.

"Don't look left, don't look right, and don't ever look behind you," General Heidkamper told his men, Heidkamper, who'd taken over now that Eidl was dead of gangrene. "The only thing behind you is thousands of men whose lives depend on you defeating what is ahead." That's what Radio Scarpa reported, and for once I was sceptical because it'd long become clear the Germans saw us as nothing more than ideal cannon fodder for the Russian tanks.

There was a panic now, a panic induced by that merciless cold and endless ocean of ice and the menace of Moskalenko chasing us through the steppe, but we vagabonds of the snow, this convoy of cowards without weapons, with stolen valenkis and blankets tied to our naked feet with telegraph wires and rifles used as crutches shuffling into the lazy dawn of the steppe on that march to Romachovo, we would not die easy.

We learned that Heidkamper's radio had received a broken message from Gruppo Armato B, from the Italian 8th Army. Novij Oskel was in German hands, and the new axis line was secure. We were a hundred kilometres from the new lines, a two-day march. Between them and us, the Russians had amassed in a town named Nikolayevka.

Nikolayevka.

Beyond that there was nothing but the steppe, nothing but the steppe all the way to the new lines … and beyond that lay home. Italy.

It should, I suppose, have meant something more to us that perfect day in January when I fell on the snow in the morning sun and the world began to spin and I sensed the blood rush from out of me and heard it pop and fizzle in my ears. Giulio, trying to hold on to me with Lago on my back, fell with me, and the three of us lay on the snow like children playing at war. We lay there with Lago between us, his breath timid on my face, and above me was a deep blue sky, so fragile and clear and I said, "I can't anymore. *Non ce la faccio più*, Giulio."

"I understand," he said.

We lay there beneath that breakable sky and it felt like childhood, it felt like those winter days when we'd climb up the Summano, lying there in the snow making snow-fairies and then, exhausted with the dusk, we'd come down to the *birreria* on the road to Schio and gorge ourselves on grilled slices of polenta with the skin seared black by the grates and fat bratwurst with fried onions and fruit mustard in nights screaming with the cicadas, and as I lay there, I could almost touch that memory, I could taste the mustard, sweet and then tart on my tongue. And then suddenly Giulio was standing over me. I could see the sun halo over his head.

"You look like a fucking saint," I told him. "Like Jesus."

He laughed. "Come on," he held his gloved hand down at me, "up you get, *Alpino*."

"*Non ce la faccio più*," I told him. "This far and no more."

He knelt in the snow, and I glanced over and saw Lago lying there beside me. Was he still alive?

"Then go," Giulio said to me, reading my thoughts.

"We're not leaving him."

"Renzo, you're not cut out to be a hero, my friend. Go."

I never was cut out to be much of anything at all, but in Giulio's shadow, John, I was something more. "We go together," I told him.

"Together," said Giulio and laughed, "the three of us are going to hell." He touched Lago's face. "Sandro—how's it going?"

"Don't leave me," he whispered. "Not here."

Giulio took a handful of snow and placed it above those trembling lips and in his gloves the snow melted and dripped, and Lago's tongue licked at the water. Around us men shuffled past, hunchbacks of the snow cutting into the cold, and we were dead, John. We had stopped. We were the dead now, and the living never see the ghosts. We were invisible to them. And as the day wore on and the light turned into that soft blue hue of dusk, the stragglers became fewer and fewer, and we were soon to be left behind with the night and whatever was chasing us. Back here death came in a dozen ways, and all of it, I suppose, was the same in the end.

Giulio, sitting on the snow, pointed at the sky. "See that?" he said suddenly, and I realised I had fallen asleep and when I looked up into the horizon, it was night and there were wisps of lit green fingers scratching the sky like words we couldn't read.

"I never saw it before," whispered Lago and we both glanced down at him and then up at the spectral sky.

"Me neither," said Giulio. "You, Renzo?"

"No," I said. "I always thought it was just a myth."

My thermometer read -50C. It didn't go any lower than that. I couldn't feel my flesh except where the pain of frostbite jabbed and when I touched my face with my gloves, I could feel a long, septic bone that ran down from my nostrils to my chin.

"We have to move," said Giulio. He stood and helped me up with one hand. My legs would not hold me anymore. They shook like stalks. I reached down for Lago and felt the world spiral and when I saw Giulio again, it was from the ice, and the blackness of the sky behind his face made him seem one of those renaissance men in an old Dutch painting I'd once seen on a school outing to Vicenza.

"Don't leave me," I heard Lago say again and Giulio was staring down at us with tears of ice. "Not here."

"If we go on ahead, we can find a sled—" I said.

"Don't," Giulio interrupted, and the strength of his voice was like a slap. He was on his knees cradling Lago's head on his thigh. "Go," he said to me. I stood and shivered in the dark. Around us was nothing now—just the clawing night with not a figure in it. Nothing. The thought came to me suddenly, and I began reaching into my pockets until I found the syrettes in my jacket, and I showed them to Giulio, and he looked into my face and then grabbed them from my palm. He looked at Lago and something unspoken passed between them before Lago shut his eyes and I saw his body shiver. Giulio lifted his arm, and he looked up at me for some reason and I shut my eyes and when I looked again, I saw Giulio's arm stab the onetime injector into Lago's throat. Three others lay spent on the snow beside him, the snow freckled by pink blood.

Lago whispered and Giulio placed his ear near his lips to listen.

"Say nothing of me, Giulio, say nothing of today to anyone—"

Giulio cradled him closer, and I don't know when the morphine took Lago into his sleep. I lay down on the snow and watched as Giulio began stripping the blankets from him until that boy lay there, splayed out in only his uniform, and we watched the fleas explode from the corpse like a river.

And it was then that Giulio fell on his knees and genuflected and I did the same and I murmured a prayer under my breath, afraid even then to disappoint Giulio.

"Say it louder," he said to me, and he shut his eyes when I recited the Lord's prayer and I looked at Lago's face and he seemed so peaceful and when I finished, Giulio began neatening Lago's uniform, flattening a collar and doing up a brass button of his jacket and then he ran a hand through the boy's hair, his fingers deep in the lice until, seemingly satisfied, he stood and looked down at the corpse lying there on the snow for the longest time before he turned and walked away into the night.

I scrambled after him and never did look back.

Romachovo we reached in the dawn and found space in an izba: Giulio found us space. He walked into the izba and when three men tried to block him, he stepped to their pointed Berettas and placed their metal on his forehead and waited. When the men didn't shoot, he pushed past them with disdain, and we fell on our asses in a corner near the oven. It was Sunday.

That afternoon, while we waited for the order to resume our march, a small wooden shack went up in flames and Don Gnocchi brought those who'd been able to crawl out into our izba. We heard him praying for the burnt, screaming boys, and we prayed they would just die so that we could sleep and then when I couldn't take the screams any longer, I walked out into the dark streets and behind a brick building, I saw a fire and a group of men surrounding it. I could smell BBQ'd meat and when I came closer, salivating like a dog, I saw what they were eating in the crackling glow of the fires, and in their eyes, sparked to life by the orange light uncertain, was a yearning so repugnant that it stilled me and I could do nothing but watch bloodstained teeth ripping and tearing at the flesh, bodies furtive and bent like the Cocui. Suddenly I saw Godin squatting with those men and in his hands was a bone of gnawed flesh that he was picking clean with his head snapping back and forth, back and forth, ripping at the last sinews of meat and our eyes met and froze and he lowered the bone slowly from his mouth and I saw his razor smile made of teeth gleaming the blood that dribbled down his chin. The horror of it made me recoil and quickly I returned to the izba where I sat and shivered with my arms around my knees as the men kept screaming and it was before dawn that those screams finally stilled and Don Gnocchi fell on his knees and prayed over the corpses.

"How much he must cry," Giulio said to me when we left in the still, cold dark.

Dawn came with the crystal beauty of an alpine lake on the march to Nitikovka and in that blue-blue sky we saw scintillas of silver that morphed into three planes buzzing over us. We thought the strafing would begin, but these were German planes, circling lower and lower like eagles until they delivered their payloads, cylinders raining down on top of the remaining German tank and troops. The Germans, John, ran their own operation—we would see them in battle, efficient and ruthless, but no one was crazy enough to approach them. We existed for them in the abstract and if needs must, they would have had us all dead, and I watched as our rabble rushed for the cylinders like *scugnizzi*. The Germans fired a volley of warning shots in response, but the men kept coming until the Germans dropped ten, twenty men, and now the rabble were running away to a safe distance from where, like shunned stepchildren at Christmas, their hungry eyes watched the Germans carve open their presents. Swiss chocolate, John, the Germans had dropped Swiss chocolate for their men from the sky, and once they'd eaten them, the hunchbacks crawled on all fours and fought one another to get a chance to lick at the tinfoil the Germans had left behind, licking the garbage as if they were stamps for our postcards bound for Italy, our postcards that once we'd posted from the Don Front that were watermarked, *Never forget—this war was caused by Great Britain.*

Giulio laughed, watching the crawling men fight for the discarded trash. *"Boia chi molla,"* he said, and I couldn't but laugh too.

The tiny village of Nitikovka had been protected by a small band of partisans who'd been quickly swept up by the Germans now rushing on their Swiss chocolate sugar-high by the time we arrived. The izbas were all occupied by the Germans and our fighting battalions, and we had to keep walking out of town looking for shelter. Radio Scarpa had it that Reverberi and Heidkamper had come to blows some hours earlier when Heidkamper had wanted to push on, to keep marching for Nikolayevka, and Reverberi had insisted the men spend the night in Nitikovka.

"If we arrive at Nikolayevka in the night," Reverberi had apparently told his German colleague, "we'll not be able to attack—we'll die waiting for the sun. Tomorrow we leave, tomorrow we fight."

We sheltered that night in an old school a way out of town where someone had trapped a cat and skinned and boiled it in a pot of snow-melt and it tasted good, and in the night came the distant sounds of battle and by dawn, we learnt that the 49th, the 46th, and X Company Command had fought running hand-to-hand battles some miles behind us in a place called Arnautovo.

On the road out of Nitikovka the next morning, Russian lay upon Italian and German and Hungarian and Romanian—who knew anymore who was who, the dead all looked the same to us buried under mounds of fresh snow like potato sacks, and no one alive gave much of a damn either except maybe Don Gnocchi. They were just naked boys flash-frozen dead on the road, their legs amputated from the calf down for that was the softest flesh. We could see Russian recon planes come over us now, trailing steam in their wake. I don't know why—they knew, surely, where we were headed. We were headed to the place where the Russians had decided to annihilate us. Our graveyard. They'd toyed with us, debilitated us, and left us to stagger in the cold, hungry and mad, to the place they'd chosen as our tomb. Curiously, John, knowing for the first time since our retreat nine days before what would come at the end of this day was like a second wind for us.

We marched to battle.

And hope, there was hope and there was a serenity, I suppose, for we were to meet our appointment with destiny. A man can hope for little less than to know that on this day one lives or dies. Perhaps I'll feel the same when you lead me to the rope, John, that rope that so pleases your soul.

The ten-kilometre-long column marched over that ice following the last of Heidkamper's tanks shadowed by the fighting men of the 6th Battalion with their gleaming, oily Breda guns. There were maybe 1,500 men still armed, most at the head of the convoy, a few guarding the rear. And us hunchbacks of the column? I don't know, John, how many were still alive, those of us who'd made it that far. We were 250,000 when the Russians broke our lines in December, and I doubt there were more than 60,000 of us left that day when we dragged our corpses to the mince-factory that awaited us. Above us the Russian planes circled like the Cocui, watching us come. Waiting for us—this convoy of broken, starving refugees, hungry and frostbitten and carrying days' worth of shit and piss in our pants and gangrene that smelt ripe and rancid, rotting flesh that made us fear every waking moment when we warmed our skin by the fire and felt the pudding-like suppleness of our skin that wanted to slide off the bone like ossobuco.

Radio Scarpa was at its most precise on that march: what waited for us were hundreds of riflemen and snipers, hundreds of machine-guns, anti-tank canons, mortars, tanks, and the entirety of the 7th Cavalry Corps of Grigori Gocholov. Thousands of men. Mongols. Killers, John. Men who we'd learnt to fear because they fought not like us. We'd been marching for nine days, had fought ten battles, walked four-hundred kilometres in temperatures that never climbed above -40C, and now we realised what awaited us.

January 26th.

That day would end one of two ways: we smashed our way through Nikolayevka. Or we died.

*O si vive o si muore.*

Reverberi had told us this day would come.

*O la va, o la spacca.*

Nikolayevka. We reached it, Giulio and I, when the pale sun had just risen above the ice steppe, turning our world into a forlorn shade of cobalt.

The town lay squat within a stretched valley, an orderly industrial town splayed out below us beyond a stretched, naked hill. It extended back from a railway station on that iced valley floor between brick buildings and dignified streets, and it could just as well as have been home, John, for me and Giulio, those brick-walled izbas that fronted neat snow-covered roads, a town they say was named after Tsar Nikolas I, but really, it could just as well have been Schio.

We stood there and gazed down that yearning slope of ice and snow leading to Nikolayevka, a slope of the most delicate, untouched, virgin snow, fresh and gleaming in the gathering light, a kilometre and more of slope that fed down from the ridge on which we stood, and it was like an amphitheatre up there above Nikolayevka from where we could see inside the bowl of the town that the Russians had chosen as our burial ground.

They had chosen well this time. There was only one way we would breach it—through a narrow red-brick tunnel that burrowed beneath the fenced-off railway tracks. And between us and that tunnel was that kilometre-long hill without as much as a shrub to protect us. There was a little red house near the grey brick railway station over to the right of the tunnel, buried in a snow drift, and the town—the largest we'd seen since our retreat—was perfectly, beautifully silent in the dawn, a town of orange-glowing streets and black crows swarming the dead-limbed trees. And silence, that muted silence of the steppe.

"They were right," Giulio said, "when they told us all roads lead to Rome."

Two railway lines beyond the tall metal fence led from the railyard, one track south to Valuki, I guessed, the other north to who knew where—Moscow, Red Square, the North Pole? Up here on the hill where thousands of vagabonds now sat on the snow as if preparing for an outdoor movie, I couldn't take my eyes off the red-brick underpass with a mouth no wider than a splayed-out man that fed out to the streets of Nikolayevka. That was our only way in. And on the other side was Italy. Home. Above the tunnel stood a water tower and, beyond that, bulky brick warehouses with their windows all smashed, and we could see there, in the rising sun, a church steeple glint in the centre of town. The glow came across the valley slanted, gorged with shadow and dread and as I sat on the hill and watched Reverberi and Signorini and Heidkamper stand behind the last of the German tanks sharing cigarettes over a splayed-out map, it was clear why the Russians had chosen this place for us.

Giulio, perhaps thinking the same, looked at me and I saw that smile in his eyes.

Men kept on coming, the stragglers and the hunchbacks and the sleds and the injured and the congealed and the mules hauling whatever was left of our heavy metal pieces, and the men who could hardly even stand anymore, could not even be called men anymore, sluggishly crested the brow of the hill to collapse there on the bowl above Nikolayevka.

John, do you believe in premonition? That day, when I gazed down that hill, it was as if a million eyes were staring back at me, and I sensed then that this was to be our tomb. I kept looking at that church with its steeple and onion-like cupola and tall belltower of red brick, and about it those handsome buildings of a town that must once have taken pride in itself, and the people, I suppose, who'd once walked those streets on a Sunday morning with their friends and their families as once we'd walked the streets of Schio, and I felt an overwhelming sense of loss.

Nothing stirred but the crows, flying silent. It was like a still-life and in the foreground of that photo was Reverberi. There was no one left but him to lead us now. And I wondered then whether he'd be able to lead his men into battle—not to survive but to attack and to die for a cause more than themselves. I couldn't help wondering if that little man there, that good-looking man with the easy sunshine smile, had the soul to lead us to our deaths.

The Russians waited patiently for us to assemble on that hill through the morning. They too were actors on this stage, and they waited until the audience was all present and the sun was up in the sky and then, at a time of their choosing, at this place of their choosing, at around eleven in the morning, with thousands of us gazing into the veiled eyes of Nikolayevka from atop the hill, they detonated our world.

Katushas and artillery, missiles and mortars from dozens and dozens of positions suddenly cooked the horizon, a tremor of hell, and the missiles could hardly miss. Exposed on the top of a hill were thousands of men and I don't think we even moved. I know I didn't. We just covered our heads and lay where we were and let the bombs fall where they would. It was pointless moving, exhausting to move. And where to? The blasts were like a golem rising from an earth bloated like an organ. and it was in God's hands now who would live and who would die, and as I was pressed to the snow, I saw a mortar land not twenty meters from me, hitting a sled full of injured men and I could see parts of them, pieces of their bodies fully formed cartwheel into the air spraying a blood-works show, and I felt that wave of bone and meat rip into my face like shrapnel and the air was concussed with the reverberation of some inhuman power that knocked me ten metres back and made the sky quake.

I sat up dazed. I must have blacked out for now there were men running down the virgin hill, about two hundred men sprinting down that hill toward the railway tracks and the underpass as our artillery, that had fought through the rabble, was now returning what little fire we had left to somehow give those poor bastards some cover, and that's when the machine-guns opened up from the railway station and the water tower and the warehouses and the little red house.

Those men who first carved a path down that hill ran like rabbits in knee-high snow, and they were razed. They were razed, John. Did I imagine it then, the screams? I remember that hill now, and I think, how can I have heard their screams so far from me? And yet I could hear their screams, those men lying on the snow now crimson with their blood, men still crawling, men dead in mid-stride, and one man, John, one man somehow just kept running toward the mouth of the underpass, and he seemed so far from us, as if he existed in a dream, one man zig-zagging down that white-white hill with the sun at his shoulders chasing his shadow as the whole of Russia seemed to be shooting at him until he was right before the tiny brick underpass. And it felt like a victory until we saw him lift as if hit by some invisible, divine force, and a second later his entire body was shredded away to ripple across the snow like rain.

I could hear Reverberi shouting, I think it was him, I'm not sure now, because the detonations had rendered me deaf, but it was time for more men, more men to make that run, to run to their slaughter in the tracks of those who had died before. Waiting for them was an entire division of Russians with unlimited ammunition, protected by a dominant position, and those of us who didn't make that run into their bullets would surely just die up here with the coming night. An army reduced to nothing but rabble, hungry and broken, unarmed, afraid, attacking in the open, disorganised, and behind us nothing but nine days' worth of the Davai, the march into -40C of ice and snow and hunger and the trail of our discarded dead. And Moskalenko, coming for us.

And before us, this place, this town—this death.

Men from the Val Chiesa and Tirona Battalions stood on the hill now like downhill skiers standing four metres apart one from the other, and there was Don Gnocchi blessing them as if they were about to storm out of the trench and the men genuflected and mouthed silent prayers and then they ran, screaming *"Oooooora! Savoia!"* and down that hill they tumbled like children and then came the fire of the 33rd Battery of the Bergamo behind us with their 75/13s and suddenly what remained of the Vicenza Battalion was running down the hill too, and the Val Camonica behind them and on the left was 255 Company, on the right the 6th with the XXX Grenadiers pouring down the hill toward the red-brick underpass with the cannons covering their flight.

And the machine-gun needle in the little red house just killed and killed and killed.

How many men died that day, John, how many men were taken by those sons of bitches manning that machine-gun in that red house. The natural protection of the railroad proved a perfect defensive structure behind which the Russians pounded us with everything they had as our men ran and died. They died so easily. I'd always imagined death to be something else: but they died so easily. A dozen, maybe more, made it down to the underpass, and they formed at the mouth of the tunnel, squeezed up against the brick, and sheltered for just a moment. Behind them was a carpet of corpses and that hill was crimson now.

A man I recognised as Ferroni—a neighbour of my uncle, from out near Torrebelvicino—and his platoon of machine gunners had managed to burrow beneath the metal fence protecting the railroad and they were now rushing for the station, running hard, crouched, and backed by a man named Baccarin and his platoon. Baccarin, who'd sold milk to our family, I knew him well, I'd fallen in love with his sister for two weeks in the winter of '39. And as they managed to get through, three men set up their 45/5 Brixia assault mortars and pounded the railway station and the water tank that suddenly began to sag and topple and fall.

Captain Zani used that moment to lead his men from the 6$^{th}$ through the underpass and I watched as the men popped out of the tunnel on the other side and sprinted onto the main street, a sizable road flanked by tall plane trees. The Russians appeared like ghosts from the izbas, and the fighting, that close, was man to man, muskets and bayonets and knives and suddenly Zani had a sword glinting in his fist and it was like theatre from up on the hill, John, it was like theatre, and Zani was our hero, he fought as if possessed and as he fought, Ferroni managed to get into the station itself, a brick building whose windows had no panes, and Baccanin was there with him now and they cleared out the station and set-up two big Breda guns in the windows and then came the thud-thud-thud that kept the Russians back as Zani and the 6$^{th}$ kept moving deeper into the town.

It was like that movie, *The Siege of Alcazar.*

The Russians turned their attention to the station now, crucial to their defence, and they began to attack it with force as Ferroni and his men kept firing from the windows. And then suddenly the Breda guns fell silent. Out of ammo, and we could see the Russians approach cautiously as back in the town, Zani was now trapped because he'd somehow managed to run his men right past the first line of Russian defence, and we watched him slow and turn as he realised he was surrounded and trapped, and now he began to fight his way *back* the way he came as the machine-gun-nest up in the piazza pinned him down behind a warehouse with his twenty, thirty men spread about him, and that's when one of his men rushed a machine-gun-needle that lay in their path behind sand-bags on the street, he rushed it on his own, drawing its fire as Zani and his men sprinted back toward the underpass.

Eros De Ros.

Who knows who he was, John, but I heard it clear, voices behind me shouting, "Eros De Ros!" Eros De Ros attacked that machine-gun-nest on his own with a grenade and was shredded a long time before he got anywhere near it. Eros De Ros, suicide bomber and dead before his grenade detonated in his cold, dead hand, but it was enough to get Zani and his men back beyond the anti-tank barricade near the tunnel, and he was now outside an izba fighting at the door with his sword, Zani, kicking and knifing and then above us we heard and then saw three MiGs cut out from the sky, and they boomed just above the ice and strafed us where we sat, ripping the column into strips of thick-boned meat. Snow and pieces of ice and shrapnel and bone, and it was impossible to do anything, to make sense of anything, the noise was just a scream made of a thousand deaths as the Germans opened fire on the planes that fled up into the blue sky and when next I looked, Ferroni in the railway station was down to a stolen Russian parabellum and his men down to their sidearms as the Russians finally broke back into the station and we saw Ferroni fall halfway out of the window dead and Baccarin was hit on his way out.

And then the strangest thing, John: One man, alone, running through the underpass and heading *up* the hill. They told me later it was Chieri, Zani's *portavoce*, and he managed to get up the hill to Reverberi and we heard him shout, "Ammunition! *Dio bono*, we need fucking ammo!"

Reverberi called for ammo to be brought up in sacks and put onto mules. Four metres apart, the mules, with one man ahead of each, were prodded down the hill, four mules who understood nothing of our world until a mortar hit them square and there was nothing left of the mules or the ammo or the men. I wonder now if Zani and his men looked up at us, the shamed there on the ridge, and what they thought of our cowardice. He was down to a dozen men, not even his own anymore, just fighting men who'd somehow got through the underpass now out of ammo but still fighting with seized Russian parabellums as they went, and a grenade exploded right in front of Zani and he fell backward in a dust-spray of pink, and rolled back into an izba, and the Russians were hunting now, they were hunting and we were soon to be swallowed up.

The men were trapped in that izba for what seemed hours and the Russians in their white uniforms began to throw grenades into it and we saw the flashes long before we heard the explosions, and then the ghosts went in, one after the other, dozens of them and it was that exact moment that I smelt it. It took a second to fully appreciate what the scent was, my nostrils flaring.

Cabbage.

I glanced at Giulio. He too had smelt it. We looked about us and there on the ridge of the hill, the Germans had fired up their field kitchen. Soup, John. They'd cooked themselves a massive pot of fucking cabbage soup. It took about ten minutes before a missile hit the kitchen and the pots went up with the chefs and we all cheered until two MiGs come streaking out of the sky, turned, and came over us again, strafing the column and our flesh soon blended with the slop of cabbage soup on the ice as the German anti-aircraft gun opened up, prepared this time, and the MiGs boosted their altitude, their engine growl like the screams they'd left behind, one trailing a long cloud of oily smoke.

When I looked back, I saw Zani was somehow still standing, injured but fighting his way *out* of the izba and firing into the street and just then I was knocked off my feet by men barging past me leading with fists and elbows.

Dozens of men with ramrod-straight backs hustled through the hunchbacks, tall and proud and following in the bootsteps of Colonel Adami, that legendary warrior from the glory days in Albania and East Africa. We watched him muscle his way through us with the disgust combatants always have for cowards in battle. Colonel Adami and his two-hundred-or-so men who'd fought in Arnautovo for twenty hours through the night and who we'd all given up as dead. I watched him march his men down to Reverberi and I could see he was injured, Adami, a big imposing man with a bandage over his head bloody and torn, and he seemed exhausted as he came to stand beside Reverberi and saluted before the two took turns with the field glasses to gaze into the killing streets of Nikolayevka.

More men were barging their way between us now—Major Maccagno and Lieutenant Piatti with the men of 48 Company, all of them fresh from their escape out of Arnautovo. There were about three hundred men standing there with Reverberi behind the German tank now, while down on the streets, Zani and his men were being hunted and killed. The sky was darkening, that short twilight of the steppe, and I began to think about what being a POW would mean, out here, and it meant certain death as it would be for most of those who were captured in the nine days of our retreat.

On that hill, spaced four metres apart, these warriors, these men stood waiting, and Don Gnocchi was beside them now, shouting, "God walks with you!" and those men were immune, it seemed to me, to fear, veterans who'd long since made peace with their mortality. They waited for the order and, when it came, when Adami shouted, *"Avanti!"*, they fell toward the underpass, four, five hundred men streaming behind Adami, and the machine-gun in the little red house wiped their lives away as if they were nothing at all, and not even fifty got down to the brick underpass as Reverberi dropped his field glasses onto the tank and peeked at his watch and up at the darkening sky and I knew, all of us knew then—we either broke through now or we were standing on our own graves.

Radio Scarpa had been reporting all day that General Moskalenko was coming. Moskalenko was coming with his army, thousands of men, Mongols, killers, and if we failed to break through now, we would be dead by the dawn and Moskalenko would have little to do but burn whatever the Cocui left behind up here on the hill above Nikolayevka.

It was then that I saw it, glinting in the sky bruised by menace, a tiny silver plane floating in the fading light and gliding toward us like a silent angel. We expected it to turn, to dive and strafe us, but I could hear men shouting, "It's an Italian plane!" and now I could see it clearly, a tiny two-seater, single-engined *cicogna*, a tailless motor glider circling like a swallow, delicate as the fragile air and somehow immune to the mortars that came flying in, immune to everything in the world as it glided in low and touched down with such precision on its two skis that it hardly even raised a snowflake, and now the wooden contraption with the cockpit under the flimsiest of wings was sliding with a meticulousness that was almost otherworldly, sliding toward us along the crimson ice ridge to come to rest not ten metres from the German tank and General Reverberi.

The door to the cabin was kicked open and out the pilot jumped onto the snow. He wore leather shoes, racing-driver shoes, small little shoes on small little feet and a time-worn leather jacket with a fur collar and green combat pants. He lifted his goggles when he hit the ground, looking down surprised and disgusted as half his legs vanished beneath the snow. Then he shifted the goggles over his forehead and trudged resentfully through the snow toward Reverberi. The pilot saluted and from his pocket handed Reverberi a chocolate bar. The men there behind the tank began to speak, Heidkamper, Reverberi, and Signorini, and the pilot was pointing behind him at the plane. It was obvious what he wanted—he was there to take Reverberi out. Reverberi and the pilot spoke for four, five minutes, surveying a map together with the man pointing at it, and then the discussion was over and the man saluted—stock-up straight he saluted—and trudged back toward the plane, and I doubt he was even aware of the thousands of men who watched him walk by, thousands of men on the bowl that led to the slaughter factory that was Nikolayevka. To him, I suppose, we were just the forgotten grey tombstones in a graveyard of a foreign land, and we watched him climb back into the cockpit and a moment later, effortlessly, his little sliver contraption picked up speed and he was off, lifting up and away.

Looking back now, John, I am convinced the battle stopped for that strange little man. And whatever it was that he'd said, it left Reverberi staring down into Nikolayevka and then up at the sky with an intensity I could perceive even at a distance, and I sensed he'd reached a decision then as the *cicogna* vanished west into the falling sun.

Edolo. The Edolo Battalion—the words came from those around me—*the Edolo is coming!* They were two kilometres behind us, they were coming from Arnautovo, they were fighting their way through the column, they were coming, Major Belotti and the Edolo!

And then suddenly they were there, Major Belotti and behind him six hundred or so men who seemed like fighters from another army, another world, elbowing the hunchbacks out of the way. Men from the Edolo Battalion and men from battalions whose leaders had long-since been killed, but those men, John, there was no mistaking their intent as they marched through the horde like movie stars marked for death. They stood silently, a phalanx of power, and waited for Reverberi and Belotti to shake hands and speak for what seemed less than a minute. Then one of Belotti's men rushed up and called for whatever was left of our big pieces to be brought out into the firing line as Belotti assembled his men.

On the right, the 51 Company of Captain Barsani, on the left the 50 Company of *Sottotenete* Poli, and as they prepared for the run down the hill, the men of the 6th under Zani were falling back toward the underpass where three or four dozen men were trying and failing to get through to rescue them, pinned by the snipers in the station and the machine-guns from the little red house.

We'd understood he'd died in Arnautovo, he'd died fighting with the Edolo, died on the march days ago, died leading his men out of Arnautovo.

And yet here he was, riding in on the back of a sled with three men pulling him through the rabble, and I heard Giulio say, "It's fucking Santa," and together the rabble stared at the small man who clambered out of the sled to tread down to General Reverberi with his coat spread like a cape behind him.

*General Martinat.*

General Martinat carrying nothing in his hands but an 1891 musket. General Martinat, the warrior who'd conquered Libya with the Edolo as a young man in 1911, Martinat who'd conquered Ethiopia in 1939 and led the conquest of Albania, Martinat, once chief of staff of the 3rd Alpine Division Julia, our Division, John, General Martinat, who'd led the second column to Arnautovo where he'd fought with whatever was left of his men for twenty hours straight, General Martinat! That name echoed around us as he came to stand before Reverberi, and the two men embraced as if they'd met after many years on a *passegiatta* down the via Veneto on a Sunday afternoon. Martinat looked over at Belotti and his men spread on the hill waiting to run, and I heard him speak then, General Martinat, heard his words so clearly.

"With the Edolo I started. And no man can be prouder to lead the Edolo today. Come on, men! Beyond the underpass is Italy."

"*Avanti Savoia!*" the men shouted, their voices like an explosion. "*Avanti Savoia!*"

And with that, Martinat, Belotti, and the fighting men of the Edolo made the run to their death with the grace of God bestowed upon them by Don Gnocchi.

"*Avanti che siete Alpini!*"

Martinat led the charge down the hill as his men ran and died beside him. Martinet himself was almost at the underpass with nothing but his musket when I saw him fall back. Fall back and then he was up, up but wounded, I could see him flopping around on his feet but he was shouting still, his arm waving his men forward as they poured on beyond him, and then he stumbled two, three paces and fell to his knees, dead before he even hit the ice face-first, and I heard Giulio laugh beside me.

But the Edolo was an unstoppable tide and the Russians bent back from the underpass for the first time, and as they fell back, the men from the Edolo rushed through with the 253 and 254 fanning across the streets headed toward Zani's trapped men as the machine-gun-needle near the station was taken out by a hastily assembled Breda *pesante*. On the snow down to Nikolayevka lay thousands of men, dead like rocks in a frozen river in the Pasubio, half a body, half a leg, valenki boots and nothing left of the man, the blood congealed into stone-like crystals as the sun shrivelled up into a red orb to the west. I imagined what it must have been like, this day ending in Italy, our mothers and our friends staring at that same sun and what did they think—did they have a presentiment that we were all about to die?

From the church a machine-gun was firing, and the mortars were coming in now too. The Russian reserves were in play, and I thought, for them it's just the next phased act in our defeat. They'd sucked our men in and now they would finish them off, the bravest of us, the best of us, for we were all in then, all of our fighting men were down there, sucked into the streets and once they were gone, once the Apaches were killed, the Russians would just walk up that hill and that would be that. Surrender and die, fight and die, it wouldn't matter.

A boy I'd known, a classmate from elementary school named Orzali, who'd been conscripted into the Bergamo artillery that'd long-since run out of ammo, turned to his men—he stood right next to me and I hadn't even recognised him under his face-scarf until his voice, calm as I always remembered it, calm and gentle—and said, "I'm going down, guys. Whoever feels like it, come with me." I listened to his words and watched the men of the Bergamo group around him—radio operators, telegraphists, medics, officers without units, men without units—rouse like lice and begin to walk down toward the hilltop. Like skiers, four metres apart, they began their suicide run down the hill on that hard-packed blood-road that'd been built by the footsteps of the dead. Three made it. The rest were dead before they reached the underpass, including Orzali, who was the first to die. What a strange thing, John, to see a man you once knew as a boy destroyed in front of you like that. He lay not five metres from General Martinat in that pasture of death.

It was then that Reverberi abandoned the shield of the tank.

He'd looked up at the coming night and down at that tomb of corpses on the hill, and then he'd turned from the tank and the fighting, turned and sluggishly trudged up the hill toward us as if Orzali's strange sacrifice had made his mind up.

He strolled toward us, Reverberi, with sick eyes observing the hunchbacks on the lip of the bowl that fed into the meat-grinder that was Nikolayevka, and he was such a fine-looking man, I could see his dimples when he unwrapped a scarf from his face, and then he took his fur hat off and his hair was silver and aglow in the glowing dusk.

Behind him, the Edolo had reached the Russian second line, and were being forced back, back toward the underpass. The Russian positions were too varied, too many. We would not break through. I watched Reverberi stand before us, naked of face, and it felt as if he were staring at me, as if God were judging me through the eyes of this man. Moskalenko coming with his tanks and the night coming with its fatal inevitability, there was nothing to it now. We surrendered. We died. *Eja, eja, alalà.*

I watched Reverberi's lips speak, but it was as if he was in a badly synched movie, and it took a moment for his words to drift up to us.

"Over there is Italy," he said, and he showed us the sunset with his hand, there beyond Nikolayevka. *"Di la c'e l'Italia,"* he repeated. And then he said it again, louder. *"Di la c'e l'Italia."* The horde was silent. Reverberi looked up at us with his face pink in the glow, looked at the hunchbacks and the crippled and the worn and the weak, the cowards and the frozen and the scared, he stood there naked-headed and spoke to all of us, thousands of men he knew to be wretched fucking cowards, he stood there as the battle edged into the night and then abruptly he turned his back on us to gaze at the setting sun and said it again, and it sounded almost like regret. *"Di la c'e l'Italia."*

And then he abandoned us, his heavy legs taking him down to the last German tank. He barked an order, and the tank kicked into life with a puff of diesel smoke.

I turned to Giulio. He looked down at Reverberi.

"He's wasted on us," he said to me.

Reverberi took his pistol from his leather holster and held it up like Tom Mix, the dying light glinting off the metal. He climbed onto the top of the armoured vehicle and, standing on it, pounded down with one boot. The machine stumbled forward almost reluctantly. Standing on the tank, Reverberi turned his back to Nikolayevka and faced us. The tank was rolling down the hill now, and Reverberi, his legs splayed apart, pistol pointing at the sky, stared back at us and we could hear him bellow, *"Avanti, Tridentina, avanti che l'Italia è lì, l'Italia è lì! Avanti che siete Alpini!"*

Alone amidst the falling missiles and mortar shells that blasted about him, his body a crimson-fringed flaming silhouette there on the tank, Reverberi bobbled down the hill with his arm waving us forward, and Giulio was laughing when he said, "What a fucking comedy."

But men had begun to stir like lice. Unarmed and exhausted, they began lumbering forward toward the tank as if magnetised by Reverberi and his flaying arm. And then I heard voices all around me, dozens of voices, weak and broken, shouting, *"Cosi, avanti, come siete, come siete!*—as you are, forward as you are!" And the men, John, the genuflecting men about me began to mass on the lip of the hill and we could hear them shout *"avanti, avanti"* and Giulio and I were being pressed forward by the mass and then beside me a German was shouting, *"avanti, Italiener, avanti!"* and I looked at Reverberi standing on his tank and rolling down the hill and punching the air with the pistol as the artillery burst about him and suddenly men began to chase him, men with dysentery whose trousers were frozen pipes of shit like concrete, men hobbling and falling and crawling and the sleds full of the injured rushing down that hill and Giulio grabbed my arm, and I looked at him through my tears and he smiled and gripped my arm tighter and drew me forward as if we were about to plunge into a frozen Alpine lake in the spring, he and I, as once we were, with that smile of his telling me it's going to be okay, and we were running down that hill now, a wave of broken men, ten, twenty thousand men and more following Reverberi and his tank spewing that whisper of blue diesel, Reverberi, who could have abandoned us and instead chose to confront his soul and our destiny on that tank scuttling toward the underpass as the artillery shells landed about him in blasts of white ice, and we were an avalanche, a mudslide of shit and shattered men pouring down toward the underpass and the railway line carrying nothing with us but our terror, and Don Gnocchi too was running and I don't know how many of us ran down that hill, we were a punishing wave of stinking cowards and we swallowed the world, and you knew how close you were to the valley floor, in amongst those countless shouting men, just by the sounds because up above the thud was of mortars and cannons and the lower down you ran, it was the hammer of machine-gun fire from the church and the station and the little red house, and as we ran through the bombs and the bullets we shouted as one, a human herd, and I remember ahead of us a priest stumbling, falling, and a man trying to help him up and the priest shouting, "Leave me, leave me and tell me mother I died a soldier," and Hungarians and Romanians and Germans and Italians, we were the herd that had scavenged on one another for nine days and now we were a mudslide of filth that rushed through the dark and swept over a blanket made of our dead and through that underpass and charged the machine-gunners and the mortar positions and we killed with our bare hands, unrelenting like shit through the sewer of Nikolayevka, and I kept running for the piazza and the church and up those stairs and finally the machine-gun up in that tower that'd killed so many fell silent as the Russians were ripped to pieces and then the little red house went up from grenades and the bells tell me, John, that it's 5AM.

Are the voices outside your men? So early? So eager.

The Russians couldn't, in the end, kill us all. They held their positions because they were brave and better men than us but they could not shoot us all and they fled that avalanche of putrid men disorderly and desperate and left their weapons on the streets and their food in the izbas and I found myself in the church that night—Giulio I had lost in the rush—and ate Russian cabbage soup and, in the silence and the wood-smoke, huddled in my blanket, I saw a man shot through the throat and I remember he was trying to eat that Russian soup and someone said to him, "Don't worry, if the food doesn't fall out, you'll be fine."

The injured were carried into the church, spread on blankets on the frozen bare-wood floor, and when there was no more space, they were carried up to the attic where the Russian machine-guns sat silent, and from up there, the blood trickled and dripped.

We left Nikolayevka before sunrise, those who could still move, and the injured we left for God and Moskalenko. We left as men, John, and only God could help those we left behind, only God and Don Gnocchi who blessed them all before leaving them to their fate.

I can't help thinking that those who were too afraid to fight, they walked out of Nikolayevka as heroes while the brave, the men who'd sacrificed everything for us, we left them for Moskalenko and the Cocui. But isn't that life, John? Isn't that the way of it?

For those who could still walk, our march endured ever westward, driven by the dawn at our backs and following our shadows toward Italy waiting for us beyond the wasteland, there as a promise just one step beyond the next within our shadows stretched. In the cold we marched, drunk after ten days and nights, drunk from pain and war and disease and mad from the lice feeding on our seeping wounds, men dragging sleds of broken men crippled by frostbite and gangrene, those bone-like icicles distended from mouths and nostrils, eyes sealed by frozen lids, and we had no idea how far we were to march. I suppose we'd expected something different to happen after Nikolayevka, some great reckoning, but to stop was to die, and so we walked anyway, and the dead in the sleds were thrown out one by one and the dying tried to cling on and were beaten and shot and stabbed and the Germans were fed by planes that dropped cylinders of chocolate for which we knew better than to beg, and I remember one man, sitting on the snow as the column slowly marched by him, saying, "Have a good trip, have a good trip now, don't stop walking," and I didn't stop, no one in that column stopped unless they fell and died and what mules remained—those skeleton mules—died soon after Nikolayevka.

We marched through snow and bleached meadows where we could see the ice clinging and glittering to the peaks of the frozen sunflower stalks like worms, and I don't know how far we walked that first day out of Nikolayevka with the Cocui circling overhead, those black-winged scavengers, but when night came, we arrived in a village near Upsenka and it was there that I found Giulio, beautiful Giulio who'd waited for me on the road into the village and in his hands was honey and milk that he'd saved for me.

"It's a long way to Portofino," he said when I shuffled by without even recognising him.

Radio Scarpa told us we were in a race now, that Russian troops were headed for Budenny, somewhere to the west. We had to continue to move, to march because Moskalenko's men were coming for us, Moskalenko's tanks. Moskalenko. The name had taken on a life of its own. Do you have a boogie man in America, John? Moskalenko was ours then. We spent less than four hours in the Upsenka. At 2AM we heard men shouting—"*Forza, move!*"—and we drifted from the izbas like dogs in the summer heat in the hope, I suppose, that something other than *this* was to happen that day.

In the dawn, in the waist-deep snow, came the shouts from men up ahead. We'd reached the *Armeestrasse*, the German-built snow-swept road that'd taken us to the Don in the summer through those vast plains of sunflowers, and on the bridge to Kosizino, an armed German vehicle stood watch. The word spread quickly, we'd been too slow, and Moskalenko had beaten us to Novij Oskol at the end of the road. We had to turn back, turn back and head southwest. Above us a small *cicogna* appeared around noon, and it began to guide us through the steppe, to Bessorab where we rested for an hour before marching on, and it was Saturday, January 30$^{th}$, just gone dawn, when we'd been marching out of Bessorab for five hours, that we saw it.

On a hill before us, a lone armoured vehicle stood silhouetted against the sky. And as we drew closer, we could see a man standing on the vehicle.

It was General Nasci, commander of the Alpini Corps.

We had reached our new lines.

Giulio and I climbed the hill. Behind Nasci stood hundreds of camions and men who seemed never to have skipped a meal in their lives, happy, healthy faces smoking their Tre Stelle cigarettes. In their eyes I saw reflected the horror of what we'd been reduced to. They stared at us wide-eyed and repulsed and, I thought then, offended somehow, offended by what we'd become and perhaps disquieted too by a vision of their own destiny. The injured were loaded onto the camions, and the rest of us were told to keep walking. But we had a road to walk on now, and it was only half-a-day's march to Sebekino where we were deloused, washed, and given food.

Food. Not too much, we were warned, but milk and honey and pasta—cooked, warm pasta and bread aplenty—it wasn't a bad death for the men who died there that day of gluttony. At Sebakino, men searched for friends and family, but like new clothes—which, we were told, remained in Voltshank because no one would authorise their release—they were impossible to find. So many had died. So many that Signorini, we were told, had died too, had died of a heart attack when he'd stood on that hill with General Nasci through the night waiting for the tens of thousands of his men who never came, who would never come home, who we'd left there for the Cocui on the steppe.

Those of us who had frostbite were loaded onto trains and sent to Kraków in hospital trains. Giulio and I were on *Treno Ospedale $^{#}3$*, he on the bunk above me, and I could smell the gangrene from his black rotting feet like potatoes left on a summer field. It was on that train that Radio Scarpa reported the end of General Paulus: he had surrendered whatever was left of his army in Stalingrad. The army whose flank we had come to protect in the summer was no more either. It was over.

The hospital was a red-brick building on the outskirts of Kraków, a cumbersome pile of brick and indented windows near the railway lines with football field-long wards and field-beds separated inches one from the other. It reminded me of the Lanerossi factory.

In the end, a factory is exactly what it proved to be: we called it the amputation factory.

I spent weeks there, John, and every day the surgeons, led by a German man, a Dr Magneven, would take the men crowded in those wards and cut and hack and sever flesh and bone and limbs and feet and toes and fingers and arms and ears and noses, and then they'd come back and cut more from you, and there was a ditch that'd been dug out beyond the building, a dump that kept swelling and smouldered from the warm aborted flesh that the orderlies would wheel away every night in wheelbarrows, the amputated bits of us that they'd dump in there for the rats that waited their feed.

I remember Giulio and I sitting on chairs in the late evening on the metal-trellis terrace that stretched around the ward to get away from the stink and the screams, and we'd watch the orderlies roll their wheelbarrows of limbs to the ditch and he saying to me, "There's our *Gioventù Italiana del Littorio.*"

"*Libro e moschetto, fascista perfetto,*" I quoted from those long lectures I learnt in this very place where I write this now, John, and Giulio and I laughed because we knew then it was over. Whatever happened after this, it was over. We'd lost the war and Italy's youth, the best of us, had been discarded in the ice of the steppe and the rest of us, we were here getting sliced and diced in the kitchen of Duce's fantasy. It was over.

Giulio left in mid-February. He had frostbite on his feet, but amputation had not been needed, and he was off back to Italy on the train that left from Kraków every two days. He sat with me on the terrace the morning of his departure with a canvas bag at his rotten feet, and we smoked and stared out at the sky that seemed so close I could pierce that greyness with my fingers. I missed Italy more than I had on the steppe, the eternal greyness of Kraków so dense about us, the fog damp like the bandage on my groin, seeping and oozing a sorrow that seemed never to clear.

"I'll see you in Schio," he said.

"Will you tell her?"

"Who?"

"Lago. His mother."

"No." Giulio's reply was immediate, and I realised that he too had thought about it as I had.

Who knows whether he was right—whether we were right? But that was Lago's wish, and I would not go against it. "Will you say hullo, when you see me back in Schio?" I asked when Giulio had flipped his cigarette over the railing and placed his arms around me.

"I'll say hullo," he said, and I hugged him while sitting on my chair. "But first I'm going to smash it all up. This rot. It all needs to be buried. It's like weeds—you need to burn it."

"What do you know about weeds?" I asked.

He laughed. "Not a fucking thing, Renzo, but you gotta burn it anyway, and you gotta teach your kids to burn it too."

"Kids, Giulio?"

He touched my face tenderly.

"Haven't you had enough?" I asked him.

"I've seen too much to ever have enough now," he replied.

I watched him leave that day, at around noon, walking with a dozen other men in the same clothes in which they'd arrived, stinking refugees on their way home, but at least they'd deloused the uniforms, and I watched him walk out onto the long icy road that led around the smouldering pit where he hesitated and glanced back at the hospital. I will never know if he saw me, but he lifted an arm and I waved at him and then he turned and walked toward the railway station.

I sat there for a longest time thinking of home.

It was in late March when I too was sent home on a train whose blinds were sealed shut before we crossed the Brennero. We came home not as heroes. We came home as vermin, and up in Trento, a group of soldiers boarded the train and I remember one saying, "Jesus Christ, you people *stink*, you're a fucking disgrace," and we threw our scraps of food at him until he left, locking the doors to our carriages.

A fucking disgrace. I suppose he had a point. There's nothing more useless than a defeated army because it's like a disease, and our disease was shame, and shame is a contagion. Late in the night we arrived in Vicenza and there was no one to welcome us on the dingy platform. We came home like secrets, and from Vicenza I walked into the dawn, to Schio, to my mother and my sisters and our farm and a spring so unbearably alive. They fussed over me, my sisters and mother, but they had little to offer aside from love expressed as sheltered whispers as if I'd lost my mind along with my health. Our farm lay in ruins that spring, my father long buried from the fever and me unable to work, and there was little we could do but suffer the hunger and listen to the wireless that reported on the Allies' slow march north, always north toward us.

The coming freedom, John. That was your promise.

And Luisa? You asked once of Luisa. Do you want to know? I won't tell you how I felt that rotten day in early April when we met outside the Lanerossi factory, and she looked at me with such pity in her crying eyes. When she hugged me and I felt the diffidence of her arms and saw the coldness in her eyes from the things that had happened to her, John, the things that had happened to her in the winter, I understood it was finished between us, and I left her that day at the factory gates knowing I had lost my one and only chance at love. But then I suppose your men have already told you, haven't they, John? Your men who shook with laughter when their probing cigarettes found nothing much left to destroy.

In May, with the sunflowers a scarred reminder of all that I wanted to forget, I travelled down to Schio, to the Rialta factory in Val Leogra. They had, I'd been told, secured a German contract and were now hiring. I remember waiting outside an office for hours along with two, three dozen other men, caps in hand, standing like peasants out there while German supervisors—strangely polite—walked around us and even offered us beer. It's a strange thing, the way the sun slanted through the windows of the factory in the silence up there where the offices were, cut-glass rays of dust-flecked light, shafts that a man could almost cut and eat like biscuits—but perhaps that was my hunger, because it was late in the afternoon when finally I was summoned toward the door of the recruiter's office by a woman who said her name was Puccini. I hadn't eaten since the night before, and my hunger was making me dizzy. So much hunger, John, always hunger.

I fought against the dizzy spell and walked through a frosted-plate door into an office where the day fell in five distinct shafts over a desk behind which a man sat in a starburst of dust and deep shadow.

I recognised him immediately, of course.

"So you made it back," he said. I said not a word, standing there before him. "I got back in February," he said. "Disabled out of the army. No bad thing."

"For the army?" I asked.

"For everyone involved," he replied, his green eyes studying me as I stood before his desk. There were no chairs there except for his, Godin's, who leaned back on it with legs splayed and hands cupped behind his head and perused me for a while as if I were a whore. "All things considered," he said eventually, "you don't look that bad. I'm told Giulio's back and up to his usual shit, too."

I shrugged. Giulio I hadn't seen since Kraków. Godin lit a smoke. Held the pack out at me. I rolled one out and he held a flame out and I leaned forward and sucked poison, too close to his soggy eyes that watched the smoke catch the rays of light violet.

"I have an opening down in the factory, storage basically, you come in at eight, you lift boxes, you go home at five."

"Okay," I said.

"You interested?"

"I need a job," I told him.

"Don't we all." Godin stood and walked around the desk and held his hand out at me as if he were a movie director planning a shot. "It's not a job that requires much of a man."

I looked at his hand.

"No hard feelings, Renzo?"

"About what?" I said when in truth I wanted nothing more than for him to ask what had happened to us, to Lago, but he just smiled, and I left his hand hanging there for a while before turning my back on him and walking back to the door.

"Renzo."

I waited with my back to him.

"You start tomorrow. Come in half an hour early and ask for Signor Buonfuoco."

"Okay," I said, reaching for the doorknob.

"And Renzo."

I opened the door.

"I'm doing you a favour. Because of what we went through together. Do you understand?"

I guess it was a good thing I was hungry, it makes a man think twice about being a fool. "Thank you," I told him.

"Viva l'Italia," he said, and he was waiting for me to turn back to him. I did so. He gave me a salute.

"Duce," I said, and saluted back and felt the shame rise with my hand.

"And do us all a favour, Renzo. Stay away from Giulio."

I worked there for ten months. At the Rialta Organisation. Lifting boxes of weapons and military-grade parts for tanks and artillery. And I kept away from Giulio. I kept away from everyone. It was as if I were a spreader of disease, a virus. And in a way, I guess we all were, those of us who'd come back from Russia with our lingering coughs and our butchered faces and our nightmares of clustered 'roaches and our amputated limbs and our sadness, and it was pointless pretending—we had seen the horror of our creation.

Giulio, I was told, had gone up to Trento from where he was organising a union for the factory workers. Madness, of course—a union for slave labour—but that was Giulio. The Germans were kinder to us than our Italian masters—they were content to collaborate with us. Not as colleagues as much as we were their trained monkeys, but sometimes they even shared their strange pasta-with-raw-apple luncheons. I suppose it was easy for them because there was an understanding that a man who stepped out of line would soon find himself disciplined by our Italian management, and if a good beating didn't help, then a man would be taken to the German management and from there it was almost always the way of the Davai that led north to the camps. To Mauthausen. To the Austrians. And worse still, to the Poles.

I worked and slept through that hot summer, and on the wireless I would listen to Radio Bari in the evenings—free Radio Bari, which the Americans had been using since the end of '43 to communicate with their men behind the lines in codes we would try to decipher—smoking my Tre Stelle cigarettes outside on the stoop on days that never seemed to cool much, waiting for the Americans. Waiting for you, John. And now I hear the bells from the Duomo. It's just gone 6AM. I should finish this. Finish this and hope your men don't beat me just for sport.

The question, John, is when does a man decide to kill? I'd killed in Nikolayevka. I found it never bothered me much. I am told that sometimes men are haunted by killing. For me, it was a release, like something a man ought to do. It was like waiting to dive into those icy lakes up in the mountains in the springtime; you stood there over the calm green water knowing you were going to dive into the cold at some point, it was just a matter of building up to it. Killing was much the same thing. It left me just as cold. But when, John, does a man decide to really kill, without ambiguity, is that the word? Without the orders of others, without the blanket of war. To kill not for survival or glory—just to kill to rid the world of a singular evil.

Was it September 8th, 1943, when the Germans became our new masters? Was it when we heard that they'd arrested Reverberi and sent him to a camp? Was it when they forced our soldiers to surrender and, disarmed, sent them to the slave camps? Thousands of men, John, sent to work the Nazi camps. Men who had survived the Russian winter, sent to die in a German winter.

Or was it when they'd fired up the gas ovens in Trieste for the partisans and the Jews and the communists—the gas chambers at Risiera di San Sabba, where they sent them all before it was too late, preparing for their new Italy without the stains of those who saw and knew?

Or was it, John, the day I came to the factory at 7AM, March 3rd, 1944, to find Buonfuoco waiting for me at the gates. I'd not been to work for three days because of the strikes—the General Strike that had been led, I'd come to understand, by Giulio—and that morning, that cool, dark Friday morning, Buonfuoco was waiting for me with my last envelope in his hand.

"I'm sorry to see you go, Renzo."

"Why?" I asked him.

"Because you're a good strong worker."

"Then why are you letting me go?"

Buonfuoco had turned his balding head and nodded at the factory, at those windows gleaming pale yellow there beyond the courtyard toward which my colleagues were ambling for another day of grind behind the red brick walls. "What can I say?" he said. "The decision wasn't mine."

"So whose was it?"

"You shouldn't have gone on strike."

"Everyone was on strike," I replied. "What was I supposed to do?"

"You're not everyone," Buonfuoco said. "You were his special dog."

I wonder now whether it was his dismissive tone or the way he turned from me convinced I'd just bow my face and accept. That's what we always do, isn't it? We accept. We bow our faces and eat our shame. I remember standing there watching him walk from me into the courtyard and recalling my father and his dignity and suddenly I was pushing past him and striding through the factory doors and I heard him shout, "He's not to be trifled with, Balbo."

I ran up the red-stone stairs to the offices on the third floor. The same office where last I'd seen Godin. The receptionist up there tried to stop me—"He's having a meeting," she said, cutting across and shielding the door—but I brushed her aside and threw open the frosted-plate door and strode into the office just as the door hit the wall inside and I saw the pane crack like a web.

Godin was sitting behind his desk. He was alone.

"Sir," said the receptionist, Puccini, behind me, "I'm sorry—"

"You should be, you stupid cow," said Godin. He waved her away. "And close the fucking door on your way out, we'll talk about this later," he told her, and I saw her blush and eat her shame, and when she shut the door, the glass pane exploded out of the frame, and she stood there staring at Godin with horror on her face.

"You'll pay for that as well," he said as she began weeping.

I strode toward him through the tunnels of soft dawn light that oozed through the windows. "This is bullshit." I held my last paycheck in my hand, my voice hollow in that yawning space. "I never saw Giulio, haven't seen him since we came back."

Godin watched me standing over his desk. Blew a trail of smoke at me. "So what do you want?" he asked. "A fucking treat?"

"I want my job," I said.

"Your job?" Godin laughed, a real laugh, it came from his soul and his shoulders shook, and we both fed on my words for a while, thick as they were, without any shame or pride. "Your job," he repeated after a while, ashing his cigarette in a tray made from a *gavetta*, our tin food bowls from Russia, "has gone the same way as your manhood, Renzo."

"Listen—none of this—" I choked on my words, and he sat back in his chair, silent, waiting for me to go on. But I'd already gone too far. "What do you want from me?"

"From you? What would I want from someone like you, Renzo?"

"I won't accept this."

"Won't you?"

"I won't accept this. You owe me."

"Owe you what?"

"You know. You fucking *know*."

He sighed and killed his cigarette, crushing it with his fingers in the *gavetta*. "You know why we lost?"

"Lost what?"

"Discipline, Renzo." He gazed up at me. "*Labour* strikes? We broke the communists here twenty fucking years ago and now you figure you can just go on strike? Just like that?"

"I'm not a communist."

"You went on strike."

"*Everyone* was on strike."

"You're not everyone, Renzo. You owed me. *You,*" he said, pointing at me, "you owed *me*. I did you a favour. I gave you a job when no one else would have *touched* you. Look at you for fuck sakes. Look at the *state* of you. And you thought you had the right to go on strike? You?"

I had words, but they were imprisoned inside of my soul—a prison made of shame, I suppose, shame and fear and hunger, John. Hunger.

"You were loyal to Giulio who has given you *nothing*. When your loyalty should have been to me. To your country. Your *people*." I remembered his face then, on that night in Romachovo, I remembered this man on his haunches with his razor teeth bloody with the meat, like an hyena, and I heard him now, distant somehow, as if I were as deaf as I had been on the steppe. "Show me," he said.

"What?"

"Show me."

I knew what he wanted. And as he sat there on his chair, his arms crossed, his gaze falling over me, I understood that there could never be redemption for this man.

"Show me."

It would, I suppose, have been better if I'd listened to my mom and been a good boy. Would have been better if I'd swallowed my shame and showed him. Instead, I looked at his face and worked it up from my throat and spit at him. A thick globule of spit that cut through the rays of dawn and flew by his smiling face like a projectile.

"Discipline, Renzo."

"Go fuck yourself," I told him.

Godin laughed. "More chance of that than you fucking anything at all. Ain't that right?"

I launched at him. You understand what it's like, John, when a man attacks from anger; the moment is lost, the memory of the next seconds misplaced in rushing adrenaline. I recall launching myself over the desk but before I could even land a blow, Godin's fist had connected with my temple. Maybe it was a lucky blow, but the hit was solid and I went wobbly and then he was pounding me with his fists and I heard the door open and voices shouting as his fist hammered my face, and I was on the floor now eating blood and suddenly I felt myself being held down with knees on my biceps and stomach and Godin was shouting—*"Ricino!"*—and arms were restraining me and then a funnel was pushed into my mouth and I kicked and shook my head violently, trying to dislodge the end of the funnel, and I felt my teeth crack and someone was pulling my hair and the pain made me cry, and through the tears I saw Godin's face sweating above me as he held a green bottle of castor oil that he shoved into the wide mouth of the funnel, and that rancid thick liquid was in my mouth and I was drowning and swallowing oil and blood and teeth, swallowing it all down and now I was being dragged down the stairs and awareness, John, it came when I found myself on my hands and knees on the road outside the gates with Buonfuoco and Godin and six or seven men watching me crawl away. I could hear their laughter and it wasn't long before the shit came from me, running down my legs as I squatted there behind the piazza by the Duomo shitting with my pants around my ankles sweating a river from the cramps and the pain that seized my guts like a vice as children stood and watched and giggled their shame away.

It took me three days at home to recover. And through it all my conviction grew stronger out there in the outhouse groaning with the cramps and the blood and the shit that came from me like sin. Hundreds had gone up into the mountains the week after the strikes had been broken by the Black Shirts and the Tagliamento militias on orders from Salò, and when they'd failed at first to get the men back to the factories, they'd smashed up homes and even shot a fifteen-year-old girl who'd been hanging her laundry out to dry, and those they'd managed to capture—the leaders of the strikes—had all been sent on a train to Risiera di San Sabba and tortured and gassed, and that afternoon I found my Russian parabellum and two Berettas in the old shed and I kissed my mother and my sisters goodbye.

*"Fa' il bono,"* my mother said, and I kissed her cheeks wet with her tears. To be good, I wanted to tell her, to be good required that evil be defeated.

Giulio I found after two days of walking. I'd gone up to Rovereto and then headed for Posina through the craggy passes I'd learnt as a boy with my dad hunting for the little birds that my mother would make into *polenta e osei*. But I suppose it would be more accurate to say that Giulio found me, up on a meadow above the Laghi surrounded by a sweet-smelling pine forest. I realised he'd been expecting me when I came out of the woods into that meadow still flecked by dirty snow to find him standing there, alone, legs wide and shadow long, his Russian parabellum slung over his shoulder and a cigarette between his grinning lips.

*"Eilá,"* he said. "You off to Portofino?"

"No," I replied, and trudged toward him, "I came to ask why you got me fired."

Giulio laughed. That laugh of his. "Way I hear it, I got hundreds fired."

"And you think that's funny?"

"Most of them are here now," he said, and waited for me to come to him. "They swapped work for liberty. And you, Renzo?"

"I'd swap liberty for a fucking meal," I told him.

"Come on," he put an arm around me. "I have grana and polenta and a bottle of Amarone, just for you. Actually, I'm hungry too—been waiting here for two hours, took you long enough to get up here."

He looked like a revolutionary then. At least what I imagined a revolutionary should look like. His beard was fully grown, his black hair down to his shoulders, and I noticed immediately he wore the summer jacket that we'd all worn on that march to the Don in the summer, the jacket he'd so meticulously groomed on Lago's corpse. But neither of us would be able to do that march again, we'd had the stuffing beat out of us, and Giulio had developed a slight limp that he tried to disguise. I never did ask him if they'd had to cut him when he'd come home.

Giulio and his group of partisans were running mostly counter-ops up in the mountains with a *contorno* of sabotage. We would blow telegraph wires and train tracks and sabotage supply lines and make a nuisance of ourselves while the Germans—who were far too occupied with the actual war coming toward them like a plague wave from the south—did little to find us. Every now and again, if we'd prove too much of an irritation, they'd raid a village and rape and kill as punishment—stand the old men up against a wall or gang-rape the women and shoot them while the kids watched, ten citizens for every German soldier killed—but they never came up to the mountains. The mountains they'd lost months ago. The mountains belonged to us, to Giulio and his Garibaldi Battalion.

With Giulio we fought a good war in those mountains, and with his battalion I marched down into Schio on April 29th, 1945, as a liberator. We liberated Schio three days before your army even got here, John. I'm told we were one of only two towns in Italy to be liberated by Italians. You can imagine our pride then when we marched on those cold April streets that I hadn't seen in over a year, everyone waving their *tricolore* flags on the streets and cheering us on and I looked for Luisa who I never saw and I searched for my mom and my sisters and saw them on the Piazza Rossi and they were crying and throwing flowers and I felt, for the first time in my life, a sense of what it could be like to be a man as I marched alongside my brothers and sisters, the guerillas from the Garibaldi Battalion with whom I'd fought and won the battles and the war that would define our lives.

But there was still one thing left and I suppose it all began—I mean what brought me here, what brought us together, John, what made me decide to kill—on a warm night in late June after I'd learned that Godin had been arrested by Marshal Svavi and was being held at the old jail.

I overheard the news in the piazza one evening—it was the talk of the town because Godin and his family we had always thought untouchable—and the next day I hitched a ride up to Trento to meet with Giulio.

He welcomed me in his apartment, a loft-like space that'd been a cigarette factory once, far up in the lush green hills with a view over the mountains that he loved so deeply, and we spoke on his terrace with the heat softening in the shadows of dusk about us, sharing cigarettes, cold beers, and too many silences as once we had on the terrace of the amputation factory in Kraków.

"So what happens now, Giulio?"

"What always happens, Renzo. They'll play at catching fascists for a while and then they'll all go back to doing what they did before, and their kids will expect ours to die for them as they expected us to die for them."

"We'll be dead by then."

"If you're lucky," he said, his eyes aflame in the setting day, and I remembered those eyes and I remembered Lago and the friends we'd left behind for the Cocui. "Otherwise, you'll be watching your kids march off to war."

"Kids?"

He took a long sip of his beer.

"I don't care about any of that shit," I told him. "But Godin doesn't deserve that."

"Doesn't deserve what?"

I had a reply, but it got stuck in my throat. I tossed my cigarette over the railing instead and finished off the beer in my hand. "You know what he deserves."

"Not sure I do."

"You *know*," I said. "Forgiving the guilty is raping their victims."

He left that alone for a while, smoking his cigarette. "Are you working?" he asked eventually.

"Godin put me on the blacklist. Undesirable. A communist."

"You?" Giulio laughed.

"It's funny except at night," I told him, "when the milk runs out and I gotta wait until my sister comes home with food."

"And would Godin's death give you food?"

"No," I said. "But I'd sure enjoy the fucking taste of it. Remember what he did to us? To Lago?"

"We left Lago as surely as he did, Renzo."

"We had no choice."

"Neither did he."

"You believe that?"

"I believe it," he said. "I saw his mom, you know. Lago. At the council. She was asking about her son."

I watched the sky and the mountains folding into darkness. "He betrayed you too," I told him. "The night the Black Shirts got Freccia. He tried to have you killed too."

I watched him draw the cigarette to his lips and take a long drag and I thought I saw him smile. "You think it was Godin? Who informed on us?"

"What do you mean? Who else? He saw us—"

"The world isn't as you think it is, Renzo. None of it is. Freccia got what he deserved that night."

I looked at him then, sitting there in the shadows congealing around us. It was getting chilly up there in the mountains and I shivered when I saw him look at me and laugh as he grabbed my face and squeezed my cheeks.

"Don't do anything stupid, Renzo. It's not worth it."

*Fa' il bono*, Renzo, don't do anything stupid, Renzo. I guess I should have listened. Maybe I would have too had it not been for what happened one afternoon a few days later. I was in the Piazza Rossi when Captain Coke—who was our English runner after Freccia was killed, do you know him?—had walked right up beside me and, without acknowledging me, dropped a box of matches in my jacket pocket, a code that we'd used during the war. I knew what it meant when I opened the box to find three burnt matches.

Coke was a man I'd trusted—he worked then for what Giulio called "Baker Street" and what I'd always assumed to be the British secret service. A spy. He was the man who organised our weapon-drops and sometimes, especially in March and April of '45, our mission targets, and I'd even stored some of that ammo' in the shed of my farm during the last weeks of the war, something my mother would surely have frowned upon had she known. I'd always believed him a fiercely loyal man to our cause though, and a far better leader than the man he'd replaced, Freccia, who, as I said, was killed in early '45. There was always something odd about Freccia, John, something untrustworthy—at least, that was Giulio's take on the man.

I met with Coke that hot night in July at 3AM as arranged, just behind the old *birreria* on the Piovene road leading out to Arsiero. The last time I'd spoken to him was on the day we'd liberated Schio. Giulio had been part of the high-ups who'd negotiated with the Nazis to surrender peacefully, and at his side that day had been Coke, the only Allied representative anywhere near Schio at the time. Together they'd promised the Nazis free passage to Piovene and the road up to Trento in exchange for immediate surrender. Coke had stood next to Giulio when we'd marched through Schio with our Russian-made weapons, standing preened with the pride of generals. I trusted Coke, trusted him with my life. We all did, once Freccia had been killed.

Here, though, standing behind the *birreria* in the heavy heat of night that smelt of pine, Coke was not smiling, as if haunted by something that hid in the darkness around us.

"I wanted to ask you something, Apache," he'd said, lighting two Dunhills with a flame that was shielded in his palms.

"It's Renzo," I told him, accepting the cigarette. "The war's over."

"The war's not over," he replied, "until justice is done."

I looked at his face framed in the cherry-light of his drawing cigarette. He was a young man, attractive, a hit with the girls—or so my sisters said.

"It's over for me, Coke."

"Do you know who betrayed Freccia?" he asked, tugging at his cigarette.

I told him what I remembered of the day when Freccia was ambushed. Giulio and I were coming back through the Laghi that afternoon. A pure coincidence it was that we ran into Godin. He was with some friends at the *trattoria* just past the church, the place where they make the gnocchi, *Dalla Sorelle*, do you know it, John? Anyway, that's where we saw Godin, smoking out on the street, a glass of wine in his hand and laughing it up with his mates. Our eyes met. I figured he'd recognised me, and once we were up in the woods headed for our camp, Giulio had said, "He saw us."

That night Freccia came to our camp with a new radio. We were to expect a signal that would indicate a drop of explosives for a mission that he said would be key to the upcoming Allied advance. He had a man, he told us, a new man named Coke who would be parachuting in that very night, if weather permitted, and it would be this new man who would give us all the details for this crucial mission. That night, Giulio had walked Freccia down toward the Laghi. And it was then that they'd been ambushed by a squadron of Black Shirts. Giulio made it back to camp with the dawn and told us he'd lost track of Freccia in the firefight and that he, Giulio, had barely made it back alive.

"Godin was the informant then?" Coke asked me that July night with the scent of pine in my nostrils as we stood in the woods behind the *birreria*, away from prying eyes.

"Giulio believed it. I suppose it could've been a coincidence."

"It wasn't," Coke told me. And then he'd put his hand on my shoulder and said, "I'm told that in two days, your old pals from the Garibaldi Battalion are going to break into the jail."

"What jail?"

"Don't be a stupid."

"In Schio?"

"You don't know?"

"Know what?"

"They want to settle scores."

"I haven't heard anything," I said.

"You will," he replied. "They're being organised by a man named Pranjic. Do you know him?"

"No."

"A revolutionary—a Marxist and a communist," he said, and it sounded as if he were cursing.

"Why are you telling me this?"

"Because Giulio will be there."

"Giulio?"

"Renzo," he said, and came so close I could smell the alcohol on his breath, "listen to me carefully. There's no appetite for this. Not with us and not with the Americans. There's been too much of it already. The killings must stop."

"They're fascists. Why would anyone care?"

"That doesn't matter anymore. If Giulio goes ahead with this, I can't protect him, do you understand? I can't protect any of you."

"From what?"

I suppose we both understand now, John.

Walking back to Schio with the moon a silver lake over the fields of summer, I came up empty. And looking back now, I came up worse than empty, didn't I? I came up wrong. I remember asking Coke, "Spell it out for me," and he replying, "What do you know about Godin?" I remember the look on his face when he said that name, as if he knew, as if he knew everything. I suppose Giulio must have told him—the two of them had been close, they were similar in their own unique ways.

"Godin's got a future, Renzo," Coke told me. "Like his father the senator in Rome, no? His family came out of the war well—they made their nest with the fascists, they made their nest with the Nazis, and now they make their nest with the Americans. Do you know what they all have in common?"

I shrugged.

"They hate you. Men like you. That's what they all have in common. Their hate."

"You sound like Giulio."

"Like a communist?" he asked. I smiled and blew smoke at his face. Coke said, "Men like Giulio, like you, the partisans who freed this country, Togliatti is ready to ride your coattails to power—him and Tito over there," he jabbed a thumb toward what I assumed was Yugoslavia, "do you follow?"

"Not really," I said.

"What the Americans want is for Togliatti to go away. And if there's another mass killing led by communists, the Americans are going to ride that all the way to the elections. Look at the commie thugs, they'll say, look at the partisans who belong to Togliatti, killing anyone they want, without due process, killing anyone they decide needs to die. A man like Giulio, the best of them, if he kills like that, if the leaders of the partisans who liberated Schio, the best of them, if they kill when and who they want, imagine what Togliatti will do."

"I don't believe Giulio capable of this," I said.

"You don't think he'd kill Godin?"

"No," I said, but I could hear the uncertainty in my voice—uncertain, too, about what Coke knew. How much had Giulio told him?

"Not even to settle an old score for a friend?"

I looked at him.

"Because Giulio," he said, "considers you a friend."

What has Giulio told you, I thought then as Coke looked at me silently, and it took me time to find words.

"I'll speak to him. With Giulio."

"You won't find him. He's gone," he said.

"What do you mean? Gone where?"

"I don't know."

"So what do you want me to do?"

"Go to the jail. Mitra is assembling the Garibaldi Battalion, on orders from Pranjic. Mitra will come to you, ask for you to join them. Say yes, go with them, and stop them. Stop Giulio."

"How?"

"Speak to him. Tell him what I've told you. Tell him Pranjic is not who he thinks he is. Tell him Pranjic is not to be trusted."

I tossed my cigarette onto the pine needles and scraped it dead. "What makes you think *I* wouldn't kill Godin?" I asked.

"Your decency, Apache."

"You don't know me."

"I know you. I saw you in the mountains. I know you. I know all of you. And you're the only one Giulio will listen to, the only one. You're the only chance he has now. He'll kill Godin for you, for that boy you left behind in Russia." He gave it a moment, for me to understand how much he really knew. "He'll kill for you, Renzo, but if you love him as I think you do, you can stop him. You're all he has now, you're his only chance."

The next morning, I hitched a ride up into Trento. At Giulio's apartment I found no one, and down by the station, where his office was, I was told he'd not come into work, and no one had a clue where he was. I left a message on his desk: "Don't go to Schio, I will explain when I see you next".

It happened as Coke said it would.

The day after, sitting on my porch in the afternoon, I watched Mitra walk through the dust that had once been our farm. Without even saying hullo, he grabbed a seat beside me and told me of his plan. When he was done, he looked me in the face and asked, "In or out?"

"In," I told him, and that night found me outside the Due Spade as instructed, wearing my red handkerchief around my throat, and waiting for the Garibaldi Battalion to arrive with the guard they'd grabbed on his way back from the bar. I lifted the handkerchief over my face and slipped into the jail with the men of the battalion, men who I knew, men who'd been educated here, John, in this place, boys who'd learnt to be good little fascists here and who'd learnt how to be men in Russia, men who'd killed in the mountains for *patria*, men with whom I'd fought and to whom I'd entrusted my life and who I believed in more than anything else in this world. Men like Giulio, who'd given me a cause that had lessened my shame. But it was only when I spoke to Mitra downstairs, looking into his strangely magnified eyes behind his gas mask and asked him where Giulio was, that I understood.

"Giulio? He's in Trento, warming up for his new life as a politician," Mitra had told me dismissively. "He wants peace and reconciliation with these pigs. Well, he can have his peace, because the dead are always passive."

I followed the men into the room where the male prisoners were being kept, about thirty, forty of them, all in a small room, and the odour reminded me of Kraków, reminded me of the amputation factory, and I thought of Giulio then as I stood watching those men cower from our guns. I turned to Mitra and said, "We can't do this, we can't kill them all, Jesus Christ," and Mitra had looked at me and said, "orders are orders."

"Whose orders?"

And Mitra said, "Pranjic, don't you know?"

And so, John, when does a man decide to kill? To really kill? In that room with the men of the battalion that had made me whole again, at least for a little while, I looked into the faces of those fascists, and recognised some of them, and I realised some had recognised me too because in that group was Buonfuoco, whose eyes met mine and I heard him say, "I know you, I fucking *know* you."

And in that instant, Mitra raised his Russian Mosin–Nagant and began firing and a moment later everyone was unloading their rifles into the men, and I raised my pistol and aimed and put a bullet right into Buonfuoco's face. One shot, John. And then I ran while they were still shooting, ran away and heard nothing but the shots. I ran into the street and kept running and when I got home, my mother was waiting for me, and when she saw the blood and the rifle, she said, "Renzo, *tagoditto di fa' il bono.*"

That night while I waited on the stoop of my farm, knowing the Americans would soon come for me, my sister told me that Giulio had been in an accident up in Trento. She told me he'd been injured on his way down to Schio. John, he was coming to stop us. To stop me. I will always believe that. He was coming to save me as he'd always saved me. I knew that then and I know now that I've been betrayed.

He was the best of us, John. Giulio. The brave and the strong, we left them for the vultures in Russia. That's what war does—it kills the best and leaves the future to the cowards and the fearful and the ones too smart to fight and die for their own bullshit. The only ones left now are cowards. Men like me, John.

And what kind of nation is built by cowards?

I don't know all the men who were there that night. I recognised only seven. But now your men are here, so I will finish this with their names, and you will hang them too I suppose, because the rope, that's your mercy in the end, isn't it, dear Joh

# SEVEN
# BELLA CIAO

*Switzerland is a country where very few things begin, but many things end.*
—F. Scott Fitzgerald

*ove*

## "Nessuno Mi Può Giudicare"
## —Caterina Caselli

The final page has been ripped out. Roughly. Casanova, I think, I sense you here now. And I understand. The clock on the wall clicks to 5.15PM. I stare at the second hand as it ticks, number after number, and return the notebook back into its Ziplock bag and slide it away on the desk. The thing that I want most now is a cigarette and to get out of this tiny room. This jail. I step to the door half-expecting it to be locked and nervously push it open. The hallway is abandoned, and I stand there reassuring myself that I'm an adult and don't need a dismissal note from the matron when I begin to walk down the hallway headed for the green exit sign, debating all the while over whether to make a lot of noise or none at all. I'm ten steps away from the partition door when the voice stops me.

"Signora Ballerin is waiting for you downstairs."

I turn. The matron, Luisa, is standing outside the office I'd just vacated. She glances in and then at me. If she's suspicious, she's not showing it. "I hope you found what you came for?"

"I guess." I'm about to step away but I have to ask, "Is this where it happened? Here, in these rooms?"

She nods as if expecting the question. "Yes, it's here where the women were being—" she allows a waved hand to do the rest. The rest. Twelve men. Machine-gun fire. A pile of dead. Here, on this floor, this tiled white floor.

"Did they board up the windows?" I ask.

"Which windows?" Her eyes are obscured by three distinct rows on her spectacles from the ceiling lights like lines of code. "There were never any windows up here. Not here," she says, shaking her head, "or downstairs. This side has always been just a wall, since I was a kid anyway, and that," she adds, "was a long time ago. I'm sure because we'd spray-paint our slogans on the wall."

"Slogans? What kind?"

"My specialty," she says with a hint of a smile, "was peace signs. I could get one done in around twenty seconds. It was a war—we'd keep spraying, they'd keep whitewashing."

"Who won?"

"Who do you think?"

It's something to consider on the way out of the library and I've worked much of it out by the time I get to the reading room. Sofia is waiting for me just by the front door from where she scans my approach, and then we're outside standing by the lone tree out there in the cold watching a group of friends laughing their way into the Caffè Roma across from the piazzetta. She doesn't say anything, so I ask, without actually looking at her, "Why are the notebooks here?"

"Can you guess?"

"Casanova gave them to Svavi before he left Schio? That was the package he brought to him, the day he left."

She nods.

"Strange thing to do."

"How do you figure?" she asks.

I shrug. "The writing left me cold, anyway."

"Your daughter would have liked that one, right?"

The mist is coming in with the night, swelling about our ankles in the twilight.

"Casanova," she says, "from what I understood of his life after—in Altoona—he wasn't the same man you'd imagine him to be. From his book, I mean. I guess not many were. Anyway, Svavi left the confession for the Schio Trust on his death."

"That must have been difficult for you." I leave her hanging for a while despite both of us knowing what's coming, but she's patient enough. "I mean, having all this suddenly exposed when I published that photo."

"Is that what you think?"

I turn to her. "You're Godin's granddaughter, no?"

"Took you this long?" She looks away from me and contemplates the cigarette between her fingers.

"And so this confession—if it became public knowledge—it would be a little troubling for you?"

"For me? Somewhat," she concedes and smiles, facing me square now. "If it got out."

"And how did you know about them? The notebooks, I mean."

She glances down at her boots and shuffles them about on the cobbles, dislodging earth.

"Who else knows?" I insist.

"Aside from you and me?" There's no humour in her smile now. Cold as dusk. "Hardly anyone."

"And why is that?"

"Because Nonno has cultivated many things in his life and gratitude is his one great bounty."

"So he made sure the notebooks were what—never made public knowledge?" I ask, and maybe she detects something in my voice.

"You can infer whatever you want, Alex. He was a powerful man once. He made his party what it is today."

"His party." I rub my hands, cold, and stick them into my pockets. "Neo-fascists and racists."

Something hard about her lips, the way they draw in a word that she won't allow to fall into the cold. "The notebooks are available for research," she says, "for approved historians and academics."

"If anyone knew they existed, you mean?"

"No one has denied their existence," she replies.

"People should know."

"People don't care," she says. "People only care if it damages. Only to that extent. All this history, it's for the old. History is just for the old."

I find a smoke and light up. Something's not squaring here. "He's retired? Your grandfather?"

"Long time now," she says.

"So who could hurt him now—who would want to?"

She throws the cigarette down onto the ground. "Why is that an issue for you?"

"It isn't," I tell her, watching as she crushes her cigarette under a black boot. "This isn't my home."

"No? So where is home for Alex?"

"Maybe, once, I wished it to be here. I read somewhere that trauma goes into the DNA of a family—we're like those little house dogs who were bred as rat catchers and three hundred years later they're still sniffing about everywhere but they've forgotten why."

"None of us," she says, "deserve to be damaged by the past."

"Damaged how? By people knowing your grandfather was a fascist?"

"That's not," she's watching me carefully now, measuring me and her words. "That's not what Nonno was, and that's not what he represents. You're trivialising, Alex. This isn't a Twitter fight." She lights another cigarette. "Fascism was not what he stood for, or his party."

"So why do you care?" I ask, watching the smoke drift from those lips.

"What happened in the war—"

"Or is it Renzo Balbo? Is that the problem?"

She shakes her head more in frustration than negation. "You have your answers now. Isn't that enough?"

Standing here, I realise that I don't care. Maybe I never did—my uncle was a man who lived only because of his death. His and a quarter-million other men from a vanished army on the steppe that no one cared about then, and no one cares about now. "You're right," I tell her, "I'm being unfair. No one gives a crap—and your grandfather being a fascist would make him even more of a hero these days."

"You people," she says, and her eyes are hard now, "and your cold certainties. This one a racist, that one a fascist, that one a neo-Nazi, as if you'd all passed some morality test and can now sit in judgment when all you do is stand in opposition, as if that was somehow a position and not a—

a—as if being opposed were somehow enough." I see the anger and she's probably right. We've come full circle. "You liberals, you're moribund, without ideas, just the smart know-it-alls who understand *nothing*. You mock the losers, those who've seen their lives stripped away by globalisation, by greed, by immigrants—you mock their pain, the deplorables, all racists and fascists, right?—you mock their poverty, their lack of education, their very humanity—might as well send them to the slave camps because what? You think you're *better*?" She takes a step closer to me and her voice lowers to a whisper. "You think being robbed of a chance, of a future—you ridicule and you deride but the working class, they don't vote for you, they vote *against* you, you vote to maintain your neo-liberal technocrats, your pro-globalist agenda, and you eat the working class alive and then you mock them for voting against you, as if they should be, what? Grateful? Grateful that you deep-sixed fifty fucking years of post-war abundance? The rich are all liberals now. And you know why? Because you want nothing but this mediocrity and your quotas and your—"

"I'm sorry," I interrupt, and look away. "But I'm not a voter so you can save your stump speech."

She frowns and meets my gaze. "Jesus," she says and laughs. "I'm sorry. Politics." A moment spent sucking her cigarette before, "That wasn't fair." We listen to the winter silence for a while before I throw my cigarette down and she says, standing on it with one boot, "So—any chance you'll meet me half-way?"

I shake my head. "The photo won't be an issue—I told you, it won't go further than in a frame on my wall."

"It really wasn't my idea."

"I'm sorry?"

"I presume you've figured out why I was at the hospice?" I can't look away from her. So beautiful. "He never even knew that photo existed. When he saw it, when I showed it to him, he was—really taken aback—I don't think I ever saw him cry before that day. He asked me to help you see the truth. About your uncle."

"He's dying?"

"Such an ugly word," she says. "Life and death, but that word is in-between, and it's so ugly. But you see, we share that, too," she says. "Our history."

I shrug it away. I'm alone here; this isn't my world. It started with my father, or maybe it had started with my grandmother heading for Paris in the early years of the last century, and she herself had been born somewhere up in Austria, and her sister dead in Zürich of consumption. We're a family of immigrants and discontents searching for something none of us will ever find and there aren't any answers here—not here or in Africa or New York or Zürich or anywhere else. There's just us, a family of no ones.

"Do you want to meet him?" she asks me now and perhaps she sees the horror in my face because she frowns as if seeing something unexpected.

"—your—you mean your grandfather? Godin?"

"I mean Nonno, yes."

In Sofia's washed-out face, here in the dusk that smells of wood-smoke, I see a longing of sorts, and I can't stop the words that bleed out of me.

"Sure," I tell her, "sure, of course," as if I'm what? Doing her a favour? But in truth, I feel nothing for Godin, just another fucking asshole in a species that doesn't produce much of anything else. It's the first time I've seen her uncertain, though, and it leaves an impression with me all the way to the hospital in Malo where I find my dad in his bed. He has oxygen pumping into his lungs at five litres now, and he's struggling to breathe. He hasn't eaten either. It's been three days that he hasn't eaten. His eyes are sharp as needles though, and he smiles at me when I walk into the room. A tired smile. Does he understand, I wonder, how close he is?

That face is so gaunt, those eyes so huge now, he's all eyes, all eyes, and too connected to be dying.

"Sandro," he says, and when he says my name as he does, as he has my whole life, my name there on his lips, the tone of it, the sound of it that reaches out through the years and my childhood and the first voices I'd ever heard, it takes all I have not to let the tears flow. My name on his lips, in the air from his lungs that have no more air to give, my name carrying me back to a time that only he remembers, and I wish my mom were here now so I could wrap myself into her chest and cry as my father struggles to breathe and my name is wheezed back inside of him on a train of created oxygen, this man who'd given me life, my name honouring a dead boy on an icy field somewhere no one will ever find and it's not, I realise suddenly, it's not for me to reveal what had happened to his brother. Not now. Not now and not ever.

I walk over to him. "You haven't eaten."

"I no hungry," he replies in English. "*Sto male*, Sandro. *Sto tanto male*," he says.

I'm the only one here now, I think, and you deserved more from this life. More than relying on a man like me who hasn't yet learnt to tie his shoelaces. How the fuck did it come to this? How the fuck is it that I'm all you have? I pull a chair closer. And smell flowers suddenly. Roses. I see a nurse walking out of the bathroom across the hallway with air freshener. He senses me and glances into the room and something crosses his face. He steps in to gaze at my dad.

"*Giovanni, come ti senti?*"

"*Male*," says my father. "*Tanto male*. So bad."

He steps closer and I stand to give him room to work—watch as he checks oxygen levels and temperature. Satisfied, he gives me a look on his way out. His face is a mask. But even masks have a purpose.

"I'm feeling so bad," my dad says. They haven't shaved him, they shave him every two days, but they haven't shaved him and his stubble is grey, and his face is yellow, his silver hair a mess, and I wish I was man enough to make him look better, I wish I could do any of the things that hide there in my heart to do, trapped in my own uncertainty, in my own weakness.

"I'll see about food, you have to eat," I tell him, and I head out into the corridor and find a nurse and she takes me back to the kitchen and ladles soup into a bowl that I take back with me and, standing beside the bed, I try to feed my father from a spoon that trembles in my hand but his cough starts up again, that sodden cough, and fluid seeps from his nose. I abandon the bowl and hand him a napkin and sit there with him as the oxygen pumps and he coughs, and the night deepens, and the nurse shuts the blinds to seal us in our tomb and my dad lies there with his eyes shut and he's asleep when I leave to call my brother on my way to the Villa Scacchi.

"He's not well," I tell him.

"I sent the doctor an email today," my brother says over Bluetooth. "She doesn't—she thinks there's nothing happening right now that need concern us."

"Really?"

Maybe it's my tone. "Fuck off," he says. "You know what I mean."

"He's not doing well. You need to come now, or it'll be too late."

I pull up at to the Villa Scacchi. The gravel driveway beneath the mist, the Palladio-style villa, the church, the pale lights and statues, it's all so familiar to me now, the crows in the campanile, it's all part of my world but not in my own context. I wonder what had ever happened to old Colonel Loller when I walk through the lobby warmed by lights from chandeliers that had once cast his shadow on this mosaic-tiled floor. I step through the rear glass doors and smoke a cigarette and stare vacantly out at the pool covered by its winter tarpaulin with Dino the night manager who comes to stand beside me, kind enough to be quiet in the night that has closed-in on all of us.

In my room, a siege of anxiety takes me by surprise. I find myself crying in the bathroom, find myself in my life so suddenly and inflexibly that I can't control neither fear nor tears. No more can I control the moon than I can control my sobs, and it's late when I finally lie in bed with the lights on telling myself I'd had a Lifetime Channel moment, Cheryl Ladd in the shower washing away the dirt of some abuse.

The phone pings late and maybe I'd fallen into one of those half-sleeps that feel like paralysis when I reach for it and notice it's 6.23AM.

It's Sofia on Messenger. *Can you make it to Thiene, to the hospice, at around 9?*

I stare at the message for a good long while. And then I sit there with my finger on the keys. And eventually I type out the usual letters.

## "Se Telefonando"—Mina

March

They started shovelling the dead six feet under during the plague. A nice deep hole to ward off the contagion. It didn't help much—the dead just kept killing anyway, right up until they didn't, and then the undertakers went back to discarding corpses into pits a few inches deep 'til gravediggers in Jack the Ripper London began exhuming bodies for fresh-faced doctors in gleaming, bloodied-leather dungarees. That's when the rich paid extra for six-foot-holes and marble mausoleums and left nothing for the corpse-raiders but the freshly dug-up poor because even in death the rich win. Money buys dignity. But that was London, and this is Italy on a bitter morning on the first day of March with the mist floating an inch above the black earth, a spectral silver lake over the soil beneath that dead-old sky, frozen and indifferent and suspended like a drawn breath when I say goodbye to Dino behind his reception desk and step out of the Villa Scacchi.

Now they just burn the corpses, I think, standing out in the cold. Like my mom who came home in a vase with a tag.

The ice has filmed over the glossy lines of the Porsche, the windscreen a pure-white carpet. Back in New York, when Natalie was a kid, she'd climb up my old Bimmer she'd christened Helmut and draw hearts on ice-encased windscreens. My memories, those she will never know once I'm gone. All those memories we carry as parents—but then who needs them now, in this new world as shallow as the graves of the poor?

The sun is cresting up on the horizon, an orange sphere, cold and lifeless, bleeding sick light that consumes shadows on the frozen plain of the Veneto alongside the long tree-lined drive that heads away from the Villa Scacchi and into the dread of day. I think of the text my brother had sent me last night from deepest, darkest, summery Africa. He said I should consider life as a nine-to-five job. *For you and me, it's just gone 1PM. For dad, it's 6.30PM.*

I think I need an espresso to get anywhere near 5PM.

It's time to go. I double-clutch to get into second down the drive, the wipers on, the engine temperature gauge still on zero and working its way up to the optimum eighty-degree range. It'll take a while this morning. But the noise, the collective clangs and whops from behind my head where the engine sits but a few inches away, is the loud conversation of a friend who talks too much but means well. The road is icy in the purple gloom and the Cayman gets nervous when the village of Lanzè meanders between a couple of deep-rooted farmhouses hard-pressed against the road. Then front tyres find some bite and the rear comes 'round under orders from my root foot, and with a quick counter-steer and a quickening heart, the back end jumps back into line and I'm powering away for the short ride to the Valdastico Autostrada onramp and the thirty-eight-kilometre strip of billiard-smooth highway to Piovene, the end of the road.

With the sunlight in my eyes, I figure agreeing to this had been ill-advised. But it's done, and I don't have the energy now to turn back. I'll be in Zürich by midnight. It's a thought that comes to me and means nothing. On Spotify, Terry Jacks comes on, *Seasons in the Sun*. It's our song, time-stamped on a white FIAT 1300 driving under a faded-blue African sky bleeding through finger-streaked windows, and it's me sitting on the backseat and Jacks playing off my dad's 8-track tape, and he's behind the wheel, my dad, a thin black plastic wheel in one hand and he's smoking with the other and my mom is pouring coffee from a thermos for him and she turns to me, and I see her face now, those dark eyes that never left much in the way of doubt as to what was going through her mind, and out of the window are mountains, the green and blue hills and the strange flushness of those trees and a man somewhere in my memory with a grapefruit cut in half, breakfast in Africa somewhere, and the man, bald and tall, burns brown sugar into the flesh of the grapefruit with a Bunsen burner and I can smell it still when I pull the Cayman up into the parking lot of the Immaculate Conception and kill the engine.

I climb out into the cold with a cigarette in my mouth and a desire not to be here. For some reason I think about William Burroughs who'd said that time-travel isn't about men carrying their shit through the stars, it's our memory that allows us to travel through time, and I recognise the truth in that because I sense my mom so close to me today, so close when I walk toward the entrance and see Sofia standing just inside the lobby watching me approach into that splash of sunlight.

"So you came," she says as I offer my hand and she ignores it and we embrace awkwardly. I feel her soft lips on my cheeks.

"Did you think I wouldn't?"

"I was sure of it," she says, and steps back. She's wearing a new scent, it smells of flowers, like the dead, and she stands so close before me after we hug that I can see the freckles on her cheeks. Her smile, her face. "Come on. Do you want some coffee? There's a machine over there."

Like in Malo, the lobby has a little automated Lavazza cafeteria, but I shake my head no, I want this over with. She leads me to the elevators, and we travel up in silence. I notice that she glances at her reflection a couple of times in the mirror, and I wonder what life is really like for someone so beautiful, what it would be like to be with someone this beautiful. We climb out on the second level. I follow her through a busy ward and an unmarked door and suddenly we're on a solitary passageway with framed photos on the walls of Thiene in the early 1900s and there's only one door here at the head of the corridor, one door that's guarded by a man in a black suit and black shades.

"What's this?" I ask, slowing.

"Just a man," she replies. "Relax. You're sweating. You okay?"

"Sure."

"Wait here." She steps around the man and says something to him I can't quite hear, and then vanishes into the room. The sunglasses watch me. I find something important to do on my phone, a minute spent trying not to acknowledge the man in the suit until Sofia's face appears in the doorway.

*"Vieni,"* she says, beckoning to me. "Come."

I take a breath and walk around sunglasses who has the good grace to pretend I don't exist and follow her through the door and into a room.

A man as thin as the air sits on a wheelchair in there. He is tethered to an IV drip on a metal stand that reminds me of a coatrack, his bald scalp slashed by open sores. He sits with his back to me staring out of a floor-to-ceiling window before him into the moist gardens below, the Cypress trees swaying in the fragile morning light that falls tenderly over the white tiles and walls and the perfectly made-up bed in the room.

"Nonno," says Sofia, standing beside him. *"È qui."*

The man turns his chair. What I think, when I see his face in full, is that age scratches everything away and leaves nothing but the soul-skin. Godin's is withered, hooded, red eyes measuring me sluggishly from my shoes and up to my face. He must be in his nineties, his flesh flabby, flaccid, dead skin mottled by open sores and liver spots, and his mouth is a damp ruby buttonhole out of which comes a sound, a whisper that I can't make out.

"I'm sorry?" I ask.

"You're so much like him. Your uncle," he says softly. "So much like him."

"Thank you," are the only words that come to mind.

Sofia stands behind his wheelchair and smiles as if he's just said something profound.

"It was all so long ago," he says, inviting me closer with a trembling hand.

"Sure."

"So long ago. I was a different man." I can hear him breathe, his voice crackling like scratched vinyl.

"I understand."

"I don't think you do," he says. "I don't think anyone understands what happened to us. Today," he looks up at me and I can see that keeping his head upright causes him pain, so that he must tilt it sideways to keep me in view, "today they would've diagnosed us all with, with that, that—PTSD, is that what you call it? All of us. The things we did—" I stare at his face ravaged by liver spots and tenderly seeping lesions. "All they had for us when we came back was shame. It was as if we'd been, been raped, as if we were guilty of some wretched sin, but we were just boys. Eighteen, nineteen years old. We were boys. And it was better in the end just to forget. For them. But for us? For us there was no forgetting—not for any of us who were there—never."

There's a TV mounted on the wall with muted talking heads, and a desk beneath it. Photos of him—with little Sofia in her bikini and a tanned woman on a boat somewhere that I figure to be from the '70s. Sofia touches his shoulder, and he lifts a hand and envelopes hers. I see the weight of it. Gnarled and stained, fingernails blackened. He looks as if he's rotting from the outside in. I step closer when he holds a hand out at me, and I squat before him, hesitant before finding the courage to touch it. Cold. Like sandpaper. In his eyes there's nothing but the yellow of fading organs.

"But Sofia tells me you—she showed you—"

I look up at Sofia standing there behind him. Her face is inscrutable. "Yes," I tell him.

"And she explained, she told you—what happened?"

"I suppose, in a way—"

"But she didn't satisfy you."

I smile. If only... "That night," I ask him, "that night at the jail, with Renzo Balbo—"

"Renzo," he says and shuts his eyes as if trying to remember, to bring him to life there in his mind. "Long gone now. Do you know I gave him a job—"

"—yes—"

"—in '58, after he was released from prison?"

"Oh, no, I didn't—"

"The man had nothing left—what the Americans did to him, that bastard, that Casanova, he was a sick man," he looks down, at his crotch. "He was a sick, cruel man. But then the war—I felt sorry for him. Renzo. *Mi faceva tanta pena.*"

"I didn't know."

"All of it so stupid. He worked for me for thirty years. More. Such a waste."

"A waste?"

"His life. Wasted by his, his education—the lack of it, you understand—and the war and his, his failings—as a man, you understand? You must remember the, the—how he was—his," Godin looks down at his crotch, "how he came back, from the war. I was told he wrote poetry—as if anyone would publish him. But why did you ask about Renzo and not Alessandro, your uncle?"

I glance up at Sofia. "It's just something I read," I reply. "That doesn't quite add up."

He slides his hand from Sofia's and folds them on his lap. "He was a tortured man, Renzo."

In every way, I think. "The thing that doesn't—I mean—that signal, the whistle, did you really hear it? The night of the shooting?"

"Whistle?" His head tilts just so and his eyes reveal nothing but caution.

"Do you remember you told Casanova, about a signal you heard, in the jail? Before they started shooting. A whistle or something like that."

"Ah," he tries to lift his face, but he doesn't have the strength, and gazes at me instead like the guy from *The Shining*. "And so you want to solve a mystery after all."

I smile. But in truth, the mystery had solved itself.

"You pieced it together, did you?" he asks.

"Some of it. I just don't understand why."

"Don't you?"

"It was a good time to stick it to the communists, was that it?"

"I suppose," he says. "I told you, we were all so young. And angry. I'd just been shot. By Giulio's men, no? That's what I was told. Shot by Russo and his men."

"Who told you that?"

"Who do you think?"

"And so you lied? About Russo?" He says nothing. "Were you asked to lie?"

"What do you think?"

"By Coke?"

I hear Sofia's voice—"Sorry, no, but—" and she seems nervous suddenly, standing there behind him, her hands on his wheelchair as if she's ready to push him away, "this isn't—"

"It's okay, *cara.*" Godin reaches back slowly and taps her fingers and I see the man he'd once been staring into my face from a few inches away. Unsettling. "Yes. I was asked to lie."

"By Coke."

"By Coke."

The lies come easily to this man. But it's easy to lie when there's a foundation of truth—to build up a lie like a narrative because that's what all stories are—lies. And so I give him more, let him stretch it, let him stretch it, I think. "What was it like," I ask, "at the jail? You were there for what, a week?" He says nothing. "It must have been terrifying."

He looks at me with those drugged-up eyes. Let him wonder. "Sofia," he says, "do you remember what I always used to tell you? About the, you remember, about the axe?"

She laughs. It sounds fake. "If I have six hours to chop down a tree," she says to me, "I'll spend four sharpening the axe."

Godin pats her hand. "Brava. You remember, you remember who—?"

"Lincoln," I tell him before Sofia can reply. "Just before he was assassinated."

"Really?" he asks. "*Just* before he was assassinated?"

I shrug. "It would make for a better story, no?"

He smiles. A strange smile—like a memory. "Do you know that I met him again?"

"Who?" I ask.

"What?"

"Who did you—"

"Coke," he says irritably. "Coke."

"At the hospital, you mean—"

"No-no, after the war," he says, "—in Rome, in eighty—eighty," he shuts his eyes and I see his lips tremble, "in eighty-three? I was down there to accept an award from Craxi. Craxi," he repeats, and I can hear his wet breath. "Can you imagine? Craxi? Giving *me* an award? This was before," he waves a hand, "well before they, before they found him in bed with, with the mafia, before he went into exile to, to Libya? Tunisia? Before we found out how rotten our republic truly was. Back when, before," he says, and I can see his confusion suddenly, "before. Now, now we don't make politics, we make money." He blinks, searching for a thread, and I sense Sofia's gaze on me.

"But—oh, I was telling you about, about Craxi, and Coke, about when I met him at that, that reception, at the British Consulate it was, when he came to me, it was late, I remember, it was so late in the evening and I was standing on the balcony smoking with Aldo and he asked, he came and he asked me if I was Godin from Schio—"

"He didn't remember you?"

"I'm sure he did," Godin says, those teeth of his as white as they are false. "But with Coke—well, you know the man he was, and he was the same then—still attractive, suave I suppose you'd say, full of himself, forty years, you know, from the last time, the last time we'd seen each other but I'm sure he knew exactly who I was. I reminded him that he'd taken my statement, that night, the night—while the doctors were extracting the bullet," he shows me his arm, "from here."

"Strange all the same—that he thought you needed reminding."

"Why strange? There were so many of us shot that night."

"But it was you he asked to lie."

His reply is immediate. "Mine was a small lie. And I wasn't the only one, I wasn't the only one he convinced to lie for him."

"He asked you to lie about the whistle?"

"The what?"

"The signal."

"Oh. Yes. The whistle. A lie of course."

"And Renzo?"

"Renzo never heard the whistle."

"But you saw him, on the night it all went down. At the jail."

"Renzo? Everyone recognised Renzo."

"And Giulio—Russo—Coke told you to lie about him too?"

Slight pause. "Yes. He asked me, told me to say, to say I heard the killers mention Russo should the Americans come, should they come to ask questions. He knew exactly what was going to happen. Coke, I mean. He knew exactly what he was doing."

Yes, he did, I think. "And what did you get for lying?"

Sofia cuts in fast like a TV attorney. "Alex, no—Nonno, you're tired—"

He taps Sofia's hand again. There's genuine affection there. "More tired than this, *cara*," he says, "and I'm in the cemetery." He smiles at me as if we share something in common. "He asked me—and I remember it to this day, so clearly, we were standing on the balcony smoking, that night, in Rome—and he, Coke, he asked me, like this, he asked me, 'Did you really betray Freccia and Russo?'" Godin gazes down at his feet. Slippers. Blue. They are the same as my dad's. "It made me wonder," he says. "It makes me wonder to this day."

"About what?"

"About the shooting. About who—about what—was really behind it. All these years, the communists blamed us, those of us who'd once been part of—well, the Italy before the war—"

"Fascists."

"Words," he says. "Names. Sofia tells me you're a, you're a writer?"

"Not really."

"Did you ever read that, that—Dostoevsky?"

"At school, sure."

"You remember that bit about how—biologically—a few men—like a virus—mutations in our species, to speed up our evolution, you remember that? And how we always end up sacrificing them because they're just rotten men who do the rotten things that must be done. Like Mussolini, no? Without him we'd be another Albania, that's what the left never understands: all of us, we all need the hard bastards to get things done."

"And bitches," says Sofia, pleased.

"And after, then we moralise, we moralise, and we tarnish them to clean our conscience. But the rewards, the rewards we keep, don't we? Even begrudgingly."

"Rewards?" I ask. "Like what?"

"I've found in my life that people do a lot of handwringing and then they go home and use the same hands to count their *schei*." He shows me his thumb and index finger and rubs them together. "Like they do in America now, no? They whine, but do you see them running away? Of course not. That's the nature of men," he says. "They whine but they understand they need the hard men to do the hard things. It was the same here after the war—they blamed us for the massacre—the communists, I mean, they always blamed us, and we, of course, we blamed them. But sitting here, you know, there's truth in what they said—the communists—there's truth in what they said because that massacre was a blessing—a cleansing—"

"*Nonno,*" hisses Sofia.

"It's fine, *cara*, we have an understanding," he says, stroking her hand. "Don't we, Sandro?"

"Sure," I reply. "A blessing how?"

"It was a blessing for, for the Americans, and for us too—Italians, I mean—because with Togliatti, my God, with that imbecile, there would never have been American money to rebuild, and without them we were finished, we were absolutely finished. Togliatti," he says and wheezes out a laugh. "The Russians, the Soviets, they called their motor-city Tolyattigrad—when FIAT built a factory there to produce Ladas for their Soviet comrades—FIAT and the Soviets—can you imagine? But it's odd that Schio, when you think about it, it's odd that ours was the only massacre that ended in, in prosecution. Of all those thousands who were *giustificati* after the war, why was our massacre different? We were the tipping point, and after it, we saw the partisans for who and what they were—a crew of bandits, communists, cut-throats. *They* were the hard bastards, and we were all ready to sacrifice them. Them and the communists." I watch his hands tremble on his lap. "But still, we all—all of us, we all got it wrong."

"Wrong?"

He rubs gunk from one eye that he examines on his finger. "Those boys, those boys from the Garibaldi Battalion, they were led there, do you understand?"

"To the jail?"

"To the jail, yes, to that slaughter, they were—think about how easy it was, no guards, the locals whipped into a frenzy, so easy. But where they—the communists, the liberals—where they go wrong is to think, to imagine this as some, some nefarious plan hatched up in a backroom somewhere by, by faceless American spies and their ex-fascist friends."

"Wrong how?"

"There was always a face to this. This was a vendetta—a personal vendetta, do you see?"

I frown. "A vendetta?"

He shakes his head irritably, the impatience of the old. "An English vendetta."

"Coke?"

His lips tremble out a tired smile. "If you think about it, everyone who was in his circle was destroyed after the massacre. Renzo, Giulio, the partisans, everyone—even Togliatti." His yellowed fingers are desiccated and bent like twigs broken on an autumn field and I can't look away. "If you accept that Coke came to Italy," he tells me, "to break the partisans and the, the communists, what happened with the massacre and after, it all makes sense. No? Context adds clarity, Sandro. Always. And that night in Rome, I always felt after as if—as if he were confessing something to me."

"Didn't Raskolnikov confess in the end? To a whore?" I ask.

His laugh catches me off guard. A genuine laugh, wet with death. "Yes, Sonia, the whore. And so you *do* understand."

"What did you say to Coke when he asked?"

"Asked what?" I give him a moment before he assembles his thoughts. "Oh. About Freccia. I told Coke the truth. I never spoke to anyone about seeing Giulio with Freccia. Why would I? We knew the war was over then. It's like that, that, Lampedusa—'If we want things to stay as they are, things will have to change'. He was a wise one, despite being a *terrone*," he says.

"*Nonno,*" Sofia admonishes.

"We're only joking, *cara*. But do you know what he said?"

"Lampedusa?"

"Coke!" he hisses, annoyed. "Coke. I was telling you about Coke, that night, in Rome." I wait. "Like this," Godin waves my face closer and whispers, "he told me, like this—'I know it was Giulio who betrayed Freccia'."

His face, disfigured by age, by a lifetime of lies and politics, reveals nothing, and when I look at his lips, all I see is white. Lies, as old as this face, as old as time. Truth and lies, all thrown out, so that the truth is a lie, and the lie is the truth and it all merges and becomes impossible to distinguish one from the other until you just give up believing that truth is even possible. And then, I think, truth is as useful as the lie—it exists only to justify the powerful.

"Why would Giulio have betrayed Freccia?" I ask, thinking that if a man like this reveals a secret, it's only to protect a bigger one that he never wants you to see.

"Why do you think?"

"Did you know him? Before Russia I mean?"

"Who, Coke?"

"Giulio."

"*Giulio?* Oh yes," he taps his knees with his palms and a laugh comes wheezing out of him, "oh God yes. We attended the *Salesiani* together, Giulio and I, until he, until, I think, yes, he left, left for the, the, what do you call it—state school. His father was—wanted Giulio to see what, you know, what the working class, what they—then we met up again at the *liceo*. We despised each other all our lives," he says, and wheezes out another laugh. "Arrogant little prick. I tell you, of all the people in the world, to get thrown together with Giulio in the war just proves God's a sadist with a sick sense of humour. If you ask me, it was those kiddy-fiddling priests that made him into a communist. And then when he met the working classes—Jesus, he never stood a chance. Fucking priests—"

"Nonno," she says, "I—"

"Give me a moment," he says, and there is steel in that voice, and she glances at me to see if I'd picked it up. "His father owned a couple of factories, had their offices here, up in Magré, still running to this day, right, Sofia? They, they were in textiles, back, before the war, but his daughter—Giulio's sister—moved them over to, to precision tools, many years back now, during the seventies. Smart decision, but she always was the brains in that family. They own a lovely villa—don't they, Sofia?"

"Yes," she says, looking at me. "In Asolo."

"In Asolo," says Godin. "Giulio came from serious money. *Tanti schei*. But he was mixed up. In the seventies they'd have called him, he'd have been a terrorist, one of those, those Red Brigades terrorists. Like that, that, what was his name, Sofia, the publisher—"

"Feltrinelli," I reply and Godin nods.

It takes a while before he finds his thread again, drifting, and I can see the loss of clarity in his eyes from the dope slipping through the IV into his blood.

"People liked him, that's the thing, people liked him. Giulio Moro. In my career, that was the hardest—being liked, that's, you can't fake that. Voters, they liked my politics, they liked what I stood for, but Giulio—Giulio was a leader, charismatic, he'd walk into a room and people would just—gravitate toward him—and they'd never be disappointed, you know? Just being with him was enough. And so deeply committed to his cause, wrong-headed as it was. I doubt anyone else could have led the strikes, those strikes in '44, that took a lot of guts—he was as brave as he was committed, and he'd have caused so much damage. And I just wonder, you know, if maybe in England, or in America, maybe there they weren't too happy to have a man like Giulio Moro around—a war a hero and armed and ready to lead some sort of, of Marxist rebellion. And like Giulio, here in the Veneto, there were so many—in Lombardy, in Alto Adige also—so many partisan leaders disappeared after the war." His shoulders falter and his head lowers. There were other men who wanted Giulio dead and for better reasons, I think. "I know how this sounds," he says. "But this was 1945. We weep over the death of a few people," he blinks, "but we lost millions then, and we're like that, we get used to things, we got used to death, that's the thing. We got used to death. It was a different world. And in that world," he says, "I can tell you honestly, it was a blessing that he died."

"Nonno doesn't mean—"

"I know *exactly* what I mean," he says, but his eyes are vague now, and he sounds petulant, like a child. "I know exactly what I mean."

"Did you see him that night?" I ask. "At the hospital?"

"Who?"

"Giulio."

A moment, too long, trying to work out his lies. "Yes," he says. "He was there."

"And at the jail?"

He shakes his head. His voice sounds slurred now. "I saw him at the hospital, as you say, the night they shot me. I saw Giulio for a second, just a second. He was sitting on a bed," his tired eyes meet mine and I see the truth there, "and Coke was with him. I was in a room across the hall, and we looked at each other, Giulio and I, long enough for him to see me and I'm sure he recognised me and then Coke closed the door, and he was gone, and I never saw him again."

"He was with Coke?"

A slight tremor runs over his lips. "Is that what you needed to know?"

That flattened nose, those eyes that had seen so much, this face—I can't hate this man, I can't even hate his lies, because he'll take them with him and there's nothing to find here but pity. I imagine this man on the sled, I picture him that night when Renzo had seen him in the firelight, and the things he did, even now, even now he's still lying, but I can't hate this man. He shuts his eyes. "Giulio was dead the moment he came down to Schio that night," he says. "You're looking for Judas when it's Pilate you should blame."

"Nonno," says Sofia. "You're tired, please—*basta adesso*." Her eyes are on me when she says it. "We should go."

I hold my hand out and he envelopes it with his cold fingers and his eyes absolve me. "Thank you for having seen me," I tell him, and I wonder what he would have done if I knew fifty years ago what I know now. How easily he'd have silenced me. And it wouldn't have mattered a damn.

"It's okay," his voice is garbled. "Snow is coming," he says. "I can feel it in the old bones. That photo, do you know where it came from?"

"Came from? Russia, it was—"

"I mean, how did your father get it?"

"Oh. I don't know."

"Did you ask?"

"No."

He looks at me from below his brows, his head unable to rise. Twenty years ago, he'd have found a way to break me too. But now he merely taps my hand twice and releases it. *"Capisco.* I've always wanted to say sorry, you know?"

"For what?"

"For Alessandro. Your uncle. I think of those days—in this place," he motions to the bed, "really, one has little to do but remember the past. Time is a soldier marching to battle."

"It doesn't matter." I look at his scalp as the weight of his head forces his face down. "No one could have saved him."

"That's not—" his eyes slowly shut. "I never felt any guilt, never, not about what happened. But it was so incredibly sad, he had no business being in that war, none of us did—" I gaze at him, at those claw-like fingers and his bone-thin face, "but him least of all."

Sofia steps around the chair. "It's the drugs." She wraps his blanket further up his legs as he sits there with his head bowed and eyes shut. "Come on," she says, and we walk out and around sunglasses and back to the elevators passing a nurse headed toward the room who nods quietly at Sofia on her way past. "Morphine. All the time now. He doesn't have long," she tells me on the journey down. "We're close."

We're close.

The elevators open and I wait for her to walk out into the lobby, and I follow her out into the wind and the cold, and we stand there by the cypress trees in the garden sharing the steam from our lungs as clouds, thick and dark, rush in from over the Pasubio.

"Do you hate him?" she asks.

"Does it matter?"

She meets my eyes. "Do you?"

"No." It's the truth, I think. "What's there to hate?"

She looks at me as if trying to determine something and then it comes. "Would you give it to me? If I asked?"

"Are you? Asking?"

She shrugs.

"No," I tell her. "But I won't do anything with the photo—I told you. I just want to keep it."

We stand there for a while in the cold. Eventually she says, "So is this goodbye then?"

She's close, almost touching me. If I was a man, I'd have her in my arms now, my lips on hers, those lips flush by the cold. If I were a man, we'd leave together and find a room and fuck our sorrows away. But I've never been man enough to be a marine. Story of my family—never seize the moment or the day; I've never seized a fucking thing, much less the moment, and so I offer her my hand and tell her, "Maybe it's just *arrivederci*," and hold her hand for far too long before I break away and head for the Porsche gleaming its welcome in the ambiguous daylight.

# "Io Non Mi Sento Italiano"—Giorgio Gaber

It's just gone eleven when I pull up below the rehab centre and park the Porsche illegally. The wash of sunlight, bright and cold, follows me in through the double doors and down the hallway where I side-step the woman with the crazy-wide eyes and pause outside my dad's room. He's lying in the bed, borrowed oxygen piping into his nostrils from its source somewhere in the bowels of the building.

"Sandro," he says when I walk in, his watery eyes gaping at me as if he's terrified and a chill runs down my spine. "You back? Help me up."

I walk to the side of his bed and lift him. He weighs nothing now. And the weight is all history. Nostalgia. Jagged bone and hot, coarse flesh. I'd like to hold him close, I'd like to hold him, I'd like to touch his forehead as he, perhaps, had once touched mine in the hospital beds of my childhood, but all I feel is the graze of his stubble. I'm going to lose you soon, I want to tell him, and there are things I've wanted to say all these years, and I know the truth now, I know what happened to your brother. He was left to die alone. And I won't let that happen to you, I'll be here for you. I can see fluid dripping from his nostrils, dense. I give him a tissue and he blows his nose.

"Have you eaten?" I ask.

He shakes his head. Lying there, entombed in his blankets and his flesh, just for a little while longer. I find the packet of biscuits on the table—McVitie's, "Nonno cookies" my daughter called them before she'd learnt the ways of her mother and now no longer calls at all—and dig two out and place them before him on a napkin. "You should try to eat."

"I have no appetite, Sandro. *Non ho fame.*"

"Try," I tell him, "try take a bite."

He does. And then begins to cough. A damp rasping cough that goes on and on as if he's trying to clean out his lungs of a lifetime. Then finally he spits into a tissue and drops it into a wastepaper basket by the side of his bed. I watch it fall. It's flecked with fluid clinging to the texture of the paper, dark and bloody. Mucus slips down his nose, dense and gleaming, and he keeps coughing. "Every time," he tells me between breaths, between coughs that are knives cutting my soul, killing him, "every time I try eat, this happen."

"I know," I hear myself say when finally he clears something from his throat and I take the tissue from his hand and throw it away without him noticing the dark fluid. The cough has dislodged a biscuit from the table, and it has shattered onto the linoleum floor. I kneel and scoop up the pieces. There are crumbs up by the wall now even after I throw the wedges into the bin with the soiled tissues.

My father is sitting and staring at something or nothing, but not at me when I sit on a chair at the foot of his bed and watch the day fold into itself out there beyond the windows of the room where he will die. He'd gone around the world and it all ends here in this fucking room without even a picture on the walls; this little square room with that window where heavy clouds blanket the afternoon that trembles to night, dense and impenetrable, a world that he will never again feel on his skin, and a bed on which he will die with my mom only a fading memory sixty years in the making. And we share not even a word. Outside the room, it's quiet as always—I suppose the dying are forgotten on a Sunday evening, washed away by thoughts of enterprise soon to come with the dawn.

"I feel bad," he says.

"I know."

"When you go home?"

"Tonight."

"What time is it?"

"Almost six."

"You should go. It will be late."

"I will. But I need some coffee."

I walk out of his room and down the hallway. I'm near the doors when the nurse sees me—the one with the tattoo, Julie—and I can see she wants to talk.

"We gave him a morphine shot," she says, showing me a finger pointed at her gut. "He was struggling."

I look into her eyes to try to understand. "Is the doctor here?"

"No—she doesn't come in on Sundays unless there's an emergency."

I wonder what kind of person would do this job, cleaning the shit from the old, watching them die, smiling, being strong. What kind of person does this? "Thank you," I tell her, and she sees my tears and her hand comes out and touches me on the wrist, holds my arm firmly. It feels strange, being touched. "You're very kind," I tell her through my tears. "All you people here, you're all so kind and brave."

I smoke outside on a bench and sip on an espresso I've bought from the machine. The night is cold, a damp Northern Italian cold that gets in your bones, and it's always dead-silent here in Malo, and I think of the drive home. I think of my mom, dead now these nine weeks, and I think it's maybe that I never mourned her, that my father's fall had taken that from me too, and he will never feel this again, this cold on his flesh, smell the winter mist of the Veneto plains, that strange-smelling mist of this flooded world, he will never touch this again, and when I get back to the room, he asks me, "When is the Monza Grand Prix? Is it next weekend?"

The season hasn't even begun. "No, they're still, no," I tell him and smile because I can't—I just can't. "It's in September. We're in March. Come on. Are you getting like the crazy people here?"

"Ah, you right," he says and frowns, puzzled by something.

I sit with him in the silence. Deep into Sunday night. Beyond his windows, there's a church all lit up, and there's a statue up above the tower that I'd never noticed before, standing tall over Monte Malo, some saint or another, lit gold from below. My father falls asleep, and I sit there and send a WhatsApp to my wife. *Natalie needs to come say goodbye.*

She replies after a while. *My daughter doesn't need to see your father die. She's 12. What's wrong with you?*

There's that, I think, placing the phone into my pocket. There's that. Shallow-happy life for the shallow-water sharks. When he wakens with a start, I try to offer him another biscuit, "Or do you want some soup? I can ask in the kitchen?"

"What time is it?"

"About nine," I tell him.

"So why you no go, Sandro, no make me worry."

All my adult life, no matter the journey, my father had always waited for my call, my text. I'd call him at 3AM with three rings on the phone, our long-ago arranged signal that I'd arrived safe and sound before the era of texts, and sometimes he'd answer unexpectedly and I'd hear him say, "Now go relax," and I'd be in a hurry to say goodbye and his brother never did come home. I understand now.

At 10PM, I stand and grab my coat. I can't anymore. "I'll be back on Wednesday," I tell him. "There are things I need to do here next week—at the bank."

"Okay Sandro," he says, watching me.

In the cold light of the room, lying on the bed that isn't his, in a room that will be someone else's tomb soon, his gasp watery and weary and so full of gunk, choking him. The good deserve a better death, but life never did give a fuck about the good or the bad because neither get what they deserve.

I head for the door. Turn to him. I think, I should hold you. He too is alone now. Him and I. On this little journey to the end of everything.

"So I'll see you on Wednesday. I'll try to bring Natalie also, she'd like to see you."

"Okay, Sandro." He turns his face and smiles at me from that sled of his bed. But his eyes are black holes of terror. He waves a weary arm. I look at the chair by the window where I'd sat through the day. At the night beyond the windows.

"Okay," I tell him, and his inscrutable gaze follows me when I walk out, out and into the night and the Porsche and the autostrada where I hit 256kmh on the run to Vicenza with the open windows rushing cold air into my face like a slap, racing back to nothing and leaving behind everything, and it's as I'm hitting the onramp for the A1 to Milano that my phone pings, and I glance at it balanced on the little cupholder by the passenger seat. Sofia on Messenger.

*Can you meet me? There's something I want to explain.*

I grab the phone and type. *Where?*

*At the house. In Asiago. Ok? Can you come now, tonight?*

I filter onto the autostrada and work out the route: about an hour out of my way. But what does it matter? There's nothing waiting for me out there at the end of the night.

## "Dettagli"—Ornella Vanoni

I seep out from the claustrophobia of the dark woods and into the clearing, headlights mixing with the warm glow oozing from the windows of the stone villa. The snow is tumbling now, moth-like flakes lumpy and cold, swirling in my headlights and burning on the windscreen. I park up next to her Ducati and brush a hand against the bike's engine—still warm—when I walk past in that hush that always falls with the snow. I'm climbing the three stairs to the porch when the door opens, and Sofia is caught in the doorway with her body silhouetted as if she were naked.

"I guess it was *arrivederci* after all," she says and steps aside to invite me into the villa, into the light. "Thank you for coming. Were you on your way home?"

You know I was, I think, but home—not quite, just a fucking bed in some miserable life I'd been too scared to save myself from when I'd been young enough to have been brave. Maybe she understands too, the way she smiles, the way her body brushes up against mine as she walks me to the couch. She's got a fire going in the cavernous hearth, but there's hardly any burnt wood at the bottom of the grate, and the windows are sweating from the sudden change of temperature.

Hastily arranged, this farce. It's what I'd assumed.

"They say we're in for snow, a foot," she says.

"A foot? That's very American."

"It sounds so much more dramatic than ten-something centimetres."

I smile. "I should probably get on the road soon," I tell her. "You're not thinking of going down tonight on the bike, right?"

"Oh no, no-no. I'll huddle up here with some hot chocolate and a book. Would you like a drink?"

"I don't drink," I reply, and sit on the couch with my coat on.

"Because you shouldn't?" she asks, standing over me.

"Because I've seen too many who shouldn't." I glance around the room. Nothing's changed under the *Star Trek* lights. Her handbag's on the couch opposite me, the phone abandoned next to it. "Coffee?" I ask.

"Sure." She's looking at me with an expression that I can't quite work out. I know why I'm here, what she wants, but her face is reflecting something else, something that instantly clicks into place the moment the Xenon headlights of an approaching car shreds through the windows white and cruel. She frowns, and when she steps to the door—all pretend surprise—I'm overwhelmed by a sorrow that I hadn't quite anticipated.

"Eva," I hear her say to the night when she's opened the door, and I can hear the lie of astonishment. But I suppose it's something—that's she either a lousy liar or a worse actress. "What are you doing here? I thought you were in Asolo."

"Nonno told me you were here," comes the voice from outside, "so I thought I'd come by and see how you're doing. I was down in Schio with—" Eva has stepped into the house, pounding her shoes of fresh snow, and she spots me suddenly—stunned pose—and pauses mid-sentence, glancing first at me and then at Sofia. She's a better actress than her sister. She's wearing her Sunday get-up, I guess—jeans and a green pullover flecked by snow and green Ellesse sneakers that are identical to mine. She hastily kisses Sofia three times on the cheeks, but her eyes are set on me like a cat seeing an allergic stranger, and now she's striding toward me, thin and tall and straight-backed, bouncing like a piston, one hand extended, her personality reaching out from her like high-priced perfume. The man from the hospital slinks in through the door behind her—black suit, black shirt, undertaker eyes that vanish the moment Eva comes between me and his gaze.

"This is my sister, Eva," says Sofia, playing this farce way past curtain close.

"So we finally meet. Sofi has told me *all* about you, Sandro."

Eva Fachin holds out her hand and I stand to accept it. I've always hated my weakness, but she's fucking gorgeous, and I can't blame myself for holding her hand until she breaks contact. She's got a good practiced warm squeeze too, and her eyes are like a movie that draw me into a universe of possibilities, and she really does resemble her posters and those spots on Facebook. Beautiful in a faded, no bullshit way. She looks a lot like Sofia, but there's a vitality about Eva, a confidence that comes only from someone who has long since convinced herself—and been encouraged by the ease with which the world has bent to her convictions—that her destiny is a special one. It's a good mix for a politician, and I try not to stare, wondering if the peanut-hard nipples had come along for the ride, and now I find I can't help the slow, inexorable lowering of my gaze.

"And your father?" she asks with just a hint of a dimpled smile on the edge of those lips that tell me she's reading my every thought. She's comfortable in the notion that she has me pegged. My reply is unimportant, so I sit down instead and try not to stare at her crotch by my face. Or the muscle in the suit who shuts the door and turns the latch under Sofia's watchful gaze.

"It's hard, all of this," Eva tells me from up there on her pedestal above me, and it's as if her acknowledging my pain makes me a better man. "It's hard to see them go. Sofi's awfully close to Nonno, aren't you, *cara*? You two suffering together, giving each other strength—it's just so positive. But in the end, this is the circle we must all accept. Death is life, not so?" She looks down at me for a moment, assessing, I suppose, whether her empathy has hit the mark. "You met Nonno, I'm told?"

"This morning."

"It's so rare that he sees anyone these days. It's quite the honour," she assures me in her bouncy voice. "One of the last of that generation of truly great Italians."

"I wouldn't know," I look up and try to ignore her crotch. "I'm African."

"*African*," she says and laughs down at me. "A white African, that's so funny." She sees my discomfort with her crotch there by my face and decides to sit down on the couch beside me. I feel the weight of her, the warmth of her, and just a brush of her leg on mine. Her leather bag she abandons beside her, just so, and she gives the muscle in the black suit by the door a feint nod, and he shuffles away into the kitchen.

"Well," she says, legs crossed, butt settled, and ready to give me her face, blank like an Instagram post, all levity and positive vibes. "Here we are."

"I'll get the coffee," says Sofia.

"Don't worry," I tell her. "I really do need to be on my way. It's going to be a bit of a nightmare with this snow." I glance out of the windows, and the snow really is pitching down now, dense and fast, a blanket silencing the world.

Eva looks at Sofia. "Sit," she says, and it's not a request. She waits for Sofia to obey, there on the couch where she'd sat that afternoon with me when she'd given me Casanova's book to read, an afternoon that had felt like freedom and has now been corrupted like everything else.

"The irony of history," Eva says, as if she's reading my mind. "That's what Nonno always says—right, Sofi? 'Defeat made us!'" She wags her finger about, imitating Godin perhaps, and Sofia seems to take pleasure in it. "'Defeat made us!'. He was special, you know, in his prime," she says, eyes inviting me into her sweet-smelling cosmos. "A singular politician: a man of vision and determination who came of age in a time when patriotism was a bad word. When God and family and *patria* were bad words." She smiles warmly. She could tell you the world was coming to an end with that smile and you'd be thrilled, those welcoming dimples and expensive white teeth and blowjob lips that seem too big for her face, and those eyes that embrace you, her body so close, and I find myself receptive to her words in an almost primordial way. There's a gleam there in those green eyes that make me want to sink inside of her forever. "Men like that changed the arc of our history and these days it's acceptable to be proud—it's no longer shameful to be in love with our country. Italians first. And we're full-up. Especially here, in the Veneto."

"Everywhere's full-up," I reply and glance at Sofia. She smiles at me encouragingly, and it's sincere—as cruel as it's sincere.

"If you're a citizen of everywhere," agrees Eva Fachin, "you're a citizen of nowhere."

"Is that a slogan?"

"A speech, actually," Eva replies. Little laugh, and it's a fun laugh, it makes me want to join in. "The irony of history. Liberals are like children who can't understand why Daddy needs to punish them sometimes." She smiles warmly as if I were an imbecile. What she sees in my face, though, makes her pause and glance at her sister, and it's clear she doesn't like what she sees reflected there either because she quickly changes tack. "But listen to me go on—*che noia!*—this is hardly the time for politics. And on a Sunday! But I have so much passion for this country of ours. And after all," she adds, finding a road back, "your uncle sacrificed everything too, didn't he? Your family has done its part for *patria*. We could ask for nothing more—"

"You asked for too much," I tell her, lost in her eyes. "It's only sacrifice if my uncle had a choice. Like between dying in Russia or a vacation on a Caribbean island."

She laughs. Hearty. Earthy. She's easy to like, I imagine, even if you're not one of her people. "I see why you like him, Sofi, he's very funny," she says, and the way she looks at me makes me feel like a million bucks, and I tingle all over when she pats my knee twice with her soft hand. "But your father came back, didn't he? To Italy, I mean. A *baia*."

"What?"

"*Baia*. Home. Home, from Africa."

"Oh. Yes. Yes, I guess he did."

"And your mother."

"She hated this place."

"And yet back she came, too. And we provided for them, am I right? A pension, and now his care. The safety of his inheritance, tax free, to you and your family, no questions asked, about whether he has money, assets in Africa. This is the promise of our country. And why we must always keep Italy for Italians. For us. No matter who we are, white or *negri*, yes?"

"My father's not much of a patriot."

"And you?"

I shrug.

"You speak with an accent," she says, "but you're Italian, no?"

"Not enough to vote for you."

That laugh again, eyes dead but staring, her hand tapping my knee again, twice. "Funny *and* honest. Sofi, he's *delightful!*"

I shiver and turn to Sofia. "I must be off," I tell her and get ready for the play I know is coming.

"Before you do," Eva says, and looks quickly toward the kitchen where the muscle stands sipping on a glass of water, watching, "there's something I'd like to—well, discuss with you. About the photo."

And so here we are. "What about it?"

"Do you have it on you?"

"I've got it on my phone if you'd like a copy?"

"I only deal in originals," she says, and I sense a dismissal there. She's not expecting to work too hard for my consent, and I hate myself when I smile and feel my lips tremble just so. I look around the room. At the fire that whispers shadows about like threats. At Sofia, lounging there on the couch scraping at the cuticle of a finger. At Eva, her breath on my face, watching me. At the snow falling silent beyond the tall windows, a white carpet already covering the terrace. And the muscle there with the empty water glass in his hand, relaxed by the door, watching me as a predator does an object of mild interest. I'm not leaving here unless they escort me out. And out, beyond the windows, is nothing but the reflected reality of this room.

I clear my throat and find myself saying, "I already told Sofia," I glance at her. "I told you I wouldn't publish it."

Sofia looks up from her troublesome fingernail, glances at me and then Eva, and something goes unsaid before she looks down again, deferring to the voice on the couch beside me.

"The thing is, Sandro," says Eva, "and I hope you'll excuse me for saying this, but why should we trust you?"

"Alex," I tell her and find I can't look away from Sofia. It's just a face, I think, but so achingly beautiful, and I'd be happy to be strung along except there's nothing on the other side of that pretty rainbow. "And I'm not sure what difference it makes, I have the image on my phone, on the cloud."

"Yes, but they're fakes—there's only one original."

"How does that make a difference?"

"It just does. Trust me," she says, "I've spoken to my legal team. But look, there's no—I mean, why make this an issue here? Sofi's been open with you, right? I figure the least we could expect is for you to be open with us."

"Open in what way?"

"In every way, if I know our Sofi." A little laugh and a little wink, and Sofia scrapes her fingernail ever harder. "Look, Sandro—Alex—that photo, it's—we would sleep better knowing it was in our possession, okay? And it's really not asking much, is it?" She's being reasonable. And yet, I think, and yet. "You have what you wanted—you know now what happened to your uncle—you have your answers. Now give us what we want, and we all make kumbaya and part as friends. More than friends, maybe, isn't that so, Sofi?"

Eva is so close we're almost touching, and I shuffle away a little. "Why are you so bothered by an eighty-year-old photo?" I ask her.

Eva keeps her smile going—an American smile, just a muscle tic, smiling away even when she's about to stick a blade in my spine. "I think you know."

"Do I?"

"Do you?" She raises her brows suggestively, but there's humour there, and I can't help but laugh. She laughs right along with me, but my laughter sounds strained, nervous.

"I guess I know enough to know what your grandfather told me was a load of bullshit," I tell her, and her laughter comes to an abrupt end.

She glances at Sofia. "Don't tell me he started in with that AIDS shit again? Sofi—"

"There was never a whistle," I tell her.

Eva's big eyes look at me, assessing. She seems confused. "Don't interrupt me," she says pleasantly, her lips wrapped in that passive-aggressive smile. "And what whistle, anyway?"

"There was no signal on the night of the killing."

"So no AIDS thing?" And then, "Because you know how it is, with men of that age—"

"There were no windows at the jail. Not in the rooms where the prisoners were being held. No windows, no signal. Because no one inside would ever have heard it through the walls. Your grandfather lied."

"Lied to you?"

"Lied to Casanova. It's what gave him away."

"Sofi? Do you know what he's on about?"

Sofia nods almost imperceptibly.

"You know what I think happened?" I ask.

Eva's eyes sweep from Sofia to mine, and I recognise her grandfather there. "This is dead history," she says.

"So's the photo."

"What?"

"Dead history. And yet here we are."

She thinks about that for a while. "And yet," she agrees eventually, and glances over at the hard man by the door, "here we all are." She sits back on the couch and recrosses those long legs and gazes at one swinging Ellesse foot and then, perhaps arriving at a decision, she glances over at Sofia who diligently ignores her and says, "Okay, Alex, why don't you tell us," and she smiles when Sofia raises her head, "what you think you know."

"I thought you didn't care?" I ask, and feel a fool, a petulant child.

Eva turns to me, that smile like the patient embrace for a stunted child. "Of *course* we care. Sofi—do you care? Do you want Alex to tell us a *bedtime* story?" They share something silent and curiously savage. "*Su, dai, forza*, Alex—tell us your story. You look as if you're dying to get it off your chest. Go on—once upon a time," she prompts, and I think fuck it—fuck you—

"There was a fascist by the name of Godin and a British spy named Coke," I tell her, "who conspired to kill ninety-nine people in a jail in Schio."

"Alex," Sofia says, "don't do this."

"*Zitta,*" says Eva, and there's nothing friendly in her tone at all now, "let him talk. I love conspiracy theories."

I think of my uncle, abandoned there on the ice like a flea, and I think fuck these people. Just for once—just this once, I can be brave. He deserves that. At least that. "He wasn't a good man—Coke I mean—he was an awful sonofabitch, but he was plenty ambitious, and he was cold and ruthless and efficient, and he found good use for your grandfather who, let's face it, was an even meaner sonofabitch."

After a moment spent listening to the fire crackle, Eva says, "I see," and I sense her words aren't meant for me, they're meant for Sofia who doesn't look up from her fingernail pruning. "So this is how you'll repay our family's kindness."

"Kindness? I think my uncle might disagree." I meet Eva's gaze and I don't look away. "But whatever. That massacre in Schio, you know when it started?"

She shrugs.

"The day Freccia walked into an ambush and was killed in January of '45. Legend has it your grandfather ratted Freccia out, did you know that?"

"That's not true," says Eva. "Nonno would never have betrayed—"

"You're right—he didn't. He saw Giulio and Renzo that day in the Laghi, but he never informed on them. It was Giulio who did that, Giulio who told the Black Shirts where he'd be that night with Freccia."

"Wasn't Freccia his friend?" asks Sofia. "His—British liaison? Why would Giulio—"

"Because everything changed the moment Coke parachuted into Italy. Coke came to Italy to win the peace, not the war, and Freccia was given his new orders when Coke arrived—take care of the Russo problem. Permanently. See, in Coke's world, Giulio was just one more partisan who needed to be removed from the postwar reshuffle: men who'd run their course, men whose debts to Russia and the Communists had become a liability. Remember," I glance at Sofia, "you told me that."

She meets my eyes and says nothing at all.

"But Giulio, he was a survivor, and he must have figured Coke had a British bullet with his name on it, and that Freccia was the triggerman. Giulio was no one's fool. He had a whole career planned for after the war, and a whole lot of money to back his ambition. Isn't that what your grandfather said? Another Feltrinelli? He wasn't some working-class grunt playing at soldier—Giulio was a war hero, like Sandro Pertini, right, except he wasn't a US-approved European socialist, he was a Communist, a hardcore believer. So what happened? Before Freccia could do the job, he was betrayed to the Black Shirts who tortured and killed him. Coke blamed Giulio for the betrayal. And he was right. And that left Coke with a thirst for vengeance. It took him a while—six months—but in late June of '45, fate delivered Coke a perfect set of circumstances that would end with Giulio dead, the Communist Party irreparably damaged, and his thirst for vengeance quenched. Revenge and duty."

Eva laughs. It's a cruel laugh—designed to injure. "I see why you write car stories," she says. "Thirst for vengeance? Vengeance quenched?" She chuckles some more. "Sofi," she jabs a thumb at me, "you sure he gets all those likes on Facebook?"

I glance away, the blush spreading on my face, feeling like a teenage boy around a group of girls, always inadequate, and I look over at the muscle by the front door. He's got a grin on his face too. I look away, shamed, out at the snow. It's tipping down now, and I need to get away from these people. "Coke's plan started when he learned that Pranjic—"

"Who's Pranjic?" asks Eva, glancing over at Sofia to see if she should register this name.

"Some crazy Marxist revolutionary," Sofia reassures her. "Long-dead. Doesn't matter."

"Yes, exactly, a Moscow-run revolutionary and the perfect fall guy for Coke's plan."

"What plan?" Eva asks, her eyes firmly on Sofia now.

"The Schio massacre, what else?" I try for sarcasm, and it sounds mean and stupid, so I drive on. "See, Coke figured the revenge killings—the *resa dei conti*—had reached a tipping point by that summer: it was front-page news, right, even the *New York Times* was talking about the tens of thousands murdered, the triangle of death, *bla bla*. And then, through his old friends in the Garibaldi Battalion, Coke found out about yet another massacre in the works—only this time, it was going to happen right there in his backyard. In Schio. And best of all, it was being led by a man named Ivo Pranjic."

"Why best of all?" Eva interrupts.

"I'm getting there. See, Coke was smart enough to figure everyone in Allied Command was going to get caught with their pants 'round their ankles on this one—Paget, Loller, all the way up the chain of command to General Dunlop, everyone was going to come out smelling like shit because they'd all been warned the massacre was coming, and once the media got wind of that, Allied Command would have no choice but to at least pretend to try to track down the killers. And when they did that, Coke would have his tailor-made fall guys all lined up for them, ready for the gallows."

Eva nods her chin at Sofia. "This was all at the library? Sofi?"

Sofia shrugs.

"You haven't read Balbo's confession?" I ask.

"Did you, Sofi?" Eva says, ignoring me.

"Yes," says Sofia, scraping her fingernail eagerly. "I read it."

"Not well enough obviously," Eva says. Her grandfather's eyes. Admonishing. I sense Sofia's unease and get a weird sense of guilt. "So who were the fall guys?" Eva asks me.

"Giulio Moro and Ivo Pranjic, who else?" I reply. "The two leaders who planned the massacre of fascists in the Schio jail."

"They weren't fascists," says Eva, "at the jail."

"You mean aside from your grandfather?" Those clear-water eyes of hers darken. I'm getting to you, I think. I'm getting to you now. "See, Pranjic was a gift from heaven for Coke because he really *was* an informer—he'd been turned by the Nazis back in '44, and Coke knew that, and if that got out, Pranjic was a dead man, dead in Italy, dead in Prague, dead in Moscow. Once Coke threatened to expose him, Pranjic was his to do with as he wanted. Coke's little puppet."

"So Pranjic planned the massacre?" asks Sofia.

"I don't know for sure. None of the partisans ever fingered him as the man who planned the raid—but that doesn't mean much. His name was mentioned in the jail, you remember, by that Dalle Valle woman?"

Sofia nods.

"But it doesn't matter. What matters is what Coke really needed Pranjic for—the part that mattered most. Killing Giulio Moro."

Sofia glances up at Eva and the two exchange a look with an intensity that makes me think I'm missing something.

"This, this Pranjic—this is who killed Giulio?" Eva asks.

"No. No-no, he was just an enabler. Pranjic's job was to go up to Trento on the evening of the massacre and bring Giulio down to Schio."

"Why?" asks Eva.

"To connect Giulio to Ivo Pranjic, why else? Coke's fall guys: Pranjic the Marxist revolutionary, and Giulio Moro, the Communist partisan hero. As I said, tailor-made scapegoats to discredit the Communist Party—cold-blooded killers with marching orders from Moscow via Togliatti in Rome. This was Coke winning the peace, and that meant making sure the Communist Party *lost* the peace—isn't that what you told me?"

Sofia slowly shakes her head when I look at her.

"But the real question you should be asking," I tell Eva, "is why would Giulio leave Trento with Pranjic? And that's where your grandfather comes into the story. See, without your grandfather, there is no massacre."

"Alex," says Sofia, and it sounds like a warning.

I ignore her. "So how does Pranjic get Giulio down to the jail?" I ask.

Eva looks from Sofia to me. "How?"

"Renzo Balbo," I tell her. "See, there's no way Giulio would've had anything to do with that shit show down at the jail. But saving Renzo Balbo, that was something else, wasn't it. Renzo was a friend, a brother—they'd come out of Russia together, they'd liberated Schio together, and Coke was fully aware of their bond—he'd been with Giulio and Renzo up in the mountains for months. Coke knew Giulio's weakness. So, all Pranjic needed to do was convince Giulio that his old friend Renzo Balbo was down in Schio with the Garibaldi Battalion, about to kill your grandfather in the jail. Poor Renzo, meanwhile, thought Giulio was about to lead the massacre to kill your grandfather because that's what Coke told him. Coke played them both because he was playing chess and everyone else didn't even know they were in a game. But your grandfather, he was the glue. If he wasn't in that jail, neither Renzo nor Giulio would ever have gone near Schio that night."

"Nonno was a victim," says Eva.

"A victim?" I try a laugh on, and it sounds pathetic. "Don't be ridiculous. Your grandfather was the only man in this whole setup who got something out of Coke. Everyone else, all they got was a cold grave."

"What did he get?" asks Sofia.

"What do you think?"

"Why don't you tell us," Eva whispers.

"I *am* telling you. So Pranjic goes up to Trento and convinces Giulio to go down to Schio with him, and off they go, Pranjic and Giulio, on Pranjic's bike, the two insurgents rushing down to Schio to the massacre for which they're about to be blamed. They don't know that of course—just like they don't know they're about to have an accident that'll leave them both dead, and with plenty of leads that will finger them as the leaders of the Schio massacre."

"What leads?" asks Eva.

"The leads your grandfather was about to feed to investigators."

"Alex," says Sofia, "you need to stop now—"

"Let him speak," whispers Eva. "Let him finish his story."

"So there they are, our fall guys, rushing down the mountain on Pranjic's bike. And guess who's also up there, waiting in the shadows," I smile, "his thirst for vengeance about to be quenched? Our old friend Coke. He sees them coming and *wham*—he runs them down with his car." I collide my fist with a palm and the impact makes the suit at the door look up, prepped for action.

"The fall guys," says Sofia. "Your daughter would have liked that."

I smile at her. So beautiful, so corrupt. "The perfect plan," I tell her. "Except that Pranjic somehow manages to survive the accident, doesn't he, and the last anyone sees of that poor bastard is when he's forced into the back of a car. My bet? Coke was in that car and Pranjic never went to Prague—he went into a hole somewhere near Trento. Giulio, meanwhile, is left for dead. Job done, and Coke's vengeance—vengeance for the death of Freccia—complete, he heads down to Schio and waits for news of the massacre to hit, and then he rushes up to Valdagno, picks Paget up, and together they hurry down to the hospital in Schio where Coke begins interviewing the survivors, making sure to establish a trail that leads beautifully back to Russo and Pranjic. And so enter," I tell Eva, "your grandfather."

Eva looks over at Sofia. "This is like, what's that thing, in those Agatha Christie movies—Sofi? A denouncement?—"

"Denouement," says Sofia.

"Yes, that. Like a murder mystery."

"Actually, that's what comes next—the murder," I tell her.

"Was it *Colonnello* Mustard in the study?" Eva asks, but her humour is uncertain now.

I have you. I have you now, I think. "No, it was Captain Coke in the hospital."

"And what did he use? The, the," she mimes it out for me, her fist falling really close to me, and it feels like a threat in that room, "lead pipe?"

"Casanova figured an injection of insulin."

The word triggers something in Eva. Surprise, yes, but something else, something I can't quite place. She looks at me for a long while. "Insulin?" she says eventually, and she and Sofia exchange a glance that I can't read. Sisters. Secrets. Women. Playing a sport whose rules I'll never understand.

"None of this has anything to do with Nonno," says Sofia, but it sounds fake, rushed, as if she's trying to throw me.

"It has everything to do with him," I tell her, but when I look up, I see a warning there, an imperceptible shake of her head as her eyes take a quick peek at the muscle at the door. Fuck it, I think. "Him and his lies."

"What lies?" asks Eva.

"The ones he told Casanova. See, Coke's plan was bulletproof—except for one small detail."

"What detail?" asks Eva, but I can see she's connecting the dots.

"Giulio Moro. You can just imagine Coke at the hospital, right, in Schio the night of the massacre, convinced everything has gone to plan—Pranjic dead, Russo dead, massacre successful, your grandfather ready to wrap it all up like a gift for the investigators—when suddenly who comes rolling into the hospital? None other than Giulio fucking Moro himself—and still *very* much alive. Can you imagine the moment Coke saw him that night? Coke was fucked and he knew it: Giulio would work out what had happened up in Trento sooner or later, especially once he got to speak to Renzo, and once he did, that was Coke fucked. As in, you know, Giulio could tie him to the massacre, and that wasn't some minor offense. This was Coke implicated in the mass murder of over fifty people. So that was that—Giulio could never be allowed to leave the hospital alive."

"So Coke murdered Giulio?" says Sofia.

Eva looks from her to me, and again I sense something's troubling Eva that doesn't fit right. And Sofia, so keen to lay this on Coke's door. Something's wrong—something ... "Right," I reply, suddenly feeling less than. "He wasn't fucking around, Coke, was he? But that's where he made his mistake."

"The whistle," Sofia says.

"The whistle," I agree.

"What whistle?"

"I'm coming to that. But we're at the hospital now. You can imagine the chaos, dozens and dozens of wounded and dead being brought in, and that's when Coke makes his move. With Giulio already injured, it couldn't have been a difficult thing to do—the opening, I mean. Or the kill, I suppose, because Coke really was a cold bastard, wasn't he, and so he takes his needle, and he murders Giulio Moro. That done, once he'd shoved that needle of insulin in Giulio's neck, it was time for your grandfather to get in on the act. But now Coke had to improvise, see, because Giulio's obviously been seen at the hospital, and that needed an explanation."

Eva stares at me silently, and I'm relieved when she looks away from me and hunts down Sofia's face instead. "You knew?" she asks Sofia with a voice that is eerily calm.

Sofia swallows and says nothing.

"Sofi. Tell me the truth. Did you know?"

Sofia rubs her fingers over her face and sighs.

"How long?" Eva asks. "How long have you known?"

I look at the two of them. Somewhere, I think, I've missed something. But I need to go—it's time to finish this. "So Coke comes up with a plan on the spot—he tells your grandfather that the story he was meant to tell the investigators has now changed. Your grandfather needs to tell them that not only had he heard the killers mention Russo's name at the prison, but now he also needs to tell them that he heard a whistle, the whistle that was the signal for the killers to open fire—the whistle that would place Russo at the scene of the killing. Can you see it, your nonno and Coke, making a deal there over Giulio's corpse. Can you imagine it? That night at the hospital? Coke the manipulator and your grandfather negotiating his new price?"

"You don't understand a thing about Nonno," Sofia says, "this is—"

"What price?" interrupts Eva, and this isn't right, I think. I've missed something here.

"Like maybe the promise of a little help for his political career from grateful allies." I glance at her. "Perhaps a few envelopes, like Craxi, like that whole mafia—"

"That's bullshit," says Eva, glancing at the muscle for a moment and toning down her voice. "You're making this shit up. Nonno hated the mafia. Bunch of *terroni*—"

"Whatever," I interrupt. "You can ask him. I don't care. But the whistle is what gave Coke away to Casanova because no window, no signal. When Casanova figured that out, he knew your grandfather had lied. And that led him to Coke. But he couldn't prove it—not really. And in the end, Allied Command, Loller, they wanted the Communist partisans to hang, and that's who Casanova gave them."

Eva sits back on the couch. She looks beyond me, at the snow falling peacefully in the dark valley beyond the windows. "I think," she says now, nodding once, "I think we've had enough."

"You sure?"

"It's a nice story, but there's one obvious flaw."

I wait, knowing what's coming.

"Nonno was shot in that jail—he could have *died*. You think he'd have let himself get shot in a massacre he knew was about to happen?"

"Who says he was in the jail when the shooting happened?"

I like that her jaw slackens. "Don't be stupid," she says. "He was *shot*." She turns to Sofia. "He was shot!"

"Not in the jail he wasn't. Balbo was there, and he never mentions your grandfather in his confession. You know why? Because he wasn't there. Coke got him out before the battalion raided the jail."

Eva blinks. But she's sharp. And she's been paying attention. "Coke was up in Trento, then he went to collect Paget in Valdagno—that's what *you* said," Eva says quickly. "So he couldn't have got Nonno out of the jail. You're *wrong*. Sofi, tell him he's wrong."

"Coke didn't get your grandfather out of the jail," I tell her. "Svavi did. On Coke's orders."

She blinks, looks over at Sofia again, then back at me.

"And Casanova figured that out," I tell her, "when Renzo wrote about shooting Buonfuoco at the jail. Your grandfather wasn't there—if he had been, Balbo would have written about it, fuck, never mind written about it, he'd have killed him because your grandfather destroyed that man's life, and Balbo despised him. And anyway, Svavi all but told Casanova the truth when they met."

"So who shot Nonno?" Eva asks.

I shrug. "Why don't you ask him? He wasn't shot in the jail, that much I can tell you, because he wasn't there. Svavi got him out, that was always the deal between your grandfather and Coke. That's why the files on the prisoners vanished from the prison—they vanished because Svavi had logged your grandfather's release in them. Who knows, maybe Coke shot him. What price do you think your grandfather got for his silence and taking a bullet for Coke?"

Eva nostrils flare as if she's just smelt shit on her lip.

"Svavi was a lucky boy, too, because the way I figure it, he was destined for a hole in the ground if it wasn't for Casanova gifting him an insurance policy—Renzo's confession. That and the photo. The photo that links your grandfather to Giulio Moro and Renzo Balbo. The photo that's a fat flashing arrow for anyone who recognises the ex-mayor of Valdagno, the leader of Italy's soon-to-be leading political party—your grandfather—and Giulio and Renzo Balbo, right there together in Russia, right there together, the great and mighty Godin with Russo the Communist and Renzo the partisan mass-murderer. You know where anyone following that trail ends up? At the library where it all began in July 1945. And Renzo Balbo's diary. Even a car writer," I tell her, "can figure that one out."

Eva focuses in on her Ellesse shoes for a while. Thinking it over, I guess. She kicks her feet up a couple of times, as if she were on a swing, this way and that. And then she sighs and looks at me. "Are you done?" she asks.

"Am I?"

"Yes," she says, nodding. "Yes, you're done." She unfolds her legs and plants her shoes firmly on the wooden floor and then places both palms on her knees. Finality. "This was quite a fairy tale, Alex. You should start writing children's fiction—those car stories are beneath you."

"I like cars," I tell her. "They ask for nothing and give freedom in return. Not like your world, the one you and your grandfather made for us, for people like me and my uncle and my father, little people whose stories don't matter because you get to write our history, don't you, people like you with your connections, and we're just not crooked enough to be the heroes or the villains—just the little people who die on an ice-field somewhere in Russia or in a bed in Malo—little decent people who just live and die without stories worth telling while you fucks get to write and publish your own glorious history. You strip our dignity and then you strip our lives with your fucking lies—men like Renzo Balbo and his poetry, and my uncle, just broken men ridiculed because theirs wasn't the right voice to glorify your, your fucking—"

Eva abruptly slaps my knee twice with the flat of her hand. Hard. It shuts me up.

"So much virtue, goodness me," she says, standing, and I've become the third person to her now. "He has all the answers, and a fine little moral speech to wrap it all up. How fucking adorable." She looks down at me. "But here's the thing, *caro*. No one cares. Not about you or your fucking dying father leeching off our health care system, or your little family of fucking nothings, or your uncle too afraid to stand and fight. You know who I am, right?"

I look at her. "I think I'm starting to learn," I reply, and look over at Sofia who stares at Eva with something like panic on her face. I frown—

"Eva, no, don't—" says Sofia.

Eva ignores her. "Giulio's sister," Eva says, staring at me, "is my fucking mother-in-law."

And then she glances down at me to see my reaction. Her face is cruel. Spiteful. But there are tears there in her eyes, and I sense the truth that comes over her face like a veil, and suddenly I understand, I understand it all, and I turn to Sofia who stares at me disgusted, and I hear Eva say, "I told you, Sofi. I *warned* you. You and Nonno, I warned you. Both of you. So *stupid*. And you knew? All this time? You knew?" Her arm lashes out and grabs the bag from beside me and she sees me cringe and it makes her laugh. "Let me just say this, *carissimo*. I'm not an enemy you want to make."

"You mean we can still be friends? Kumbaya and all that?"

*"Fuck off."*

"Your Nonno," I tell her, because suddenly it comes to me, what I'd missed—how the hell had I missed it?—"he's a diabetic, isn't he?"

"Alex, no," whispers Sofia. "No more."

Eva stares at me with a loathing that makes my heart take a rattle. "Fuck you," she whispers.

"Was he on insulin? In 1945?"

Eva's about to say something but Sofia talks over her, deflecting quickly. "How did your father get the photo?"

"He is, isn't he?" I insist. "He was a fucking diabetic—"

"Yes," says Eva.

"Eva," Sofia gets to her feet, "no, this, this isn't—Eva, Alex is just—"

"Yes," Eva repeats. "He came back from Russia a diabetic—*didn't* he, Sofia?"

"Yes, but so what, Eva—"

I'm late to the scene, always slow and late. "Your—your—Godin? He killed Giulio—your fucking grandfather?"

Sofia shakes her head. But not in denial. "You can't know," she says, looking at Eva almost despairingly, "you can't know, none of us can ever know."

I get to my feet and stand in front of Eva, and she squares up to me, her hands fist at her sides and for a moment I think she's going to take a swing at me. *"You* know," I tell her, and I watch the muscle in the suit push toward me, "and I know. And you know what else I know? I know people never get what they deserve, and if anyone deserves you and your grandfather and your miserable lies, then fuck them. Fuck them and *fuck you*." I turn to Sofia. "Fuck *both* of you, actually, and fuck *him* as well," I add, pointing at the muscle who's close enough to touch now, "and stay the *fuck* away from my hotel. I'm not some peasant you get to push around, *mate*."

"Alex, *basta*, stop this," says Sofia and I glance at her and there's a sadness there, as if I were a wayward child, and I can't make out if she's angry or disappointed, and I wait for her to say something more but she's just staring at me now with that look only a woman is capable of holding, and I turn from her repulsed, sickened with all of it and most of all with myself, and stride away toward the door. The muscle, standing in front of me, is caught without orders, and he tries to block without touching me, and we do a tango there together until I feint right and brush right by him.

His hand reaches out and I swing around to face him. "Don't fucking touch me."

He frowns. Before his arm coils out and his palm wraps itself around my face and he drives me back hard against the door and I feel my head bang against it and stars fly like the Northern Lights.

"*Basta!*" Sofia shouts.

The muscle steps back from me as if surprised by his own actions, and I see him glance back at Eva as I get woozy from the fear and the adrenaline. I need out of this place.

I grab the photo from my jacket. "Is this what you want?" My voice sounds alien to me—high-pitched and panicky. *"Is this what you want?"* I shout, waving it about. I frisbee it at Eva's head. It slices through her hair on the way past to spin onto the floor. The muscle tenses, and I can see his hand balled into a fist as Sofia jostles between us. Eva gets onto her knees to scoop the photo up and it's then that she looks at me, there on her knees, and I smile at her because I can see she's crying and this is all the winning I'm ever going to get, and I'm walking away now, wrestling open the latch and throwing open the door to the cold and the snow and my sweat freezes up and makes me shiver and Eva says, "Let him go. *Mi fa pena. You're pitiful!* You hear me? You're fucking pitiful! As if you're the only prick who's ever lost a father. *Mi fai pena!*"

I slip and slide through the slushy snow on the porch and then in an instant my trainers lose traction and I fall backwards into the snow. I slide around trying to get back up and crawl away on all fours until I grab onto the bike and push myself up and now I'm half-skating away through the ankle-deep snow feeling the ice get into my shoes and down my socks and I can hear the whistle of air as I scrunch my way toward the Porsche, all white and pure and waiting to save me. I click the locks open and see the orange lights blink under a deep covering of snow. I jump into the cockpit, slam the door, and snow collapses from the windscreen like an imploding building. I fire the engine up and turn on the wipers, clearing the windscreen, and suck in air when I see them.

The three of them.

They're standing just outside the front door, there in the pale porch light, three dark shapes as still as the night, watching.

I stick the Porsche into reverse and begin to back up. My tyres lose traction and I sense them spinning. I modulate the throttle but I'm stuck now and I think, those fuckers will see me dead if I get trapped out here, and it's then, when the tyres find some bite, that I realise I've stopped breathing as I head into the impermeable woods, the snow falling hard, and in the rearview I see the three figures step through the door and shut it behind them and then the lights on the porch go dark.

# "Senza Fine"—Ornella Vanoni

## March 11

The call comes at 6.12PM on the Monday. The number is +27. Italy.

"Signor Lago?"

"Dr Marcon? What's happened?"

"Signor Lago, I wanted to inform you," she's using formal Italian and there's no language that sounds so threatening and so clinical, and I sense the truth in her voice, in her words, when she says into my ear, "your father's condition has deteriorated significantly during the day. I thought it prudent to advise you."

"What do you—"

"We will do what we can this week for him, to make him comfortable. But we—"

"I'll leave now," I tell her.

I drive through the Swiss autobahns headed south for the Gotthard Pass. Cameras everywhere, they send the guilty back to where they come from, the Swiss, and it's a slow ride up into the Alps. The illness, I imagine, had come with the dusk, with the cold, and it won't let go now. My brother calls and I tell him I'm on my way.

"Okay," he says. "I guess I'll have to sort a flight out."

I drive through Rotkreuz where my daughter goes to international school, cryptocurrency paradise hidden behind glitzy glass skyscrapers lit like Christmas trees in the night and just past Luzern I get onto the meandering road that leads up, always up for the Gotthard Tunnel. The night is flecked by snow, trifling angels in the flare of my headlamps, and I wonder how bad it will be up in the Alps. I realise I don't have a hotel for the night. And just as quickly, I realise I don't care. I just want to keep driving, riding into that night that comes at me with a whoosh through my open windows. Just to drive and keep driving.

It's just gone nine and I'm outside Faido with the snow gloopy on the windscreen and the road a white dusty track when my brother calls me back.

"Hey. I'm just through the Gotthard," I tell him.

"He's gone," he says.

"I'll be there at about two, stuck in shitty traffic at the moment, snow's crazy."

"He's gone."

"No," I tell him. I can hear him choke up. "No, because I'm on my way and I told him I'd be there on Wednesday." And then. "Tell them. Tell them to wait for me."

I'm almost through the border at Chiasso when he calls back. "They're waiting for you," he says, and his voice is as soft as the snow that floats like butterflies in the lights of the Porsche. "Any time you get there is fine. They're waiting."

The main road to the autostrada through the old tunnels just beyond Chiasso is closed, and there are signs for a deviation into Como. Italian deviation, signs that lead nowhere, signs that end when I'm halfway through some village on the hills above Lake Como, and soon enough there are hundreds of cars circulating through the night with licenses from all over Europe trying to find their way back to the motorway on narrow roads meandering between tall solid walls of villas long abandoned to the winter. I think fucking Italians, and then I'm shouting, "Fucking Italians! *Italiani di merda!*"

It takes two hours and more to find my way onto the onramp of the autostrada and I rush down to the tollgate. It's then that I see the sign. Lit bright, white on green.

MONZA.

The wind is blowing hard, and the Porsche on the motorway is seriously unsteady at 250kmh, weaving about the lanes and buffeted about by the trucks headed east to Trieste and on into Eastern Europe. But I'm hours late—I'm too late—and it's close to two now and I just keep the throttle flat and push through the night, counting down the cities—Brescia, Bergamo, Verona, always fascist Verona—and it's just the trucks I need to watch for dancing with their spindly red lights and really, if I ended up under their wheels, who is left to remember, anyway? In all the time my father had been in the hospital, it'd only been me. He'd had no friends. Maybe he'd outlived them all. Or maybe he never had many to begin with. A life scarred by war, by loss. I will die the same. The same but even more alone, I suppose. But there's no walking away from that. He'd died alone. And I'd failed even at this. When all that was required was for me to just be, I'd failed.

It's past four on the clock when I park the Porsche outside the building in Malo and climb out. Cold. A silence that crushes my soul. The moon is hiding behind the circle on the concrete up there in the black sky. So cold, so quiet. Broken only by my footsteps. There's an intercom by the revolving front door downstairs and I take a moment before pressing it.

"*Si?*"

"*Sono il figlio di—*"

"*Vengo,*" the voice says, and it takes about a minute before I see an orderly walk through the pilot-lit lobby toward me and he uses a key to unlock the door.

I step inside.

"My condolences," he says. I follow him in the silence to the elevators, and he leaves me alone to ascend to the third floor. There's a mirror here. In the elevator. I use it to stare at my face. I see my father. I walk out and push through the two double doors and there's a nurse waiting for me, right there by the radiator, she's waiting for me, the blonde, Julia, she's waiting in the dim light where once my father had waited and her hand reaches out and I see the tattoo on her arm, and I shake her hand and notice my arm is shaking.

"He was complaining," she says to me, trying to meet my gaze, "but when we left him, he was tranquil. Then when we returned, he'd passed. It's often like that; they always pass when they're alone."

I hold on to her hand.

"Come," she says, and I follow her down the hallway.

The rooms are all dark. Silent. The hallway has pilot lights, sharp like pens. But from his room, from his room there is light that washes out onto the hallway, soft light that spills out onto my shoes in a stain of gold.

I pause at the door. The nurse stands beside me. Waiting.

I walk in.

My father lies on his bed. They've made up his sheets and blanket so that only his face is visible. It's good they didn't leave him in the dark. I think, it will be morning soon, and the worst will be over when the light comes. I had seen this with my mother. They've been kind; they've combed his silver hair. His eyes are shut. His mouth is tight, as if he'd been in pain. Old. So old. The dead don't look like themselves. The dead look like the dead. A family of their own. Unmoving. Just a layer of bone and withered flesh stretched like a mask. And yet there's a respite now—as if all the muscles that'd masked the secrets of a man and the shame that he must have endured were no longer needed and now a man could be seen in full. A death mask that is the only true reflection of a man.

On his little tray are his personal belongings. And a biscuit. One biscuit. The one I'd left behind. He had eaten a piece of it. Just a nibble. I touch it, and then I lift his iPhone from the tray. There are missed calls, four, two from me, an hour before he died, two from my brother. I wish that he'd answered. But what would I have said? Nothing. I'd said nothing. I'd been trusted to bring him to—this. And I had failed, I hadn't even been there, that's the truth of it. I stare at him. Ashamed that I'm not strong enough to touch him even now. Not even in death, I think, not even in death do I have the courage. I take his phone and his Bosch wristwatch and his spectacles and slide them into my jacket pocket. "I'm sorry." I'm not sure that the words don't spill from my mouth. I look at him then, lying there, I look at him so still, so still, and then I turn and walk out of the room. I walk out the room and don't turn around and the nurse accompanies me back to the elevators and when we get there she says, "We'll put his things together for you, you can come collect them when you wish."

"Thank you."

"I'm so sorry," she says, and we wait for the elevator.

"Thank you," I tell her. "Thank you for what you did—for speaking English to him, for being kind, for—"

"He was a good, kind man."

"He was kind," I tell her when the elevator doors open. "He was kind, and he was good."

I am outside. Just outside the revolving doors. I stand there in the night. It's close to five. Silent. Absolutely silent. And when the tears come, when the pain spools, I can do nothing but hold on to a pillar. There's no word for it. For that sound that comes from my soul. And no control. Pain that flees. Not from me. From my soul. It's what's inside me. It's that which fucking howls. And I'm just flesh, holding onto the pillar, trying hard not to fall away into the night. And what comes out of me then I know will never again find its way back.

# EIGHT
# THE LAST GOTTHARD RUN

*With maternal love, life makes a promise at dawn that it can never hold. You are forced to eat cold food until your days end. After that, each time a woman holds you in her arms and against her chest, these are merely condolences. You always come back to yell at your mother's grave like an abandoned dog. Never again, never again, never again.*

—Romain Gary

## "Azzurro"—Adriano Celentano

June
A *ligne claire* paper plane soars into a blue sky over an impossibly green meadow. I run after it. Next to me is Natalie. My daughter, she's about ten. She wears a yellow dress. We run and laugh. And then we see the enemy—they are coming down a green-green hill in canary-yellow camions. There's a river between the camions and us. A blue-white milky river. And they begin to sink. Then the enemy are friends in ancient white trucks. Bright clothes. And one truck is taking me home. Home is a cobbled street that reminds me of a movie set, somewhere in France, a cobblestone village. It's night. Cold and silent. But I'm not afraid. I see my mother standing in front of a shop. She wears a red dress with sequins on it. She's young. Forties. Maybe fifties. I walk slowly toward her. And she hugs me. It aches it feels so good. Then the lights in the shop switch on. Yellow, dim, full of shadow. Bay windows. Leaded and distortion-thick. And my father is in there now. Beyond the windows. In a beige sweater. I recognise him suddenly as a toymaker. He sees me and I see that smile of his. So rare that smile. He too comes for a hug. And we hug. And it feels so good. And then a big sedan pulls up, a sixties sedan sweating night-light, French and blue, and I wake up crying. Tears running down my face. I sat up in my little room in Zürich and I stared into the dark and I said goodbye because I knew then they were leaving me, and in my tears there was joy and I wished I could have this dream every night, and instead I'd walked to the bathroom and checked the time and it was 2.20AM and by three I'd showered and left the apartment and was on the road up into the Alps.

Now, deep in the late afternoon, the revs stumble and the engine rattles and everything sounds as if it's about to explode around me. The temperature gauge on the dashboard is way up high, and I'm sure if the warning lights on the car worked, they'd be flashing danger. The car is about to seize—I can taste its looming death.

We'd buried them, my brother and I, we'd buried our parents together in a south-facing wall of the Piovene cemetery, both their ashes in two colourful urns, red and blue, and I'd said goodbye to my brother at the cemetery on a warm day near the end of March, me on my way back to Zürich and he to Joburg.

I'd come back to my father the day after he'd died, back to his room. He was gone. I'd walked out with two white garbage bags that contained his life. They'd given me a key to the morgue, downstairs in the basement, and I'd gone down there trying to find him, down in the bowels of the building where they made the oxygen, and I'd got lost down there until I'd found the room that I'd mistaken, at first, for a utility room, and I'd unlocked the door and walked in and it was, I thought, like a changing room, tiles on the floor, tiles on the walls, and there were two rooms in there split by a single wall without any doors, and my father was in the second room and he was in a coffin under Hansa lights, so white there wasn't a shadow anywhere, and I looked at my father in the clothes that I'd left behind for the undertakers.

I'd dressed my mom too, for the very last time.

Seven weeks ago, I think now, as I listen to the engine rattling and the power fading fast under my foot up here in the Alps in the late afternoon.

Sofia had sent a couple of messages in the week after I'd left Asiago. I'd ignored the first two. I'd replied to her third because it read, "Nonno died today." I'd replied with my condolences. That was the day Facebook used its algorithm to show me a post by Eva Fachin, freshly elected to some portfolio or another in the new far-right-led coalition government. Italy's rising star. A future prime minister waiting in the wings.

*Like my nonno always said, Italians can have their parades and the Communists can love their partisans and the patriots can honour their Duce and the gays can love their partners but we are in 2024 and the only thing I care about is our Italy, our one and only beloved Italy, and clearing the swamp of the mafiosi in Rome and the immigrants in your streets and the drugs from your cities and the crime from your towns. The rest of it, the rubbish from the past, belongs there. #ItaliaFirst!*

The post had come with an asset I recognised: the photo. Except the only person on that photo now was Godin, standing there staring back at the camera. I guess a photo of her granddad standing with a Communist partisan and a mass killer and a boy they'd all left behind to die like a dog on the Russian steppe was best left forgotten. So he stood there alone. A hero. A survivor. A warrior. And the rest had simply been erased from history. It's like that with the winners; they're winners because they have no moral compunction to address the sins of the past. After all, if they can walk away from the guilt then surely the victims should be able to walk away from their shame.

And then I'd come to Piovene with the first hot days of June, the day I'd woken in tears from my dream. And it's true what they say, that home isn't where you choose to live—it's where you find peace. I came with the sun, and I stood below the plaque in the cemetery with the fresh light of a new day and cried. And then I'd gone back to their apartment, warm now in the late spring, and rifled through their personal possessions with the intention of cleaning up. My brother wanted to sell the apartment, and I went along with it because there was nothing there but pain and memories and that red chair. I'd found a real estate broker who told me the apartment was worth less than when they'd bought it a quarter of a century ago, and the concrete was rotting, the neighbourhood was going to shit, and I'd agreed to a small price for a quick sale and I'd come to clean it all up and found that I couldn't do it, I just couldn't do it and so I'd left it all there. And it was while the Porsche was failing to ignite on that Sunday afternoon down by the garages that she'd called. I'd almost ignored it but at the last I'd surrendered and touched the green button and placed the phone to my ear.

"Ciao," said Sofia.

"Hey. I'm—I should've called. I'm sorry. For your loss—there aren't words that, that—"

"I know," she said.

"Everything's changed," I sat on the hood of the Porsche, hot in the Italian sun. "Nothing's the same anymore."

"Nothing. No."

"You have your family. That should give you strength."

"And you?"

"I'm married," I said.

"It's the happily part," she said, "that was missing."

The insurance company tow-truck turned down the long drive and headed toward me then. "I should go," I told her. "I'm sorry again, about, about—"

"You're a good man, Alex."

"My wife's friends would disagree."

"Tell her to get better friends."

"She wouldn't agree either."

"Then get a better wife."

I didn't have any more words. I'd lost enough.

"Do you know," she said, "that Svavi lived in South Africa for a few years, back in the sixties?"

I waved the truck over, and I guess she senses my indifference.

"What do you miss most?" she asked after a moment.

"Their voice," I replied. "I miss their voices."

I listened to the silence for a while until she said, "So, you think we'll ever meet again?"

"You remember what Casanova said, to Snyder?"

I listen to her breathe. "Well," she said, eventually, "I thought I'd just check in. If you wanted to meet."

"I'm leaving," I told her, stepping toward the tow truck. "I'm going back now."

It'd taken twenty minutes for the tow truck guys to lift the broken Porsche onto the truck bed and drive away. Back to Switzerland. And watching the black Porsche bounce lifelessly away before me on the bed of the truck, I realised she was the best friend I'd had through it all. That black hunk of German metal. She was my best and only friend; true and courageous. She'd taken me up the Alps in the snow and I'd put 87,000 kilometres on the clock in eleven months. And all the way through, she'd remained true. Until today. And that, too, was an act of love, I thought when I'd opened the metal door to the garage and climbed inside the old FIAT.

*La Vecchia.*

She'd refused to start, of course, but I'd pushed her out of the garage on my own and then, when she'd picked up a little speed, I'd jumped behind the wheel and kicked out the clutch and the thing had risen from the dead with a fearsome and eager buck and an explosion of pale blue smoke and now, up here on the Stelvio, two thousand metres up into the sky, six hours later and in the fading light of a warm spring day, *La Vecchia* stumbles.

She stumbles with the most diabolical sounds coming from her frying innards. I keep the throttle down and I can hear metal things punting and screeching up front in the engine bay until finally a stream of smoke jets up from the bonnet as the engine seizes up the front wheels and she bounces once, twice, and once more when I dump the clutch in and allow her to roll off onto the apron of the meandering mountain pass. I lift the handbrake, engage the gear, turn the ignition off, and climb out.

Smoke is billowing up into the evening. I stand next to her, on an apron that sits tight to the precipice, and before me are the silver tipped Ortler Alps piercing the fragile sky like teeth, and I can see where the tree line ends and the rocks begin, up there where nothing grows. It's Africa up there. African soil, and the snow has yet to melt, black and filthy and not two hundred metres on is the Swiss border. Just two hundred metres. The smoke from the engine wafts up and I watch for a while, smoking my own cigarette. It smells of fried clutch. It smells of mechanical engineering, of oil and metal, of racetracks on hot summer days. It smells of history—of a time when men like my dad could work and raise a family. She reeks of dignity.

I run my hand on the red FIAT's hood. Scorching. I imagine my mom and dad, imagine them as they once were, driving to the boot of Italy in *La Vecchia*. I imagine them there on the front seats, alone and ageing, just the two of them, their kids so far away, just the two of them and the years closing in fast, and I remember them as they were, two Italians in Africa driving through the bush, I imagine them, those two faces there beyond this windscreen, together, the way they were when they'd come pick me and

Natalie up from the airport in Venice, my mom with her cookies and fresh milk in a sippy cup, and my dad distracted and yet somehow always there, driving *La Vecchia* to their apartment, so excited to see their boy, to see their only grandkid. When Natalie was a child, and I had a make-believe family. I imagine them there as cars pass me on the Stelvio, Porsches and Lamborghinis on their way home after a jaunt up the mountain passes, throaty engines rising to high-whine crescendos. I lean back on the rear of the FIAT and watch the twilight so infected with colour. It's beautiful up here on the Stelvio. Up on the ridge, the patchy snow is turning crimson like a night rose. A campervan with Netherlands plates stretches around the turn before me like an oil tanker, glacial speed enabling the driver to wind down her window without braking to shout, "Do you need help?" as she sloths her way by. I smile and shake my head and wave her on her way, and she's got a couple of kids staring at me from the back and they're waving at me from behind finger-streaked windows and I smile, and I wave back, I wave back like I'm pushing them up the Stelvio.

I would do anything to be them.

With death comes the loss of fear. I've learnt this now. The edges of life become muted, and I'm marooned on this rock, spiralling on without history or context or love. When they died, my mom and dad, nine weeks apart, when they died, it was as if someone had swapped the movie reel twenty minutes from the end of a comedy and replaced it with a slasher flick. That history should guide us to the end is certain; those of us who have a history. For me, up here on the Stelvio in the gathering night, there is no home. Home had been my mother's love. While she lived, I had a home. Now ... now home is as transient as the mountains vanishing into the dark. My father had chosen to be an immigrant; a refugee from his own history, his own scars. I'd merely continued his path. Lonely, unloved, unwelcome. There's no time for those who don't belong anywhere. Old men who'd never done anything much one way or the other; just stamped on as most men are. My history is gone. It'd died the night my father died. And standing here in the night beside his broken-down FIAT, I realise it makes no difference what happens next. I should never have left him. I should have been there for him when he died, but maybe he'd have preferred how it ended. To die alone. Without fuss. To die like a man with the dignity afforded to so few. And maybe, just maybe, in my presence every weekend for those nine weeks of winter, just maybe, he understood that in his life he'd had a son that had loved him to the end.

The dead linger as if they're forever dying.

My phone buzzes. I slide it out from my pocket. Natalie's number.

"Hi," I reply.

"Hi, Dad. Are you on your way home?"

"Kinda. How you doin', Nats?"

"Good. You?"

"Been better."

"I finally found that Eevee. Can't wait to show you."

"Can't wait to see it."

"I miss you, Dad."

"I miss you more. Is your mother there?"

"Yup, hang on. Mom. *Mom!* It's Dad—on the phone."

Silence for a moment. Then, "Hullo?"

"Hey."

"Where are you? You on your way back?"

"I'm near the top of the Stelvio. The FIAT broke down."

"The ... FIAT? Where's—what's happened to the Porsche?"

"Broken too. On its way to Switzerland on the back of a truck."

Silence. "So now what?"

I stand there in the night and stare into the dark. "I don't rightly know," I confess and smile.

"We're coming," says the voice.

"It's a long way."

"It's a long way from here, yes," says my wife. "But we'll leave now. Wait for us. We're coming."

*Zürich*

## Thank You

Massimo Bordoni. Grazie.

Fabrice Offranc, for a cynical French eye to soapy Italian sentimentality.

Ian Bell, for generosity.

The doctors and nurses at Casa Mužan in Malo: your compassion will always inspire and humble.

Dr Oliviero Puccetti, Oncology, Ospedale Santorso, who told me I would suffer.

Dr Gianpaolo Marchetti, Geriatrics, Ospedale Santorso, who tried.

Dr Alex Sherman in New York—because you always asked.

Dr Paolo Gasparini, who called me at 7am on a cold December morning to break my heart.

Violetta, who appeared when she was needed like an angel.

And my Aunt Elisa, who was the last of us who left in the summer of 2024 …


## A Last Word

I couldn't write this book while my dad was alive—I tried and always ran into false dawns.

Instead, this book took shape, after a decade of research, one cold afternoon in February of 2019 when, with my dad dying in Malo, I went to find my uncle Alessandro's name that my dad had told me was engraved at the *Chiesa SS Trinità Sacrario Militare* in Schio.

My father had always said he'd take me, but we never got around to it. Isn't that the way of it? While searching for his name, there amongst the tombstones, I chanced upon the grave of a partisan named Germano "Turco" Baron. His mysterious death on the night of the Schio massacre was the spark that ignited the voice of this book.

My daughter Natalie then came up with the central conceit while I was driving her home one cold afternoon from school that winter.

The first draft of this book happened quickly. In truth, though, I hardly recall writing it at all. It came out like a wound.

And so that's that.

If you've read this far, thank you. Books come with dedications and all sorts of acknowledgements. But they mean nothing if the book is never read. You reading these lines matters more than me writing them. So, thank you, and maybe we meet each other again in another book one day…

# GLOSSARY

| | |
|---|---|
| A baia | To go home. Venetian dialect. |
| Al fogo | Fire. Fogo is Venetian dialect for "fuoco". |
| Ardenti | Stragglers. |
| Armata scomparsa | Vanished army. |
| Avanti | Forward. |
| Avanti che siete Alpini! | "Forward. You're Alpini!" |
| Boia chi molla | Fascist slogan: he who gives up is a dirty traitor. |
| Bono | Good. |
| Che noia | So boring! |
| Commissione d'Epurazione | The "purge commission". Established after the fall of fascism and given the task of removing people judged to be too closely associated with the regime from their positions. |
| Cosa fai | What are you doing? |
| Credere, Obbedire, Combattere | "Believe, Obey, Fight": Fascist motto. |
| Da dove sito | "Where are you from?" Venetian dialect. |
| Dal Po in giù l'Italia non c'è più! | Anything south of the Po River is not Italy. |
| Dio can' | Venetian expletive (literally, "God's a dog"). |
| Disgraziati | Bastards (in this context). |
| Domani si vedrà | Tomorrow is another day. |
| Eja, eja, alalà | Fascist war-cry invented by Gabriele D'Annunzio in 1917. |
| El me scuxa | "Excuse me". Venetian dialect. |
| Fa' il bono | "Be good". Venetian dialect. |
| Fanculo | Go fuck yourself. |
| Flebo | IV drip. |
| Gavetta | Mess tin. But also, apprenticeship. See Giulio Bedeschi. |

| | |
|---|---|
| Gente | People. |
| Gheto capio | "Do you understand?" Venetian dialect. The accent is on the i. |
| Giustificati/giustiziare | Literally "justiced". Fascists killed after the war. |
| Guastatori | Assault engineers |
| Guerra | War. |
| La brava gente | "The good people": A cliché of what it is to be Italian. |
| Lascia stare | Leave it alone. |
| La vaca de to mare | "That cow of your mother." Venetian dialect. |
| Libro e moschetto, fascista perfetto | "Book and musket make the perfect fascist". |
| Magnagatti | Cat eaters. |
| Mi fai pena | "I pity you". |
| Na lengua sola no la xé mai bastansa | One language is never enough. Venetian dialect. |
| O la va, o la spacca | Either it works or we're done for. Italian expression. Literally: either it fits, or it breaks. |
| Pàrlitu | "Do you speak?" Venetian dialect. |
| Patria | Homeland |
| Pasa na bona xornada | Having a good day? |
| Pennichella | Siesta. |
| Pesante | Heavy metal. |
| Polenta e osei | Polenta with bird (not to be confused with the desert from Bergamo!). |
| Porca troia | Fucking whore. |
| Portavoce | Spokesperson. |
| Resa dei conti | "Settling scores" in post-war Italy. |
| Sbadanti | The damned. |
| Schei | Money: Venetian dialect. |
| Sciccoso | Italian for "chic". |
| Scopa | Italian card game using the Italian 40-card deck. |

| | |
|---|---|
| Scugnizzo | Street urchin. |
| Semoventi | Armoured vehicle. |
| Sempre lo spiritoso | Smart alec, but in an endearing way. |
| Sottotenete | Second lieutenant. |
| Spaghettata | A meal of spaghetti! |
| Stronzate | Bullshit. |
| Tagoditto | "I told you". Venetian dialect. |
| Te si furbo come na quaja | "You're sly like a fox". Venetian dialect. |
| Terrone | Epithet for southern Italians. |
| Terroni Trains | Racist depiction of southern Italians embarking on trains for the north looking for work in the post-war boom. |
| Zitta | Be quiet. |

# About the Author

Sandro Martini has worked as a word monkey on three continents. He's the author of *Tracks: Racing the Sun*, an award-winning historical novel. He grew up in Africa to immigrant parents, studied law in Italy, chased literary dreams in London, hustled American dollars in New York City, and is now hiding out in Switzerland, where he moonlights as a Comms guy and tries hard not to speak German. You can find him either uber-driving his daughter, chasing faster cars on the autobahn, or swimming in Lake Zurich with a cockapoo named Tintin.

## Note from Sandro Martini

Word-of-mouth is crucial for any author to succeed. If you enjoyed *CIAO, AMORE, CIAO*, please leave a review online—anywhere you are able. Even if it's just a sentence or two. It would make all the difference and would be very much appreciated.

Thanks!
Sandro Martini

We hope you enjoyed reading this title from:

# BLACK ROSE
## writing

www.blackrosewriting.com

Subscribe to our mailing list – *The Rosevine* – and receive **FREE** books, daily deals, and stay current with news about upcoming releases and our hottest authors.
Scan the QR code below to sign up.

Already a subscriber? Please accept a sincere thank you for being a fan of Black Rose Writing authors.

View other Black Rose Writing titles at www.blackrosewriting.com/books and use promo code **PRINT** to receive a **20% discount** when purchasing.

Printed in Dunstable, United Kingdom